THE AGENT:
THE SPY

ROBIN ESCHLIMAN

ISBN 978-0-9982847-0-5
ISBN 978-0-9982847-1-2 (electronic)

This is a work of fiction. Names, characters, places and incidents are the product of the author's wildly overactive imagination and are used fictitiously, and any resemblance to actual persons, living or dead, businesses, companies, events, or locales is entirely coincidental.

The publisher and author do not have any control over, and do not assume any responsibility for, author or third-party websites or their content.

Library of Congress Control Number: 2016918241
Eschliman, Robin.
    The Agent: The Spy / Robin Eschliman. – 1st ed.

Editor: Keith Heckman

Printed in the United States of America
2016

Book Design by Jeff Beckenbach

Dedicated to CIA employees who bear burdens daily that are massively chilling and weighty.

Fourteen thousand Middle East antiquities were looted from the Iraqi National Museum in 2003 as the American invasion began, including valuable artifacts that Saddam Hussein himself attempted to steal. Many were located and returned.

Today, eight thousand five hundred pieces remain missing.

ISIS also reportedly looted antiquities and sold them on the black market.

PROLOGUE
Camp Peary, "The Farm"
Williamsburg, Virginia

*T*he sound of mock gunshots in the trees alerted the instructors in the Career Trainee Program that the final remaining two students were completing the Crash and Burn simulation.

This was it. The instructors could call it a day.

The second-to-last car wheeled around the final orange barrel and came to a stop. The male trainee emerged gingerly from the vehicle with his paramilitary gear, panting, stopping to collect himself for a moment. He looked over his shoulder and then stood and waited for the car with the last student, some distance behind him. The female trainee in the car, Liu Chen, was more hesitant, pulling slowly towards the orange barrel. She pulled to a stop and exited the vehicle and walked over to join him.

The male trainee slapped the back of the shoulders of the female with his free arm and said some words of encouragement to her. She shook her head, disheartened, but he kept encouraging her. The two stragglers climbed the hill towards the instructors, huffing and puffing with the weight of their equipment.

"He always looks out for Liu, doesn't he? Treats her like a little sister or something. She's not going to make the cut, is she?" predicted the instructor-in-training to the older instructor, observing the tiny, slight figure of the Asian-American girl struggling with her gear.

"No. Maybe she could be Military Affairs, given her background. Or a CIA analyst. We definitely need more officers of Chinese heritage."

"You think Ryan will make the cut?" asked the instructor-in-training. "Thirty-five year-old architect. Isn't that pushing it in age?"

"Yeah. He has to go through the same rigor anyone has to go through that wants to be in Covert Operations, but he's more mature than the rest of the class. Plus, he has folks in high places in his corner," said the older instructor. "Shhh, here they come."

The male trainee with the Midwestern accent was never called by his real name, Josh Evans. He went by the CIA-created identity of Ryan Taylor. There was a cut over his left eye from a bump

1

against the window during simulation. The young, petite Asian-American trainee with short-cut hair fought to remain dignified but was clearly fighting back tears. She had scratches all over her arms, which had been cut by brambles when she jumped out of the car during a simulated explosion down by the river.

"That's enough defensive driving for one day. You can load up on the truck and go to the barracks and clean up and eat." The instructors offered their palms in a high-five gesture.

Ryan, in a burst of energy, dropped his gear and leaped up with both feet and met the high-five. "Hey Liu, you made it."

But the girl didn't give a high-five. She made a crisp salute to the instructors, then her eyes dropped to the ground in disappointment. Liu Chen knew she wouldn't make the cut.

"Ryan, a word with you first. Liu, go on," said the older instructor.

They watched as she picked up her gear and trudged in exhaustion towards the truck where the other trainees were waiting. The older instructor said, "Ryan, it's not your responsibility to carry her buckets. This is the big leagues. It's every man for himself. Focus on getting through this."

For a moment Ryan looked as if he were about to disagree, but he remained silent and kept his face expressionless.

"You can go now."

"Yes sir." He, too, picked up his gear, slung it over his shoulder, and followed Liu to the truck.

"So," asked the younger instructor, "What do you mean, Ryan has 'folks in high places'?"

"According to Langley, he was once an agent for both the CIA and the MI6."

"Shit, he spied for both? He's never said a word about it!" Contrary to the popular misperception by the general public, a CIA agent was not a CIA employee. An agent, also known as an asset, was a private citizen recruited by CIA case officers. The CIA quietly contracted independently with the agent in order to perform covert ground work in another country.

"Remember a few years back there was a militant Muslim branch of Uyghur Chinese involved in a plot to assassinate Prime Minister Evans and plant a bomb for the royal wedding?"

The younger instructor thought for a moment. "I had forgotten all about that."

"Both the Secretary of State and the U.K. were offering a reward. Ryan worked for a technology firm in London that helped track the militant leader and catch him."

The junior instructor asked, "So did he apply to the CIA on his own, or did Headquarters recruit him?"

"I don't know, but he knows some Chinese and some other languages, and he has impressive international connections. He scored high in Magnatism, Versatility, and Steadfastness. Excellent traits for a case officer. Come on, let's go get some grub."

Part I

Josh and Chelsea

1
Chelsea

Chelsea Evans, a forty-two-year-old mother and commercial real estate agent, blearily poured herself another half cup of coffee. The past week had been interminably long and dull at the Mizrahi & Associates office in McLean, Virginia, a suburb of Washington, D.C. There had been no appointments all week, and just one this morning. This was crazy. She really should look for another job! Oh well, it was almost the weekend, and if she could just get through today, it was going to be a weekend to remember. Her good-looking, sexy husband, Josh Evans, was coming home in the middle of the night from an operation with the CIA, where he was an undercover case officer who operated with fake identities.

She allowed the television in the kitchen to fully and completely annoy her and thus jolt her all the way awake. It blared with the "Peppermint Pinkey" cartoon that seven-year-old Atalaya had turned on. Peppermint Pinkey was the most annoying cartoon character ever, a children's series based out of China, translated for an American audience. Everything was all about the Chinese these days. It got old.

The goofy-looking Peppermint Pinkey doll, with its strange short, black chunks of hair and somewhat Asian looking features, had taken America and other countries around the world by storm, resulting in shortages and brawls in the children's toy department during the holidays. The cartoon character had an inquisitive, nasal voice and had sparked a crop of cheap, copycat Chinese factory-produced Peppermint Pinkey dolls, clothes, sheets, pillowcases, comforters, pillows, and a line of dancewear. Chelsea's husband Josh, on his return home from the last covert CIA operation overseas, dryly remarked that Atalaya's bedroom looked like a bottle of Peppermint Pinkey Pepto-Bismol had exploded. Josh's best friend, technology wizard Clinton Radcliffe, always bought something horrible to add to the collection whenever he came to town to work on secret CIA contracts.

Peppermint Pinkey doll perched in her Peppermint Pinkey high chair next to Atalaya's place at the table, just like a real family member. Atalaya, with her dark curly hair and long eyelashes that fluttered over adorable brown eyes, fed the doll its breakfast and sang the irritating song along with the television:

Now it's time to go to school, time to learn and play.
Make our bodies smart and strong, on this happy day.

The television Peppermint Pinkey waved goodbye. Atalaya mimicked in unison with the cartoon character. *"Z`aiji`an!* Goodbye, everyone!" Because the show was translated from Chinese, only Chinese words seemed to come anywhere close to matching the movement of the cartoon character's mouth.

Atalaya unhooked Peppermint Pinkey doll from its high chair. "Come on, honey," she crooned like a little mother, "I'm in first grade now. It's time to brush our teeth and go to school."

As Atalaya lovingly carried the doll up the stairs, Chelsea set down the coffee cup, hastily grabbed the remote, pointed it to the television, and with relief switched the channel to *Good Morning America with Milo and Giordano.*

Angela Stevens Giordano's sculpted face dominated the screen. Chelsea watched the show because the attractive blond anchor was now married to Governor Tony Giordano, with whom Chelsea had briefly had a volatile relationship in her stodgy, inbred Midwest hometown of Columbia in the early part of his political career, back when he was an alderman and a mayor. Governor Giordano's best friend since childhood was now Vice President of the United States, Vice President Russo....

"Members of the human rights protest group, Hollywood For Humanitarianism, continue with Day Three of their hunger strike outside of the Chinese Embassy in Washington, D.C. The activist group is protesting Chinese human rights abuses against the citizens of Iraq," Angela Giordano proclaimed. "The spokesman for the group, Hollywood movie star Tyler Tischner, joins us in our studio. Good morning, Mr. Tischner." The camera zoomed in close to Tischner, with his thick, light brown, feathered-back hair and strong jawline with sexy razor stubble.

"Good morning, Angela. I just want your viewers to know that China continues its sex trafficking of Eastern European and Southeast Asian women. It has utilized shocking brutality in its peacekeeping efforts in Iraq. Just the other day they rounded up and shot fifty-nine protestors. We need to call on the United Nations to put pressure on China for a total ban on capital punishment in Iraq." Tyler Tischner had a minimal amount of

6

buttoned shirt, enough to get a great glimpse of his chest and pecs; Chelsea thought to herself that he was sufficient to stop you dead in your tracks and fire you up in the morning when you should be getting ready for work.

Chelsea left the kitchen, one ear still on the TV. Her heels clicked on the tile in the marble foyer in front of the circular stairwell. Early October morning sunlight streamed in the windows and a few leaves fluttered to the ground. This was Chelsea's dream house, a beautiful, expensive Georgian mansion that she had redecorated from top to bottom, and she was prouder of it than any house she had ever lived in. She primped in front of the hall mirror, frowning. Her own looks were so average. Her blond highlights were fading, and the boring light brown with the bits of gray at the roots was peeking through. The straight cut was losing its shape—she needed a cut to give it more volume....

"But Mr. Tischner, when we tolerate a group of people that take a vow of intolerance, peace is only a temporary phase. We learned that with ISIS, and it is repeating itself again with Black Lightening. One thing you have to acknowledge is, at least the Chinese are getting the job done. They succeeded in preventing the Uyghur Muslims to destabilize its own borders, and now they are refusing to tolerate destabilization in Iraq."

Angela Stevens Giordano was tough. Chelsea spun slowly around in front of the mirror, smoothing her hands on her waist. She hadn't been to the gym much with Josh being out of the country on assignment, and she would never be happy with her hips. She walked back to the television. What was taking Atalaya so long?

Tyler Tischner was not going to take this from Angela Stevens Giordano. "We can't condone brutality just because we defaulted on our national debt to the Chinese. Here's the bottom line. China thinks that since they are the strongest economy in the world, now they can be a bully."

Angela leaned forward and squinted at Tyler Tischner in a manner very reminiscent of Diane Sawyer, as if she could not quite comprehend. "But Mr. Tischner, our national debt to China is so large now that in lieu of payment, they are demanding we turn over our military bases. What is our leverage, and how many more days do you personally plan to engage in your hunger strike?"

7

"Our leverage is our shared, common humanity. We need to stand up to them. Personally, I'm not on the hunger strike because I'm filming my movie, Angela, it's—"

"You're not participating in your own hunger strike?" Angela missed nothing, especially opportunities to make stupid, self-interested people look dumb.

"It's called 'Avenging Conspiracy' and should be released next spring—"

"Sure to be a great hit. Thank you Mr. Tischner," Angela cut him off.

The camera went back to the *Good Morning America* news desk. The distinguished-looking Brett Milo said, "I've been tracking the comments to this interview online, Angela. I don't think America agrees with Tyler Tischner. It appears from our social media comments that Americans support the use of Chinese force in Iraq in order to keep the lid on the proverbial pot from blowing in the Middle East and to protect us from nuclear weapons."

Angela said, "It's time to go to a commercial break, and this *Good Morning America* segment has been brought to you by Peppermint Pinkey, the Chinese doll that is bringing children together around the globe—"

Chelsea snapped off the TV. "Atalaya," she called. "Hurry up. The carpool is waiting for us and Mommy has an appointment at work." She noticed that Yappie, her beloved old Sheltie, who was sleeping by the front door as she usually did when Josh was out of town, didn't even lift her head when Chelsea called loudly. Yappie was nearly deaf.

Something unintelligible wafted down from the bathroom. She got her purse, thinking dismally that she really ought to go apply for a more challenging job, even if it didn't pay as well. She stood at the base of the stairs, jangling her car keys. "AT-A-LAY-A!" she yelled impatiently. "You're going to make us late for school!"

Atalaya slunk guiltily around the corner, and Chelsea let out a shriek so loud that Yappie raised her head curiously.

Most, but not all, of Atalaya's long, beautiful, black curls were gone, and uneven, ragged chunks and spikes stood out on her head.

"WHAT…ARE…YOU…DOING???" Chelsea screeched. She strode up the stairs two at a time, surveying the mass of butchered curls on the floor in horror.

Atalaya burst into tears and sobbed loudly, clutching her doll under one arm. "I was cutting my hair." 'Hair' came out slurred, sort of like 'hey-oo'.

"WHAT WERE YOU THINKING?"

"Just wike Peppermint Pinkey," Atalaya blubbered in baby-talk explanation, one fist jammed in her mouth. It was a habit since babyhood, whenever she was upset.

Chelsea frantically danced on the bathroom floor, helplessly surveying the mess under her feet. "GET! IN! THE! CAR!" she ordered with clenched teeth.

"No!" Atalaya babbled.

"Get in the car! There's no time to clean this up!"

She hauled her daughter to the garage, opening the car door and planting Atalaya onto the booster seat, and she took off down the residential streets. She careened into the circle and skidded to a stop in front of the Feldmans' house, nearly covered in trees with yellow fall leaves. Attorney Kimberly Feldman, Chelsea's close friend and fellow carpool mom, did not come to the door. Maybe Kimberly was having just as crazy a day as Chelsea was. Kimberly's son, who was in Atalaya's grade, lumbered across the lawn unconcernedly as if first grade could simply wait for them all. Chelsea gunned the engine before he even had time to finish buckling and whirled around to the block to the north, feeling remorseful about wasting gasoline and trying to think what she should do: keep Atalaya home today, clean the mess, and take Atalaya to the beauty shop the minute it opened? No! She couldn't! She had a showing with a client in exactly forty-five minutes, the only appointment this whole entire week!

"What happened to your hair?" Kimberly's son asked Atalaya bluntly, then nearly bumped his head on the dashboard in front of him as Chelsea screeched to a stop at a stop sign. Atalaya burst into fresh sobs and covered her head with her hands in humiliation. They careened down the street and up to the school drop-off. The car pulled to a stop, and the children unbuckled and hastily climbed out, Atalaya sniffling.

Chelsea leaped out of the car and grabbed Atalaya's hand, leaving the car idling at the curb and blocking an angry mother in the vehicle behind them. She marched into the school, checked in at security, and stomped to Atalaya's classroom. "Atalaya cut her hair," she explained to Miss Monroe, Atalaya's new teacher this term. "I have a meeting and I don't have time to do anything about it. She'll just have to keep it like it is until I can come and get her and take her to the beauty shop."

To her credit, Miss Monroe did not laugh, and she took Atalaya's hand. "Everything is going to be okay. Let me get you a tissue," she said professionally to her little student.

Chelsea spun on her heel and walked out of the classroom at top speed, hearing the teacher's voice in the distance behind her, "You don't need to cry. We'll take you to the office and maybe they can pin the rest of your hair up."

Chelsea hurried down the hall, shoulders slumping. This was far from the first encounter with teachers about Atalaya's behavior. Things had improved a little bit this year, but still, Atalaya struggled to overcome the effects of fetal alcohol syndrome inherited from her birth mom. School was challenging. Life was challenging.

She exited out the front door and into the bright morning sun, overcome with mom guilt.

2
The Office

The clock on Chelsea Evans's computer blinked, moving up one more digit. Two minutes until three o'clock p.m. Chelsea leaned on one elbow and yawned with boredom. She looked out the floor-to-ceiling window at the campus of Monument Metroplex, the beautiful office, retail, and condominium project in McLean, Virginia, developed by her boss, Levi Mizrahi, and financed by China National Bank. Through the trees on the courtyard with their leaves that were changing to fall color, she could see the glint of the sunlight down below on the monument of the small replica of Shanghai's Oriental Pearl Tower. At this time of the year, the sunlight angle hit the colorful red spheres such that they glowed this time of day. All architecture lately was Chinese-inspired trendy-fad. It was the rage. Her office clients wanted their newly finished offices to have Asian décor, and she was already tired of it.

She turned to stare bleakly at the walls in her office, attractive with their bright contemporary paint colors, but emblematic of confinement. She just wanted to hug her daughter that she had screamed at this morning. There was absolutely nothing to do today, this entire week. Would Mr. Mizrahi EVER get to the office? He was supposed to have flown into town for a noon property management and leasing meeting with all of them but had to take a later flight.

All of a sudden she heard a screech of laughter from the next office. "Who DID this to my business cards?" howled the property manager.

Eager for a diversion, the Mizrahi & Associates team members popped out of their lavishly appointed offices and work stations to catch the latest prank inflicted on a member of the office staff.

"*Someone* substituted business cards for me and changed my title from 'Property Manager' to 'Psychic Mind Reader.' How long ago did this happen? How many people did I give a business card recently? Ok, everyone. Time to fess up. Who was it?"

"Not me," echoed Chelsea and several others.

"Guilty." Dane Schwartz, the thirty-something accountant from Wyoming with thinning blond hair, was red with embarrassed satisfaction as he confessed. "It was two months ago. I wondered if you would ever notice—"

"TWO MONTHS AGO?" the property manager shrieked again, and then doubled over her desk in gales of laughter again, burying her head in her arms. "So that means I passed them out at the Chamber of Commerce reception…."

Dane Schwartz was behind the prank? Dane was bouncing back! Today he was at it again, displaying his corny sense of humor. Dane's wife had been killed when she was deployed with the U.S. Army to Sudan. Only recently had his spirit begun to improve.

The Mizrahi & Associates team members erupted in laughter, which was pleasantly muffled by the plush white carpet and soft office chairs. For a good fifteen minutes time passed a little faster in the dull real estate office. Then they drifted back to their desks, back to leasing and property management reports, or in reality, social media, waiting for Mr. Mizrahi's arrival and staff meeting to start. Any other Friday afternoon, they would have all cut loose early to go to the '80s retro decor vape bar and lounge at Shangri-La hotel in Monument Metroplex (which was called "Just the Fax"). Chelsea didn't vape but there was still strong peer pressure to come along anyway. It was a friendly group of co-workers. All of them were younger transplants from other states and with no immediate family in the area.

Chelsea went back to her own office. Bored, she logged into the secure site from the CIA and pulled up the NoitaLever game on her computer. She knew she shouldn't do this at work. Her husband, Josh, and his enigmatic technology friend, Clinton Radcliffe, who developed the game for the CIA, wouldn't like it. They would worry that as secure as it was, someone might find the cache on her work computer. But the game was so addictive!

The phone beeped. It was the receptionist. "Mr. Mizrahi is here! Everyone to the conference room."

The office team scrambled out of their desks and to their places. Levi Mizrahi, aged somewhere between seventy and ninety years old, but sharp and fit as a man half his age, sat down at the head of the conference table wearing his golf shirt and shorts. Mr. Mizrahi had homes and hotel complexes in New York, Florida, Ontario, and Tel Aviv. He spent a lot of time on cruises to the Mediterranean. "How are my Washingtonians?" he clucked fondly in his thick East Coast accent as they all settled into place. "Tell me what you got today!" Mr. Mizrahi jumped right into the meeting. "Dane?" he turned for a report to the studious-looking staff CPA with thinning blond hair.

"You know why the cash accountant committed suicide, don't you? It's an accrual world," Dane quipped.

Mr. Mizrahi guffawed and clapped his hands delightedly at the pun. "Accrual world! That's a good one!" The team members obligingly laughed. Dane, who had gradually returned after personal tragedy to his role as the purveyor of awful, corny office jokes, proceeded to give a report on his accounting. Bored, Chelsea's mind began to wander, thinking about Josh coming home from his latest CIA assignment.

Her job at Mizrahi & Associates had been a dream job when she started it. It was only a twenty-five minute commute on a bad day, which was pretty good for NOVA, the locals' nickname for Northern Virginia. Monument Metroplex had been newly constructed and had needed a real estate agent. The team members were not snotty and stuffy like other big-city professionals, they were informal and extremely friendly, like a family. The first two years on the job had been awesome. She had sold luxury condos, leased space to national retail chains in the retail mall, and landed a lease for a large government contractor. It was a salary job— almost unheard of in the world of commercial real estate. The company prizes were good, and Mr. Mizrahi had flown her and her husband Josh to Martha's Vineyard as a reward for good work.

But eventually she discovered the reason for the unusually high salary arrangement: Once the project was sixty percent leased, Mr. Mizrahi basically quit caring. He was paying for someone else to care. The property was cash flowing. He was on to the next thing, a development in Pennsylvania. If he had time to think about leases in McLean, Virginia, that was nice; but if he was busy—well, phone calls with offers went unanswered. This was the first time the office workers at Monument Metroplex had seen him in person for four months. No straight commission commercial real estate broker would put up with that for very long. No third party real estate management company could make financial decisions with such an absent owner. This was why he had to pay for a quality staff—and pay them well, with daily catered luncheons and luxurious office space and free parking and onsite health club privileges—to stay interested in their jobs.

"Whatcha got for me, Chelsea?" It was her turn and he greeted her as if he didn't remember that he had ignored offers on the real estate for an entire month. She handed him the hard copy of a lease proposal, blowing some dust off it. Mr. Mizrahi waited so long to respond to offers that the prospects frequently gave up and went to another building.

She explained the terms of the offer. It was a Chinese insurance company that wanted a good-sized amount of office space. "Their broker from Goldberger Hewitt called and yelled at me last week about how long this is taking. I don't want to lose them."

"Goldberger Hewitt? Cheaters and liars," he grumbled. His pen trailed down the proposal and he made marks here and there. She knew he expected her to affirm out loud that the competitive brokers were indeed criminals, but she didn't bite.

She had once worked for Goldberger Hewitt back in her provincial and inbred Midwestern hometown, Columbia, and also for a very exciting but short time in the London branch office. Her work had been more motivating and challenging than this job at Mizrahi & Associates. She should have tried to get a commission job with Goldberger Hewitt in McLean, Virginia, instead....

"Tell the dickhead broker to keep his pretty little Goldberger Hewitt pants on. Counter back and tell him we're cutting the remodeling request down to three hundred thousand dollars," Mr. Mizrahi said, scratching here and there with his pen, pounding the document with his little fist, and handing the proposal back to Chelsea with a flourish of his hand.

It was exactly what she had expected. Once you nabbed Mr. Mizrahi and got his gears turning about a negotiation, he was pretty good to work with. It was just that it was almost impossible to get his attention when it was a brand new offer. If only he would just raise her latitude to negotiate and sign leases up to a higher amount....

"You're such a good girl! Great job, great job." He stuck his hand down in his pocket and then stood up, as he did at the end of every meeting, to shake hands and personally thank all the employees. They all scrambled to their feet and Chelsea gathered her purse up with her free arm. "Chelsea," he reached for a handshake with her first, and they clasped hands.

"AAAAAAAAACK!" Chelsea let out a yell and jumped backwards. Her purse flew up in the air and landed on the floor, and her conference table chair scooted backwards, slapping the wall.

Mr. Mizrahi let out an uproarious belly laugh. "This time I gotcha, Chelsea Evans!" He winked and pointed a finger at her. Eyes twinkling, he turned his hand and opened his palm for everyone to see. A buzzer was suspended inside his hand via what looked like a regular ring on his middle finger.

The rest of the staff burst out laughing: "The old hand buzzer trick!"

Dane, who had been sitting next to her, helped her pick up the contents of her purse. Her face flamed scarlet as she ruefully scrambled to get everything back in place. It was Chelsea = four deflections, Mr. Mizrahi = one victory. At long last, after several failed attempts, Mr. Mizrahi had finally succeeded in pranking her.

He wriggled the ring with the buzzer off and put it back in his pocket. "I'm headed to Canada next week for some hunting," he announced as he shook hands with each person in the room, launching into a story about a moose that kept eating his flowers in Canada. The story was long, they were standing, and they were hungry. Finally he concluded the meeting. "Let's go eat, everyone. I have reservations for all of us at The Capital Grille."

It was the most expensive restaurant in McLean. Chelsea held back behind the others and squeezed his arm. "Mr. Mizrahi, I am so sorry. My husband comes home from a long assignment at 2:00 in the morning. I'm going to miss your amazing dinner."

"What, my dear? You're going to miss? Why, it won't be the same without you! You say Josh is coming home?"

"Yes!" she replied, her eyes lighting up. Josh had charmed the pants off Mr. Mizrahi at the holiday parties and the trip to Hilton Head. They had conferred for hours, and Mr. Mizrahi had no idea, but Josh had made a key recruit for the CIA due to a name that Mr. Mizrahi had unknowingly dropped.

"Oh, that's wonderful, just wonderful. He's such a fine young man. Tell him hello from me and Miriam and give him and your daughter our love. How is my little Attie?" Her boss was a ruthless

15

businessman, but he treated his employees like family, even if he didn't see them or talk to them much.

"She cut off her hair this morning with play scissors, and it has these horribly ugly chunks all over her head…."

Her boss chuckled amusedly as Chelsea shared the story. "Dane, give Chelsea her present, she has to go," he said. The office CPA scrambled and collected an envelope. "Chelsea, we're so sorry you can't hang with us tonight," Dane said sincerely, handing it to her. His Adam's apple bobbed up and down in his thin accountant's throat and he seemed genuinely disappointed that the team would be incomplete without her this evening.

"That is so kind!" Chelsea said. She knew what was in the envelope. It was a random bonus, and it was the kind of thing Mr. Mizrahi did for his employees. He was so funny and so generous. For the thousandth time she put away thoughts of looking for a more interesting and challenging job. How could she even consider leaving such an agreeable, funny, caring group?

She tucked the bonus in her purse and slipped away from the rest of the team members, who would probably be wined and dined until 10:00 or 11:00 tonight, and went for her purse and car keys. She was going to hit McLean rush hour traffic, which was not going to be fun; but she couldn't wait to start the weekend. Josh would be home and they would be a family of three once again.

3
Josh

After right-sizing Atalaya's hair at the children's salon to the extent feasible, making supper, and putting Atalaya to bed, Chelsea wandered around the house, wondering if she could fall asleep before Josh got in.

Doing bills would make her sleepy! She went to the desk in the living room to go through mail. Household chores and decisions were the drudgery part of being a CIA wife. It was all up to her to organize. Josh was mostly too far removed, too detached from being constantly gone, to help very much with decisions. It was boring to work all day at a do-nothing job. Then there was a rush to beat traffic and pick up Atalaya, and after that it was on to the nightly homework struggle, boring bills, boring housework, and boring laundry. She telecommuted and worked at home one or two days a week, but that was lonely until Atalaya came home from school. It was monotonous, day after endless day until Josh came home. Then it got a lot more interesting. They got to go to government functions and parties. She settled into the comfortable desk chair for a dull hour of clicking, paying, sending, more clicking, more payments, more sending. Then she began to yawn. She looked at the clock. Three hours until Josh would be home!

She decided to try to crawl into bed and attempt to sleep so the time would pass.

She awoke when she heard the soft clicks as Josh locked up his hand gun, a Browning, in the safe in the closet. The light in the bathroom turned on and the shower began to run, and she stretched, coming awake. The water stopped and Josh stepped out of the shower into the light with the towel around his waist. She blinked, her eyes adjusting, and watched as he crossed to the bureau and ruffled through for some shorts.

The towel dropped, and his naked muscular silhouette woke her up more fully. She squirmed and re-adjusted the sexy little white negligee she had tugged out of the back of the bureau drawer earlier. She propped herself up seductively on the pillows. He turned around and in the light cast by the bathroom light saw she was awake.

"Babe!" His voice was low and thick with desire. He crossed the distance to the bed, pulling her into his arms; and there she was, finally pressing next to his skin and smelling him and kissing him and running her fingers through his dark curly hair at the back of his wet neck. She touched her forehead to his and kissed the freckles on his nose. Every time Josh came home, it was a strange process of re-acclimating. In some ways it was as comfortable as pulling out a favorite coat that had been stored away since last season; in other ways it was like getting reacquainted with a stranger.

"Did I tell you how much I want you?" he breathed.

They clung together and he took her mouth in his and kissed her, then his lips traveled down her neck and tickled her collarbone, traveling across her shoulders to the back of her neck. Even in her grogginess, she felt longing for him. He groaned softly into her ear as he eased her onto her back with her head on the pillows. He ran his hands down her waist and under her hips and thighs, wriggling over her. Then he lowered down over her, tasting her throat and neck with his mouth.

4
The Assignment

Josh and Chelsea talked softly in the darkness, their arms and legs intertwined. The sexy little white negligee she had fished out of the back corner of the bureau drawer was tangled somewhere down in the bottom of the sheets. She rolled over on her side, running a hand down his stomach. "Tell me about your trip. How long are you back? Are you all finished with the op? I thought it was going to last a little longer."

"Headquarters cabled me that a SAD personnel got killed. I came back for the funeral."

"Oh no. That's why you came back early?" SAD was the CIA's version of Special Ops, sent in to kill, if necessary. A funeral was hard on the CIA family. "So will you go back after the memorial service?"

"I'll be back here for a little while but they said that they need me to fill a case officer position on an emergency basis." Few case officers went on more than one or two tours; since he did undercover architectural work, Josh was unusual. His cover had never been blown. He hadn't been a victim of any departmental budget cutbacks, and he was fortunate that he wasn't permanently stuck in a cubicle in Langley where CIA headquarters drones worked, like the remainder of his classmates from The Farm.

"Wouldn't that be a dream come true if you could get a post to Western Europe? I would love to live there again." She reached up and stroked his cheek and pressed a kiss on his jaw.

"I'm going to make another request."

"Honey," she spoke in the dark, "Do you think you'll have to do Africa to bargain for Europe?" Every CIA wife spent sleepless nights worried that her spouse would be asked to serve some country in Africa, especially if the spouse had low seniority. Militant groups and tribes that had procured biological warfare weapons were warring with each other, poisoning rivers, scorching the African plains and the forests, and raining the greatest scourge of human genocide the world had ever witnessed across a continent. Her co-worker, Dane in the accounting department, had a wife who had served in the Army. The wife had been killed when a suicidal group of Muslim extremists launched a highly toxic bacteria into the water supply.

"Not Africa. They are pulling people out, not putting them in," he reassured her. His finger traced a line along the sensitive area of her collarbone and down between her breasts. "My next assignment's in the Middle East." His voice dropped as he pulled away from her, got up, and turned off the bathroom light.

When he came back to the darkness of the bed, he withdrew into that part of himself that was married to the CIA, the part that the government would not allow him to share, because it was classified work. There were terrible things he knew that were happening all over the world—horrifying things. From time to time he told her some of it—by and large, he probably told her more than what most CIA husbands told their wives—but there were still so many secrets.

That was the other Josh, the one with a darker side, who lived a double life and whose life, for the safety of the country, was a lie.

5

Omar Al Ghamdi
Arlington, Virginia
Two Years Earlier

*T*he string group finished playing the classical piece, and gentle clapping rippled across the house as the employees of Mizrahi & Associates gathered for the holiday party carefully balanced their drink glasses. The lights of a menorah twinkled in the frosty window, casting delicate sparkles off Chelsea's wine glass.

"Babe," Josh said in a low, sensual voice, moving his lips towards her ear, "did I tell you how beautiful you are tonight?"

She actually had to bend down a tiny bit to hear him. She and Josh were close to the same height, but tonight her newly highlighted hair was piled into an up-do and her stiletto high heels put her two inches taller than him. She grinned seductively at him. He was dressed smartly in the black tux and red cummerbund he had worn to their wedding. "Yes, you did, at least twice. And you, honey, are hot!" Despite the fact they were nearly forty years old, the chemistry between them was as strong as ever, and she knew that people still thought they were a good looking couple.

Her outspoken boss, Levi Mizrahi, was at the dining room bar, wearing a Santa elf hat that fell down comically over one eye. It was a bit of a peculiar juxtaposition to the Tallit prayer shawl draped around his shoulders. He was conversing loudly with a Middle-Eastern man she had never seen before with striking salt-and-pepper hair: "Of course the Chinese are allies of the United States, and especially Israel! The Arabs want to annihilate all of us, and anyone who is an enemy of our enemy is our friend! And besides—" Chelsea's boss poked his guest in the ribs and winked—"China National Bank made me a great loan so I could hire engineers like you to design my shopping center."

"Hi Mr. Mizrahi," she said at the first break in the conversation.

Her boss turned to her and Josh, who was still at her elbow, and his face beamed with pleasure. "Chelsea, you brought Josh with you. How are you, my dear boy? I want you to know how much Miriam and I enjoyed having you at Martha's Vineyard!" Mr. Mizrahi embraced Josh with effusiveness that nearly made the

21

other guests blush. His friend from the Middle East regarded them with polite curiosity. "Omar, this is Chelsea, my star leasing agent for my commercial real estate properties at Monument Metroplex. And her husband Josh. You and Josh will have quite a bit to talk about," Mr. Mizrahi explained to the man. "Josh is a simply spectacular architect for Crestedon Global Architectural and Engineering. Josh and Chelsea, this is Omar Al Ghamdi, an acquaintance of mine from Saudi Arabia. He's a structural engineer that I met on the shopping center project in Canada. He does projects in the Middle East."

With his gentle, soft-spoken voice and earnest brown eyes, Josh launched easily and quickly into a conversation with Omar, and Chelsea felt the wine settle warmly all the way down to her toes. Josh and the Saudi engineer soon engaged in an animated conversation about the increasingly troubled relationship between the Saudis and the United States.

She drifted away over to Dane Schwartz, who was standing alone on the other side of the drinks station with a whiskey sour in his hand. "Hi Dane, you didn't have to come. But I'm glad you did."

"Oh, uh, thanks. I really didn't want to miss."

"How are you doing? I mean, honestly, how are you doing?"

"It's ok. Really." His Adam's apple constricted uncomfortably in his throat. The funeral for Dane's wife, who was killed while on duty with the military in Sudan, had only been two weeks ago. He was pale tonight, obviously lonely and adrift.

"We miss her this holiday, completely."

"Thank you, Chelsea. When you're in college and it's about weddings, everyone jabs you in the ribs and tells you you're going to be next. It's a little different with funerals. I'm not a 'mourning person', but I had to attend that one," he lamely quipped.

"It's good for you to get out of the house, Dane." They hugged awkwardly; his pain was obvious. Just then one of their co-workers interrupted to introduce his latest girlfriend. Dane recovered quickly and went on with corny witticisms, but Chelsea could tell he was making an effort. "I'm Dane. I'm an accountant, not an actuary. You know the difference? An accountant has a sense of humor. You know how actuaries put some zip into their holiday party? They invite an accountant."

Suddenly she saw a flash of red cummerbund and black. Josh was signaling her, the sign that he used when he was onto a potential CIA recruit and needed her help. She excused herself and made her way back to him.

He slipped an arm around her and drew her cheek down to his lips and kissed it. She heard him murmur, "Omar's wife. Her name is Laila. Make her comfortable." He inclined his head towards the kitchen, where Mr. Mizrahi's wife, Miriam, was arranging rugelach on a tray on the marble kitchen island and conversing to a group gathered around the food. A lovely Middle Eastern Saudi woman with huge, beautifully made-up eyes and perfect brows stood by the kitchen wall a little apart from the others.

Helping herself to another drink, Chelsea went to Laila and touched her gently on the arm. "Hi, Laila? My name is Chelsea. I just met your husband over there with Mr. Mizrahi. Welcome to the United States!"

The Saudi woman responded eagerly, delighted to converse with Americans.

In the car, when it was over, Josh turned on the engine. He held up his hand in a high-five and Chelsea gave it a slap, and then they fist-bumped. Josh and Chelsea were a team, continually working a crowd, always trying to identify a target that Josh could cultivate so that the Agency could recruit an overseas spy. Josh's ultimate job was to peddle treason against rogue governments.

It had started out as simply a holiday party for work, but it had turned into a productive evening. Laila had accepted an invitation for coffee with Chelsea at their house for next weekend.

Josh would transmit a secure cable from home tonight asking for traces on the couple. Next, he would have to write a formal request to cold-pitch the Saudi target. It would be sent back to him and re-written a few times to make dozens of American bureaucrats from Langley and Saudi Arabia happy. Then it would take a month or longer to do traces on Laila's husband, ok everything with the CIA referent for the country of Saudi Arabia, double check everything with the FBI, and run it through Josh's bosses and on up to Headquarters, before Omar could be approached by the CIA. By then, as many as nine months would have passed.

The CIA would never know that by then Chelsea already had Laila in her trust for nine months and that Josh had already collected intel from Laila's husband. Josh had those rare and sought-after qualities of a CIA case officer: a deep respect for the institution and love for country, yet at the same time, an autonomous, individualistic, and creative problem-solver.

6
The Gunman

Just outside the auditorium overlooking the narthex of Fairfax Community Church was a coffee and gift shop with warm wood floors and bags and crafts for sale, handmade by rescued sex-trafficking victims from China. Fairfax was a megachurch that pumped thousands of people from NOVA—the northern part of Virginia near D.C.—through four services every week: two on Saturdays and two on Sunday. The music was great, but Chelsea and Josh really didn't know hardly anybody at the church. Josh had spent too much time on tours to get involved. The narthex and gift shop were mostly cleared now because the service was underway. Atalaya was downstairs in Sunday School. The music was finished and the sermon had just started, but they remained sitting at a small, round table, sipping coffee. It was so good to be together, to go to church as a family and just sit and enjoy some downtime before Josh's next overseas tour.

His eyes were always darting behind and around, even in relaxing moments, looking everywhere, assessing every situation, wary of something unusual. It was second nature to CIA case workers, especially when they just came back from an assignment. Josh watched as a bored security guard for the church wandered over from the entry door to the direction of the coffee shop. The officer stopped to chat with a woman sitting alone behind a charity booth.

"What should we do about Atalaya?" Chelsea asked.

"I don't know."

The school counselor had met with them and said their daughter was caught in a social rut, labeled as "different" by her mainstream classmates. Changing to a different first grade class might help, but after a few weeks or months, the labeling could start all over again. Atalaya might catch up with the others socially and developmentally—indeed, she had improved some already— or she may always be a step behind the rest of society. There were support groups and plenty of online material to read up on, but at the end of the day you had to do what you thought was best for your family, and sometimes the answer wasn't obvious.

The coffee shop had a large screen television turned on, airing the service via closed circuit. "Now, guys, let's deja-vu last week's sermon: We told you that Babylon was destroyed centuries ago." The young, good-looking Pastor Rouch was pacing energetically across the stage, and the camera zoomed in close to his face, showing a close-up of his wavy red hair, slightly long and feathered back, the way the young guys were doing their hair now. Youthful and vigorous, he could form a torrent of words destined to raise an audience onto its feet. "Hyper-caffeinated with a splash of spiritual sexiness," was the way Josh described Pastor Rouch.

"They've tried to rebuild Babylon nineteen times," Pastor Rouch shouted. "I know some of you don't believe me about this. But listen to this prophecy from TWO THOUSAND YEARS AGO!" He fairly leaped up into air and then squatted down on the heels of his yellow and orange sneakers, reading the words from the teleprompter. The camera guys were clearly challenged, trying to keep up with his movements.

The words the youthful minister was reading aloud flashed up on the screen, scrolling down so the congregants could follow along. "Woe! Woe to you, great city, you mighty city of Babylon! In one hour your doom has come! The merchants of the earth will weep and mourn over her because no one buys their cargoes anymore. The merchants who sold these things and gained their wealth from her will stand far off, terrified at her torment. They will weep and mourn and cry out. In one hour such great wealth has been brought to ruin! When they see the smoke of her burning, they will exclaim, 'Was there ever a city like this great city?' Buckle up your seatbelts, everyone. This is for real, it's going to happen!" Pastor Rouch was gesticulating with his arms wildly now.

Josh and Chelsea watched the closed-circuit TV screen with interest. Pastor Rouch was fascinating. There were some things you heard about in those ancient prophecies in church and you weren't sure if they were literal. You neither disbelieved nor believed them.

A door hinge squeaked down at the end of the narthex, vaguely distracting them from Pastor Rouch's leaping and bouncing across the stage. The security guard that had been talking to the woman at the charity booth went into the men's bathroom. Josh's eyes scanned the area one more time and then he turned back to Chelsea. "Speaking of the Middle East, he said, "do you ever hear from Laila Al Ghamdi anymore?"

26

Chelsea had to think for a moment, it had been so long. "Who—oh, you mean the wife of that structural engineer that you were trying to recruit for the Agency? Um, no. She quit posting pictures of her kids on social media. I bet I haven't heard from her for a year."

"I didn't think so," he said. He paused for a bit and then said, "I need to talk to you about my new op."

Usually, from what he described, Josh had an occasional assignment with the State Department building operations rehabbing a graciously designed foreign embassy, or providing architectural services for undercover officers with alternate professions and fake offices, or legitimate architectural assignments for nondescript, dull government buildings in foreign countries. It was always his covert job to be looking for locals to recruit as spies.

"Where is it this time?" she asked.

Once again he looked around to make sure no one was listening. By now the coffee shop was mostly deserted, except for the girls who were cleaning up in the back kitchen. At the far end of the narthex a door opened, and a man entered with dark hair, a dark complexion, a light windbreaker; but he was too far away to hear their conversation.

"I'm going to Iraq. I'm being assigned there. " Josh's voice was so low she could barely make out the words. He turned to watch the man in the narthex again for a moment.

Her shoulders slumped with disappointment. "Still no assignment in Western Europe! How long will you be there?"

"Don't know. I've put in five years; I can't believe they are sending me off to that godforsaken place to do this stuff."

"If it turns into something long, will we go over there to live?" She didn't want to raise her child in the Middle East, but their family needed to be together more.

"No." His voice was definitive, final. "No, I don't want you there. There's a veneer of civility in the business and tourist areas, but if you drive down the wrong highway out of town or get crosswise with the wrong people, you get your eyes gouged out or your hands or your head get cut off. Maybe you might permanently disappear, or you might even get nuked."

"Oh…." She physically shrunk back at his strong reaction. "You can refuse, you know. You have employee rights."

"And end up in a cubicle in Langley. Then we'll never get to London until we retire, and by then we'll be too old and arthritic to enjoy it."

The dark-complexioned man who had entered the narthex stopped before the auditorium door, seemingly hesitant about going into the auditorium to sit down.

Pastor Rouch was still talking on the closed-circuit television about the futility of trying to rebuild Babylon, and you could hear the echo of his sermon out in the narthex, too. "Therefore wild beasts of the desert shall dwell in Babylon with the jackals, and ostriches shall dwell there. And it shall never again be inhabited with people, even from generation to generation! Fallen is Babylon the Great! She has become a dwelling for demons and a haunt for every impure spirit, a haunt for every unclean bird, a haunt for every unclean and detestable animal."

It was awfully hard to imagine THAT ever happening when you saw the pictures on *Good Morning America* of the gleaming office buildings and hotels and casinos in the new, modern metropolis similar to Las Vegas that the Chinese peacekeepers dubbed Babylon Metro. She started to speculate about it to Josh, but he was watching over his shoulder. The man in the windbreaker had just opened the door of the auditorium to go inside, his hand in the coat pocket.

"Stay right here! Don't move!" Josh hissed. He slipped to his feet and padded quietly across the carpeted narthex behind the man. Puzzled, Chelsea watched as Josh cupped his eyes, peering in the crack between the auditorium doors where the man had gone in.

All of a sudden Josh wildly whipped open the auditorium door and leaped through it like a cat, his hand on his pocket where he usually kept his Browning, disappearing into the darkness inside. A frantic male voice filtered back into the narthex: "....Jew lovers! Allah is the enemy of unbelievers! Do not take the Jews and Christians for friends!" The door slowly began to swing shut behind Josh and the man.

On the television screen, Pastor Rouch paused in confusion, turning sideways to squint towards the back of the auditorium. "Uh, hey there, folks, we seem to have an audience malfunction of some kind, if we could have the ushers—"

By now the security guard had crashed through the men's bathroom door and was propelling towards the auditorium. He was a conceal-carry guard and had pulled out a weapon, but as he opened the doors, from somewhere deep within the auditorium itself there was the sound of a gun going off, again, and again, and again. Screams rose from behind the doors and then a different gun went off.

With an instinctively garbled wince and half-scream of her own, Chelsea leaped up and scrambled backwards towards the cash register counter, knocking violently into chairs and tables on the way. She ran around the cash register counter, crouching down on the floor and covering her head. All of a sudden the row of doors in the auditorium simultaneously burst open and a stampede of congregants exited. She heard another security guard yelling at the crowd, "Everyone down on the floor! Protect your heads!" But the crowd ignored him and fled.

Her heart was beating so hard she thought it would burst, and she began to panic. Atalaya was separated from her! She was all the way downstairs in the Sunday School room in her little chair, coloring at the little kids' table.....

And Josh! He was in there with those gun shots! Her breath came in ragged hulks as terror swept her. Crawling on her hands and knees, she peered around the corner of the cash register, but all she could see was stampeding feet. Wildly she thought about her own gun she had at home in the safe that Josh had given her, the gun she didn't want to use and didn't like.

Over the din she could hear Pastor Rouch praying on the television in a rapid-fire, tense voice, "Lord protect us! Lord, please bring your hand of peace upon us and make everybody in this auditorium calm right now—" and it occurred to her that it was strange that he was still standing at the mic. Why didn't he drop and roll on the floor?

Hide in the kitchen! her instincts told her. If there was a hostage situation, it may be safer in there. Frantically she crawled on her hands and knees from the cash register to the kitchen door and scrambled inside onto the cool tile.

"Oh my gosh, did she get hit?" wailed one of the coffee servers inside the kitchen as she crawled in.

"No, I'm ok!" Chelsea managed in a croaking voice.

"Grab her! Get her under this table!" Hands reached out and clutched her, yanking her violently, and when she righted herself and bumped her head on the steel table above her, she found herself surrounded by the three frightened coffee servers.

Someone set off the fire alarms. Josh…was he alive? Or were they in there, their bodies a mass of blood and carnage? She felt nausea in her stomach and wanted to throw up. She felt the gag reflex and tried to stifle it because there was no way she was leaving the shelter of the steel table to reach the trash can and throw up.

Someone grabbed her hands. The coffee shop girls began praying as they listened to the horrible sounds of pandemonium — people screaming and yelling, stumbling, falling to the floor and being trampled. Through the roar they could hear a man's voice over the sound system, "Attention ladies and gentlemen, this is security. We have the situation under control. The gunman has been contained. Please do not panic. Please exit in an orderly manner. I repeat, the gunman has been contained."

"But what if there are more of them outside?" moaned one of the girls.

This thought hadn't occurred to Chelsea, and she felt her stomach roll with nausea once again. She choked back the bile in her throat and fought to take a deep, slow breath. A wild motherly instinct made her want to jump up and race out into the narthex and down the corridor to the children's wing, grab Atalaya, and run with all her might to the car. Except they couldn't leave Josh….

Outside they heard the distant sound of sirens.

7
Enemy to the Disbelievers

The attendees of Fairfax Community Church and their crying children poured out of the building towards their vehicles and vacated the property in a spider web of confused traffic, cutting across the grass and the sidewalk, horns honking. Chelsea crawled out of the kitchen, joined the teeming mass, and finally reached the Sunday school room downstairs. The frightened Sunday school teachers were reluctant to unlock the doors of the children's wing, but as the parents pounded and yelled, they finally did, and she rushed in to Atalaya, falling down on her neck and trying to muffle her own sobs, as did the other parents entering the first grade Sunday school room. The Sunday school teachers, clutching the children and barely containing their own panic, attempted unsuccessfully to verify the identity of the parents grabbing their children.

She scooped the seven-year-old in her arms and carried her up the stairs in a burst of superhuman strength. And then at the top of the stairs, just inside the narthex, she stopped, panting vigorously and repeating over and over in a broken, relieved voice, "Daddy is ok, Attie! Daddy is ok!" She could see him down the hallway standing near a gurney with the police officers and firemen, along with the other security guards and congregants who had been in closest proximity to the shooter. The police were taking statements. "JOSH!" she shouted, waving her free arm.

Josh turned and saw her and Atalaya and then excused himself to the policeman. He crossed the distance in less than five strides, bumping into oncoming elbows, and she and Atalaya threw themselves into his arms, crying.

"Thank God," he murmured, and she could feel spasms in his arms as he fought to control his emotions. "Thank you, God, thank you, God, thank you, thank you..." he repeated endlessly.

"What happened?" she pleaded, turning a tear-stained face to him. He kissed her nose and pressed his forehead to her forehead, Atalaya nearly crushed between them.

"It was dark inside and my eyes were having a hard time adjusting, but I took him out," he said, squeezing his eyes tightly shut at the memory. "Security was right behind me. They also took a shot at him."

She could smell the gunpowder on his clothes. "Did he kill anyone?"

"Yes."

The policeman that had been interviewing Josh had come up to finish. Josh turned to the policeman and finished answering a question that the officer had apparently asked. "No, I didn't hear what he was mumbling, not until he started shouting the Quran at Pastor Rouch."

Chelsea waited, trying to halt her own shaking and calm Atalaya while the police continued to question Josh. It went on forever, and the questions made her nervous. They were lucky to be alive, and more than anything in the world, all she wanted to do was go home. The police were asking questions that might lead to blowing Josh's cover. Why was he carrying a weapon at church? Where was he trained to use it? Did he have military training?

When the interviews with the police were over, they headed to the car. Reporters still roamed the parking lot, looking for a story. One of them spotted the small family and raced over, waving a mic. "Excuse me, sir, ma'am, can you tell us what happened there?"

Josh shook his head and covered his face with his hand as they hustled towards the car. In the car, Atalaya sniffled tears in the booster seat on the back seat and Josh positioned his weapon in his lap, at the ready, the whole way home.

The next morning, Chelsea watched the report on *Good Morning America with Milo and Giordano*. The pretty, blond, blue-eyed Angela Stevens Giordano opened the show with the story. "Three people were killed and thirteen injured when a gunman fired shots inside a church in suburban Washington, D.C., yesterday. Fairfax Community mega church is a congregation located in Arlington, a pleasant neighborhood suburb in Virginia. During Sunday morning services, witnesses reported that a gunman shouting, 'Allah is an enemy to the disbelievers' sprayed bullets in the auditorium and trained a gun in the direction of head pastor Jake Rouch. The gunman was stopped by the church security and a congregation member with a conceal carry weapon. We go live on the ground to where the local ABC affiliate is reporting."

The station went to the local reporter standing in front of the church. On the television screen the trees were the vibrant gold of autumn, and the lawn looked so big green and stretched out. You could see the ruts in the grass from all the cars that had fled. "I'm standing in front of the church, which as you can see is a crime scene. Investigators are combing the building. The gunman's identity has not been released, pending notification of relatives."

"We are hearing reports," Brett Milo said to the reporter, "that the church pastor was engaging in racial stereotyping by presenting sermons about prophecies in the Middle East that painted Babylon Metro in a negative light."

The reporter was having trouble hearing and hesitated while adjusting the small earphone on her ear. "I didn't quite catch that, Brett? Witnesses report that the gunman was screaming quotes from the Quran, including, 'Do not take the Jews and Christians for friends'. The quotes are found—" unfamiliar with the Quran, the reporter had to pause and read her notes. "The quotes are found in a part of the Quran called 'The Dinner Table' verse 5.51."

"We seem to be having trouble with our audio. Thank you, that was our ABC affiliate reporting live from Fairfax Community Church in Arlington, Virginia," smoothly interrupted Brett Milo. "Coming up after the break, *Good Morning America* interviews a moderate Muslim cleric about yesterday's events."

Chelsea turned the volume down. "How long will you be able to stay out of the media?"

"I don't know," Josh replied. "Wouldn't it be ironic if my cover was blown, not because of some bungle-up during an operation, but because I tried to be a good citizen and ended up as a witness at a trial?"

"Maybe you can pull it off. Could you say you are an architect who has had job sites in high-crime neighborhoods, and that you carry it out of habit?" Chelsea suggested, trying to be optimistic.

"Headquarters is handling it."

Covers were blown fairly often at the CIA. They were usually a slip-up overseas. Not at home, nor in such a spectacular way.

She opened the safe in the bedroom and pulled out the weapon in a little box, the gun Josh bought for her five years earlier.

"I don't like it and I don't want to keep it," she said, after the first lesson, when she had removed her ear protection and they

33

were walking back to the car. "That was terrible. It's heavy and I'm clumsy. I feel have no control over it."

"We'll get out to the firing range a few more times and work on it."

"Do you really think I need this? I don't think I can ever get good enough to shoot somebody, and for sure not in the right part of their body. And besides, what are the odds that someone whose cover is an architect and businessman is ever going to have his cover blown and his family threatened?"

"You never know, it could happen. You need to be prepared. Don't worry, you'll get better at it."

She took the box down to the garage. She opened the door of the car and slid it under the car seat. Then she went to the kitchen and opened a bottle of wine, trying to muffle the echoes of screams of panicky church members from thudding in her ears.

Spiffily dressed in an expensive suit and designer shoes from one of the most popular men's stores in Georgetown, Josh Evans unlocked the sporty-looking car in the garage and set a large, non-descript briefcase in the trunk underneath the cover which was supposed to contain a spare tire. It was intentionally typical of a car that an architect in the Washington-Baltimore area would drive: a silver, somewhat sporty looking Mazda with dark tinted windows.

Opening the passenger door, he threw a roll of blueprints in the passenger seat, slid into the driver's seat, and started up the engine.

He backed the car out of the driveway. Out of habit, he carefully observed the activity around him. The neighbor across the street appeared to be following his normal routine, idling his truck engine while he picked up his coffee and took a sip, then taking off down the lane towards the stop sign.

Josh wound his way through the curving, tree-lined streets of McLean to Route 123, Dolley Madison Boulevard. The morning sun glinted off on the waters of the Potomac between the trees along George Washington Memorial Parkway in little flashes, and his car slowly made its way along with the morning commuters to downtown Washington, D.C.

He dictated some notes for his CIA reports, frequently checking out the mirror and the sides of the car. He recognized the same white natural gas-conversion truck and the same tiny red smart car that ordinarily took the commute at this later time.

He headed towards M Street and Pennsylvania Avenue, going east in the direction of his cover office, Crestedon Global Architectural and Engineering offices. It was a company he had worked for in his private sector days in London and in the United States. The Washington, D.C., office was located past rows of concrete block and brick condos and office buildings, sprinkled in with an occasional hotel. He pulled the car into the underground parking garage.

He emerged a few minutes later, at 0851, on the fourth floor, pausing for a moment to say hello to the receptionist.

"Welcome back, Josh! Did you have a good trip?" she perked.

"Yes, but sounds like I'm going to have to go on another assignment right away."

"Did I see you on the news this morning?" she hissed with curiosity.

He stopped to speak courteously to her a moment in his soft-spoken voice and then passed through the rest of the office, greeting co-workers, pausing to talk briefly, and then headed to his office on the eastern end of the suite. He unlocked the opaque glass door and swung it open, closing it once again behind him. He set the heavy briefcase on the desk and also let the floor plans fall on the desk with a thud. A thin layer of dust floated up into the air in the dark, windowless office.

Dust was always a good sign.

He unlocked the briefcase and pulled out detection equipment and made a sweep of the room. Satisfied, he packed it back into the briefcase, closed and locked it, and opened the opaque glass door.

The CIA had done careful due diligence before they approached CEO Kelly Dunberry of Crestedon. They eventually secured a top secret arrangement for pseudo work for Josh—architectural design along with real continuing education classes, international conferences, and inspections of projects in key cities around the world where Crestedon had branch offices.

A paycheck was cut for Josh in the Crestedon payroll department, but the annual amount was creatively reimbursed by the CIA via the formation of artificial architectural clients complete with fake Federal EIN numbers. Josh's enclosed office room had been carefully chosen and meticulously planned due to proximity to the stairwell and garage. The office was completely soundproof, containing a separate HVAC system and the latest high-tech security. Obtaining the office space in D.C. meant that Crestedon (with CIA money, of course) had to approach the landlord with buyout funds and moving costs for the neighboring tenant's office space so that Josh could be situated at the end of the offices near the stairwell.

Josh's elaborate cover as a private architect with Crestedon was costing the CIA upwards of three million dollars. It was the perfect cover. Only Kelly Dunberry and the top legal counsel in the corporation knew of the arrangement. If Josh's cover was ever blown, the CIA would deny that Josh was on its payroll or that they knew him.

Josh logged into the company computer to work on reports until time to check in with CEO Dunberry.

When the meeting with Kelly Dunberry was done, Josh went back to the office and once again closed the door. There was a locked closet to the left of the desk. He opened it, snapped on the small light, and pulled out the Clark Kent props: the wig—a lighter shade of brown with straight hair, not dark and curly like his own—and glasses, along with a change of clothes—a black suit from J.C. Penney, a blue shirt, a pleasant but unmemorable tie, and shiny but moderately priced black men's dress shoes. He hurriedly put them on, checking the full-length mirror nailed to the inside of the closet door.

He grabbed the large, non-descript briefcase and cracked open the second door behind his desk, the back door that exited out into the common area hallway.

He heard the sound of two women coming down the hall and hurriedly clicked it shut, waiting until they had passed. Then he cracked the door open one more time and glanced quickly down the hall.

No one was coming.

He slipped into the hallway and into the fire exit stairwell. He could hear the women's voices down on first floor, then the fire exit door slammed shut behind them. His shoes echoed softly throughout the stairwell as he hurried down towards the basement.

Once back in the parking garage, he made his way to a different car. This car was a larger, older, less expensive dark sedan. Like his personal car, this one also had heavily tinted windows. It was parked in a back corner of the garage that the security cameras conveniently missed.

No one else was in the garage this morning. Good.

He scrutinized the car for tampering or explosives, pretending to check the oil dipstick. Then he locked the briefcase in the trunk under a blanket and set out of the garage, onto the street and then to Pennsylvania Avenue, looking in the rear view mirror to see if anyone unusual was following him. He used an SDR, a surveillance detection route, to make sure he wasn't being followed. Instead of heading west past the condos and office spaces and hotels he had driven past two hours ago, he detoured south towards George Washington University. He looped through the campus streets until he was positive that no one could possibly be following and then headed across the Potomac—this time on Key Bridge—back to the wooded and forested Parkway, and towards McLean and Route 123.

This time, he pulled off just a little before I-93, to the road that led to the CIA headquarters.

First he stopped at the camera and microphone box, pulling out the badge with his Agency-assigned alias and dropping it over his head. When cleared, he pulled forward into the vast concrete sea of parking, pulling around to the West Lot.

Jumping out of the car with his briefcase, he crossed the parking lot and went up the steps into the cool gray marble of the building, across the great seal and past Memorial Wall with its gold stars that symbolized agency officers and assets who had been killed in service of America. A wreath was hung on the wall today to commemorate the death in the CIA family, and there was a distinctly subdued mood on the part of the employees that hurried past the wreath. His fellow employee, Case Officer Matthew Logan, had lost his life in Iraq. Officer Logan would receive a star on Memorial Wall. However, it would be followed by a blank space, and his name would not be written in the Book of Honor, either. He was a member of the Special Operations Group, one of the most secret departments of the Special Activities Division. Officially, the United States denied knowledge of the operation.

It was 1050 hours. He checked in his weapon with the security guard. "Good morning, Mister….Taylor," said the guard, reading his blue badge. Josh, known at the CIA by his cover name, Case Officer Ryan Taylor, rarely set foot in the actual CIA offices. It was too risky.

Josh briefly responded and then headed down through the immense building in the direction of Directorate of Operations which ran the National Clandestine Service, and to the Technical Services Unit of Nonofficial Cover. He would meet with his bosses to discuss the shooting yesterday and to debrief from his tour. Then he was headed to the Box, because it was routine after overseas trips for CIA operatives to undergo a polygraph test.

Sunlight streamed in the majestic glass windows. A flag flew at half-mast in the garden outside, commemorating the slain Officer Logan.

9

Operation AuCHFOP

With the looming memorial service of a fellow CIA employee to be held this afternoon, a tense and tight-lipped group took the elevator from the basement of Langley to the seventh floor where management resided. To be summoned to meet with the Deputy Director of the National Clandestine Service signaled a sell job for a risky operation—the only higher ranking summons could come from the Director of the CIA, the Director of National Intelligence, or President Maly himself.

The Deputy Director began the meeting at 1100 hours in a crowded conference room that overlooked the George Washington Memorial Parkway with the Potomac in the distance. "Everyone, thanks for coming. Ryan, first of all, we extend our admiration for your patriotic duty yesterday." Like most everyone in the CIA, the director used Josh's cover name, not his real name. "In a difficult split-second decision, you saved the lives of dozens of people with your quick action, and you risked your career to do it. We will do everything we can to minimize the news cycle and protect your covert identity."

The people gathered in the room applauded.

"Thank you, sir." Josh had spent all his remaining hours of the weekend on a secure phone line talking with his superiors and writing reports on the incident.

"We have a very unique problem, and it requires a unique individual to fulfill our request." He flipped on a screen, and the title of the presentation appeared on the wall, *"Operation AuCHFOP."*

"Let's fill Ryan in on operation AuCHFOP. Ryan, this is about one of your recruits a couple years ago, Omar Al Ghamdi. His cryptonym is 'Excav8.' Do you remember him?"

"Yes. He was a Saudi engineer I identified for recruitment at my wife's company party. He was upset about the hardline anti-Western regime in Saudi Arabia. He had information that a new Saudi extremist group called Black Lightening was infiltrating and funding mosques in Iraq."

"We assigned Excav8 to Dave." the Deputy Director said, nodding to the man sitting at the end of the table. Dave had diplomatic cover. Josh did not. By batoning off Omar to Dave for actual recruitment, Josh did not have to break cover and was able to continue his work as an architectural businessperson undiscovered. This was Josh's role with the CIA.

Dave, Omar's handler from the Office of Central Cover, was normally salty and flippant, a rogue employee who always carried a Browning pistol. But Dave was now on the hot seat for having lost control of his asset. "I took over recruitment and tradecraft after you identified him. Omar—handle name Excav8—was assigned a cover job to hide what he was doing. The location for the cover job was an archaeological site just outside of Babylon Metro, Iraq, which used to be under control of Saddam Hussein. That was one of Saddam's palaces before the American invasion." A brief series of photos flashed on the wall. "Then the damn locals started making threats and I began experiencing problems with him."

The Deputy Director interjected some background. "Excav8 and his engineering company were 'restoring' a portion of the palace. Subsequent to the destruction that occurred in two Gulf Wars, our mission has long been to assist the Iraqis in rebuilding."

Josh was taking notes but paused and looked up as the director raised his arms and used air quotes when he spoke the word 'restoring.' "And were you successful in obtaining actionable intel?"

"Yes." Dave answered. "Excav8 gave me intel indicating that Black Lightening was planning to direct jihadist attacks in and around Babylon Metro. But then Excav8 started cutting communications short with me, began turning in reports late and incomplete. He withdrew a large sum from the secret fund account we set up for him and didn't show up for work. His guys were on the job site without any direction, and then we had counterintelligence that a Black Lightening gang was going to target either the palace or the team for destruction."

The Deputy Director concluded, "It was a very dangerous situation. The safety of our assets is paramount. We sent in Special Ops. You know the rest: we did a sting and took Black Lightening down, but in the firefight Officer Matthew Logan lost his life."

"Why weren't the Chinese notified? Why did we try to take Black Lightening down?" Josh questioned. "That's a violation of

United Nations treaty. The Chinese are the peacekeepers in Iraq now."

"Because of the nature of the archaeological 'rehabbing' that we were trying to do." Second set of air quotes from the Deputy Director. "An accidental discovery was made during the cover job. We found some interesting things down in there. We didn't, and still don't want, the Chinese to know what our military team is planning to remove from the archaeological site. It could be a political mess. Anyway, back to Excav8. Dave, go ahead."

Omar's CIA handler, Dave, picked back up with the story. "There's been no covcom contact with my asset for two weeks." Covcom was Headquarters lingo for covert communication via satellite burst transmission. "We started checking it out and my asset told his neighbor that he and his family were going to leave for a few weeks to visit his sick mother in Saudi Arabia. That's when I knew I was screwed." The coarse, street-smart covert officer dropped his hands loudly down on the conference room table. "His wife and children went back, but he never went there. There was no sick mother. Now Counterintelligence is picking up intel that he's still in Babylon Metro. I think either he's been blackmailed by these son-of-a-bitch militants, or he's turned."

It happened sometimes. Assets turned and became double agents. It was obvious from his demeanor that Dave feared being the bureaucratic fall guy; after all, it was on his watch that a spy had disappeared. If he became the sacrificial lamb, he would be kicked out of station.

Josh's immediate supervisor, Rich Novak, sat on Josh's right. Rich had failed an overseas assignment many years ago and had been sent back to Langley; he was now an aged bureaucrat. "Ryan, the Agency does everything it can to protect its foreign spies, and we need to make sure he's ok. We're tasking you with an op to Babylon Metro to be the action officer that helps track Excav8 down."

Josh's eyebrows shot up in alarm. "But once I identify a potential asset and gain his trust, I turn his name over to you. I'm supposed to be out of the picture," he objected. "I'm the one who finds the guy. Then it's up to the rest of you to make him a spy." This was the reason Josh's cover had worked so well for five years.

"From everything we can determine, Ryan, he never knew that you are a spook. That's why we need you there."

42

10
The Negotiation

The CIA handler for Omar Al Ghamdi, Dave, tried in his gruff voice to trivialize the risk involved in the tricky assignment that the Agency was trying to task Josh with. "Hell, don't worry. My asset trusts you. He simply thinks you work for a global architectural and engineering firm and that you are a socialite gadfly who loves to network and has impressive international connections." It was a left-handed compliment. In Dave's territorial paradigm, Josh had the cushy CIA job while Dave risked identity, safety, and his very life while wrestling with bears in a denied area.

Josh's boss, Rich, detailed how the op would be undertaken. "Here's the plan. You'll go to Babylon Metro under your cover company, Crestedon Global Architectural and Engineering. You'll search for Excav8 in Babylon Metro and 'coincidentally' run into him, strike up a conversation. See if he'll socialize with you. We'll take it from there. If it's just that the horses have been startled, it's our job to protect him. We want to calm him down and convince him to go on the box—and if he's clean, resume operations with us."

The box was, of course, a polygraph test.

"If he's in actual danger, we have an exfil contingency plan to get him out of there and resettle him in another country. On the other hand, he might be playing the system and planning to ask us for more money. We may have to withdraw him short of tour for cause. It's also possible he could have turned on us. If so, the security team will bring him in. Meanwhile, you'll coordinate with Crestedon to finish up the reconstruction project at the archaeological site that Excav8's company started."

The Deputy Director took over the narration. "Liu Chen just flew back yesterday from Iraq, where she did some background work for you. She was able to scope out the landscape. Liu, go ahead with your presentation."

"Good morning, Ryan. Good morning, team members," Liu said in her small, tentative voice, giving a polite nod to him and to the others.

"Hi, Liu." Josh gave Liu an encouraging smile; she was noticeably nervous in front of the Deputy Director.

Josh and Liu had been through CIA training at The Farm at the same time. Josh had gotten a job in NOC, but unfortunately Liu did not make the cut for undercover work. Disappointed, she took a job as a CIA analyst. She could have resented Josh, but she never did. Comradery from the tough training at The Farm prevailed, and the friendship remained intact.

Liu flashed a photo of an imam on the screen. "We believe this target, a mufti named Mohammad Al-Issa from Saudi Arabia, ordered the uprising that killed Officer Logan. He is in hiding now, raising money for Iraqi mosques and planning more jihadist attacks. According to internet chatter he is the leader of 'Black Lightening.' He represents another wave of extremism being exported from Saudi Arabia to Iraqi youths. He's well-funded and making his rounds, calling the faithful to jihad against the Chinese." She clicked through several photos, then turned on audio of the mufti speaking.

Josh studied the pictures and listened carefully to the Saudi voice, memorizing every detail.

The analyst clicked the remote to another picture. "You will work there." It was Babylon Metro's new, mind-blowing skyline. Babylon Metro was the Chinese creation rivaling Las Vegas, Monte Carlo, and Macau. She pointed the laser towards one particularly stunning high-rise building in the center of the picture.

Josh's boss interjected, "This," he said, "is the office Excav8 and his team were operating out of before he disappeared. Facilities and Procurement made a nice little pad there for him. For the cover job, the State Department coordinated with a non-profit on the funds for restoration work to Saddam's palace. The nature of the cover job was to insure the structural and architectural integrity of the existing buildings during the rehabilitation."

Josh was taking notes. He asked, "Where's the dig site?"

"Ancient Babylon, which is just outside of Babylon Metro and the historic city of Hillah, by a branch of the Euphrates River." Liu clicked to an aerial of a ziggurat and several surrounding buildings with the Euphrates River winding away into the distance. Office skyscrapers, hotels and condos towered in the background, overlooking the ziggurat.

Then Liu clicked the remote again, and suddenly photos appeared of what appeared to be museum pieces of jewelry: necklaces, bracelets, and gold goblets. "These are some of

Nimrud's treasures taken from Iraq's national museum during the first Gulf war. Many have been accounted for, but not all. ISIS found some and used them to fund its operation. We have intel from local Iraqis that some antiquities are hidden in Ancient Babylon. Maybe Saddam Hussein put them there. It has been the American mission for a long time to return them where they belong."

Josh no longer felt the urge to yawn. The operation had an interesting twist.

The Deputy Director gave instructions. "If the antiquities are found on site, you'll report back so the military division can remove them. However, it would be a very delicate operation for a couple of reasons."

Dave the handler spoke. "You can't just march into the Euphrates basin to supervise an archaeological project, and if you happen upon some 8th century Assyrian antiquities, ship them back to Baghdad. There's a lot more to it. The Chinese will try to intercept them and might even claim ownership."

"Also," the director said, "We've been picking up more intelligence lately about a particular local superstition. Liu, find the slide."

Liu searched on her laptop and then flashed a passage from the sacred accompaniment to the Quran onto the screen: *Hadith Number 6918--The Last Hour would not come before the Euphrates uncovers a mountain of gold, for which people would fight. Ninety-nine out of each one hundred would die but every man amongst them would say that perhaps he would be the one who would be saved and thus possess this gold.*

"This is a Muslim prophecy," she explained. "It is about the last days, the end of the world. There will be fight over gold. We must proceed cautiously with the antiquities and not cause a big fight and make the prophecy come true."

"Do the Chinese know about these artifacts?" Josh asked. "How are we going to remove them if the Chinese have military control of Iraq?"

Liu did not answer. She turned to the director. The director replied, "We don't know what the Chinese know, or what they don't know. We know they've heard the legends. We're not sure if they believe them."

Josh persisted. "Wait a minute. Didn't the United Nations agreement with China cover stuff like this? Didn't somebody already work out a plan to take antiquities back to museums where they belong?"

An officer from the military division, who had been silent during the whole meeting, spoke for the first time. "Antiquities are always accompanied by weapons. Removal would be...sensitive. If you run into any of them, you'll report back to us."

The Deputy Director said, "Ryan, you're the best man for the job and we're preparing things so that you can ship out."

There was a pause, and the team looked at Josh expectantly. This was the moment Josh was expected to accept the assignment. The Deputy Director had even been brought in to convince him.

"Let me get this straight," Josh said slowly. "You're asking me to risk breaking my cover by going to foreign soil and engaging face-to-face with one of our spies. If we can't find him, you're asking me to risk an international incident with the Chinese by smuggling relics out of an architectural rehabilitation zone. The CIA and the military have pulled so many resources out of Iraq since China took over peacekeeping that I'll be out there with almost no support. How much staff will I have? How much counter surveillance?" In Washington, D.C., the preferred assignments were the ones with visibility and resources, not sparsely-funded assignments in the hinterlands.

"Hold on a minute. You won't be the one to remove anything. You don't know anything about what's in there, right? You're just supervising the renovation project for as long as it takes for others to get the things out," said the Deputy Director.

"The embassy and the local station is in Baghdad, and that's a two-hour drive away from the dig. I don't want to report to them. I want to report directly to Headquarters so I can get in there and out of there fast."

There was an angry rustle from Rich's direction at the request to jump the levels of reporting.

"We have to go through channels in Baghdad," the director replied obliquely.

But Josh pushed, negotiating hard. "Then when I get back— *if* I get back and don't get purged from clandestine operations due to my cover being blown, I don't want to end up in a cubicle in Langley, and especially not in the Oakwood." The Oakwood was the Hades destination for CIA overseas operatives with failed missions. "I want an assignment in Western Europe. Preferably London."

Dave the handler puffed and swelled. There was an uncomfortable silence as the other team members soaked in the audacity of this request, a lower level case officer making such a direct entreaty of a high-level bureaucrat.

The Deputy Director's eyes swept the table, resting briefly on Rich Novak, and then back to Josh. He gave a slight nod. "Do your duty for your country. Then maybe later I think that can be arranged. Good enough, let's call the meeting to a close."

They filed out of the room and Josh walked down the gray corridors contemplating the brevity of the operation. A Special Ops officer was dead in Iraq, and an asset was unaccounted for and refusing to communicate with his handler.

He caught up with Liu in the hallway after the meeting and slowed her down until the others were too far ahead to hear them speak. "Liu, I don't see how this operation can possibly move me up the food chain! Iraq's been raped and pillaged for decades, so what makes us think ISIS didn't get the last of the antiquities anyway?"

Liu appeared uneasy. "This is a good project. The team has looked at this. I have been there, and the locals are quite sure the items are hidden there and afraid the Chinese will take them. The Americans promised long ago to do what they can to return items to the Iraqi people that belong to them."

"On top of it, my cover is paper-thin and Omar is probably going to figure out immediately that the CIA sent me."

She looked torn. "You are judged by how you protect your agents. You need to help Omar."

"Liu, I need your help if something goes down. Remember our agreement."

"It is going to be okay, Ryan. You will see. You must trust the team." But her face was solemn. Worried.

47

11
The Reprimand

Josh parted ways with Liu and hurried down to the basement of the building to the offices of the Technical Services Unit of Nonofficial Cover. His immediate supervisor found him. "In my office. Now."

Josh followed Rich Novak through the secure, sterile, windowless maze and into his high-walled cubicle. Rich closed the door and crossed his arms, glaring. "What the hell was that all about?" he demanded resentfully, eyes slit. "You rolled over on me. Do you think that just because you saved lives in a local church you can go over my head asking the Deputy Director for a Western Europe assignment?"

Josh's voice was soft-spoken and calm. "Rich, let's face it, the handler got screwed and you're asking me to fix it to save his ass. I've been asking for a Western Europe assignment ever since I joined the Agency and you know it."

"Everyone wants Western Europe and the only guys that get it are the ones near retirement. You only have five years' seniority. That was insubordination and I'm going to write up a report on you." Rich was a non-descript, unmemorable CIA officer who had no real history on the street. He was simply marking his time, writing reports until retirement in a few short years.

Josh made the instantaneous decision to play on his boss's sympathy. "I just got back. I'm tired. I was told I would get some down time. I have a child stateside—" Josh began and then stopped. Actually, it would be a show of weakness to mention a child with special needs with problems at school, and it could complicate future career steps abroad. "This is a low level op and it's setting me up to blow my cover for—what? A gold hunt? The CIA is a civilian organization. I don't have to do this. If I refuse, you have to find something else for me."

Rich's attitude changed swiftly to fear, because it was his job to accomplish the will of the Deputy Director of National Clandestine Service. "If you take this, you get to office out of Babylon Metro, Ryan. Facilities and Procurement has burned some real money on that place. A lot of case officers would kill for this op. Not only guys in the field, but also a lot of guys stuck behind a desk in the United States."

"Then give it to them if they want to hang out in one hundred twenty-degree heat in that godforsaken shrine to Chinese ego."

"We aren't exactly overrun with NOC case officers who are architects that can fill posts in the Middle East. You know Excav8 personally. You can keep the operation running if he turned. The director is right, Ryan. You're the best person." His expression softened. "Tell you what. We'll have the CIA Chief of Station personally come down from Baghdad to Babylon Metro when you get there and spend time with you and the team, give you the support you need. Look, I know you need a break. It'll take Facilities and Procurement a little while to re-open this operation and to get all the operational levels of approval. Take some time off at home with your family before you ship out. Work on your Arabic and Chinese."

If Josh took the time off and took this assignment, there would be plenty of time to put together another written request to be transferred. If he negotiated carefully, he could probably get the promotion he wanted.

If he refused this operation, his off-the-record hall file—his reputation in the back channels in the CIA—would be soured, and he could kiss any hopes of getting as assignment in London, or anywhere close to it, goodbye.

The Memorial Service

The CIA delayed, and even contemplated pulling the plug on, Josh's new assignment to the Middle East while it did its own internal investigation of the church shooting. Discharging a weapon in the line of duty was rare; discharging it during off time was even rarer, and minimizing the part of the story involving Josh was very tricky for the CIA. "The Agency practically treats me like I'm the one that's guilty," Josh grumbled.

His cover, fortunately, was not blown. He completely avoided the press except for one brief statement that he released in writing about the shooting, which had actually been written by Office of Public Affairs staff in Langley.

The press and social media largely ignored the fact that the perpetrator was diagnosed as mentally ill and had failed to take his anti-psychotic medication. Some of the media labeled Pastor Rouch as a racist and focused on the lack of gun control laws which "encourage disenfranchised minorities to act out on their aggression against law enforcement and authority figures." Other social media and gun rights advocates responded back vociferously that all parishioners needed to carry guns to church.

On Tuesday night Josh and Chelsea went to a prayer service at the church for all victims' families. They did not really have friends at the church because it was so large and their attendance was hit-and-miss, but there was something inside them that pulled them back to the church and would not let them rest until they had re-convened with its congregants. Chelsea, the coffee shop girls, and the Sunday school teachers who had been a part of the shared experience and had survived, held onto each other and hugged.

Every inch of the church was packed with people and their children, and Pastor Rouch gave a moving tribute to those who were lost, as well as an exhortation to forgive. But the act of driving the route to and from the church gave Chelsea heart palpitations and made her dizzy and caused her ears to ring, because it reminded her of the nerve-wracking and traumatic ride home after the incident was over. "I was glad to see the people who survived. I feel a solidarity with them. But at the same time, I don't want to go back there again. I don't want to re-live it," she told Josh after the memorial service was over.

He protested mildly, saying that Atalaya needed to go to Sunday School, but his own weekends with family were rare enough that it seemed easier to stay home.

"**U**NCLE CLINTON! We have Daddy and Uncle Clinton home at the SAME TIME!" Atalaya shrieked to Chelsea. The tall, wealthy forty-year-old technology genius waited outside on the Evans front porch with its soaring white columns and brick archway, grinning through the glass at Atalaya. Clinton Radcliffe's long, sandy-blond ponytail flapped in a light mid-October wind, and his pink forehead glistened in the Saturday sun. It was a beautiful, perfect day, and the leaves were turning.

"Come on in, Clinton." Chelsea pushed the glass door open for Josh's best friend, an expat from the U.K. who had flown in this weekend. Clinton loped a brotherly arm around her and kissed her on the forehead.

"Hey, Balls, you ejit!" Josh said, coming into the foyer where Atalaya stood holding her Peppermint Pinkey doll and beaming. Josh always went Brit when talking to Clinton.

"You pikey," Clinton shot back. Clinton delivered a punch in the shoulder to Josh, which Josh returned. Soon they were slugging each other, ultimately landing on the marble foyer in a brawl. Josh, short, slim and agile, maneuvered his way on top, punching Clinton until Clinton begged for mercy. "Ok, Bags. Off me now."

"Mommy! Look at Daddy and Uncle Clinton! They're beating each other up again! Mommy, why does Uncle Clinton call Daddy names?" asked Atalaya.

Chelsea replied, "Clinton always called Daddy 'Bags' and 'pikey' because when they were roommates in college, Daddy needed his alone time and would take off on the train on the weekends to some country in Europe so he could get away from people.

"Oh." The little forehead wrinkled. "Balls is not a nice word," Atalaya whispered reprovingly. Chelsea blushed, hoping the child wouldn't ask how Clinton got that nickname, back in his wild college days.

"Well, my chum, like a cat you landed on your feet after that shooting," Clinton said. He gave Josh another little slug in the arm, Clinton's way of showing emotion. The church shooting had finally pried Clinton from his California office—and his newlywed wife—onto a plane and out to Washington, D.C., to be with his best friend again.

Yappie, the Sheltie, limped her way to the foyer where the men stood up brushing themselves off. "Yappie, old girl, you're slowing down. I see a lot of gray hair on that furry face of yours," Clinton said to the deaf old dog. Over the years Clinton had lost some of his British accent, but it was still there.

"I guess I don't notice it as much as you do, since I see her every day, but she's definitely got arthritis," Chelsea agreed. Clinton bent down to pat the dog and then handed a gift box to Atalaya.

"How was your flight from San Francisco? Where's your luggage? Come on in and sit down," Chelsea offered. "What do you want? A beer? I'll have a glass of wine."

"Diet soda for me," Josh said quickly before she could offer him a beer also. Josh had never been much of a drinker and almost seemed condescending about it at times. Now that he was back from tour she was reminded that in this area Josh just wasn't very fun. But at least she could have a drink with Clinton. She poured the drinks in the kitchen and took them to the living room.

"Mommy! Daddy! Uncle Clinton got me a Peppermint Pinkey Talky Watch!"

"What the hell happened to your hair?" Clinton asked Atalaya, noting the lopsided chunks as they sat down on the beautiful leather couches.

"She was trying to copy Peppermint Pinkey, weren't you Attie?" Josh said.

"Why do you talk funny, Uncle Clinton?" asked Atalaya.

Interesting, Chelsea thought. Atalaya's listening skills had developed enough now to notice things liked that. "He used to live in London, England, on the other side of the ocean. They talk differently there, honey," she explained. "Daddy went to college there and that is how he and Uncle Clinton became friends. Someday we'll take you there."

"Attie," said Clinton "Let's take a look at your new Talky Watch and get it going." Clinton had purchased a very age-appropriate gift for Atalaya, a Peppermint Pinkey watch messaging set. It was a fairly realistic looking watch phone for little girls and a miniature one for Atalaya's doll. Computer chips

53

made it possible for the girls and the dolls to call and message each other. Within minutes Clinton had removed the product out of the packaging, set up a password, and had the set operational.

Clinton and Josh immediately launched into conversation about Clinton's government work.

Josh and Clinton were former business partners in a small technology firm before Josh entered government service. Clinton had gotten into gaming and was a millionaire now, flying between the coasts on government contracts. He thought about, lived for, and breathed work and money, and the CIA had been good to him.

While they talked, Chelsea sipped her glass of wine and watched her husband, feeling the relaxation waft down to her toes. Josh was sunburned from his latest operation. He was good looking, although when she first met him, she had overlooked him, because he was short—barely taller than her. His hairline had receded in recent months, and there was a little more salt and pepper in his sideburns and more crinkles around the edges of his eyes. He had turned forty and gravity was starting to set in. But he still worked out every day and still had the lithe, muscular body of a gymnast, as well as curious, soft brown eyes that lit up and drew you in when you talked to him. She was shaken and rattled from the church shooting, but it was like Christmas to have Josh and Clinton home again in the house.

Abruptly Clinton stopped talking to Josh and pulled out his mobile device. They waited, but Clinton continued messaging.

"Earth to Bags," Josh finally said.

"It's Jennifer," Clinton said, as if that was the only necessary explanation, and continued messaging. Josh shrugged. Chelsea chalked it up to the oblivious state of being a newlywed. Clinton hadn't been out here to visit since before the wedding to his wealthy and enigmatic venture capitalist wife, Jennifer, who posted pictures on social media that showcased her wealth but never made any comments.

Clinton continued messaging and Chelsea stretched restlessly. She could hear Atalaya, who was upstairs, talking to her Peppermint Pinkey doll, which was downstairs. The rumpled doll sat on a bar stool in the kitchen with one of Chelsea's dirty wine glasses from yesterday. Embarrassed, Chelsea jumped to her feet, snatched the wine glass away, and put it in back the dishwasher. It was too late; Josh saw it, and his eyes rolled. "Looks like Peppermint Pinkey has a drinking problem," he said wryly.

Clinton came out of his Jennifer trance and looked up to see what they were talking about. "Oh, by the way, the Talky Watch has GPS in case the watches go missing. And a long life battery. You probably won't ever have to replace it, she'll grow out of the toy first," he pointed out. "Here, let me send you the password for the website."

"I have to concede," Josh observed with grudging admiration, "that The Talky Watch is an improvement over the mindless little girl junk the Peppermint Pinkey franchise usually produces."

The doorbell rang and the babysitter arrived. "We're headed off for supper, Atalaya," called Chelsea. "We'll be back at bedtime."

They drove to a very hip dance club for thirty-somethings in muggy, hot downtown Washington D.C. on U Street, about a half hour away. The downtown bar district was packed with cars and people. The dance club on U Street had three levels. The first floor had a speakeasy and was less crowded. It served high quality bar food, and the thumping and pulsing of music and the sound of the noisy dance crowd from the second and third levels drifted down a curving staircase. Chelsea ordered a cocktail and felt the slow buzz. "So Clinton, when you compare, where do you like living in better? Silicon Valley or London?" The wings were excellent and the deep fried cheese appetizer tray was to die for.

"I'll take the Yanks any day," said Clinton. "Silicon Valley moves at warp speed, you can do anything you want. I don't think so much about Blighty." That was an old-fashioned term for the U.K.

"Do you hear anything from Sophie and the kids?" Chelsea ventured. Clinton had no immediate family in the United States.

"Just doing their thing in Brighton, I guess," Clinton answered in a non-committal voice. He offered no further information. He never did when Chelsea gave him openings to talk about it. Sophie, his first wife, hadn't adjusted to the United States and had taken the twins back to England and filed for divorce. It had left Clinton detached, mechanical and devoid of emotion. Chelsea and Josh's own families were four hundred miles away. Clinton used to visit frequently and regularly when he was single and looking for government contracts in D.C. that Josh could lead him to, and Josh and Chelsea were his only family.

"I miss London. It seems so long ago," Josh said simply. "Someday I want to move back. I want Atalaya to have the chance to live where we lived."

Clinton blinked and changed the subject. "Bags, when we get done here tonight, I'll show you and Chels our latest update to the NoitaLever game. We're testing a new feature at the end. We'll do a tourney."

A grin broke out on Josh's face. Josh was an immensely talented architect by trade, but he was also a serial entrepreneur. Being an angel investor in Clinton's software company, CRAJE Technologies, was a happy accident he stumbled into as a college student. CRAJE stood for Clinton Radcliffe and Josh Evans. But they'd had a quarrel a few years ago, and Josh had sold his company shares. Chelsea knew that Josh missed being a part of the various breakthroughs that Clinton's company made in its development of technology.

"It's about time you came out with an update to the game," Josh admonished Clinton. "You've got to keep it fresh. There are copycats being introduced."

By now Clinton was on his second or third beer for the evening, and his voice was a little slurred with even more British accent, and louder. "The new feature we're launching with the next update is really cool and designed to hook them into playing much longer," Clinton said. "You—" he added with a wink "are the first two people outside of CRAJE Technologies to see this. Bags, you can show it to your Middle East targets that the CIA is trying to recruit and it will keep them online longer..."

It was risky enough for Josh to talk CIA recruiting around Chelsea, and around Clinton, who was developing proprietary products the CIA could use. It was foolhardy to talk about it in public. The work both men did was highly confidential. "Bags. Stop." Josh's voice, low and severe, cut Clinton off.

Even through her happy alcohol buzz, Chelsea reacted with alarm. "Clinton! Not here! Not in public!" Dizzily she looked around at the other tables to see if anyone had heard their conversation.

What in the world was Clinton thinking, talking about Josh's job in public? It could blow Josh's cover!

Chill. Nobody can hear us," Clinton responded, shrugging carelessly.

They weren't really done with their food yet, but Josh stood up from the table. "I'm done eating. Chelsea, let's go upstairs and dance. Bags, come along with us." The dance floor would be noisy. It would be impossible to carry on a conversation.

They were definitely at the upper end of the age group that frequented the night club, but it was still fun to move to the music. They hadn't gone dancing in months, maybe even years. Josh had the nimble, graceful body of a gymnast. They danced to the beat and Josh took her hands and twirled her around a couple of times. She felt the buzz, the room spinning from the alcohol, her ambitions melted away. "Let's show off like we used to when we first got married!"

"OK, Babe."

They'd had lessons long ago, and they began twirling each other, swaying and bending, until gradually the crowd began to notice and step back a little to watch. They heard a hoot and some clapping as they dramatically spun, twisted, and arced.

Josh leaned over her, his lips traveling down her throat, and they heard catcalls and clapping. By now the crowd had pressed back and was watching with fascination. He pressed his face into her chest, and then suddenly dropped one hand and supported her with the other hand under her back. He lifted her up, put her down, let go, bent backwards, and did a back flip. Like a cat he landed on his feet and slid down to the floor almost as if he were going to do a split, except he was wearing blue jeans.

The crowd howled and burst into applause and the DJ congratulated them. They exited the room before the DJ could get their names. Because of Josh's job and the recent publicity with the church shooting, it was just better to stay below the radar when they were out in public.

Back at home in McLean, it was past Atalaya's bedtime. The very drowsy seven-year-old put down her Peppermint Pinkey doll and the Talky Watch on the floor and went with open arms to the family friend. "Nighty night, Uncle Clinton."

Clinton reached down and engulfed her in a bear hug. Atalaya was his soft spot, the only thing about him that seemed to represent an emotional connection.

Once Atalaya was down for the night, downstairs in the main level TV room on the cool leather furniture with the soft lamp lighting and cozy rugs covering the hardwood floor and the ceiling fan overhead cooling them, Josh opened the cover for the big screen TV. They pulled out their mobile devices and started a group game of NoitaLever on the large screen. They were going to feel the effects of dancing tomorrow morning. Yappie curled up under an end table and studied them with cautionary interest.

"Clinton, this video game you created—it's like crack!" Chelsea exclaimed, punching the lever icon for the game on the home screen as she played. She was playing the horses tonight, red with splashes of hyacinth blue and sulphur yellow accents. The graphics and bright colors grabbed her and sucked her in—it was more compelling on the TV screen than it was on her phone. The sound effects were even more amazing.

The grasshoppers advanced towards her horses, gobbling up blades of grass and drawing dangerously close. It looked so real! Her score plunged. She tapped on the lever on the screen, shooting at the grasshoppers.

BOOM! The screen exploded.

The advance slowed! She wished she could bargain even more energy credits from the good Eagle that she could trade for more weapons….then the Eagle in the video game dropped her horses an interest payment. She would use it to build schools in rural provinces and purchase some of the Eagle's toll roads.

Clinton studied the way she played the game—every move that she made on the "lever" on her phone—observing her expression and her reaction. "So you like it?" He smiled a lopsided, satisfied smile. "I never thought of you as a gamer. It's exactly what we like to see at CRAJE Technologies, new game players."

"Love, love, love it! I'm addicted. Will it ever be released in the United States so my co-workers can play it?" she complained, working the controls with her thumbs.

"He shouldn't even be giving the secure link to you. Promise you won't give it to anybody," Josh warned.

"I know, but why?"

Clinton explained, "Military guys all over the world, in any country, love to game. The games I'm developing are specifically designed to overtly and subliminally propagandize them to a favorable opinion of America. It's psychological warfare."

"However," Josh explained, "there's a line in the sand. CIA isn't allowed to propagandize its own populace. It won't ever be released in America."

Chelsea rolled her eyes. Apparently it was okay for the rest of the world to be patriotic about America, just not American citizens. No question about it, once the game drew you in, it certainly did propagandize. The Eagle in the video game, which was fairly obviously the United States of America, was always saving the day. The ads contained good looking Arab youths in excellent fitting clothes made by American designers.

"I still want to take it to market in the United States," Clinton said flippantly.

"You can't, Bags," Josh said.

"Sure I can. I'll find a way." Clinton was reckless. He always had been, and it had gotten him into trouble in the past. Josh was often the one who brought him back to reality. While doing reconnaissance of a Chinese Muslim extremist group in London, Clinton was nearly ambushed in his garden at his home. He had hurriedly immigrated, moving his company from East London to their hometown in Columbia.

But tonight was not good gaming for Chelsea. Clinton seized her oil fields, Josh's insurgents bombed her village schools, and intelligence agents hacked her news organization. "Ok, this isn't my night," Chelsea said after it had gone on painfully long. She stretched and yawned. "I'm going to have to commit suicide and end the misery."

"Wait, before you go out in a blaze of jihadist glory. Here's where the new update comes in. So let's say you're playing the game and you're a Middle Eastern jihadist on a suicide mission like Chels here, only you have—shall we say—second thoughts about Istishhad."

"Is-tish-what?" Chelsea asked.

"Istishhad. Suicide. Martyrdom." Clinton used the lever icon to point to a palm tree on the right hand of the screen with a decrepit ladder dangling from it. It was something you wouldn't necessarily notice, at least not at first. "You don't have to drop out of the game, you can keep playing. There's always a way of escape. So…you turn yourself over to the Eagle for refuge. The second way will be a rope. The third way will be a green circle. One of the three options will always be on the screen somewhere, you just have to look to find it."

Chelsea clicked on the Eagle. Up popped Chelsea's profile picture and a list of choices. The first option was "New Identity: Where would you like to live? Pick a vacation photo from your camera roll."

She selected a pretty picture of Tulum, Mexico, where she and Josh had once visited. Chelsea's profile picture began to morph, presumably due to plastic surgery or something, and her face took on slight Hispanic characteristics and attached to a virtual computer body. Then the character shrunk to the proportions of the picture, and there she was, her new plastic surgery self, bouncing happily on the Mexican sand. She giggled.

"Or, let's say that you, in your ambivalence about being the leader of a rogue nation, would rather have money. Tick off the 'Cash' option," Clinton continued to explain. Realistic looking bars of gold and currency popped up on the screen, with Chelsea's animated self, happily bouncing around on piles of money, which you could receive from the Eagle in exchange for all of your remaining assets.

"On the other hand, if you are a warmhearted and caring terrorist, and if you have concern for your troops and your nation, you can click on 'Medicine For Your People' as an option. We're also rolling out ads convincing players to think about joining the CIA." Clinton played one of the ads; her animated character dropped into a dark, dingy alleyway, and bad guys ran after her, shooting. Out of a side door burst an American CIA operative to save the day. The CIA jobs website flashed up on the screen.

This, then, was the heart of the NoitaLever propaganda campaign: to slowly and subconsciously convince gamers in Middle East countries that the Eagle, America, was good, and had them and their country's best interests at heart; and if they became an agent of America, they could have a safer and better life.

"I'm going to head out for the night, everyone," he said.

"Head out for the night?" repeated Chelsea in confusion. "Aren't you bringing in your luggage? Aren't you staying in the apartment?" Clinton had helped her and Josh buy the McLean,

Virginia, home. The deal was that Clinton put up part of the money and in return had the use of the gorgeous guest apartment in their lower level during his trips to the Beltway to secure government contracts.

"Nah, I won't be staying in the apartment. I'm going to National Harbor tonight," Clinton said. "I'm not going to be in D.C. very long."

There was an awkward silence. Chelsea knew what this meant: Clinton was gambling again. He was going to glistening, bustling MGM Casino, located in the waterfront development about a half-hour away from McLean on the Maryland side of the Potomac. She felt another flash of annoyance at him. She had been up last night late, straightening up his beautiful apartment with wood floors and contemporary design that overlooked the custom patio and outdoor kitchen in the back yard.

She glanced at Josh. His face was expressionless. Gambling was the wedge that had driven the business partners apart and caused Josh to sell out his technology shares.

Josh's mobile started buzzing, and the way he answered, Chelsea could tell that it was from the Agency. He melted into the back of the house to take the call as Clinton left.

15
Recruiting a Spy
Arlington, Virginia
Two Years Earlier

"*Have another hot chocolate, Laila.*" *Chelsea handed a steaming Styrofoam cup to the wife of the potential spy recruit, who leaned over the plexi-glass fence, watching. Out on the ice rink, Josh and Omar held hands with the children, helping to guide their clumsy feet. Twilight was setting in at Pentagon Row Outdoor Skating, and beautiful white lights flickered on for the evening at the upscale retail shops that encircled the rink.*

"*What do you think of the cold?*" *Chelsea asked merrily.*

"*Brrr!*" *Laila shivered in her thick, white down coat, her dark eyes sparkling. "The children love it. I must become accustomed."*

"*Even grownups who've lived here all their lives aren't used to it,*" *Chelsea reassured her.*

On the ice, Josh had Atalaya in one mitten hand and one of Laila's children in the other. As he swung around the corner of the ice rink, the children screeched and shrieked with glee, wobbling and balancing themselves.

"*Your family is kind and hospitable. It is nice to know someone in America who also works in architectural and engineering business.*" *Laila said.*

"*And it's fun for us to meet an engineer all the way from Saudi Arabia. I hope your husband enjoys his work here in America for my boss, Levi. He is great. Look, Josh is going to show off. He's such an entertainer.*" *Chelsea pointed. Josh let go of the children's hands, checked his position, and then whipped around and skated backwards, flamboyantly throwing his arms up to the sky in a dramatic flourish. He nearly crashed into another skater, and Omar let out a belly laugh that echoed across the ice. Josh finished his exhibition with a grand bow and flourish.*

"*Josh used to be a gymnast,*" *Chelsea explained to Laila.*

With a whoosh, Josh emerged from the ice into the seating area with benches and tables, and Omar followed behind. Their cheeks and noses were red with cold and exertion as they sat down with Chelsea and Laila under the heat lamps, took their hot chocolate, and pulled out their mobile devices. Darkness was setting in, and the children shuffled along on the ice, catching on to ice skating and huffing and puffing shouts of excitement to each other. One by one, pinpoints of lights appeared in the windows of the condos with their little white balconies above the retail shops that overlooked Pentagon Row Outdoor Skating, and the large, outdoor clock face on the clock tower turned on for the night.

A rapid-fire burst of laughter broke out where Omar and Josh were holding their phones. They were playing the new video game that was being test-marketed for overseas play for the first time: NoitaLever. "This game so addictive, Josh, it could take all my sleeping time at nights!" The light from the mobile devices and its dancing colors reflected off of Omar's face.

"Omar, the game causes food to be cold. Enjoy the drink that Chelsea bought you," Laila told her husband with amusement.

Noises and beeps came from his mobile device. "Now take that. America just come to my rescue and I just unleash a weapon on your artillery base. You about to go BOOM, my friend Josh."

"So you like the new NoitaLever game, Omar?"

Omar had churned over the idea of betraying Saudi Arabian radicals even before he met Josh. What Omar did not know was that the information he plugged into his online gaming profile had been sent to the NSA. His activity was being tracked as a larger pattern of big data and predictive analysis.

As their children skated on the ice, Josh, with his easygoing, approachable style and his intense, sincere interest in everyone around him, was calmly and deftly taking Omar into his confidence.

Josh was learning his potential recruit's routine and habits. Omar, Josh had told Chelsea earlier, was alarmed at progressively hostile American sentiment in Saudi Arabia. Omar had strong potential as a candidate! He had already dropped some comments, some decent and legitimate intel about Wahhabi extremists from Saudi Arabia cultivating the newest Jihadist cells in Iraq. He had also talked about office space he'd been involved in constructing. It was Omar's suspicion that it involved Chinese and Iranian researchers collaborating on some type of nuclear project.

It was Josh's job to identify potential assets, foreigners who could be recruited to be spies for the United States. The CIA would evaluate and approve Josh's request to cold pitch. A handler from the CIA would "bump" into Omar in a supposedly "chance" meeting and would also begin a relationship with him. The handler would suggest that Omar consider working for an international organization—and try to formally recruit him as a foreign agent.

The CIA would never know that Josh had already been getting specific, valuable intel from Omar about Wahhabi extremists' attempts to fund Iraqi uprisings. Josh's supervisor, a slow-moving bureaucrat, would not realize that Josh had already found creative ways to pass this intel around to the appropriate divisions within the Agency.

Chelsea chewed a hangnail on her thumb, torn with indecision, feeling horribly disloyal to Mr. Mizrahi. Tuesday was her day to telecommute from home. There wasn't much going on at work this week. Nothing, actually. The only exciting thing other than Josh being home was that she had started going back to the gun range to practice, now holding the viewpoint that carrying a gun around and possibly having to use it on somebody was repugnant but essential. This time she resolved to raise her marksmanship skills from poor to at least the bottom tier of average.

She logged onto the employment sites, weighing her generous salary and the bonus Mr. Mizrahi had given her against how bored she was with her job. Maybe there was something available at the nearby CIA Headquarters. She knew there would be extra hoops if you had a spouse that worked at the CIA, in order to prove there wasn't nepotism that could occur. She logged on, but the only thing available was a facilities job opening offices in the Middle East and Asia.

With a husband who was perpetually restless and adventurous and always flying off to a foreign country on a mysterious operation and who worked all hours and missed holidays, didn't her daughter deserve to have some stability? And wasn't part of a child's learning process watching a parent in an 8 to 5 job who had to deal with boredom?

Well, what would it hurt to apply? Something different might come up. She clicked on the keyboard, working her way around the job application information on the website. She logged onto the website of the Goldberger Hewitt commercial real estate office in downtown Washington, D.C., and wondered for the millionth time about applying with them. Back when they lived in Columbia, she had worked for Goldberger Hewitt. But she had been fired because she missed too much time due to Josh's government work. Columbia was a place she tried not to think much about anymore.

She had also worked briefly for the Goldberger Hewitt office in London. She had a good recommendation from Ian Clark there.

She weighed the potential embarrassment and possible benefits and decided to apply at the Washington, D.C., Goldberger

Hewitt office. Bravely she picked up the phone and left a message for the local branch manager.

Josh, just about to receive final clearance for his next tour, had gone to the gym to work out, to the men's clothing store, and to the hardware store, a place he hadn't been for months or maybe even years. Tonight was a bright spot. She and Josh were going to one of those Washington, D.C., receptions with lobbyists in the architectural and construction community. Josh was constantly working the circuit and cultivating contacts useful towards recruiting foreign agents on overseas construction jobs, plus those events were good networking for her business, too. They would get to dress up; he in his black tux with the red cummerbund that he had worn at their wedding, and she in the long blue dress that matched her eyes.

Her socks nestled softly into the fur of Yappie, the old Sheltie dog, who slept under the desk today instead of her usual position by the front door. Yappie slept all of the time and limped on her way to go potty, and Chelsea wondered how much longer they would have the dog with them. She paused to lean down and stroke her pet's head. Yappie had been with her longer than Josh had.

At 2:00 p.m. the phone rang. She could tell from the first few digits on the caller ID that it was the elementary school, but it was not any of the usual numbers from the school.

"Mrs. Evans? This is the vice principal's office. We would like to know if you gave anyone permission to come and pick up your daughter?"

"No, not me," Chelsea answered in confusion. She jerked straight up in the chair, accidentally hitting Yappie with her feet. The dog yipped painfully and slunk out from under the desk.

"I need to let you know that Atalaya did not come back to the class after recess at lunch time. We have been unable to locate her and wanted to check and see if she is with you or your spouse?"

"No, she's not!" Chelsea felt a flash of fear grip her.

"Could you please come to the school as soon as possible?"

Her heart nearly stopped. She grabbed her purse and flew out the door to the car, debating whether to tell Josh when she knew so little, when it might be some silly little thing. Every CIA parent's worst nightmare was that a rogue group would target the CIA employee's family members…yes, she needed to tell him! Her heart pounding, she pulled over to the side of the street to leave him the message. Then she messaged Kimberly Feldman, the mom from the car pool.

She arrived at the school simultaneously with the police. Her mobile buzzed from Kimberly, who called back live.

"WHAT HAPPENED?" Kimberly thundered on the phone. Kimberly's lawyer voice was naturally loud enough that you had to hold the phone away from your ear slightly when she called. Today the distance was more like a foot. Josh always said it was a voice both capable of taking control of a courtroom and scraping chalkboards.

"I—I don't know for sure!" Chelsea gulped. "She disappeared at recess." She turned off the engine and slammed the car door shut. "I'll know more in just a few, and I'll call you back, Kimberly."

The school was in lockdown. They steered Chelsea into the vice principal's office where a group of apprehensive adults were gathered.

"Your daughter did not come back in with the others at the end of recess," the vice-principal explained gravely. "The Neighborhood Watch group is on the way to search the playground and streets. Security is combing the building."

"Did any of the children say where they last saw her?" Chelsea asked with a sinking heart, already sure of the answer. Atalaya, due to her learning and social problems, was an outlier in the class and had no real friends.

"The class teacher is interviewing every child, trying to find an answer," was the reply.

"We'll find her." A kindly Neighborhood Watch volunteer patted her shoulder.

"The police would like to ask you a few questions."

"Please," Chelsea managed to squawk. She choked back panic. "Can you make it fast, because right now there is no place I would rather be than outside searching for my child."

She answered their questions in a daze of disbelief. No, nothing out of the ordinary had happened before school this morning. No, they were no family members or ex-spouses living in the area who might want to take Atalaya. Her natural father, who gave her up for adoption shortly after birth, lived in Arizona; her birth mother who gave her up had been deported. There had been no contact for years.

67

Josh arrived after a record-breaking drive. His jaw was clamped. He listened to the story without comment. She knew what was churning in his mind. He had to contact the CIA immediately and let them know in case this was a kidnapping.

17
The Talky Watch

*W*here could a child hide? There are a million places.

Chelsea slowly drove down the nearest tree-lined street. Red was starting to pop on the leaves of the trees, and the temperature and humidity were noticeably lower. A movement in a driveway caught her eye, until she realized it was a wandering cat, its tail slinking along behind him. Her friend Kimberly was on the speaker phone from her law office, scrutinizing an aerial map of McLean and offering suggestions.

The task seemed impossible. Chelsea wondered about every free-standing garage or storage shed, conjectured about every bush, speculated about the back of each home. Then suddenly she remembered something.

The Talky Watch had GPS…

She pulled over to the curb and looked up the password from Clinton Radcliffe, the giver of the Talky Watch gift, and logged into the website. Had Atalaya worn the watch this morning? She honestly could not remember at all. Would the GPS location signal even work?

The map popped open with two side-by-side red, pulsing dots. It appeared that Atalaya was standing in the road somewhat near the school, probably holding her Peppermint Pinkey doll!

She studied the map and called Josh. Then she turned onto the school road and neared the far fenced boundary of the school playground, at the end of the school softball field where the two red pulses indicated. She looked carefully but saw Atalaya nowhere.

She drove over the area indicated, and even past it, her heart sick. Had a kidnapper known that Peppermint Pinkey Talky watches had GPS? Had he thrown the watches into grass and weeds along the street?

She pulled to the side of the road, and Josh met her coming from the other direction. With a squeal of tires, they both jumped out of the car.

"According to the map, it's supposed to be right here!" she wailed. "Damn it, why isn't the Talky Watch GPS working right?"

"Something must be interfering with the signal," Josh said. "Cheap Chinese crap."

"Wait, what's that noise?"

Somewhere down below them, muffled and with an echo, they heard Atalaya. Josh cocked his head and then hoisted himself up and over the schoolyard fence at the side of the road. He dropped to the ground and ran down the short embankment to a drainage culvert underneath the residential road.

"She's down here!" he yelled.

Chelsea hoisted herself much more slowly up over the fence, tearing her clothes as she climbed over the top and back down. Unlike Josh, she did not have benefit of his training at the CIA Farm. She stumbled towards him down the embankment in the direction of a washout area. A low-rising gnarled tree at the entry point of the drainage culvert ran under the road. Iron bars secured the culvert and prevented students from wandering under the street and off school property. Atalaya perched amidst the tree branches. Stuffed up on the inside of the iron bars was Peppermint Pinkey with its Talky Watch around its doll wrist.

"C'mon honey, jump down." Josh held his arms up, and after protests and a long hesitation, Atalaya cautiously dropped down into them. Chelsea ran over and grabbed them both in her arms, her heart hammering.

"Attie," Josh squatted down eye level with his daughter. "Tell Daddy something very important. Who told you to go to leave the playground? Who told you to go to here?"

Atalaya did not answer, she only stared back guiltily with her own dark brown eyes and sucked her available wrist with her mouth.

"Atalaya, did someone take your Peppermint Pinkey and put it in the storm drain?" Chelsea asked, fear sticking to the inside of her throat.

A fist emerged from the little mouth. "No," said Atalaya.

"Did you put Peppermint Pinkey in the storm drain?"

Atalaya nodded, and the fist went back in the mouth.

"Let's get back to the school." Chelsea tugged the doll out of the dirty, rusty bars covering the drain.

At other points across the school yard, they could see people who were probably hunting for their child. They hurried with Atalaya to the school where the police resource officer accompanied them to the principal's office. A very pale and shaky Miss Monroe stood in the office with tears in her eyes.

"We found her at the far end of the property, by a culvert," Josh explained. "She had climbed a tree and her doll was in the drain."

"The Hole. Is that right?" The principal frowned, forehead creasing. He turned to the staff. "How did she get out of the fenced area and all the way over to The Hole without someone noticing her?"

"The Hole?" Chelsea asked.

"That's what the children call it," explained the principal. "The children are told to stay near the playground equipment and not go over there. These are our rules. Sometimes the older children do anyway, such as when they are kicking a ball around and it gets loose."

"Honey, I think you need to tell the principal that you are sorry," Chelsea reprimanded her daughter.

"Climbing a tree," Miss Monroe said carefully, "is also against our rules."

Atalaya regarded her parents uncomfortably, as if there might be repercussions to this additional trespass, and turned to bury her face into Chelsea's slacks.

"We will have a full investigation of this," promised the principal after the interview was complete. "We will take steps to find out why this happened and prevent it from happening again. We hope that you will be willing to return her to our school and let her continue her education here."

It hadn't occurred to Chelsea to think about tomorrow, or changing schools. She just wanted to get Atalaya home.

The school lockdown had reached the blogosphere and news reporters were in the security area. "Please, no questions from the press," Josh begged the principal. "We'll work on a statement and send it to them."

That meant, Chelsea knew, that the CIA would do an investigation and work on a statement. Or more likely, put a lid on the story.

Josh called the Agency and the CIA opened an investigation, sending an officer out immediately for an interview. Despite repeated questions that afternoon, Atalaya offered no explanation of why she played near The Hole and climbed the tree. "I tell Peppermint Pinkey there are very bad guys out there," was the only explanation.

Worry swept Josh's freckled face. It was the kind of statement he made often. Atalaya was just mimicking something she had heard at home. Atalaya had no answer to repeated queries about stranger danger. From everything the other children said and from what Atalaya said, it appeared that Atalaya had chosen on her own to play near the storm drain. Had Josh's constant worry and protection over his family spilled out into a little girl's imagination, causing her to run off and hide? Or was Peppermint Pinkey simply the "bad actor" in the child's imaginary world, and had been sent behind bars?

"I suppose we should stay home tonight from the reception," Chelsea said.

"Actually, to tell you the truth, if someone is after her, I feel better if she's not at home. Although I don't think anyone is after her or us," Josh concluded. "It seems pretty clear she did this on her own." Atalaya often played alone since starting elementary school, according to the teachers. Chelsea's heart gave a little wrench as she thought about a child who was a bit behind and at times a social misfit, and how catty other children could be.

Once they made the final decision to go to the reception after all, they scrambled to feed Atalaya supper and get dressed in the "monkey suits", as Josh called them.

"She's getting older. We have to do something about what she did. We need to impress on her she can't just run off alone," Chelsea fretted, standing at the kitchen sink in her high heels, scrubbing the dirt from The Hole off the Peppermint Pinkey doll.

"Come on, Attie, let's load up in the car and go stay with Kimberly while Mommy and Daddy go to a reception," Josh called. He took the little girl by the arm and once again squatted down to her level, his soft brown eyes serious. "You cannot leave the others and run off to play with Peppermint Pinkey. Just to remind you of this, I am going to take away the Peppermint Pinkey Talky Watch that Uncle Clinton gave you. You can have it back when you've shown me that you are a big girl and you will play with the other children at recess and not run away to The Hole. Don't keep asking me and Mommy to have your Talky Watch

72

back. You are going to have to show us first that you will follow the rules."

Ruefully, Atalaya handed over the Pepto-Bismol pink communication device.

"We're running late." As they headed to the car, Josh stuffed Talky Watch deep into the bottom of one of his tux pockets.

18
Goodbye

Josh was perfectly fine if concern about the church shooting, combined with Atalaya's brief disappearance, caused the CIA to completely pull the plug on Operation AuCHFOP. He was content to work his cover job at Crestedon Global Architect and Engineering until a different assignment could be organized for him. As the month of October wound down, the trees in NOVA turned brilliant colors of crimson, and the air took on an autumn, woodsy smell. But then his formal assignment cable from headquarters came, along with a welcome note from the Chief of Station of Iraq. Omar Al Ghamdi, the Saudi spy recruit who had gone missing, had been observed by Counterintelligence walking along Wangfujing Avenue in Babylon Metro! Josh would be shipped off to the Middle East after all to try to make contact with Omar and to re-engage the architectural mission.

He called his parents back home in Columbia and talked to them for a long time, something he did if he was going to be overseas for a long tour, or a dangerous one. His attitude shifted from indifference to the operation, to becoming decidedly focused on it, and to being completely committed.

"Are you going to Halloween parties?" Chelsea asked, noticing that he was packing his tuxedo in a garment bag.

"I suppose. I'll be cleaning up messes and making the Americans look good on this trip." It was all he said, because of course he should not tell her what he was doing. He took her into his arms and gave her a long, tight hug. "Still haven't heard from Omar and Al Ghamdi's wife? Laila?"

"Laila? Um, no."

"Keep an eye open for news from her while I'm gone, okay? If you get something, send me a message that says 'you'll never guess who sent us a Christmas card.'"

"Oh! I don't think they do Christmas...." Chelsea wondered if Josh's tour involved something with Omar since she wasn't supposed to use the Al Ghamdi's names in communication.

"I am going to miss every single inch of you," he breathed into her ear, his hands traveling over her body.

They stood holding and touching each other and then he kissed her and pulled away. Downstairs, he picked Atalaya up and swung her around until she squealed. "I don't know how long I'll be gone. It might be just a few days or it could be a very long time. Attie, can you take care of Mommy? Do everything you can to make things easy for her, okay? And no matter what, you promise to always, always remember how very much Daddy loves you?"

"Yes, I love you, Daddy."

He pressed the ragged chunks of black curly hair to his chest for a long time and while he was holding her, he looked up at Chelsea. "Contact Kimberly in case anything happens to me." Kimberly was not only a fellow carpool mom, she was their estate planner.

Chelsea felt the familiar anxiety she experienced every time he left for an operation without her, although the worry lessened over the years. Putting Atalaya down, he picked up his garment bag and his keys and headed towards the car out in the garage. She watched through the glass of the front door as end-of-October leaves fluttered to the grass.

19

Babylon Metro

T he CIA Chief of Station from the embassy in Baghdad, referred to by CIA personnel as the COS, met Josh in the airport to pick him up. The hot desert sun shone down on the black, four-wheel drive Suburban with the dark-tinted windows.

The COS was a tight, disciplined individual with perfectly trimmed hair and meticulous clothing, even though today was a Saturday. He was dedicated to the mission of the CIA and obviously very much a bureaucrat. The non-descript Suburban wound its way along the Babylon Metro freeway past hastily constructed and bustling warehouses that went for miles. In the desert, they passed a cluster of camels in the sand along the road. In the distance, the newly built skyscrapers of Babylon Metro pierced the blue sky, shimmering and glimmering with spectacular colors in the desert heat.

"Amazing." Josh sucked in his breath, peering out the front of the limousine as the buildings came into better view. His pulse raced; it was an architect's dream. The population and the skyline wasn't nearly the size of Dubai or Mecca, but what was incredible was that the tourist and business addition to the ancient city of Hillah was only a decade old and was attracting every banking and oil headquarters from around the world and already rivaled Las Vegas and Monte Carlo.

When the war-weary United States, hung over with trillions in budget deficits—a good share of which was owed to China— pulled out of Iraq, a very worried United Nations had been faced with the unpleasant prospect of Russia taking charge of Iraq. Sending troops to get Iraq under control wasn't something China had wanted to do, but China did want repayment from the U.S., and it was hungry for oil, so China got the U.S. oil leases and the responsibility. With the money from the oil, they built Babylon Metro.

"What's making it work," the COS explained, "is that unlike Dubai, foreigners are granted long-term residency rights. And of course, no other major business center in the world can touch the tax structure in Babylon Metro. Still, the egotistical sheiks that own these buildings are crazy. A lot of the buildings are sitting mostly empty. But that's ok. The sheiks have money to set on fire."

As a commercial real estate agent, Chelsea would be fascinated. He wished he could tell her all about it.

On both sides of the superhighway, vehicle loaders hauled conveyances and every conceivable type of construction materials. Trucks of every kind brought in merchandise from two seas: the Mediterranean to the northwest, and the Persian Gulf to the southeast. They snaked back and forth along the freeway, exited the loops, and unloaded their goods along the various points—cattle, sheep, wheat, grapes, olives.

A digital billboard overhead proclaimed *"Welcome to Babylon Metro, Forever a Happy Place!"* in Arabic, English, and Chinese. The gleaming white billboard had a sparkling cartoon image of a fat, happy queen with a scepter in her hand, from which seven stars were bursting with a kaleidoscope of colors.

"What is it, Chinese Disneyland?" Josh made a jab at the odd billboard. "Do the Chinese really think that even though Iraq's been torn apart by war for the last three thousand years, if you put it on a billboard and flash it at people enough times, they'll believe it?"

"The opening of new oil fields around Hillah—enough oil to feed hungry Iraqis, not to mention hungry vehicles in China—has made everyone rich," said the COS confidently. "And with all the other industry here now, even if the oil dries up in hundreds of years, Babylon Metro and Iraq will still be secure."

The freeway turned into a concrete jungle of roads. "This is Exit 3, where a lot of the sensitive things come in. It's a secure area, but we have clearance," said the COS, turning the steering wheel. His fingernails were perfectly groomed, almost as if they had been manicured, a sign of meticulous vanity. Ahead of them was a line of five armored vehicles, "probably jewelry, from the looks of it," he observed. "Bahrain and Basra pearls are highly valued, some of the best in the world. They truck them in from the Gulf. There's a lot of gold and silver trading around here, now, also." The exit was heavily patrolled with security. They stopped at the booth and were ordered to exit the vehicle while the Chinese guards inspected it from hood to trunk and checked their permits.

They pulled into the newer-looking warehouse park and saw behind them in the rear-view mirrors a huge bus that looked like a tour bus. "What's that doing in here?" asked Josh.

The station chief replied. "You'll be interested in this," he said to Josh. He pulled off the service road at a driveway and let the tour bus with heavily tinted windows pass; but it didn't appear to be a tour bus. Whatever tour it had been on, the name had been painted over.

"It's the women," the station chief explained knowingly.

"Which women?"

"Let me put it this way. You can't have the genocide of girl babies in China for decades without creating a need. This is the market from Eastern Europe and Southeast Asia that helps fill that need. Look closely."

Josh removed his sunglasses and squinted at the darkly tinted bus windows. Only faint shadows could be detected moving about on the inside, but a few curious face pressed to the glass, gawking at the surroundings or snapping pictures with a camera. They were the faces of mail order brides for the Chinese, the prostitutes.

T he nondescript bus turned into a highly secured facility with a scattering of anemic looking date palms and mounds of barbed wire. "We're pulling up to a processing facility for the escorts," explained the station chief. "They come here to be checked in." He idled the Suburban. "The buses pull inside the terminal, so no one ever sees the women. Then they transport to the hotels in town to meet the men."

"How much of it is voluntary and how much of it is human trafficking?" Josh asked. Human trafficking had been a top human rights issue for the last two decades. Compounding the testy relations between the United States and China, the stories that Chelsea watched on *Good Morning America* had focused particularly on Chinese human trafficking.

"Prostitution puts the local imams and clerics' panties in a bunch, so the Chinese narrative is that they are 'wives'. They get statements on record from them."

"Is the FBI doing any work on it?"

"Not unless American women get kidnapped. Works like this: if you are China, and if you've been developing from a third-world country into second-world or first-world country, you are probably better off centralizing your human trafficking over here in this part of the planet, which isn't exactly cutting edge when it comes to women's rights."

Josh commented, "There's allegations that some FEEBs and CIA operatives are actually in on it," then put his sunglasses back on and studied the station chief's reaction.

"Does it happen? Maybe. Probably. And of course, the western countries pass resolutions, and say they are concerned blah blah blah; but hey, if China is your banker and you can't pay back your country's trillions of dollars of deficits, what are you going to do about it?" The station chief cleared his throat. "I'm showing you this because while your office is being set up, I'd like you to go to work recruiting foreign spies so we can infiltrate some Chinese officials."

Josh quickly assessed his new superior: impeccably groomed and dressed, even though it was the weekend. Vain, easily impressed by power and opulence. Did the COS have an appetite for womanizing, porn, or CIA honey traps? "My assignment is supposed to be temporary," Josh finally replied cautiously.

Recruiting foreign spies was Josh's task. Or at least, from the CIA's standpoint, starting paperwork and working his way through forms and reports in an effort to recruit foreign spies—even if you didn't ever quite actually recruit any, was adequate enough busywork. Josh, however, preferred to get actual foreign spies fully recruited, and it was the part of his job that he loved.

The station chief shrugged. "You can make some inroads. It will give you something to do so you don't get bored."

Was this more than a fascination with honey traps? Was this a fetish of a work superior possibly suffering from sexual addiction?

They pulled out of Exit 3 and waited for a cattle truck to pass; but it wasn't the snouts of cattle they saw poking through the ventilation holes in the sides of the truck, it was horses' noses. "That's for the Chinese. They have stables north of town for their decorated guard. Absolutely amazing to see. On your day off, it's worth taking a tour of it." The station chief checked the time. "Well, let's get you to the safe house and then to your job site."

The safe house was a two-story villa in a part of Babylon Metro that was relatively less expensive but still secure. The station chief accompanied while Josh did an electronics sweep of the inside, and then they immediately left for the cover job offices.

They made their way into the new business district, with its achingly tall skyscrapers competing with each other to pierce the sky and cast shadows on the street below. Just as they had completed a surge of construction in Shanghai, the Chinese had expanded, rebuilt and renamed Hillah, Iraq, which until the entrance of the Chinese had been a war-torn city of somewhere around 400,000 people without a decent mall or so much as a four-star hotel. Beefing up the existing sewer, water, and roads and infrastructure, the Chinese had located the gleaming, powerful Babylon Metro just outside the bounds of the historic site of Ancient Babylon. Prime office space users paid money to look out over the Euphrates River valley with its farms, burning oil wells, and ancient dig sites.

Despite his disdain for undiluted greed that the city represented, Josh craned his neck in fascination. The truck pulled up to the Tomorrow Globe Financial Plaza. The middle of

Tomorrow Globe Financial Center was shaped like the sail of a ship and revolved—not just one floor with a restaurant, but the whole entire *middle* of the building, one hundred floors of office space! The top of the tower glinted in the sun with accents of gold and brass and pierced the clouds.

"Here you are. Your office space is in the Tower of Babel," joked the station chief as the vehicle pulled up to a circular entrance surrounded by date palms.

Josh whistled, looking out the window of the vehicle. "Hasn't that always been the game ever since the beginning of time, to build the tallest building in the world?"

The station chief rifled through his bag for the proper identification pass cards and they exited the truck, passed through security, and took a series of elevators up to the 95th floor. An endlessly long hallway finally brought them to a windowless suite. On the door was very plain lettering:

Pyramids and Palaces Architectural Renovation
A Non-Profit Corporation

Josh swiped the magnetic card and they entered. They fumbled and flipped on the lights. It was a very small, dark suite with a tiny reception area and three small rooms. There was no exterior window. There were desks and furniture, but no employees. Ever since Omar Al Ghamdi went off the grid and disappeared, no one had worked in the office. Josh walked through examining, again sweeping for bugs, noting the security panel and next to it a mechanical door. It probably led to the mechanical shaft of the building directly behind the space.

The construction of the building was glitzy and opulent, but when you looked at it close up, it was cheap and shoddy with shortcuts, like Las Vegas. Josh pointed to a crack appearing in the drywall. "Babylon will go down. Everything from the foundations of buildings constructed on sand, to the political system, is built on a desert mirage."

The COS laughed. "That's what everyone says, that it was built too fast. Never fear, every bank in the world is flocking here to take advantage of the tax structure and the ability to own 100% of the business they establish in Iraq. Babylon Metro will never be a sad widow. She'll be the queen." He pulled out his mobile and looked at the time. "Let's go down to the casino and get something to eat and play a few rounds of blackjack," he said. "Oh, and by the way, if you are still here at Christmas, you can come to the holiday party at the Embassy in Baghdad. We invite any nationals stuck in Iraq working over Christmas who are missing their families. It's a huge party and you don't have to wear your disguise. You'll blend in just like all the other American contractors."

"Thanks, but my op should be wrapped up by then," Josh replied.

They secured the space and headed back to the elevator. Soon work for the front company, Pyramids and Palaces Architectural Renovation, would resume with its new contractor, Crestedon, at a hot, dusty dig site down the river. But in reality, the tiny air conditioned office space in the Iraqi sky would quietly and secretly be the nerve center for CIA Operation AuCHFOP.

21
The Prostitute

Fairly soon after Josh had arrived, he detected surveillance following him, a man who appeared to be local. The man wore a couple of disguises but Josh ultimately recognized him by his shoes. Few Americans were "black", or off the radar of Iraqi's secret service. Josh would be followed for at least a little while when he first arrived in Iraq, maybe always. Josh manipulated the tail into showing himself, and the tail disappeared. But that didn't mean there wouldn't be another one soon, and Josh stayed on the highest alert.

To pass the time while the Crestedon office was being set up, the Baghdad Chief of Station requested—or ordered—that while waiting for Operation AuCHFOP to resume, it would be useful for Josh to cultivate relationships in Babylon Metro with prospective assets that the CIA could eventually recruit. The assets would hopefully become CIA spies, reporting to a new handler coming from D.C. who would replace Dave, who had bungled up the operation with the Saudi informant, Omar Al Ghamdi. The new handler would meet with sources with useful information.

"Like I said the day you arrived, I want you to work the mail-order 'brides'. They are good targets. For a good price, I'm sure some would be willing to spy on the Chinese. Provide your daily after-action reports directly to me."

It was a trippy assignment, and the request not to make reports to Langley further added to Josh's theory that the COS had a sexual fetish. And of course the architecture of Babylon Metro was a never-ending source of fascination, especially given how hastily constructed it was.

Josh worked the streets under a viaduct where solicitation was generally known to occur. The temperatures gradually changed to more comfortable levels as the November days drifted by. The area was near the Chinese military compound by a freeway overpass. He searched for a prostitute with reasonably good English. Just under the other side of the overpass was the pearl factory, where pearls came by truck from the Gulf and were cleaned and assembled and distributed around the world. In the back of the factory was a dormitory with iron bars on the window.

No buildings in Babylon Metro were old, but this one looked as old as it could possibly be, already worn with dirt, lack of maintenance, and peeling plaster. In a little curtained-off cubicle in the dorm that contained only a chair, bed, dresser, and mirror packed tightly together, and with the sounds of sex all around them, he pulled out a wad of bills and sat on the chair by her bed and handed money to "Ana," a prostitute from Romania. Neither unattractive nor attractive, she was thin and strained looking, with thick but dull brown hair and hazel eyes that darted everywhere.

"I am only looking for companionship."

She sat cross legged on the bed. "You want to talk only, yes? Some men talk only, but price is equal. My time is the same," she informed him indifferently. With her hand, she flipped her dull brown hair back from her eyes.

"I'm an architect and businessman who has come to Babylon Metro in search of money in a new city." He handed her his card with his front company and phone number that, unknown to callers, was answered by a back office in the CIA in Langley. "But this is not always a good place. I see bad things here. There are a lot of people but it is a lonely place." He dangled the empathetic sentiments to her, watching her reaction carefully, hoping to win her confidence.

"How do I know? I am always working," she shrugged neutrally. Ana was guarded.

He may have to interview several women before he found one who would cooperate. And he probably wouldn't have time to see the project very far along.

Back at the safe house, where signal receivers, computers, and encrypted communication devices were set up, he sent a secure night action cable with encrypted text to the COS and to Langley via his covert CIA identity:

Formal request of Headquarters to run traces on target to see if she can be recruited. Video and coordinates to follow. Please utilize restricted handling channels. C/O Taylor awaits instructions.

A response came back: *Headquarters pleased with Station's attention to this matter and efficient work of case officer.*

The ops plan was in motion. A non-descript van idled in the alley which included Excav8's handler, Dave, and two counterterrorism operations officers. The van had full surveillance equipment, encryption devices, and communications equipment poised to transmit information to Langley in a matter of seconds. The security team was prepared to take Omar in if he failed to cooperate.

Nights were cold in the desert, but it warmed up pleasantly in the sunshine. Josh wore American tourist garb—a Kansas City Royals baseball cap, tourist clothes, and a large lanyard which read "BABYLONIAN TOURS". The lanyard was a carefully disguised recording device. For extra effect, a round sticker was on his collar with the number 43, to complete the tourist effect. He was constantly aware, always on edge, eyes darting about, looking for disturbances, carefully observing anyone who was watching. But he seemed to be black—there was no apparent evidence of Iraq security teams following him today.

He ambled along Wangfujing Avenue at tourist speed, supposedly perusing the junky trinkets offered by street side merchants, all the time keeping a sharp eye out for Omar who might possibly be stopping by again for supper. The tourist groups were thinner this time of year, but Babylon Metro was still a congested city, and merchants sold food, aromatic spices, incense, perfumes, and other items out of vendor stalls. He passed a cobbler playing a tinny recording of Turkish music. The music in Babylon Metro was fascinating. You never knew what nationality of music you might hear in a restaurant or a street corner, and he stopped to study it and to analyze the chord structures and the rhythms.

Sure enough, Omar moved into the area, sampling a kebab cart in a different part of the bazaar. A tall truck filled with cages that had little holes and the sound of bleating goats rolled to a stop at an intersection.

"Excav8 just ahead," Josh breathed into the mic. He moved up the street quickly. "Approaching. Ten yards…five yards."

"We're on it. Go."

"Is that you, Omar?" Josh called out, breaking into an awkward tourist lope. With a silly grin on his face, he waved eagerly.

Omar turned around with a start. For a micro-second his face was a mixture of surprise and alarm.

"It's me, Josh Evans, from America! Levi Mizrahi's friend!" Josh leaped up next to the gyro stand, touching his chest over the heart, the Middle Eastern greeting. "How are you, man? How's it going?"

"Josh my friend! You surprise me!" answered Omar, fighting to compose his facial expression. His eyes squinted to read the lanyard and sticker. "You are a tourist?"

"It's the trip of a lifetime. I've always wanted to come!" Josh lied glibly in the manner of CIA operatives, chattering easily and happily about the construction in Babylon Metro while Omar stood, hesitantly taking a bite of his rapidly cooling kebabs. "And what are you doing in Babylon Metro, Omar? Are you a tourist, too? Or are you here on business?"

The Saudi's eyes darted around the street and he answered carefully, "I'm not with my old company any more. I am into business for myself."

If Omar was abandoning the CIA and starting a new life, a structural engineer with his world experience could certainly find work here. Or hide here.

"Do you want me to help you?" Josh asked eagerly, putting on a puppy dog persona. "I can talk to my architect friends. They could lead you to a high-profile American project somewhere here in the city. You know I'd be glad to help you." Like a good recruiter, Josh had found Omar's Achilles heel while building a relationship two years ago: attention from Americans.

"Of course. Of course. I need to have some work." Omar said. And then he asked, "And how is your lovely wife, Chelsea?"

"She is fine. And Laila?"

"Laila is—" Omar licked his lips and replied carefully, "she is back in Saudi Arabia with her family."

Were they permanently separated because Omar was on the run from the CIA? Or still together, just temporarily apart while Omar was scrambling for work?

A harpist and horn player were setting up next to them in preparation for performance music on the street this evening. A truck roared by, spewing smoke. It was going to become noisy. "Tell you what," Josh said, sticking to the plan set out by Covert Operations. "Why don't you come with me to my hotel? We will catch up on old times! Then I will contact everyone I know and help you find some engineering work."

"Ah...Yes, of course that would be nice."

"Where are you staying?" Josh pressed. "Do you have a new number? I lost track of you long ago."

"I'm, ah, getting a different mobile. That is why I come here to bazaar, to look for new one," Omar said evasively. He rattled off the address of a hotel, but it was different than the one Josh and Counterintelligence knew he was actually staying at.

"What time can you meet?" Josh pressed. "Now?"

Omar hesitated.

"I will buy," Josh added. "It will be a fine dinner."

"Is ok," Omar agreed, but his reluctance was transparent.

"Shall we catch a cab to the mall? It's almost sunset and it's getting chilly." Josh hailed a cab, knowing that the Agency van would pull around a distance behind and meet them at the hotel. The mall and hotel had adequate parking and even more ideally, a back alley that made it easy to load and take off fast.

Josh talked easily in the cab about his own job in Washington, D.C. with Crestedon, and some of the legitimate projects he had worked on in the last couple of years. Omar nodded without comment and without smiling.

They arrived at the beautiful hotel attached to the shopping mall and casino, a hastily constructed building, and headed to the dining room. Josh ordered expensive appetizers, and they studied the dinner menu.

By now, the van should be parked in the alley, and the officers should be surrounding the hotel in the setting sun. Hidden surveillance devices in Josh's attaché case and embedded on his mobile, which lay casually on the table, recorded and taped the interview and transmitted video back to Langley, where dozens of analysts would study it. "I need to go to the men's room," Josh said according to plan. He took his mobile and left the table. Out of sight of Omar he inserted the earpiece into his ear as he moved towards the bathroom. "Operation AuCHFOP. Can you read me?"

He heard his associate reply into the mic. "We've been in an accident! Fender bender. No one is injured but personnel have to proceed by foot. Buy time with Excav8!"

"How far away are you?"

"We only got two blocks away from the bazaar. Eat supper. We will get there as soon as possible."

Immediately Josh yanked the earpiece out, stuffed it back in his pocket, and hurried back to the dining room. But there was no Omar; he had left the table!

Josh let out a breath of exasperation. He rushed to the front of the restaurant and the front lobby of the hotel. He opened the front door; the cool night air blew into the lobby from outside. Up and down the street in the fading light he looked but there was no Omar. He made his way back to the hallway where the bathrooms were, considering Omar's options.

Was that Omar's voice down the hall and around the corner?

He snatched off his shoes so that the squeaking could not be heard on the marble, tucked them under his arms, and raced down lengthy hallway in his socks towards direction of the fire exit. He turned a corner. There Omar was, about halfway way down another lengthy hallway, his back to Josh, talking on the phone. At the very far end of the second hallway was a fire exit door and alley. Josh could hear little but he detected Arabic. One phrase he did understand, because he had listened to it and practiced it on the recordings of a number of dialects and languages:

Black Lightening.

The group headed by Mufti Mohammad Al-Issa, the jihadist on the CIA wanted list!

Josh spun around in his socks, turned the corner, and raced back to the bathroom, hissing, "Operation AuCHFOP! Operation AuCHFOP! Do you read me? Heard the target discussing 'Black Lightening' in Arabic.

"Find a way to stall him. Keep him in the restaurant until backup gets there."

Once again, Josh raced down the long hallway, his shoes still under his arms, planning to make up an innocent story about desert sand irritating his feet. He turned came around the corner. Omar, at the distant end of the hallway now, had his hand on the fire exit door now, finishing the phone conversation.

"Omar? Do you have to leave? What about our dinner?" Josh's voice echoed in the hallway. He tried to suppress his own panting as well as the urgency in his voice, and to simply sound curious.

Omar whirled around to see Josh. He disconnected the phone and put a hand down to his hip, raw fear on his face.

A weapon?

Josh felt his heart stop and tried to maintain a normal posture while surreptitiously sliding his free hand towards his own weapon. He had practiced poor tradecraft; he should not have completely rounded the corner! The only way to get protection was to back up!

Omar pulled out a Viper Jaws pistol from his pocket, his hand on the crash bar of the door. Reflexively Josh drew his own weapon out and pointed the gun on Omar.

But the Saudi spy had turned around was not looking at Josh anymore. He did not point his gun in Josh's direction or pull the trigger. With a bang of his fist against the crash bar, he flew out the fire exit door.

Josh spoke frantically into the communication piece. "Target armed and on the run. Request permission to discharge a weapon!"

There was a crackle and he could hear a blur of voices in the background, including a request for second source confirmation.

"No. Stand down. Repeat: orders are to stand down."

Once again, the asset had gone missing.

Using the very training that the CIA had provided him, Omar Al Ghamdi had eluded the Agency. He had never returned to his hotel; and as far as Josh knew, he had vanished from, or somewhere deep within, Babylon Metro. The CIA sent Dave, who had mis-handled the operation with Omar, back short of tour in disgrace to a cubicle in Langley and a boring job of reviewing the case reports of agents working in the Mideast. Pretty much everyone from the Consulate, the Baghdad Embassy, and the State Department, not to mention the Office of Security, investigated the meltdown. Until the CIA could launch the rush contract with private company Crestedon Global Architectural and Engineering to take over the work abandoned by Omar's former engineering firm, there was little that Josh could do to further the goals of operation AuCHFOP specifically.

He went to visit Ana a second time, the prostitute who worked the underpass below the freeway. He followed her into the brothel, and upstairs into her curtained-off room. He seated himself on the chair beside her bed and handed her a large wad of cash from the CIA. "Here. I am paying you a fee for the time you talk to me," he said.

"Do you wish to have the sex today?"

"Maybe. Maybe no. I mostly want female companionship and someone who will listen to me about my work."

"Suit yourself. It makes no difference to me."

Josh was not looking for sex, he was peddling subversion. Trying to connect with her by using humor, he launched into a funny story about a building he was designing in Babylon Metro where he forgot to design the area for an air conditioner. It wasn't really a building in Babylon Metro, it was something that actually happened two decades ago when he was an architectural student in London. Ana never laughed. All she cared about was survival.

He asked, "How long have you worked at this place?"

"Two years," she replied.

"Do you like it?"

"Of course. My clients are very exciting." Her voice was monotone.

He lowered his own voice and leaned in close to her. "Are any of your clients American architects like me?" He composed his face into a look of potentially worried jealousy.

She grasped a piece of her long, straggly, light brown hair and flipped it around her finger. "I think not. They are from many countries. Mostly they are Chinese military."

He furrowed his brow as if deeply concerned about this. "How do they treat you?"

"They have much money. Sometimes one take me to his, what you say..." she struggled for the translation. "Villa. It has swimming pool. Our time is almost over. I have another customer."

"Would you like to go to the swimming pool at my hotel? It is one of the best hotels in Babylon Metro." Entertaining Ana the prostitute at an expensive hotel pool would only further add to the perception of any surveillance that Josh was a typical playboy business man having fun after hours, and it would give Ana the impression that he could compete with top-level Chinese military.

"It will have to be cleared with my boss. How much will you pay?"

It would also most certainly have to be cleared by Josh's superior. The Chief of Station would no doubt be more than happy to oblige and would also probably personally show up at the hotel swimming pool deck chairs to leer behind dark sunglasses. Bureaucrats in cubicles at Langley would stay busy for a few days double checking clearances for expenditures in pricey hotels and analyzing Josh's expense reports, thus insuring their government jobs.

Josh pulled out a little gift for her, lip gloss and an attractive headband wrapped in a gold foil box. "I must go. If the Chinese ever treat you shitty, call me, ok? I will come here."

She gave a little twitch looked at him with odd surprise.

"If they ever hurt you, call me," he repeated.

She did not answer, obviously wondering whether to believe him. She turned away from him, opened the lip gloss and held up a mirror.

He left the depressing brothel, scanning the faces of the various Chinese men scurrying in and out of the building with caps or sunglasses, faces averted, dodging notice and conversation. Were they high level officials? He caught a cab back to a restaurant in a different part of Babylon Metro. He had planned a circuitous route back to the safe house so that he could eventually return undetected by local Iraqi surveillance.

Conceivably, the CIA could waste months working to recruit Ana. Even though he liked to see projects through, he decided that wasn't really his problem. His mission was to find a guy, and it was the new incoming handler's job to make him—or in this case her—a spy. Ana's Achilles' heel might be a desire for safety. It was also obviously money, and she was becoming a developmental prospect. Hopefully it all resulted in brownie points with his immediate superiors, as well as affirmative talk about him in the back halls of Langley. And optimistically, it would ultimately get him where he and Chelsea really wanted to go.

24

The Micro Drone

While he readied the offices of Pyramids and Palaces Architectural Renovation, finalizing everything for the arrival of the new excavating team, Josh continued to study computer records left behind by Omar Al-Ghamdi—handle Excav8—about the palace restoration job. The records had probably already been reviewed, catalogued, analyzed, and partially scrubbed by countless bureaucratic lackeys in Baghdad and Langley. Josh had to request them, because as soon as Omar broke contact, Headquarters had cleared out the office. He came upon a computer file of Omar's containing a curiosity.

It was a document with a bland name, a single blueprint of a portion of what appeared to be a new, state-of-the-art building mechanical system. Something on the drawing caught his eye. He zoomed in and enlarged, moving around the image, trying to figure out what building it was. Certainly nothing to do with Saddam's palace.

Could it be *this* floor, high up in the Tomorrow Globe Financial Center?

Curiously he stood up from his desk and went over to the security panel on the wall. The small, institutional metal hatch door that led to the building mechanical system was directly beside it. He returned to the desk for some tools and picked at the lock. There was a noisy swoosh of air as the metal door, large enough for a man to stoop and crawl through, swung open, exposing the shaft and the mechanical system that served this portion of the Tomorrow Globe Financial Center complex. Once Josh's eyes adjusted, he stepped onto a catwalk, which was dimly lit by an emergency light. It ran all the way around the circular shaft; and unless he wished to tear through drywall, the catwalk was essentially a longer, circuitous pathway for a human to get to a spot where the wiring on the drawing eventually connected with a duct.

He wriggled back through the metal doorway to his office computer and studied and measured the mechanical drawing for a very, very long time, memorizing details. He closed his eyes, repeated a series of landmarks, and opened his eyes again to study the drawing, checking his memory. Then he climbed through the metal door again. He made his way around the circular catwalk and to a duct large enough for a man to slide into and shone his light carefully around the inside, blowing away some dust.

Yes, there was a wire, and Josh immediately suspected surveillance. He had never been briefed on any of this. Had Headquarters tasked Omar with installing it? Or had Omar discovered it? If he discovered it, had he reported it?

Josh followed the line, crawling through the duct work on his hands and knees, occasionally catching bits of clothing on protrusions in the metal, marking his way by recalling various notations on the mechanical drawing. As he got closer to the endpoint of the installation notated on the architectural plans, he realized where he probably was: just past a large, vacant space in the building and right over the suite occupied by another office tenant on the floor, Iran Central Industries Group. He halted, and then panting in the stifled air, crawled like a cat in the darkness as close as he could to the voices, but he could only make out bits of Farsi. A pinpoint of light shone up from what must be a hole in the tenants' ceiling tile. His hands followed the wire with his fingers as he crawled further, and then there it was, the little box that had been noted on the floor plan. He could hear it hum. He touched it with his hand and felt its warmth and everything about it—the size and the vibration emitted—told him exactly what it was.

It was a micro drone!

He did not dare try to disassemble the box in his cramped, dark position in an air duct. It most likely resembled a large insect and had probably been programmed to collect information through the small hole in the ceiling tile. If Iran Central Industries Group did any kind of security sweep, they would probably find it.

His best friend Clinton Radcliffe had worked on micro drones seven years ago, successfully marketing an aerial one that collected DNA samples. It was short-lived—the technology had been copied fairly quickly by the Chinese and the size reduced— but Clinton had made quite a bit of money on it at first.

He needed to get out of here and report this immediately.

Breathlessly he waited for an interminable length of time, afraid to move, afraid they would hear him rustling in the ceiling.

What if Iran Central Industries stayed open all night? What if the support gave way and he plunged through the white ceiling tile into the office suite below, right into the laps of bewildered Iranian foreign workers?

94

25

The Call to Liu Chen

J osh eventually heard the voices fade in the Iran Central Industries Group offices and the soft clicks of security being set for the night. The light below him went out. Scrambling backwards, he maneuvered his way through the duct and into the catwalk, and then he ran for the metal door. Hastily he locked down his office and set the security system for the night. Mindful of security cams in the common area hallway, he slipped into the men's room, shut himself in a toilet, and tried his best to brush off the dust and debris from his snagged clothes. Then he quickly made his exit from the massive complex, trying not to bring attention to himself.

Once he was back at the CIA safe house in the part of Babylon Metro that bordered the old city, Hillah, he immediately sent a satellite burst transmission: *Possible security breach. Wiring for drone discovered which runs to adjacent space. Notated in Excav8 computer file. Please confirm if authorized.*

His heart pounded as he thought of all the things that could go wrong from this: if the drone had been placed by a hostile state, it would become apparent to the placers that someone had discovered it. It might not take much time to figure out who. Cover eroded over time, and time was the enemy.

To his relief a message came back from his satellite transmission burst. Someone eating a donut and downing coffee in the middle of the night in Langley was definitely on their game: *Confirmed that project was formerly authorized for Excav8 to investigate. Operation AuCHOP does not have security clearance for continued investigation of this project. Precautions will be taken. Congratulations on excellent tradecraft.*

Enough brownie points to help score a tour in London? A long-term post in Western Europe? Probably not enough, but a guy could keep wishing.

The next day, with no explanation of what Omar had been investigating, and with no words of appreciation as there had been from Headquarters, the COS in Baghdad abruptly called and ordered Josh to remove the surveillance device.

Josh waited until after midnight to execute the assignment; fortunately, no one was working on the floor, and this time the mission was completed without incident.

He went back to the safe house, too wired to sleep. He tried to web chat Chelsea in the United States, but she didn't answer. She was probably in a real estate showing.

He did what he could to help Crestedon get the office open, but there was still ample time to do some of his own personal research. Via the security clearances he had, he collected information from back channels on what Omar had been investigating with Iran Central Industries. He read and re-read traffic and cables, researching the highest clearance levels that Agency sources permitted to him, as well as open sources online.

Iran and China collaborated on anti-ship surface-to-surface missiles.

China supplied chemical weapons to Iran, an enemy state of U.S. ally Israel.

Chinese scientists verified to be working in Iran on nuclear energy

Chinese predilection for non-military measures and neutrality has resulted in securing Iranian oil fields

It was time to call in a favor to get even more information. He had gone through his initial CIA training at The Farm with Liu Chen. He had been kind to her, even though for the other trainees it was a dog-eat dog environment. She couldn't cut it; Liu would never be a covert officer, a position she had desired; but she had been hired as a well-paid CIA Analyst. She returned Josh's kindness over the years by sharing back channel information.

He made a secure call to her after hours at her private residence. Their conversation was of necessity very brief, oblique, and coded. "It seems obvious what this probably is," he said.

"I do not know for sure, but I think there are very few other possibilities," she confirmed. She connected the dots for him:

Israel, caught between three giants—the U.S., China, and Iran—has increased trade and renewed defense industry technology transfers with China in order to assure protection from Muslim attackers.

Trying to settle his mind so he could relax, he loaded up the NoitaLever game to play a few rounds.

From the list of online identities in his group of gamers, he pinged his best friend Clinton, sending a greeting via his own online identity. In college, the methodical and logical Clinton, and Josh, a creative and somewhat wild architectural student, had been roommates who stumbled into financial success with technology for movies and then hit the big time with government surveillance contracts. Josh and Clinton parted ways shortly before Josh joined the CIA.

Clinton immediately pinged back: *Insomnia?*

Yah. Where did you get the name, NoitaLever?

Backwards for the book of Revelation. All characters from Chapter 9.

Clinton had a philosophical streak that rarely emerged in front of other people. They chatted briefly and logged off. Josh did a computer search for Revelation 9, and read the imagery. Locusts with tails like stingers...horses of red, blue and yellow...armies...Clinton had worked it all into the game. Josh studied the prophecy, written over twenty centuries ago. It was something that he neither literally believed nor disbelieved, and something he had mostly forgotten about for many years. *The agony they suffered was like that of the sting of a scorpion when it strikes...I heard a voice... "Release the four angels who are bound at the great river Euphrates." And the four angels who had been kept ready for this very hour and day and month and year were released to kill a third of mankind. The number of the mounted troops was twice ten thousand times ten thousand."*

Now the words seemed prescient. Two millennia ago, an uneducated, untrained, imprisoned fisherman penned them. This fisherman had no concept of an ancient civilization clashing with a highly technological western civilization, of tribal and religious conflict in the Middle East and Africa which would ultimately climax to a boiling point, unleashing global chemical and nuclear warfare. Josh thought about the Chinese equestrian mounted troops, admired for their pageantry but poised to savagely kill Iraqis with their AK-74Ms.

He disconnected and sat for a very, very long time, turning the gravity of the situation over in his mind, immersed in deep philosophical thoughts and unanswerable questions about the future.

His career had made church attendance in recent years nearly impossible, but he had not forgotten the ancient predictions; and now some of the mysterious teachings of his childhood haunted him.

He made a personal call to his favorite pastor, the one he knew during the times he lived in London.

26
The Arrest

Inside the luxurious bedroom of a villa just outside of Babylon Metro overlooking the Euphrates River, Ana kneeled beside the bed, facing it, with the Chinese officer's legs draped on either side of her as she worked. He grunted and moaned with pleasure.

His cell phone rang, four, six, eight rings, and finally went silent. But then it started ringing again. Annoyed, he reluctantly ended their activity, mumbling some Chinese cussing. He snatched up the phone with irritation. Ana sat back on the floor and wiped a straggly piece of brownish hair with her finger back out of her face, waiting for him to finish the call.

As the voice on the phone jabbered with frantic warning, it dawned on him what was actually happening, and at the same time commotion sounded down the hallway of the compound. He lurched for his gun and yelled something in Chinese to Ana. Frantically he grabbed his pants, struggling to get them up his short legs as someone began banging on the bedroom door, and then kicked it. The door flew open.

"Iraqi police! You are arrested for prostitution!"

The Chinese officer pointed his gun back at them, but it wasn't unlocked and ready to discharge, and four police officers immediately stormed into the room, brandishing their weapons. He was outnumbered.

"DROP IT!" The sergeant of the police force fired a shot into the drywall just beyond his head, and Ana screamed in terror. The Chinese military officer dropped the weapon onto the carpet and threw his arms up over his head. An officer grabbed Ana and yanked her off the floor, angrily throwing her clothes at her and yelling at her in Arabic. The two other policemen took custody of the Chinese officer.

"This is not a prostitute! This is my bride!" the Chinese military officer insisted angrily in a botched Arabic accent.

"Show us the proof! How do we know she is your bride?"

"I have a sworn statement! It is in the safe!" Once again the accent was awful, but the phrase was well rehearsed.

"Let him make proof," snapped the sergeant of the unit to his police comrades. "But even if he has the paperwork, he and the girl will come with us to the police station!"

27
The Dig Site

Josh and the new team from Crestedon Global Architectural and Engineering rolled up in a jeep on the sandy road flanked with palm trees to take over the rehabilitation project abandoned by structural engineer Omar Al Ghamdi.

Ancient Babylon stood on a wind-swept, sandy expanse just outside of Babylon Metro and ancient Hillah, and eighty miles southeast of Baghdad. The legends grew larger than life as the years passed by—in the 1980s, Saddam Hussein had channeled the spirit of King Nebuchadnezzar II, evacuated a thousand local villagers, and tried to rebuild Babylon and its seventh wonder of the ancient world, the Hanging Gardens, literally on top of the old ruins.

"There was supposed to be a cable car that went to Baghdad," the archaeologist told them as they bumped along in the jeep. "Saddam Hussein was just about to start building it in 2003 when the Americans invaded."

The odd, blue Ishtar Gate was the first stop. The jeep pulled up to a checkpoint and they presented their credentials, *Pyramids and Palaces Architectural Renovation.*

"Unbelievable," Josh said to the group when they climbed out and examined the gate up close. It was one of Saddam Hussein's narcissistic architectural monstrosities. The archeologist with them narrated, "This was a reconstruction of a long-removed double gate from 575 B.C. Note the reliefs of the deities, aurochs and dragons emblazoned in gold in tidy, straight rows."

They mingled about with the other tourists. A gust of wind picked up and blew sand everywhere around them—in their shoes and in their hair and in their clothes. It disturbed a group of huge, black birds that were feeding on a dead owl in the court yard, and the birds fluttered away for protection in the crevices of the building. Spitting sand out of their mouths, the team climbed back into the jeep for the second stop.

Saddam's massive palace, built in the shape of a ziggurat, was a tourist attraction that had become unkempt and run down due to lack of funds; or rather, a lack of priority of funds. "It was either a national monument to a legendary hero, or a disgrace, depending on which strain of Muslim you were," the archaeologist said of the Saddam era.

Conveniently deferring to the superstition that Ancient Babylon was cursed, the Chinese, with their vast sums of money to invest from the oil they were extracting from Iraq, didn't bother to renovate Ancient Babylon. The Chinese were far more interested in investing in Babylon Metro and the oil pipeline in the east portion of Ancient Babylon than they were in historic preservation.

"Saddam's palace," the archaeologist told them as they climbed out of the jeep into the burning hot parking lot, "was built on ancient two thousand six hundred year-old ruins. The effort to restore the Ancient Babylon ruins was hit and miss over the decades—primarily a miss that appalls our profession." On the ceiling above them, the archaeologist pointed out the colors of the paint on the ceiling, a mural with elephants and wild animals. They stopped to read the inscription on some bricks: *"This was built by Saddam Hussein, son of Nebuchadnezzar, to glorify Iraq."*

"What an ego," one of the members of the team shook his head.

The archaeologist explained that each attempt over the centuries to rebuild and restore Ancient Babylon had been beset by any of a number of problems: wars and skirmishes, inconvenience and distraction caused by flooding of the river; and more recently, failed cell phone towers, faulty electric lines, inadequate sewer infrastructure…the list went on.

He showed them to the basement of the palace where the prison was, with a damaged kitchen area above it, which they would be restoring for a future tourist entertainment area. "This is ridiculous," said the structural engineer who had been brought in to replace Omar Al Ghamdi. He was sweating and cranky from the desert heat. "We're supposed to repair a shoddy reconstruction on top of shoddy ruins? It's crazy. None of it is stable."

They climbed over broken tile and concrete from the kitchen down into the dark, musky stairwell; and with the use of searchlights, they made their way to the clammy prison below ground.

"Look at the cracks in the floor," Josh pointed to the concrete.

The structural engineer bent down, shining his light on some of the cracks to examine them. He replied, "I doubt there is sand underneath the floor of this prison. I bet there's more archaeological ruins underneath and we're going to need some extra structural support."

"Hmm. Might be one of those secret passageways where the ancient sultans went to visit their mistresses," suggested the archeologist.

"We need to spend some time down here and figure this out. I need some help getting some decent lighting down here," the engineer appealed to Josh.

The next morning, Josh and the structural engineer sweated in the dank heat of the prison. The lighting that they were stringing was bright enough that it allowed them to move foot by foot throughout, examining every inch of it. They could see Arabic, American, and Polish graffiti on the walls.

"Here you go," the engineer spoke, holding up one of the light fixtures over his head and gesturing straight ahead towards a concrete block wall at the far end of a rather wide hallway. "What do you want to bet this is what Omar was working on?"

Josh held the string of lights up closer to the wall. "Yep. It's new. Or false. See, the concrete blocks don't really match the adjacent walls."

"The grout has been cut. Somebody sawed into these blocks and put them back in place." The structural engineer dug into the crevices with a pen. "They didn't re-grout."

Josh scratched his head in puzzlement. "Our next trick: to get some help pulling these blocks out. Suppose we can we find locals that don't know the superstitions and who won't talk?"

While waiting for Crestedon to hire some locals to examine the wall in Saddam's palace, Josh went back to his project of developing Ana the prostitute for potential recruiting as a spy by the new CIA handler, who would be flying in from D.C. shortly. He immediately noted a marked change in her demeanor. She had clearly been traumatized recently.

"What has happened to you?" he asked. "You are not yourself. Why are you wearing long sleeves and slacks on such a nice day?"

She pulled up her sleeves and showed the discreet architect with the earnest, inquisitive brown eyes the bruises and scratches on the insides of her arms, clearly hinting that she needed more money from him. "I come to Babylon Metro on promises of a good life, she said. "I must work until my debt to come here is paid off or I cannot leave." She took a deep breath, and with her finger she twirled back a clump of straggly light brown hair that had drifted over bitter eyes. "I know a girl, she tries to leave here and live on the streets. Black Lightening do not like prostitutes. They drag her through the street and beat her. All of her teeth gone, and she has the scars that will never heal. They are on the police force. They come to the villa and beat me."

Now Josh was getting real information from her, although he had to lean on the chair over the bed to hear her low voice. Most of her clients, she said, were Chinese military and security officers. There were about a half-dozen of them that came to see her regularly.

"Are they elevated ranking?" he asked. She didn't understand his English. "Big? Important? Famous?" he tried different synonyms.

"Yes. Some important clients go upstairs to Isabella, my boss. They say they protect us from Black Lightening police officers on the Iraqi police force.

"Do the Chinese military officers have lots of money? Maybe I can design nice offices or a home for them." Josh never designed homes except for himself and his family, but Ana would never know.

She licked her lips. "You pay me if I get you some work?"

"Absolutely." If all went well, she would end up on the payroll of the CIA. She had given Josh the information he needed. He did not need to come back and ask her any more questions about the Chinese. He studied her for a minute; had he finally earned her trust?

In a barely audible voice he said, "You want a better life than this place? You want to be safe with no more worry? You can find a much better life than this in America. You will be far away from Black Lightening there."

Ana was ripe for recruitment, and there might be multiple candidates for the CIA in this building. It was time to go back to the safe house, write a summary, and flip things back to the Chief of Station in Baghdad so that the new handler replacing Dave could figure out a way to actually do it.

29
The Discovery

Within a few days Josh's cover operation, Pyramids and Palaces Architectural Renovation, identified and hired some non-Iraqi internationals who had come to do construction in town. They hadn't been in Babylon Metro long enough to know the local superstitions and prophecies about gold in the Euphrates that must not be moved.

Josh and the engineer stayed on site the entire time the young men maneuvered the blocks out of the lower part of the wall, bracing the row above it with metal supports. And when enough had been removed that a man could crawl inside, they dismissed the workers and called down two United States Marine Security Guards.

One Marine went ahead, pulling the light string through the opening in the bricks. Josh, the engineer, and the second Marine followed behind. Even though the prison was subterranean and somewhat cooler, it was still stifling.

A stairwell of newer construction descended downwards into a sub-basement, and they could see on the sides of the stairwell very clearly where the newer Saddam Hussein reconstruction had been built on top of a very ancient structure.

At the bottom of the stairwell, below the prison, a short doorway had been blocked up, then sawn open and left that way, with a dusty pile of debris left in the hallway.

"Midgets. They were sure short back in the old days. I wonder," asked the engineer, "why somebody would leave this mess down here at the bottom of the stairs but carefully fix the concrete blocks at the top of the steps?"

The Marine cocked his rifle, climbed up on the little pile of rubble and stepped down and through the low door, shining his light into the mysterious chamber. "Sonuvabitch!" he exclaimed suddenly, jumping backwards into the rubble. He swayed and nearly stumbled. "Step back everyone! Do not approach! This is damn fucking unbelievable!"

Josh peered over the shoulder of the Marine into the chamber where the spotlight was still shining, feeling the hair stand up on the back of his neck. "So did Omar know this, I wonder?" he managed to ask, his eyes widening.

"Don't ask questions you don't want to know the answer to. According to what I see down here, your Saudi Arabian informant found out too much," the Marine replied, swooping the light around the objects in the chamber. "Way, way too much!"

The temperatures in Iraq had cooled with the approach of winter. It was nearly twilight as Ana the prostitute stood pressed behind a neatly manicured Hawthorn bush along the cream-colored concrete wall at the far end of the American Embassy compound in Baghdad.

As the embassy attaché walked briskly towards the direction of the main entry gate, she spoke aloud in a plaintive voice.

"*Am nevoie de ajutor.*"

Startled, the man stepped sideways.

"I need help," Ana repeated in English. He turned his face and moved on but she stepped out from behind the Hawthorn bush onto the sidewalk behind him. "Please. I am in danger. Black Lightening men try to kill me."

The embassy attaché threw a look over his shoulder, warily noting a suspicious backpack she was carrying. In the twilight he could also see that she was unkempt and was shivering in the cool of the desert night. She pushed a long, brown piece of straggly hair out of her eyes with her hand so he could clearly see her face.

"Water, please sir."

"Who are you? Where are you from?"

"My name is Ana. I am from Romania." she said and held out empty hands, her long dirty hair trailing down her shoulders, "Water, please, *ajutor*! Black Lightening try to kill me but I run. I will give you informations if you will help me go to America."

"Put your weapons down," he said sharply.

They locked eyes and he pointed at her backpack. She threw it onto the ground without breaking eye contact. Across the street a Chinese security officer saw what was happening. In a few strides he was across the street, his AK-74MS drawn.

"On your knees. Open it. Put everything onto the sidewalk."

She knelt and unzipped the bag and dumped the contents. Darkness was overtaking Baghdad rapidly and pinpoints of starlight were popping in the eastern sky. There were a few personal toiletries and one change of clothes sprawled on the sidewalk.

"Black Lightening take all my money," she said.

"Stand up. Raise your arms and turn around."

She hesitated, processing his instructions. Slowly she turned, twisting her head to keep an eye on him. "They beat me."

The Chinese officer patted her down, searching her jeans and sleeves for weapons, exposing red marks and bruises on her skin. He examined her backpack. There was nothing suspicious.

The attaché dialed on his cell phone to the Marine Guard stationed at the front entrance. "I have a walk-in. A Romanian woman on the northwest corner, victim of Black Lightening beating and intimidation, asking for water. She has no weapons and no money." He disconnected and nodded his thanks to the Chinese officer. "Come and walk in front of me," he ordered her, pointing ahead of himself on the sidewalk. "We will go to the embassy and get water and food for you."

Even though it was a school night, Atalaya got to stay up later to talk to Daddy on web chat. Occasionally they used sec-vid, or secure video, but to keep up the cover of a normal American architect and his family, they primarily used conventional web chatting for brief conversations. Iraqi or Chinese National Intelligence Services could be watching their conversation. Clues in the background could give away Josh's location, and an associate could stop in to see him at any time and accidentally be observed. Even with her own husband, Chelsea preferred phone because cameras made her edgy and self-conscious. Nonetheless, she felt a familiar sense of relief when he appeared on the screen.

"How is school, Attie?" he asked. Atalaya shrugged, looking down at her doll and turning it over in her lap.

"About the same," Chelsea answered for her daughter. School was neither bad nor good for Atalaya, just uncomfortable. "Atalaya, show Daddy our Christmas tree." She followed Atalaya with the camera to the spacious foyer where Atalaya pointed to the decorations that had just gone up. Chelsea was glad she splurged on a real tree this year, one that soared high. If Josh didn't come home in time for Christmas, they could at least enjoy the homey pine smell. If he did make it, it would be an extra special celebration.

Josh extrapolated short bits of information from his daughter about her daily life, getting her to giggle about the latest Peppermint Pinkey episode on TV while Chelsea quickly lit a cinnamon Christmas candle. When Atalaya was done with the camera, Chelsea sent her off to bed and continued the online conversation.

It was always like getting reacquainted right at first. She hated how her image looked on a computer screen. Josh could never say anything about what he was doing. So she kept a list handy for whenever he could chat: mundane household stuff and questions first, then a frustrated monologue about work that was usually short because her job was boring. "It was hard enough for me to pick up the phone in the first place and call, and I don't understand why none of the other commercial real estate firms will even return my call about my resume and job application! I know Goldberger Hewitt Columbia dismissed me a few years ago when I kept missing work because of your government projects, but Goldberger Hewitt's policy is to never say anything bad, they just verify employment. For crying out loud, I've even owned my own real estate company. And Goldberger Hewitt London has a good reference for me."

"Maybe that's intimidating to employers," Josh guessed.

If someone was intercepting their conversation, it was important to keep it sounding like that of a normal American couple where the husband was overseas for a brief work assignment. She heard a slurping sound. "Yappie, do not drink the Christmas tree water!" But the Sheltie appeared to ignore her and continued drinking. "I keep forgetting she's deaf," Chelsea said, maneuvering over to the tree with the phone in one hand and physically removing the dog with the other. Yappie licked her lips and settled down under the tree, and Chelsea pointed the camera towards the dog staring out from under the lower branches. The rich aroma of the cinnamon candle drifted through the first floor and made her feel warm and cozy.

"So show me the three wise men decorations," Josh said.

"Huh?" she asked. That was a strange request.

"The three kings. The wise men. It's my favorite Christmas decoration."

She never knew that. "You mean my manger scene?" She focused the camera to the three kings bowing to the crèche, which sat on a coffee table in the living room.

"Tradition says the wise men came from Persia, Mesopotamia," Josh said. "Did you know that?" His hand moved across the screen casually, but it was the signal they used when they were working a room at a social for possible recruitment to the CIA. She jerked to attention. This wasn't small talk. He was obliquely bringing up something relating to his work.

He said, "There's something about the Christmas story that reminds me of a Muslim story. Something about the gifts they brought. I forget what all those gifts were?"

On the surface it was ridiculous. Any little boy growing up in a Baptist home sang the songs at Christmas and knew the story. "Gold, frankincense, and myrrh," she replied carefully, as if she were reminding him of something. Their eyes locked. He was trying to tell her something.

"Yeah, right. That's what I thought. Gold. There's a Muslim legend about gold, too. It's in the Hadith."

Chelsea tried to hold the camera steady while she went for a pen. She gave a loud, fake yawn. "It's where, honey?" she asked, trying to sound casual and vaguely disinterested, but she was fully alert, and she did not take her eyes off his.

"The Hadith, the prophetic commentary on the Quran. Hadith Number 6918. A lady in a tourist shop was telling me all about it today. She went on and on. I couldn't get away from her."

"Oh. That's nice." Chelsea was quite certain that there was no woman in a tourist shop telling him this, but she wrote down "hadeeth 6,918" on the back of a piece of junk mail. Josh did not offer any more clues, so she asked, "Will you be home before we put the holiday decorations away?"

"I'm not sure. We're busy. It's not going to be a short assignment."

"Oh," she said, disappointed, thinking of long weeks or maybe even months ahead. Of course he could not tell her about the schedule involved in a CIA tour, but she read his meaning. Mom and Dad had flown out for Thanksgiving, so they wouldn't be here for Christmas either, and Clinton was going to celebrate the holidays away, with Jennifer's family. It was lonely now that Clinton was married. He used to be such a solid rock and a comforting presence to her and Atalaya during his visits to D.C, especially when Josh was out of the country on assignment. Clinton would always give advice on problems around the house and would entertain Atalaya.

The dryer buzzer went off loudly in the laundry room, startling her. She righted the camera so he could see her again.

"Those blue eyes of yours suck me in, make me want to fly right home on the next plane and rip off your clothes," he said.

She giggled. Her hair was a mess and her makeup had worn off hours ago. "Want me to rip them off right now?" If someone from foreign intelligence services was spying on the conversation, they were probably leaning into the screen right now, hoping for a thrill.

He grinned ruefully. "I suppose I better take off and go to work." There were eight hours' time difference between them. "I love you."

"Love you too." Chelsea said reassuringly. Was Josh's assignment this tour more dangerous than usual? "Stay out of trouble," she said lightly.

"I'm a cat, I always land on my feet," he answered.

"Bye, Babe."

"Bye."

They logged off. She went to the dryer and put the two shirts on a hanger under her arm, and she trudged up the stairs with them to put them away. Then she came back to the desk with the piece of junk mail on which she had made her notes and did an online search.

She spelled it all wrong, but it self-corrected and came up. According to internet sources, it was a Muslim prophecy: *The Last Hour would not come before the Euphrates uncovers a mountain of gold, for which people would fight. Ninety-nine out of each one hundred would die but every man amongst them would say that perhaps he would be the one who would be saved (and thus possess this gold).*

She recoiled when she read the words. This was not a sentimental, heartwarming, triumphant tradition about a baby, like the Christmas story. She clicked on some of the other references and read the cryptic interpretations. It was a portent of the end times, of man's greed and final bloodshed, which some Muslim scholars interpreted as being over modern-day oil and some interpreted as being over literal gold.

What did this have to do with Saudi Arabian Omar Al Ghamdi and his pretty wife, Leila, whom Josh seemed anxious to hear from?

She leaned back in the chair and squirmed and stretched; her back was tired. Yappie was still asleep under the Christmas tree.

Was Josh doing some architectural job involving gold or oil? Did he have intelligence about an imminent military attack and was trying to prepare her? She scrolled through her mobile, making sure it was set up with alerts from Middle East news bureaus. A pensive mood of disquiet settled over her. What exactly did Josh want her to do with this information?

Under the canopy of the curving driveway, Josh handed the rental car keys to the valet at the Marine Guard booth at the massive American Embassy complex in Baghdad, fifty-seven miles north of Babylon Metro. Once on foot, Josh stopped at the second security booth and showed his ID.

He entered a marble foyer with a huge holiday wreath that was positioned between the entrance with security booth Number Two and the lobby with security checkpoint Number Three. His tuxedo hung in a plastic dry cleaning bag over his arm. The plastic had made the rental car stink. He was arriving early for the holiday party for United States workers and contractors who were stuck in Iraq on Christmas day. He planned to hit the embassy gym and pool this afternoon before the party started.

The tux was becoming tighter and more uncomfortable as the years passed. It held sentimental meaning, but it was time to retire it to the back of the closet at home. Next year he would definitely be purchasing a new one....

A young woman in a burka head covering and a mop plopped it into a bucket of water and slid a yellow "CAUTION" stanchion across the wet marble floor. She stood up and turned around. A long piece of hair fell in front of her eyes and with a sweaty hand she pushed it away, tucking it inside the burka. Their eyes met in an immediate flash of recognition.

"Oh, hi," Josh said, startled.

"*Buna seara,*" she mumbled back in greeting.

"I know you. What are you doing here?" Josh started to ask, but then realized he could not think where he knew her from. It was always tough with the burkas.

"*Scuza ma.*" She diverted her gaze and melted away with the bucket behind a large, thick column, exiting to the outside of the building. It was what most Muslim women usually did around men.

He watched her disappear, trying to place how he knew her. The American Embassy building didn't seem right at all. It was the wrong building and she shouldn't be here. It was at some other building they had met and talked. It had been about architecture.

And she wasn't an Iraqi Muslim, she must be some other kind of ethnic Muslim, because the language was different.

"Step forward with your ID." The voice at the third checkpoint interrupted his thoughts about the identity of the woman. He entered the halls of the embassy and spotted some familiar CIA faces from the local station. Despite being far from family on a holiday, the mood in the room was lighthearted and cheery.

The Chief of Station, meticulously dressed in a black tuxedo with his hair slicked and glossy, held his wineglass up in the air with perfectly manicured hands as he proposed the toast. The guests invited to the evening holiday party cleared their throats and turned towards him expectantly. It was a surprisingly large group, and the room was warm.

"To our loyal, hardworking staff, safety and peace. To our vendors and contractors from America and Western Europe who are missing your families this evening, may you be blessed with fortune and success! May all of you have Happy Holidays and a prosperous New Year."

"Hear, hear!" the crowd of guests clinked their glasses with each other. The music started up again.

All of a sudden the left pocket of Josh's tuxedo began to buzz. Unobtrusively he pulled it out, pretending to adjust his bright red cummerbund while rapidly reading the message, then abruptly shoved it back into his pocket, annoyed. Last time this happened, it had been a false alarm, but he could not take any chances.

He moved through the crowd of embassy staffers, ambassadors, dignitaries, and highly paid government contractors towards the Chief of Station. He tapped the COS on the arm. "May I have your attention for a moment?" He pulled the COS to the side and explained the situation.

"Absolutely," the COS nodded and summoned a staffer. "Please see our guest safely to his vehicle."

A security patrolmen accompanied Josh to his car, their shoes echoing down the marble corridor and the sounds of the party fading behind them.

Josh exited the security gates of the embassy in the rental car, entered the Qadasaya Expressway, and then merged onto the Babylon Metro freeway. Fortunately the traffic was relatively light, but he was still grumpy. A rare evening in the company of Americans was abruptly ended, plus he was in for an hour and a half drive for what would probably be a false alarm.

As his rental car left Baghdad and entered the desert, he sped up as fast as he dared drive, wanting to get it over with. In the darkness of night, the traffic was lighter on the freeway than during the day—which at the worst times was a virtual parking lot between the two cities—but tonight traffic was just barely heavy enough to keep him alert and from getting drowsy.

The miles rolled by through the dark of the desert dotted by the headlights and tail lights of vehicles on the freeway and an occasional oil pipeline burning in the distance, until the lights of the Babylon Metro came into view. The view of the city skyline at night was stunning as Tomorrow Globe Financial Center twisted imperceptibly, radiating its pastel green, pink, and yellow colors in the night, the pinpoints of light from its upper floors blending in with the stars in the sky. He passed the gleaming white digital billboard with the glittering cartoon of the fat, happy queen with a scepter in her hand, from which a kaleidoscope of seven colorful stars were bursting, welcoming him into town. Palm trees lined the freeway, under lit with tall, thin decorative spikes that looked like ice crystals for the benefit of visitors from colder climes.

He utilized a surveillance detection route to throw off anyone who might be following, turning off the major exit of the freeway with a conglomeration of exit ramps that intertwined like a pit of snakes. He passed the gleaming digital photos advertising clothing on the outside of the mall and the splashy blinking of the casino and headed to the grid system east of the Tomorrow Globe Financial Center, where the central business district was located, so that if anyone had vehicular surveillance on him, they would have a perplexing series of intersections to navigate. He watched his rear view and side view mirrors the whole time.

No one was following him. He doubled back.

As he drove into the parking garage, the upper floors of Tomorrow Globe Financial Center switched to reduced energy lighting for the evening.

In the dim light of the hallway Josh slid the card into the door of the Pyramids and Palaces Architectural Renovation office and opened it silently. The lights automatically turned on, flooding the small area, and his voice boomed. "Who's there?"

There was no sound except for the HVAC system. Nobody was in the office. Nothing appeared to be disturbed since they closed this afternoon. This was probably a stupid false alarm, but he needed to do more checking.

He heard the elevator. Quickly he closed and locked the door to the hallway. In the back of the office by the air handler, he checked the controls. He pushed a series of keystrokes and performed a scan. All of a sudden he heard loud pounding on the door of the office and the command, "Security! Open up!" in Arabic and English.

He stood perfectly still, his skin prickling. There were multiple voices coming from the hall. He heard a rattling sound as they tried to open the mag lock; but he frequently changed it without alerting building security, so they began kicking the door.

It might be a legitimate building emergency, but he doubted it. He would take no chances.

In a flash he disabled the system. Quickly he opened the desk and grabbed a tool, then picked the lock of the small maintenance door that entered the shaft and opened it and stepped through onto the catwalk where the HVAC system was, at the same time hearing the splinter of wood coming from the front reception area.

What the hell was going on?

He pushed the catwalk door shut and pressed his ear to it to try to hear, but the HVAC system was running at full speed with a roar.

He stuck the tool that he had used to pick the lock into another deep pocket in his tuxedo jacket and felt a piece of bendable plastic. He did not remember what it was, and in his state of apprehension, it jolted him like an alarm, and he snatched it out of his pocket.

It was the Peppermint Pinkey Talky Watch, confiscated from Atalaya just before the last party at which he wore this tux. So, Talky Watch had traveled another ocean….He stuffed it back deep down into the pocket, fished around, and found his Agency mobile from his other tux pocket. It lit up and he quickly sent an encrypted message to Langley:

Operation AuCHFOP compromised.

And then he heard their voices in his office, just on the other side of the door, and he broke out into a sweat. Was someone trying to break into the office, or had he walked into some kind of trap?

117

It was only a matter of time before they tried the small maintenance door to see if he had exited that way.

He ran nearly one hundred eighty degrees around the circumference of the catwalk to the very low door on the other side and picked that lock. There was no alternative but to exit the building shaft, crawl into the duct system, and hide in there.

Dust and small wires snagged at his tux as he wriggled through on his hands and knees, and a pang of regret went through him. It was the tux he'd married Chelsea in! Nonetheless, if it hadn't been for the pockets holding his identification, remote starter for the car, small tools and a place to put his mobile in when he finished, he would have shed the jacket.

He was now approximately in the same area over the space occupied by Iran Central Industries Group. He had no desire to be discovered by them, either. He waited for a while and heard no noises, so he began to inch his way backwards from the direction that he came, trying to drag himself through the vent without making a sound. There was nothing he wanted worse than to escape the building, head for the safe house, and get the hell out. His CIA cover may very well have been blown this evening. As he inched his way backwards, he worked out a plan to escape the building and catch a cab, because using the car would be too risky.

He worried less about being heard as he got further away from Iran Central Industries Group and approached the mechanical room door; the HVAC shaft was still noisy. He checked his messages, and there was one, from Headquarters: *"Standing by to offer consultation on next step."*

With relief he popped the low door open and stepped out onto the catwalk that curved around the building shaft towards his office suite, blinking at the emergency light and four uniformed officers pointing their guns at him: *"Khalass!"*

They were telling him it was all over.

He had been set up!

Josh quickly shut down the expensive, incriminating Agency-issued mobile device and hurled it down the shaft, and then he threw both hands up in the air.

As a case officer, he was on the brink of flaming out....

The Iraqi security officers screamed at him to get down; he heard the mobile clattering its way hundreds of feet to the abyss below as he dropped to his knees.

33
Missing

S he thought Atalaya would never go to sleep.

Chelsea downed a glass of wine in four gulps and set the empty glass on the nightstand. Across the street, the neighbors' house, still lit with Christmas lights, blinked and twinkled through the slats of the mini-blinds. She crawled into bed under the covers, tucking her knees under her abdomen in a fetal position. Lifetimes had passed since they showed up at the door with the news.

Josh hadn't replied to any messages since Christmas. A liaison had come to the house from Headquarters, accompanied by a chaplain. The liaison's name was Connie. She had gray-blond hair, and she looked like surely she must be retirement age. Connie was obese and had huffed and shivered as she set down her briefcase in the living room floor, her large glasses fogging up. "We have come to talk to you about your husband." Her face was red from the cold outside, sympathetic and kind, but professional.

Chelsea squeezed her eyes shut, sliding the pillow over her head, trying to make the words go away that echoed with loud thuds in her ears:

"...a CIA operation was compromised and your husband disappeared while on duty in the Middle East..."

"...his mobile lost power in Babylon Metro..."

"....I'll be your contact throughout this and will provide you with information and updates..."

"...at this point there is no reason to suspect the abductors know who his family is, but if you see any suspicious activity in the neighborhood, call the police..."

"...trained to deny that he works for the government..."

"...his highest obligation is to protect the United States and protect our asset over there..."

"...unfortunately, if his identity is discovered, we may be facing the worst of outcomes."

Babylon Metro was the place in Iraq where Josh had been stationed. The full impact slammed into her violently. Sick apprehension welled up in the pit of her stomach as she remembered the various news reports about business exploitation, prostitution, and insurgent uprisings. What if the prophecies of doom about Babylon that their young church pastor had preached about were literally true? She threw the covers back and swung her legs over the bed, standing up. The room was woozy. In the darkness she staggered across the floor to the closet, rummaged through until she reached one of Josh's shirts. The faint odor of him, along with a little bit of cinnamon gum, still clung to the clothing. She stumbled back to bed, taking another drink directly from the bottle of wine and felt it burn her stomach. She set it on the nightstand, next to her handgun. Then she curled back under the covers with her nose pressed into the fabric of Josh's shirt.

"…We have many resources available to our CIA family. The Employee Assistance Program and the Family Advisory Board can be found on the Benefits page of the Agency website…"

"The Office of Medical Services has psychiatrists and psychologists available who are well-integrated into our overall objectives…."

"…it would be unproductive for anyone to know that he was on a CIA mission…"

Part II

Hakim

34
Hakim
Hillah, Southern Iraq
1 year earlier

There was nobody else nearby in the trailer park this afternoon who would watch what direction they went. It was payday, their day off, and the three housemates were going to indulge in forbidden pleasures.

Good-looking nineteen-year-old Hakim Al-Obaidi flexed his muscles as he peered vainly at himself in the cracked mirror in the bathroom. He twisted, looking back down at his butt in the tight American jeans. He reached for the bottle of gel, spiking up black chunks of his hair with his fingers. He stared at himself, turning to the left and to the right, pleased that for today's adventure he had his mother's eyes—striking hazel ones, which made it easier to pretend to be American. Mischievously he grinned at his reflection. Then he exited the bathroom.

"Ha, ha," his housemate Ali laughed at him. "You look like a genuine corrupt Westerner." Ali had a wide, prominent forehead with black goat-like eyebrows. Ali was as quick and agile. The other quiet housemate, Yazen, was thick, muscular, and lumbering.

Hakim checked out the window at the front of the trailer. "All clear, nobody's watching us."

They went around back to the shed where their bikes were stored and unlocked it, Jumping on their bikes, the housemates inhaled the strange mixture of smells in the neighborhood—grilled goat meat, vehicle fumes, and the dank odor of Al-Hillah River, a shallow tributary of the Euphrates River in south central Iraq. They followed Hakim as he led the way and pedaled swiftly through the development, a conglomeration of cheap trailers that housed Governorate of Babil construction workers for the mind-boggling, fantastical new skyscrapers in Babylon Metro. Babylon Metro was the catchy name for the monumentally explosive new commerce and tourist area on the other side of the river, the place of gambling and evil that the imams preached against.

The three youths pedaled along the access road to the end of the village, past Governorate of Babil Prison where they worked. They had just graduated from Chinese security training and moved here to take jobs with the new prison. The prison was constructed in the older part of Hillah. It would not be a good image for the Chinese occupation to have a prison in shiny, pristine Babylon Metro.

The sky was a beautiful blue today and the sun was a hot white ball overhead, searing the desert and streets. The bikes jounced and bumped until they hit the level path by the river, occasionally passing a cluster of workers or a small cadre of Chinese peacekeeping troops lounging in the shade with their cigs, gaping at them warily through their thin eyes.

They biked past the new oil refinery and the old petrochemical plant and the fertilizer factory, towards the loading docks, and in the direction of the incredible new skyscrapers that twisted and shimmered against the blue dessert sky. They crossed the railroad, and instead of old, rusty industrial buildings, date palms waved along the sandy shore. No more gravel—they rode smoothly and luxuriously on brand new asphalt without pot holes and without hot, sticky tar patches. The Chinese occupation wanted international visitors to be impressed with its stunning economic development triumph.

Panting and sweating in the heat, they pushed their bikes to the supports underneath the modern new dock and locked them up, coming up a back exit to the passenger area. A Chinese military security officer confiscated their backpacks, examined the contents, and shoved them back, waving them through.

Hakim guided the housemates through the gathering throng waiting for the shallow barge that ferried passengers across the Euphrates to Babylon Metro, the city of sin. The barge appeared to contain some business people but mostly tourists today. Hakim fantasized that he fit in with them, as if he were an American tourist...The barge engine sputtered and came to life and drifted across the shallow, dirty brown water to the direction of the towers.

Yazen and Ali leaned over the railing, gaping at the view of the newly built, shining, asymmetrical edifices with an endless array of construction cranes. They had never been inside Babylon Metro before. It was a dazzling and unbelievable sight. "What decadence has sprouted up in the desert!" burst out Ali. "It is just as with the ancient city of Babylon. The Chinese act as if they can make buildings that reach to Allah! How silly and conceited. No one can reach Allah. Yet Allah does not smite them!"

Ali and Yazen had lived their childhood in a more distant, small Sunni village three hours away. But Hakim had grown up in a village much closer to Hillah than the other two housemates. He could remember when he was a boy and there were no buildings on this side of the river—just river, bare pinkish-tan colored sand and brown-green scrub with an occasional cluster of date palms or an ancient ziggurat temple piercing the blue sky. He'd had many more opportunities than his housemates to witness the awe of the various stages of Babylon Metro's construction by the Chinese, and many locals had gotten jobs.

The lavish shopping center with its immense photos of young men and women in decadent western clothing and underwear and signs in the window that said "AS SEEN IN THE NOITALEVER GAME" (because the game featured ads with the clothing), and the casino with its huge arches, gold plating, and bright colors and noises, gleamed with splendid shimmery and spherical design. As they glided into the shady dock, date palms and huge fans cooled them. Chinese peacekeeping security forces were stationed on colorfully decorated and stunning horses all along the dock.

Thrilled, the housemates bounded out the boat and up the ramp, stopping for yet another security pat-down by the Chinese, and then they were free to enter the mall.

"Welcome to Babylon Metro, Forever a Happy Place!" proclaimed a glossy new digital billboard at the boat dock in Arabic, English, and Chinese. The billboard was gleaming white with a sparkling cartoon image of a cheerful, benevolent queen with a scepter in her hand, blessing the Governorate of Babil with seven colorful exploding stars, a symbol of prosperity.

They gave shouts and whoops, dizzy at the opulence and the western influence which was even more stunning than the shopping malls in Baghdad. Across the walkway, the casino sang and beckoned and flashed enticing colorful lights, summoning all of its evil power to lure man's money away. Some women wore the hijab on their heads, but most did not, and most of the men wore tight western clothing.

Hakim's new American sneakers, soft and foamy, bounced like air across the cool marble floor as they entered the mall. He blended in with them! He was indiscernible from the Westerners! "This way!" He pointed the direction and they hurried across the mall to the darkened chirping, blinking gaming arcade, paid their money, and headed straight to the long line of young men waiting for the 3-D NoitaLever booth. All of them pulled out their phones and played the game while they stood in line.

"You go first," Hakim generously allowed Yazen, even though Hakim could barely stand it and wanted to begin playing immediately. Yazen swiped the door with the pass card, swung it open, and shut the door.

"Watch him as he comes out," Hakim told Ali.

It seemed like forever but finally Yazen emerged, a stupid grin on his face as he took off the state-of-the-art 3-D glasses and wobbled down the ramp. Immediately their housemate, a normally placid computer technician, burst into a broken stream of description. "The music! The colors!" Yazen teetered, regaining his balance. The door closed for one minute behind him while the smoke eater unit vaporized the odor particles for the next player. "The sounds and images…rushing at you!"

Never, in the time that Hakim had known Yazen, had Yazen been able to manage more than three or four words at a time without a gulp of air.

"The smells that are pumped…into the booth! Ali, my friend, Hakim…has shown us a miracle!" Yazen sucked in a deep breath and his eyes nearly crossed with delight. "No other game in the world…is like this!"

"Let me go next, then. Hakim has had his turns at other visits!" Housemate Ali elbowed right passed Hakim and ran into the booth.

They all eventually emerged from the 3-D NoitaLever booth, their budget for their addiction exhausted, euphoric at the experience which rivaled amusement park rides. Around them in the arcade the other games beeped and sang, luring them to spend more treasure, but they must be careful of their budget.

"So, Ali, will we be safe from the imams finding out we played NoitaLever?" Hakim gloated naughtily, but it was actually a challenge to the housemate who sometimes feigned a good game of following Islamic rules.

"How will they know?" shrugged Ali.

At a technology kiosk, housemate Yazen bought a new pair of tiny, nearly invisible earbuds. With his big hands he pried open the plastic box. Yazen connected the buds to his music device, popping them into his ears and squeezing his eyes shut with sheer delight at the sound quality. Yazen loved music and there were no judgmental clerics and imams around to criticize.

They made their way out into the concourse, smelling the delicious odor of food wafting from the urban eatery. They passed a bar that served liquor, staring curiously at the men drinking in public without shame. A pretty girl with luxuriously long black hair and western clothing, low cut at the chest with the soft tops of her breasts peeking out, crossed Hakim's path, staring at him brazenly, rather than casting her eyes aside. Hakim, with his perfectly symmetrical features, full, thick hair and hazel eyes, was constantly giggled at by girls everywhere who thought he was handsome. He did not cast his own eyes aside as Islamic rules dictated, but instead, stared right back at her.

"See how she lures you," snorted Ali.

"I'm hungry and I…" poor Yazen still could not articulate his desires in a single sentence without taking a breath, "want to eat!" Yazen was fleshy and a little round in the tummy and always hungry.

"Is it Halal? Is it fit for Muslims?" Ali asked.

"There are no signs to tell us," Hakim replied carelessly, "And besides, we are not given a choice."

"It isn't illicit if…" rationalized the hungry Yazen, sucking in air in order to finish his sentence, "if we don't know."

They ordered a lamb kebab at the urban eatery. They were hungrier than they realized and wolfed down the food and drink without even speaking.

A military-mandated sign hung next to the fire exit just off the eatery. The sign said, in Chinese translated clumsily into Arabic:

BABYLON METRO IS RELIGION NEUTRAL ZONE

This was what it was like for the infidels to live without prayers five times a day and to live without rules!

His elbows resting on the table, Hakim stuffed his face with French fries and chewed as he studied the sign. Outside of Babylon Metro, it was time for the mid-afternoon Asr prayer. But today the housemates ignored it. No Muslim prayers were allowed in the hallways, bathrooms, or stairwells of the mall, or any public place in Babylon Metro. The Chinese didn't believe in Allah. The Chinese science and technology channel that Hakim secretly listened to on his computer taught that mankind evolved from a big bang, and everything that came after that was a slow metamorphosis into what we have today. Suppose the Chinese were right and there was no Allah, and all of the effort to walk the righteous path to eternal Paradise was a waste of time?

But on the other hand, it was written in the Quran that Satan was always seeking to plant doubt in mankind except for those who were Allah's chosen slaves.....

At the table behind them, they heard the snicker of two younger Iraqi youths, dressed in the expensive western garb of well-to-do Babylonian Metro parents. "Ignorant Hillah hillbillies!" they heard the first boy taunt them. The second boy laughed. Then the two boys jumped up and left the table, and the first used his hand to flip an insulting obscenity at them. Then the two broke into a run for the fire exit just outside the urban eatery where the sign hung.

Ali jumped from the table and took off after them, and Hakim and Yazen quickly wiped their faces and hands with the napkin and leaped up from the table to follow. Into the dimly lit fire exit hall they went in full pursuit of the youths, their feet echoing as they clattered down the steps. Ali reached the first and grabbed him by the hair. "What name did you call us, you foolish child?"

The youth struggled, arms flailing, and Hakim got there just in time to grab the arms of the second youth and pull him backwards in a painful twist. Ali pinned the first youth to the wall. The two perpetrators howled and kicked.

"Beg me for mercy!" ordered Ali. He took the youth's head and slammed it against the concrete block wall of the stairwell. For good measure, Yazen came from the behind and also kicked the youth in the legs. For all of his inability to get through a sentence without additional air, Yazen had heft.

The boy crumpled to the floor, wincing and bawling. "You didn't know we are Chinese-trained security guards. You will never call us 'Hillah hillbillies' again, will you?" snarled Ali.

All of a sudden they heard the fire exit door open. "HALT!" a voice echoed down the stairwell in Chinese and then in Arabic. At the top of the steps appeared a Chinese security guard, his yellow face and slit eyes even more yellow and thin in the odd light of the stairwell.

They released the two offenders with a thump on the concrete landing and raced down the stairs as fast as they could, nearly sliding down the hand rails the final way as the security guard pursued them.

35
Unrest in the Mosque

Hakim and his housemates reached the fire exit door and burst out into the bright sunlight and scorching heat of a parking lot. As the door slammed behind them and they cut across the loading zone to the cover of a dark parking garage, they burst out with shrill laughter. They kept running across the gravel to the rear of the property and beyond, to an area which changed abruptly to a conglomeration of warehouses surrounded by barbed wire as they neared the underpass of the freeway.

Up above their heads, the traffic roared, but it was shady down below. They dodged oncoming service vehicles full of loaded goods and dropped to a concrete island in exhaustion. In this desert heat, they needed water soon.

"I'm Ana," said a seductive voice.

Hakim turned, and his eyes widened. A thin, eastern European woman with tight-fit clothing, bare legs, and a very clear view of cleavage stood studying them. One sandaled foot with multiple colors of toenail polish swung back and forth seductively on the sidewalk. For the second time today, Hakim's eyes locked on cleavage and he was unable to move them away.

"What is your name?" she persisted, and seeing Hakim's eyes glued to her breast, she stepped closer to him and swaggered her hips.

"Hakim," he fumbled.

"You fool, do not tell her your name! She is a prostitute!" snarled Ali bossily. Hakim scooted backwards from her on all fours with a mixture of horror and fascination. He had only seen prostitutes on video before. He had heard of the growing number in the back alleys of Babylon Metro, but this was the first time he had seen a live one.

Ana the prostitute continued to stand by the large concrete support pillar of the freeway with her hands on her hips, foot swinging, pursing her seductive lipstick, and studying the three young men with hazel eyes. She was not glamorous like the ones on videos. She had a hard look to her face. Apparently deciding they were hardly worth the effort, she flipped her long, dull brown hair out of her eyes with her hand, turned, and walked away.

"We must—must run!" wailed the fearful Yazen.

More than finished with their covert trip to Babylon Metro, the three housemates sought water to drink from a nearby stall peddling merchandise and hastily made their way back to the ferry back to where their bikes were stored. They pedaled to central Hillah, the old part of the city, and to the mosque for prayers. It was a Sunni mosque. Hakim wasn't Sunni, he was Shiite, and his parents would not be pleased to know about this, but it was where his housemates and some of their friends worshiped. They passed the Chinese soldier who monitored the services. The room was packed with people ready to hear the special address from a visiting cleric, the notable Mohammad Al-Issa from Saudi Arabia, known in whispered circles as leader of the newest Wahhabi Muslim group, "Black Lightening." Normally Iraqi Sunnis did not accept Wahhabis because of the Wahhabi's misguided thoughts and harsh actions; but the Sunnis were increasingly making exceptions because of the Chinese occupation of Iraq. The Wahhabi monetary contributions also had a great effect.

There was no time to wash, and they barely made it in time to initiate the salut. The imam who was in charge of leading the prayers cast them a disapproving look. "Alahu Akbar!" the room intonated. Hakim scrambled into place, then let the familiar repetition of the ritual calm him. His mind wandered, as it frequently did during the prayers. He had seen and heard and smelled beautiful things today. How he had loved the escape from the rules and the monotony of life! It was so hard to be a good Muslim. Today it had been so fun for a few hours to pretend that they were powerful and lived in a fast-paced world of commerce and success, and they had even seen a prostitute ....

"Peace be upon you, and the mercy of Allah." The prayers finally concluded. Hakim drifted into a pleasant daydream trance and nearly missed the fact that no one else had their heads turned to the left anymore; they were looking straight ahead now and waiting for the address from the mufti, an expert scholar who ruled on questions about, and direction from, the Quran. Stupidly, he scrambled into a cross-legged position.

When the prayer was complete, from behind the lectern, the black-turbaned visiting cleric from Saudi Arabia with the messy, graying eyebrows like a ragged bottle brush who was traveling to the mosques to strengthen the faithful delivered a lecture on pork, drinking, cigarettes, lust, homosexuality, and western consumerism. With the Chinese monitoring the mosques for violence, the visiting mufti's address tonight would be fairly benign. The call to jihad would only come when the mufti secretly visited neighbors' houses and met with small groups of men.

"You say you believe in the Quran, but do you obey its every word? Avert your eyes downward when you see a temptation! The Quran says, 'you will be awarded the punishment of humiliation because you were arrogant upon the earth without right and because you were defiantly disobedient.' These are the words of the Prophet—peace and blessings upon him!"

Hakim thought of the girl in the mall with the smooth, curvy tops of her breasts bared and the prostitute named Ana who worked under the overpass. He felt shamed. It was as if the mufti read his thoughts.

The mufti continued. "What does the Quran say? 'O you who have attained to faith! Intoxicants, and games of chance, and idolatrous practices, and the divining of the future are but a loathsome evil of Satan's doing.' But some of you have participated in the drinking and gambling of this city!"

The mufti paused to take a drink from his water bottle, his eyes traveling the hot, crowded room, and continued with his lecture. "You will never be satisfied until you meet death, do you not understand this? Do not look at and want the things that they have! Do not wish for their cars, their houses! Do not look at the women! Give up your earthly desires and follow the way of Allah!"

Hakim knew he had been a very bad Muslim today. He must try harder to do what was right! Allah would honor a heart that was truly repentant.

The mufti scrutinized Hakim and the other two housemates, and his graying brows furrowed together critically. "The prophet says that he who abandons his prayers is a disbeliever. You must beat a woman or a man who refuses to pray and is in danger of the fires of hell!"

Hakim sucked in his breath in shame. Did the mufti somehow know that they had skipped their prayers? His face went crimson. On the prayer mat next to him, Ali's face burned with mortification. Yazen, in front of him, looked downright frightened.

131

Hakim felt conflicted. He wanted to fit in with his new friends at the prison, and he knew he needed to be a better Muslim. But since the Chinese had tightened their grip during the peacekeeping occupation and Black Lightening subsequently began donating large sums of money to the mosques, everyone had become horribly strict lately, trying to take away the fun. Was it possible to melt away and forget about them?

36
The Initiation

akim's housemate, Ali, operated the rusty motorboat with Hakim and his other housemate, Yazen, behind him as they propelled up the Al-Hillah River, the eastern branch of the Euphrates River. The sun diminished itself into an orange ball behind the ragged rocks to the west, preparing to hide someplace in that distance beyond the desert scrub and the main branch of the Euphrates River. Darkness crept over the water and the stars popped out against the blue-black sky.

They lay on the bottom of the boat on their backs, using their sleeping bags and backpacks as cushions with their legs suspended up over the edge, carefully balancing the boat. Cigarette smoke curled up into the warm, humid night.

"Ok, it is dark enough now for the Hillah Hillbillies," Hakim finally pronounced, making fun of the name that youths at the mall had coined him and his housemates. Four months had passed since their outing to the forbidden pleasures of Babylon Metro, and they were ready for another adventure.

He popped open the cooler and passed out cans of Farida. They snorted and laughed. It was a good thing the visiting cleric from Saudi Arabia, with all of his rules and fatwahs and demands to return to Sharia law, could not see them! They were definitely committing more sins now, but he cast it out of his mind.

Ali cut down the motor, because they were almost to Ancient Babylon, and they couldn't risk that Chinese security guards would hear the boat while they embarked on their initiation. Hakim lounged on his back, gazing at the stars, allowing the fire of the beer to seep through his young body. He felt happy and relaxed right now and refused to think about Islam denying beer to men. It wouldn't really make them forget their prayers, as the imams claimed!

The boat drifted up the river, hugging the west shoreline as far as possible from the scrutiny of security or late night workers. Ali hunched as low as he could go over the steering wheel, his dark eyes peering out under his heavy eyebrows and thick forehead, watching for sandbars in the shallow water as they rounded a bend in the river and approached the cluster of commercial buildings on the east side. The river was used less for transportation since so much water had been diverted for irrigation in Babylon Metro, and many of the older buildings were abandoned now. An occasional rusty light pole on the shoreline still worked, casting meager light. They were about to glide past the run-down Garden of Babylon. They were almost to their destination.

The floated along, sipping more beer and waiting expectantly for the signal. Then Ali pulled the boat up to a pier overgrown with bulrushes and cut the engine off. He took the paddles and used them to steer and push. His friends helped him lash the boat; and then hoisting their gear on their backs, they slipped out of the boat as quietly as possible and onto the pier, their hearts racing with nervous excitement. Ali took the lead, hoisting his AK-47 over his shoulder.

They were taking The Dare!

The Dare was the initiation expected of all new housemates in the trailer park who worked for the prison system. Their challenge: to spend tonight in Ancient Babylon without being caught by Chinese security. You could camp anywhere on the site, but you got the most respect if you got away with spending the night at Saddam Hussein's 600-room ziggurat, known as Saddam's palace. It was a taunt at the Chinese occupation.

They knew where to go. It had been carefully planned. They had taken a tour of Ancient Babylon with a tourist group earlier in the week. It was long spoken by the Jewish and the Christian prophets that there was a curse on Ancient Babylon—that no one would ever live there again. Even some of the Muslims believed the legend.

Now the Hillah Hillbilly housemates were following the instructions of those in the trailer park who had gone before them: Park the boat here....hike across the gardens to the spiral road...look for the crumbled section of wall by the rose garden and enter....head to the northeast...the guard does a round just before dark....

Somewhere in the distance on the shoreline, an owl hooted, and even further away, the howl of a wild animal answered back. There was no sign of Chinese security guards.

Surreptitiously they raced in the direction of the road, their backpacks and coolers jouncing roughly against their bodies, past a rectangular compound to their right that sat between the river and the palace.

"Shhh!" Ali hissed, put a warning finger to his lips. The compound was thought to be where security was stationed. If they could make it past, then follow the road, they would be to the hill.

They slunk towards the north, but all of a sudden a man's shout rang out in the compound, reverberating among its largely empty walls, and a searchlight pierced the night.

A gunshot rang out!

Hakim caught a glimpse of the panic in Yazen's face as they all dropped to the ground. Ali pointed the gun in the direction of the shots while the rest of them covered their heads. Hakim's heart pounded in fear. If Ali shot a Chinese soldier, he would be guaranteed death.

They all might die!

37

The Curse of Ancient Babylon

The search light traveled in a slow circle, and as it moved away from them, Ali hissed, "Run!" The three housemates dispersed somewhat from each other, crawling on their hands and knees in the general direction of north as fast as they could with their gear. If they could make their way between the date palms and vegetation, hopefully they could hide effectively from the searchlight....Slowly it continued in its circular motion, coming frighteningly close to them. Hakim's heart beat so hard with fear he thought it might explode in his chest, and he mouthed a prayer to Allah begging for protection.

Ali, somewhat off to his left, suddenly stood up to his full height and hurled a rock with all of his might behind them. It landed a ways back down the hill with a thud.

The rock deflection was effective. The searchlight stopped in the wrong spot and a volley of shots rang behind them where the rock had fallen. It gave them time to run, and they zig-zagged from date palm to poplar tree.

Hakim worked his way to the base of Saddam Hill where the palace was located and began to climb upwards, sweating and panting from the exertion of the sleeping bag and food rations he was carrying. The spotlight started to circle again, and he flattened himself on the sand amidst a cluster of licorice plants, sweating with terror.

What if he was shot dead by Chinese patrols? What would his beautiful mother say? Her heart would break. His father would be shamed that his eldest son was lost in a silly initiation prank....

The searchlight apparently did not disclose their whereabouts. It circled a little while longer and then finally shut off.

His racing pulse slowly turned to normal, and he began creeping up the hill again, occasionally snagging his clothes on landscape rose bushes, but his fear turned to exhilaration as he moved higher and higher.

Now he either had to locate his housemates, or find his own chink in the palace wall and enter. He crept along the wall and then made a howling sound like an animal, hoping his housemates might recognize his voice, rather than be frightened.

In the darkness a hyena howled back, far away among the ruins on the eastern side of Ancient Babylon, its shriek reverberating across the vacant stone ruins. He felt goose bumps prickle his skin and his hair stand on end. What if his own howl attracted the hyena to the site, or what if Ali thought he was an animal and shot at him with the AK-47?

Then, far to his left, he heard a more human howling sound respond, which surely must be Ali, and he crept along the wall in that direction.

A chink in the wall!

He whistled low and waited. Soon there was a rustling sound and Ali emerged in the moonlight. They gave each other a jubilant, silent high five and dived through the hole in the palace wall.

The moonlight only cast so much light for them, and they stumbled their way across rocks and rubble towards the shadows of the palace. They gingerly stepped onto the large courtyard made of brick and carefully made their way across it. The missing bricks in the courtyard caused them to occasionally stumble and bang their backpacks hard against their bodies, and they headed for a section of standing wall with a tall archway, whispering to each other in excitement.

"Let's stop here and rest until Yazen finds us," Hakim panted with exhaustion, throwing his gear down onto the ground. They slid down on their butts to the courtyard, grasping for water bottles and gulping water down.

"We must say our prayers," Ali said, observing the time. "We are late and it is a sin to miss them. Allah has been merciful and he has spared us tonight."

They performed the ritual and settled down to wait. After about half an hour, they heard the sound of footsteps in the distance and jerked to attention, listening closely. Yes, they were the ambling footsteps of Yazen.

"The stupid Chinese infidels, they did not even find us!" Ali mocked.

"We are the victorious Hillah Hillbillies. We made it into the palace," said Hakim gleefully.

The housemates clustered together in the cathedral style entry way of the mysteriously dark and shadowy Saddam's palace, gobbling down the military food rations that they had secreted from the basement storage facility in the prison where they worked during the day. Ali's AK-47 was propped up against the wall behind them. Adrenaline was still surging from their narrow escape from gunshots, but they were euphoric about their adventure. It was the middle of the night and sleepiness had not quite settled in, although their sleeping bags were unrolled and in place on a marble floor, and mosquito netting had been positioned over the sleep area. They were gathered at the base of a wooden palm tree sculpture, from which dangled the stripped remnants of a chandelier. They guzzled down the rest of the beer and were happy.

Hakim had lost his inhibitions and this was the evening to bring up the subject of visiting the shopping mall again. "Time for some NoitaLever." He pulled out his mobile and loaded up the game.

"Did you hear? The clerics warned against it the other day. It is an addiction," Ali informed them. "The Chinese are also suspicious of it and think it is propaganda. I've heard they might ban it."

Of all of them, Ali was the most devoted to Islam. He was also careful and calculating.

"Then we'd better play before it gets banned. And you, Yazen?" Hakim challenged.

"Uh, I will play if…if both of you will do it," replied Yazen uncertainly. Yazen was the most nervous and tentative of the three housemates. "I have to go to the bathroom," he announced suddenly, tossing his can of Farida, letting it roll along the marble floor. This, too, was the dangerous initiation into the trailer park: to litter your beer cans brazenly around the Ancient Babylon historic site. "I will locate a place." He jumped up from his sleeping bag, grabbed the roll of toilet paper they were to share, and headed into the darkness.

Yazen was gone for what seemed like a long time, and then all of a sudden they heard the howl of jackals, and Yazen's yell tore through the night, echoing in the walls of the palace. There was a horrible sound of snarling and barking. Fearfully Ali grabbed the weapon and they leaped to their feet, flashing their lights in the direction he had gone. Then they heard Yazen's feet pounding unevenly towards their direction and then another grunt and a yell as he fell over a broken portion of palace pillar. They raced over to him and helped him up.

"His thigh is bleeding," Hakim said shining his light over Yazen, pressing his hand to the Yazen's jeans. Swiftly, without even thinking twice, Hakim removed his t-shirt with a fast swipe, took his teeth and chewed a hole in the fabric, then ripped a strip off the bottom portion. "Unzip," he ordered. Yazen struggled painfully out of his jeans. There were puncture marks on Yazen's legs. Quickly Hakim lashed the t-shirt strip around Yazen's thigh, which was starting to bleed.

"Oww!" Yazen moaned, rocking back and forth.

"What happened?" they asked. Hakim tore another strip from the t-shirt and wrapped Yazen's leg.

"A nest of jackals, a…mother and her babies. I disturbed their rest and….the mother ran across….the palace grounds and… charged me, howling and snapping. The legends are true, this…this place is cursed!" Yazen could hardly string together a complete sentence without taking a breath in the wrong place.

This was the whole point of the initiation in the trailer park, to exploit the legend that Babylon was cursed, and to see if you could last the night without harm.

Ali took off in the night towards the direction of the jackal. Hakim hoisted Yazen up and helped him back to the camp site in the room they had settled in, inside the dark palace. Hakim grabbed a water bottle, washing sticky blood from his hands. Yazen had been bitten by an unclean animal, a type of dog.

"Where is the toilet paper? Did you lose it? Now we will all…be unclean," worried Yazen.

A gunshot rang in the night and the animal fell to the ground, howling in pain. A chorus of barking went up from miles further away, other jackals who knew the cry. Quickly the boys turned off their lights. What if the Chinese guards had heard the gunshot and came to investigate?

Ali emerged in the darkness and sat the weapon down and fell to his sleeping bag with relief. Quietly they listened and watched, but there was no spotlight against the night sky and no sound of security vehicles approaching.

A somber mood replaced the sense of adventure. Not only was this place dangerous at night, they had a comrade with an injury. The initiation required them in the morning light to take as many pictures as possible of the parts of Ancient Babylon to prove they had been there before the Chinese guards and tour guides caught them. Would Yazen be able to have his pictures taken?

Eventually they ceased their worried talking and drifted off into slumber under their mosquito netting, but it was punctuated by the eerie howling of owls and the occasional cries of the hungry jackal pups, which caused them to wake up in a state of alertness and then fall back into an uneasy sleep.

Hakim rolled over in the morning with a grunt, trying to hide his head, distinctly discerning that it had been an awful night's sleep. Ali was awake already and stirring around the encampment. Ali's rustling about was irritating.

Hakim's dreams had been filled with the nightmares of his childhood. In his dreams, ISIS soldiers lurked behind the columns and broken walls in Nebuchadnezzar's palace, the ruins adjacent to them; the Chinese were rolling up the hill in their tanks in pursuit, and the housemates completing their trailer park initiation were caught in the middle.

He peeked at the world through exhausted eyelids. He stumbled to his feet and made his way towards the general direction that Yazen had gone last night in order to find a place to relieve himself. There was the barest hint of sunrise in the east.

The pink dawn cast dim light on the ghostly broken columns and chipped brick. Occasional graffiti spattered the palace walls. Towards the end of the courtyard and in a cluster of date trees, he spotted jackal dung and knew that this must have been where the nest was. A distance away, the dead jackal lay on its side in a pool of blood. Disgusting unclean birds had already discovered it, and flies. He circumvented it and found a different spot to do his personal business.

After finishing the breakfast rations, the sun was further up, and they set out for picture-taking, leaving Yazen and his bandaged thigh with the camp gear. Thank goodness Hakim had packed a second shirt in his backpack. It would not do to look ragged in photos meant to impress the trailer park community.

There was a fascinating part of the underground palace they had wanted to explore during the tour last week, but the tour guide wouldn't let them go into it. A historic preservationist group with the sign "Pyramids and Palaces Architectural Renovation" was doing some renovation work and had assembled scaffolding over the top of it. Below the restoration project was a prison. Turning their lights on, they ignored the No Trespassing signs in Arabic and Chinese and clambered down the stairs into the cool corridor below ground.

The small prison had been used very little, if ever, and most of the plumbing had been stripped. Hakim explored each cell, beaming his light everywhere, suddenly stopping with surprise at one cell near the end of the row.

It still had a key dangling from the door! When the Americans and the Polish occupied the palace, they must have utilized it to hold an insurgent!

Quickly he pilfered the key and stuffed it into his pocket. It would be the proof of their adventures back in the trailer park, and also a treasured souvenir.

"I want tea," complained Yazen as they trudged down Saddam Hill to the east in the direction of Ishtar Gate. They hadn't bothered to try to bring tea. There was no way to easily heat it up and brew it. What irony, to spend the night in the heart of the ancient empire that brought tea to the entire world, but to have none of their own to drink!

They cut across the circular road that spiraled around the palace and headed for their first photo, the Lion of Babylon. It was a sculpture of a giant stone lion trampling a man, and you simply *had* to climb up on the back of the lion to get a really good picture, then they could post it to social media that the Hillah Hillbillies were successful....

They moved on and stopped for another picture. The rest of the mounds scattered around a few square miles in area were a rosy tan brick. Ishtar Gate was a popular target for vandalism and was destined to lose the war against time. The brick structure was glazed with a gaudy navy blue color that was fading and peeling. During the invasion, the Americans had damaged the gate, and now tourists and Saddam haters frequently defaced it. The half-hearted Chinese effort to secure history was often stationed at this point of ancient Babylon, and the two kept their eyes peeled for guards up unusually early.

The fascinating ruins of Nebuchadnezzar's palace was south of Ishtar Gate and east of Saddam's palace, and they made their way through the rubble, once towering to the sky but now largely no more than hip-high. They paused at one point as they came over the crest of a hill and peered over the edge. All of a sudden down there was a flurry of white feathers. Two ostriches went running down the hill.

They burst out laughing at the funny animals. A wolf was in pursuit of them, looking for breakfast.

Down in the valley Hakim caught sight of a car turning into the parking lot near the gate of Ishtar. He grabbed Ali's arm in alarm. "Hurry! Someone is coming to work for the day! We must go before they find us!"

They set off in a run, jumping over rocks and bricks and ruins, back to Saddam's Hill to rescue Yazen and head back to the boat before the tourists arrived.

The meeting house with the visiting mufti from Saudi Arabia, Mohammad Al-Issa, was located in the outskirts of the city at the personal compound of a rural wealthy smuggler, because religious and political meetings were forbidden by the Chinese inside Metro limits and watched suspiciously everywhere else. The Chinese constantly monitored for indications of local violence. An under-the radar, door-to-door walk had been organized through the trailer park, and Hakim and his housemates had been summoned to a meeting of the teachings of Allah. The meeting was held after dark, so that the Chinese would not question the large number of cars and bicycles, and so the mufti could sneak into the compound without being noticed.

The host, a shifty looking industrialist with a hard expression, grouped them in the largest room in the center of the compound. It was packed with men. Even though it was cool outside, the room smelled of body odor and sweat.

Listening to a mufti's lecture wasn't the first choice of a nineteen-year old young man on his night off. It was housemate Ali's idea to attend. Ali was the most devout Muslim, or at least, devout when he felt its importance. Hakim and Yazen went along with it. When they arrived, they found themselves caught up in the excitement as the mufti and his body guards arrived and the group met them with fanfare.

Hakim had been lucky enough to secure a spot by a narrow support column and therefore had something to lean against, but the rest of the men stood. The mufti was pushed through the crowd to the center of the room, and he grasped and shook the hands of the people in the room as he passed. "*Salaam alaikum.*" Peace be upon you.

"*Alaikum salaam,*" the group responded. And upon you peace. Hakim studied the mufti. You could tell a lot about a person from their eyes. The mufti's eyes were piercing, and Hakim instinctively shrunk closer to the narrow column that was supporting his back.

"We will have our caliphate, and the servant of Muhammad— peace and blessing upon him—will rule the world! We have already bled the Great Satan, America, to death," intoned the mufti, beginning his speech. "We have successfully drained away its money, and most of all, we have drained away America's patience!"

The men applauded, warming up for the night.

"But the Great Satan has been replaced by China! The Chinese, who have come to keep the order and to distribute our oil, are infidels who do not honor Allah! They have taken away our Sharia law and replaced it with laws created by their own delusional minds! They have taken our right to execute adulterers, homosexuals, traitors, and criminals for crimes they have committed! Allah's messenger—peace be upon him—says, 'As to those who reject faith, I will punish them with terrible agony in this world and in the Hereafter, nor will they have anyone to help.'"

Hakim thought back to when he was a little boy, when the terrorists had swept through his village. Most of his relatives had been killed. His family was hungry, always, always hungry. His baby sister, Rukiya, had cried for food. At least when the United Nations sent the Chinese peacekeeping troops, for the most part, Muslim against Muslim killing stopped and there was more food. But this mufti was appointed by Allah, right? If so, then his message should be heeded!

"You say that you believe the Quran. But do you follow its every word, or do you only obey what you choose? You have become complacent. You must not let China continue its occupation of Iraq. You must rise up and fight the Chinese and defeat them!" exhorted the mufti.

There was a muttering in the room at this sudden, direct pronouncement. Hakim and his housemates glanced at each other nervously. Like most of the people in the trailer park, they were all on the payroll of the Chinese.

The mufti let this sink in and then continued. "They are infidels who do not believe in Allah. The Quran says, 'Fight those who believe not in Allah nor the Last Day.'"

"Yes!" Housemate Ali spoke the word out loud and pumped a fist. Sweat glistened on his thick, prominent forehead and his eyes underneath his black eyebrows were wild. Other heads in the room nodded in agreement.

Hakim felt the energy in the room as a buzz began to spread. This was something larger, something greater! Oh, how he wanted to be a part of Black Lightening! But it would mean betraying his

Chinese employers, which could have no possible outcome except for extreme violence.

As the mood in the compound became more fervent and the mob grew angrier at the injustice of the Chinese occupation, Hakim tried to think of a compromise.

There was simply no argument with the sacred words of the Quran and the writings of the Hadith! All Muslims were called to fight unbelievers. That is, unless there was another verse in the Quran or the Hadith with which to argue....He thought hard. One finally popped in his head. "I have a question." He bravely raised his hand.

All heads in the room turned. The teacher swiveled and fastened his eyes onto Hakim, eyes that were suddenly interested and receptive. "Yes, please, my boy," said the mufti encouragingly. "I am here to answer your questions and to ease your concerns."

Hakim felt his face turn red from the attention fastened upon himself. He felt breathless and hot, challenging this famous Mohammad Al-Issa. He took a deep breath. "Teacher, the Prophet says that we can grant mercy to the infidels, and if they 'pay the poor-rate, leave their way free to them.' The Chinese are providing food to our poor."

There was a little rustle as several of his work colleagues from the prison nodded their heads and mumbled their agreement. The Chinese were occasionally harsh, ruthlessly gunning down insurgent groups involved in killing. They had recently co-opted this practice for themselves alone, forcing the halt of Iraqi-inflicted capital punishment. But as much as practical, they left the locals alone and stayed out of politics. They frequently made quite an international display of the generosity they showed to poor Iraqi beggars on television. They had made few promises, but unlike Americans, so far they hadn't broken any of them.

The kindness melted from the mufti's eyes and they flashed with angry discernment, narrow and calculating. "You are quoting from Quran Al-Tawba 9:5, are you not? But you have forgotten the first part. What does the first part say, my son?"

Hakim felt his face redden. He couldn't remember the rest of Al-Tawba 9:5....

The mufti's voice snapped with sudden impatience. "It says, 'if they repent and keep up prayer and pay the poor-rate, leave their way free to them.' That is *three* things that are required, not two, young brother! The Chinese have not repented! They have not kept up prayer! They have banned prayer in Babylon Metro! Do you not see that it is only a matter of months before they ban it everywhere? They pay the poor rate, but it is part of their propaganda! You see, you have become used to them. You say that you believe the Quran. But do you follow its every word, or do you only obey what you choose? You have accepted them into your midst because of the false peace they offer, because of the money from your own oil fields that they give to you!"

As the mufti went on and on, determined to wear them down, Hakim slunk back against his pole, studying the brothers in the room. It was a good thing there were no exterior windows in this compound, or surely Chinese police, curious about an extraordinarily large meeting that did not appear to be a birthday party or wedding, would drift past to investigate.

"Here is how you are to fight when the time is right. 'Therefore when you meet in battle those who disbelieve, then smite the necks until you have overcome them, then make them prisoners.' The instruction in Quran is clear: 'I will cast terror into the hearts of those who disbelieve. Therefore strike off their heads and strike off every fingertip of them.' Brothers, remember that if it is the will of Allah, nuclear annihilation cannot be avoided."

Hakim's memory flashed back to childhood, to the young men in the village who eagerly signed up for the military, jumping into the back of trucks and tanks with their guns and black t-shirts. They were mostly never seen again. If he joined the mujahedin, they would all be brothers who might die together. They would receive their reward at the same time, the delights of Paradise, and the troubles of this world would be gone.

But was there an in-between path? Could he find a job that didn't involve war and death, a profession that raised his social status? Getting a position in a Chinese jail had been lucky because one out of six Iraqi men had no job. Selling video games like NoitaLever would be his dream! Or even being a trader or retailer of fine goods in Babylon Metro.

The mufti was making him feel guilty, so he decided to stop listening and began to daydream.

147

"How dare you question the teacher?" Ali had barked when they arrived back to the trailer. His eyes had glared suspiciously at Hakim under his thick, expansive forehead and dense black eyebrows. "Are you not loyal to the brothers? Do you seek the easy way out?"

"You are not Allah. You do not know the heart of man," Hakim had retorted.

But the seeds of distrust had been sown, and the result of the heated exchange had been that in order to prove his piety, Hakim had been required to report regularly to the meetings of the brothers for seven months, including meetings where the names of betrayers were named aloud, and then to complete a task. It was a specific assignment—another initiation to prove the loyalty to the group; this one, a deadly serious initiation, not a prank of Hillah Hillbilly boys.

A betrayer to the faith had been hunted down, a Saudi businessman. A Hillah brother highly skilled in marksmanship would lure him and take him out tonight. Hakim, Ali, and Yazen, in order to prove their loyalty, were required to dispose of the body.

They waited in the middle of night in a decrepit pickup truck owned by a brother in the trailer park. They parked on a quiet southern portion of Route 8 well outside the checkpoints of Babylon Metro and near the caves where they had secret meetings from time to time. It was a remote area littered with explosives from the Gulf Wars, and with their flashlights they could identify the short wire stakes with faded fabric flags that surreptitiously indicated a safe route for the brotherhood to walk and park.

Soon a van pulled in, turning its low beams off and on two times as per the pre-arranged signal. The occupants in both vehicles opened the doors and emerged.

"There is no strength nor power except Allah," Ali gave the code phrase.

"To Allah we belong and to Allah we return," they heard the return code phrase.

Satisfied, Ali went to the back of the truck and removed the lid from the oil drum while Hakim and Yazen went forward to collect the body of the betrayer from the van.

The dead Saudi had been hastily wrapped in a large sheet of plastic laying on the back of the van, and they could see with their flashlights that it had rolled during the transport and was covered in a sticky, oozy mass of blood and brains. "Where's a blanket? We need a blanket to cover him or we will get his blood all over ourselves," Hakim said in disgust.

"There is none," said the brothers who had made the gruesome delivery.

"Hurry!" urged Ali in an impatient voice that did not leave room for personal vanity or hygiene.

Together Hakim and Yazen lifted the dripping corpse, which was barely cold, and maneuvered it to the oil drum, which lay on its side with the opening to the back of the pickup. Grunting with the weight, they hoisted it up and stuffed it in. Hakim recoiled as a loose arm slapped against his face in a macabre fashion and gulped at the sight of the betrayer's blown-off side of the head visible in the moonlight.

"May God protect you," the deliverers of the corpse said. They turned to leave, got in the van, and drove away.

Ali secured the oil drum lid, and then they tied it down. Hakim's arms were sticky with the foul, fetid blood. "What if blood has dripped onto the ground?" he worried.

They beamed their flashlights onto the sand and rocks, and indeed there were some dark drops and splatters. Yazen procured the shovel from the pickup, and they did their best to redistribute sand and nudge rocks upside down. Then they climbed into the pickup. Ali drove further down Route 8 to a point where the Euphrates came close to the road. They stopped the truck once again, dropped the oil drum to the ground, re-opened the lid, and hoisted up a number of nearby rocks. The rocks and stones fell on top of the body with a series gruesome thumps, and they secured the drum lid one last time.

"Ready?" Hakim said, taking a deep breath. "One, two, three!"

Together they shoved the drum down the embankment. They ran after it, panting. It slowed a few times, and with mighty heaves they nudged it over obstacles, grunting and sweating from the heavy exertion.

At last the container rolled into the water, and they shone their flashlights upon it as it sunk down into the heavy reeds and mud.

41

Governorate of Babil Prison

The following day, the prison employees packed into the meeting room as fat, old, heavy-joweled Commander Yang Chunying addressed them on the latest boring developments in Chinese policy at the prison. The three housemates, Hakim, Ali, and Yazen, shuffled their feet and tried not to yawn after their late night test of loyalty.

"As for your further instructions," the commander droned on in his awful accent and terrible excuse for the Arabic language, "there is to be no more playing of game 'NoitaLever' on government property. It offend imams and is American game corrupt with military propaganda and Western capitalism!"

A grumble arose in the room. "Is it to be banned in Babylon Metro?" asked one of the guards, "and in our trailer park?"

"Very soon," replied the commander. "You do not play it on your phones anymore here at prison, yes?"

Another round of anger rumbled throughout the room. Many of the guards had become addicted to it in recent month, challenging each other in playoffs and brackets. "Be quiet. Not done," the ugly commander rose up his hand. "Is time to announce promotion. Hakim Al-Obaidi, step to front please."

"Who, me?" In an instant Hakim was jolted out of his rebellious resentment about the banning of the NoitaLever. His friends gasped in surprise. In a flash he stood up straighter and tucked in his uniform shirt tighter, fluffing up his hair nervously with his fingers as he moved in a daze to where the commander stood.

"Hakim rewarded for good ordering of supplies and saving money and willing to work extra shifts and night hours," Commander Yang read from a set of notes. "You promoted to manager. You will come to my office after this." With his fat fingers, he held a superintendent service ribbon up for all to see. Hakim blushed. Commander Yang clumsily pinned the service ribbon onto Hakim's uniform. Hakim held his breath at the odor of cheap Chinese aftershave as the commander bent over him.

"*Shukran*," Hakim stammered. The senior officer grunted an acknowledgement to the thanks.

The room broke out into polite applause, and out of the corner of his eye he could not help but notice Ali in the back of the crowd, his face filled with jealousy. Ali had also wanted the promotion to manager and a raise, but Ali had not volunteered to work extra graveyard shifts like Hakim had.

He ignored it. He was their supervisor now! He pulled up to his full height and stuck his chest out proudly, nodding magnanimously to his co-workers.

Now that he had higher responsibilities, Hakim made a habit of lurking in the offices of Commander Yang Chunying at various times during his shift. The Chinese may be loathsome *Kafir* occupiers who denied the truth of Allah; but the good thing was that they had hired and promoted himself and several other locals, so it was clever to continue to be seen and noticed. Mostly he was curious about the new prisoner that had been brought in last night. What was so intriguing to Hakim was that this prisoner was not a local, he was American.

According to Yazen, who did the data inputting this morning, the prisoner had been picked up by an Iraqi police unit which was demanding the death penalty. The Chinese, who had taken over peace-keeping efforts from the United Nations reluctantly in the first place (and only with the promise of oil field leases and economic opportunity), were now under tremendous human rights pressure to suspend the death penalty and felt that their hands were being tied behind their backs by the international community. The resentful Iraqi police force often cited charges against their captives for everything from adultery and homosexuality (stoning), to treason against Iraq or China, to murder (hanging). The Iraqi brothers on the local police did this to make an angry and outraged point about their Sharia law being taken away. No one ever really never knew if the Iraqi brothers just had a personal grudge against somebody and if the charges were trumped up or not.

All of this was the commander's fun problem to sort out, and that of the local Chinese-run courts. In the meantime, the commander had discovered that it was an ingenious opportunity to raise bribe money from the prisoners' families while the subject was in prison waiting for the death penalty to be resumed.

Hakim was in this afternoon under the guise of reporting a problem that he had solved: a shortage of linens, and how he, Hakim, had gone to great lengths to get an emergency supply quickly. Shamelessly he bragged.

"Is good," the commander replied gruffly and dismissively, but Hakim was used to this, and continued to hang around the desk, asking what he hoped was an intelligent question about bidding out the job in the future, when suddenly Ali burst in the door.

"The new prisoner from America that was checked in last night!" Ali exclaimed. Ali had changed to his going-home clothes, obviously trying to make a point that he, too, was working late in hopes of impressing the commander. "I found this deep inside a pocket of his clothes! He is a spy!" Ali triumphantly held up a little pink plastic watch in the air and held his finger on the screen for a few seconds.

"We are finished with our homework. Is it time to go play?" the watch asked itself in both English and Mandarin Chinese.

Eyes narrowing, the commander skeptically reached for the watch dangling from Ali's fingers and studied it, turning it over and shaking it. He poked at its screen with his fat fingertip, and again it spoke: *"I can't hear what you said. Do you want to go play?"*

The commander's face broke into the closest thing to a smile that Hakim had ever seen. "Peppermint Pinkey. Yes, yes, Peppermint Pinkey. My granddaughter have one. No answer today for you, Talky Watch? No little girl close by?"

He opened the desk drawer and reached for a tiny tool. Quickly he popped open the back of the device, his heavy jowls dangling as he examined the inside. He muttered to himself in Mandarin while Ali and Hakim stood waiting. He closed it back up and waited for it to reset. The Talky Watch came to life again. *"We are finished with our homework. Is it time to go play?"*

"Is not the device of a spy," pronounced the commander.

Ali's face reddened with embarrassment and disappointment. He glared at Hakim, as if it were Hakim's fault that the device was benign. Ali had been cranky ever since the death penalty had been suspended and the commander increasingly mistrusted Iraqi police accusations against prisoners. Ali had been even crankier since Hakim's promotion.

"Ghost guy, he probably father of small girl, see," said the commander to Ali. 'Ghost guy' was the term that the Chinese used to describe Americans. Chuckling, he took the watch and set it on its stiff plastic side on top of an ancient filing cabinet facing his desk. "Peppermint Pinkey watch over my work," he said mischievously. "Very good. You can go now."

They shuffled towards the door, deflated at the lack of drama. "Ghost guy my prisoner," the dour commander reminded them as they walked out the door. "I will handle this American. Must be very, very quiet."

The longer the wait, the higher the reward price for the release of an American prisoner.

The American with the freckles and innocent brown eyes who said he was an architect had begun his stay in the Governorate of Babil Prison as an eccentric curiosity but immediately became official entertainment for the mixture of Chinese and Iraqi guards that worked in the prison, especially Hakim, who was fascinated by anything having to do with America.

Each day the prisoners were chained together and loaded up in vans in a loading area by the exercise yard. Then they were conveyed to work, in accordance with the Chinese philosophy that prisoners needed to pay their own way. Some of them tended to the horses and carriages of the Chinese equestrian guard; others worked in vegetable fields or loaded wheat or citron wood off or onto trucks and barges. Josh was never taken offsite. He was given cleaning duties, and often he was left alone in his cell for several hours. Evidently the prison commander, Yang Chungying, or someone higher up, was going to special lengths to insure that Ghost Guy's presence would not be observed by outsiders.

One of the things the prisoner did every day was gymnastics and break dancing. He was really quite good and it was fascinating to watch him walk on his hands, gyrate, and work on his splits in the small cell without ever hitting the walls, and to watch him do flips out in the courtyard during exercise time. One night one of the Chinese guards even set up recorded Chinese music with a western beat in the corridor outside the cell, and the staff gathered to watch the prisoner perform moves to real music. However, Hakim's housemate and co-worker, Ali, along with some of the other more conservative Sunni and Black Lightening guards, objected to the debasing influence of western music. Commander Yang Chungying barked at the Chinese staff not to play western music anymore and upset the locals.

The prisoner knew some Arabic but not well enough to say *Tabaašiir*, the word for chalk, nor the Mandarin word for it, either; after wild gesticulations which included blowing a puff of air into the sky and an erasing motion, Hakim had finally understood what he was requesting and brought a set of colored chalks for him, just to see what he would do. At first, the prisoner had drawn pictures to communicate and to pass the time. They were funny pictures of the prison guards retching on prison food, and cartoons of the other inmates.

One day Hakim persuaded the commander to catch a performance exhibit and led him towards Josh's cell. Hakim and the commander peeked around the corner past the bars and Hakim pointed. The prisoner was squatted on the floor cross legged with a piece of colored chalk, working on his drawing on the pitifully narrow, gray concrete block wall at the opposite end of the small cell.

The prisoner was working on a city skyline sketch of Babylon Metro with the chalks. The prisoner was singing in Mandarin and had a very good voice, a high tenor: "Now we go to school to learn, so we can grow up and earn."

The commander, in a rare display of humor, began to sing the words very off-key along with the prisoner, who turned around from his cross-legged position in surprise. He paused his song, and quickly recovered, standing up and saluting. *"Nǐ hǎo sīlìng,"* Josh said with a pronounced American accent, Mandarin for 'hello, commander.'

"Peppermint Pinkey song, yes," the commander replied. "Picture good. Mandarin need much work." He paused to study the latest in the chalk project. The skyline was really quite remarkable, and it was interesting what the ghost guy could do with a child's set of chalk bits. Ghost Guy was drawing it from memory and some of the buildings were in the wrong place or improvised, but for the most part the detail was amazing.

The commander moved on. Hakim trotted along behind. "Ghost Guy crazy," summarized the commander.

That was pretty much the consensus of most of the guards, except of course for Ali, who had a rabid hatred and distrust of anyone from America. To Hakim and most of the guards, this prisoner seemed quite harmless, one of those military and political mistakes that was rather unfortunate but frequent.

From Josh's cell all of a sudden came a burst of beeping and musical sounds oddly similar to the noises on the NoitaLever game. Hakim snorted, trying to stifle his own laughter. The prisoner had apparently heard the guards playing the game on their phones and imitated the sound effects of the game precisely. The ghost guy was fascinating, obviously artistic and imaginative and even athletic. He had warm, curious brown eyes that seemed so innocent. Most of all he was funny.

Out of the corner of his eye, Josh watched every single thing that happened at Governorate of Babylon Prison. Thus far, he had acted like he did not know hardly any Chinese or Arabic. He deliberately chose to convey the impression that he was funny and slightly crazy, so that he would seem harmless to the staff. Chalk art, break dancing, high school gymnastics, and humor weren't just entertainment. They were for his mental health, in order to combat the sterile gray coldness of the prison walls with music and memories of beautiful architecture outside the walls, and to put out of his mind the unthinkable mistake that may have handed him over to his captors. The exercise was part of his plan to stay in shape and strength train until he found an opportunity to escape.

The crazy act didn't last very long. Iraqi police accused Josh of every possible crime from adultery to shooting a Muslim brother in an American church to changing his name. He was interrogated through means of an interpreter. In the dark, concrete block interrogation cells deep in the heart of the prison, his captors subjected him to a series of techniques including sleep deprivation, bright lights, questioning, and punches.

The Career Trainee Program at the Farm had been invaluable. He had been trained how to resist interrogation and he gave up no information, sticking to the story that he was an architect from America, hired to renovate an old palace at Ancient Babylon. He talked a lot without giving any information, holding his ground, maintaining wide-eyed, innocent eye contact. "I am the wrong person," he claimed. "The police have made a mistake. I am not bitter about this. Perhaps I can help you find the person you are looking for that assassinated your Muslim brother in the church? You say it was an American? I do confess one bad thing. I took a brick with Saddam Hussein's initials carved in it for a souvenir. However, it was too heavy to carry and I threw it under a date palm."

His inquisitors snorted at this. Their interrogation was meant to make him feel out of control and to get him to confess, but his calm statements seemed to turn the tables and change the tone of who had control.

The fat, ugly commander of the prison, dressed in full Chinese military uniform, came in to observe Josh during interrogation one day, personally barking harsh questions at the ghost guy in several languages, but finally calling off punches that approached beatings.

Then abruptly the interrogations stopped.

This seemed to anger one guard in particular, Ali, who then targeted personal hatred towards Josh. The prison bully taunted him at every opportunity, pointing a rifle at him in the yard during exercise or coming up behind him and shoving or tripping him. Josh was astute enough to gather that Ali did not particularly seem to be liked by the other guards, who occasionally razzed him—Ali's voice could be heard rising in a whine above theirs, letting out a stream of rapid Arabic protests tinged with vehemence.

Conditions were noisy and crowded and the food was pitiful, often lacking protein. Josh began craving foods—at first the ones that would be expected, such as A Pizza Me Pizza with Thick Crust Pepperoni, and chocolate chip cookies; and then odd, ordinary American food cravings like peanut butter, macaroni and cheese, and mashed potatoes.

Prisoners of every kind of crime and non-crime were congregated together, and some of them were dangerous. Strangely, Josh appeared to benefit from something of a protected status, no doubt because he was American—the Chinese supervisors ensured he was never alone with the dangerous ones.

Hakim, the vain, good-looking Iraqi assigned to oversee Josh, seemed interested in American songs, products, and culture; and he was one of few Iraqi guards who wasn't mean. He watched with interest as Josh did gymnastic routines on the double rings in the prison yard. Sniffing out opportunity, Josh discreetly began dropping tantalizing tidbits about America. "The people that invented NoitaLever game in America are very rich," he told Hakim on day. "They all live in mansions and have swimming pools in their back yards. The people that work for the company come from around the world." It was somewhat true. Six of them had come from London.

"You know the men that made the NoitaLever game?" Hakim's eyes nearly popped out of his head with wonder.

Josh evaded the question. "You can do anything you dream in America. Everyone knows that. There are no limits."

160

Hakim huffed defensively, "America, it is corrupt!" and walked away from the prisoner. But he planned to look up some articles on the internet about rich American gaming creators after his shift.

Josh began assessing Hakim and decided to try to gain his trust and recruit him as a spy. Hakim frequently pummeled Josh with question after question about America, some apparently genuine and some pointedly rude: "Do all Americans play NoitaLever?" "Why do Americans support our enemy Israel, even when Israel do terrible thing to Muslims?" "Why do American women dress like harlot?" "How are Americans so rich and only work five days in the week?" "How do refugees to America get the cars and the houses?"

Manipulating Hakim's apparent vulnerabilities, Josh answered each question patiently, always describing American prosperity and generosity in great detail to the debonair youth. Sometimes prisoners nearby overheard the conversations and guffawed and scorned. Other times they fell silent, listening enviously without comment.

Josh was aware that he was facing a trial of some sort. He elicited bits of information from Hakim. Hakim did not know when, or where it would be held, saying it was the decision of Baghdad and Beijing. Josh seemed to be caught in some uncertain bureaucratic quagmire.

The days in the prison plodded on monotonously. The CIA and the State Department may or may not know his whereabouts, but since he had no diplomatic immunity, he knew they would keep up appearances that they were doing no more for him than any other normal American citizen. He was an architect by trade and a hobbyist musician; the lack of beauty and the harshness of prison life slowly drained him.

Bloom where you are planted. It was something his mother had said, over and over when he was growing up. If you were unhappy, you should make the best of it and learn the most you could. It was what got him through the utterly boring years of high school in Columbia, where he dreamed constantly of leaving the Midwest for a more exciting life. And he had made the best of it by excelling in gymnastics, winning the state competition two years in a row, and impressing cute girls.

So he listened carefully and tried to soak up every bit of Chinese and Arabic he could. He examined every inch of his cell, learned every sound and movement of the guards, and sucked up to them, charming them with his chalk drawings and voice impressions. He kept track of the days and dates and counted each one that he had survived.

Chelsea was his best hope, and every day he thought of his wife and daughter in order to stay positive and hopeful. His wife would not let the matter rest, he knew; she would follow every clue. But he knew Headquarters would be blunt with her about the odds and discourage her—most nationals who disappeared in Iraq were never seen and heard of again. He also knew that the longer time went on, the more likely his case would bog down in bureaucracy and the less attention it would receive.

45
Kimberly

The days crept by, a slow torture of nightmare; a purgatory on earth.

Atalaya was out of school for winter break. Mercifully, Chelsea had requested the week off for the holidays. The day following the visit from Connie and the chaplain, she stayed up in her bedroom hiding, watching C-Span and CNN on the bedroom television. Connie called to check on her. There was nothing new to report, and it was a serious situation. Nonetheless, it was comforting to know that the Agency had this. They knew what to do in these situations. Chelsea slunk downstairs and somehow managed to throw meals together. She paced through the house restlessly, checking social media reports for anything that might be happening in Babylon Metro that might affect Josh. She tried to go to bed and sleep that night but woke up repeatedly to make sure she had not missed a call on her cell phone.

What horrible, unthinkable torture might he be enduring? In the dark of the night, with no one awake to reach out to, she was so overwhelmed with anxiety that she raced to the toilet, hung over and retched.

The following morning she gathered up her nerve and told Atalaya that she was worried about Daddy, that he hadn't called them. Atalaya took it with the typical straightforward literalism of a seven-year old. "Don't worry Mommy, Daddy will call us soon."

She phoned their parents that night. Mom and Dad were shocked and saddened. She could hear the worry in their voices, and she knew they feared that once again she might be a widow. "We love you and support you. What is the CIA doing about this? Surely they are experienced in dealing with these things. Do you need us to come out there? We will come right away." She told them to wait to come until she knew more, in case the worse happened.

The conversation with Josh's parents went differently than with her parents, as it always did. It was the worst fear of parents of a CIA covert officer, and it was happening to them now. Dr. Evans took the news soberly, almost with a sense of fatalism. It had taken a while to warm up to Dr. Evans when she and Josh got married, but now they got along well. However, there would never

163

be a warming up with Josh's mother, Judge Mary Duncan-Evans, whom Chelsea had never gotten along with.

Josh's mother rattled off rapid-fire questions. "What day and time did you last talk to him? What was the very last thing he said? Why do you think he was talking about Muslim legends to you? Did it have something to do with his assignment? What is the CIA doing about it? Did they indicate how long he can be declared missing before they change his status? Are you entitled to a settlement?" The barrage of queries, as if Chelsea was a witness in a court room, angered her. It was all she could do to be civil and not hang up. Then out of the blue Judge Duncan-Evans suggested to her husband, "Let's pause before the throne and ask the One who knows all things to bring our son home," and as the judge prayed over the phone line, Chelsea was smitten with guilt over the aversion she had for her mother-in-law.

Each day, Connie the liaison from the CIA called, solicitous and kind; but because of the holidays there were few updates and little new information. Yes, he had a mobile, but they could never pick up a signal from the battery. And each day, Chelsea had new questions for Connie, who always said, "I will check into that for you and get back to you with an answer." There were things they couldn't tell her. She expected that. She was a CIA wife and she knew that they knew what they were doing.

The days ticked by, agonizingly slow with waiting, and simultaneously they moved rapidly, due to her anxiety. She couldn't eat and began rapidly losing weight. Laundry and dirty dishes piled up in heaps. She sought to escape by sleeping and watching television, sometimes waking up in front of the TV with Atalaya shaking her and saying, "Mommy? Mommy?" Every day that passed, the chances of finding Josh diminished. No word, nothing to report, no further clues. Josh had never gone more than a week without making contact with her.

The day after New Year's was back to school and back to work. She dragged out of bed, resenting having to re-enter a hectic and indifferent world but at the same time missing her normal schedule. It was her week to drive to school in the mornings, and she loaded Atalaya up in the car in her warm Peppermint Pinkey coat and drove to Kimberly's house. The door flew open and Kimberly's son ran out through the frigid air, across the icy lawn, and towards the warm car. Chelsea got out of the car and went up to the sidewalk to the door. She rang for the sturdy and athletically built Kimberly, who came to the front door, still putting in earrings.

"Oh, hi Chelsea. How was your Christmas?" Kimberly's resonant voice boomed cheerfully, so loudly that it reverberated across the street and Chelsea had to take one step back on the porch. But then the loud voice trailed at the sight of Chelsea's tormented expression.

"Josh has disappeared somewhere in the Middle East. We—I don't know where he is, and he said if something ever happened, to go to your office."

"Damn." Kimberly sucked in her breath, one earring left to go. Her voice was subdued, as if she may have expected that this might happen someday. "Chelsea, that's—that's not good. Not good at all. I am so, so sorry to hear that. Are you ok?"

"No."

"He left something for you in case this ever happened. I have court this morning. Step inside and let me check my schedule." Kimberly went to retrieve her mobile and came back to the front door. "Be at my office at two o'clock," she ordered solidly.

The drive to school and work and the ride up the office elevator was eerily routine, a startling reminder of normalcy. Inside Mizrahi and Associates, someone had already started taking down the holiday decorations. They greeted her with morning pleasantries, but her reply was brief and she did not engage in their laughing chit-chat about the holidays when she went to the breakroom for a mug for some coffee. She felt exhausted. No matter how much she slept, no matter how much coffee she drank, it did no good; she felt tired, drained, and barely able to get anything done.

She waited until it died down and everyone was starting to talk shop again and ready to go back to their desks, and then she said, "Hey guys, I have something to share. Sorry to be all gloom and doom. I'm afraid this isn't—well, it isn't very funny."

It was a carefully constructed story with lots of omissions but one that would protect the CIA and others working on Josh's project. She told them that his company, Crestedon, sent him to Iraq to work on a confidential building project for a few months.

He left his apartment on Christmas and never came back. His company was searching for him.

As she spoke, it was so quiet that a pin dropping on the breakroom tile floor would have produced an echo, and the faces of the employees were concerned and shocked. But the minute she finished, they peppered her with questions that were tricky to answer.

Dane's face drained of its color. "I'm really sorry Chels. That's bad stuff, really bad stuff." Of everyone in the office, Dane alone knew the helpless agony of losing a spouse overseas.

Ignoring end-of-year property management invoices and budgets, the property manager ran to her office, her fingers flying over the computer keyboard, doing web searches for tips on locating missing persons overseas and articles about Chinese-Iraqi law enforcement, immediately filling up Chelsea's email with links.

Chelsea warmed up the lukewarm cup of coffee in the microwave and then took it back to her computer to work, but she could hear snatches of her co-workers' low voices with each other.

"Aren't you supposed to contact your congressman when someone disappears?"

"Are you allowed to fly to Iraq and look for someone, now that the Chinese are in control? Is it safer now than it used to be, or more dangerous?"

"What if he's alive? Will someone try to extort ransom money from her?"

"This is really strange. It happened a whole week ago? If it was me, I'd be plastering his picture all over social media the same day! Should I offer to do it for her?"

"No, don't. She never talked about any marriage problems, but what if he met another woman and wanted to disappear? My cousin knew someone once who…"

She clapped her hands over her ears, huddling over her desk, cringing. This was the social price you paid when your spouse worked for one of the most powerful, most respected, yet secretive government agencies on earth and something went terribly wrong.

Then she picked up the phone and called her boss to let him know. Levi had not been in the office since Clinton had come to visit, and this week Levi and Miriam were on a Mediterranean cruise to Palma Majorca. Astoundingly, he called back from the

ship quickly. He had been fond of Josh and took the news hard—
a reaction that almost seemed over the top. "Oh my God, oh my
God! Joshie disappeared somewhere in the Middle East? You
don't know where he is? Oh, this is terrible, this is terrible! What
are we going to do?" Levi wailed. "I must tell Miriam, this is
tragic!" It unnerved her and just made things even worse.

At two o'clock in the afternoon she packed up her laptop and
some homework for the day and drove to the small boutique law
offices on L Street. Kimberly came to the reception area and they
hugged. Kimberly's voice was so deep and loud, and the business
suit and heels made her even more of a commander. Someone
competent and in control needed to take charge, and Chelsea
suddenly felt that her burden was being shared by someone
stronger.

Kimberly piloted her into the modest conference room that
looked out over the street and closed the conference room door.
On the conference room table was a thick file and a box of
Kleenex. "Usually whenever Josh went on an out-of-town trip, he
would drop an envelope off and take the previous one. I was never
supposed to open them, so I never knew what the contents were. I
have an envelope from him. The second item in this file is a hard
copy of your will. I want you to sit down and open these. You are
welcome to study them, make phone calls, look things up, and take
as long as you need. I'm here to answer any questions that I can."

Kimberly opened the file and drew out a small, bulky
envelope with an object inside. She handed it to Chelsea.

Chelsea felt her stomach thud sickeningly, to see it in black
and white like this:

For Chelsea Evans
To be opened if I am missing or presumed
dead / J. E.

46

The Mysterious Letters

It was Josh's handwriting, his architect's scrawl. Chelsea felt her heart stop. She carefully tore open the manila packet. Inside was an encryption device. Her fingers shook as she pulled it out.

Kimberly spoke, reading her thoughts. "Josh never told me anything about what it is or how to work it. All he did was drop off the envelope with instructions that if he was ever missing or k—" she caught herself and quickly exchanged the word, "or lost his life—to give it to you.

Chelsea swallowed. "I need to put this on my laptop."

"Would you like to be alone?" Kimberly surmised.

"I—I don't know. Yeah, I probably should. I don't know what might be on here."

"Come out front and ask for me when you are ready."

Kimberly left the conference room, and even through the soundproof walls Chelsea could still hear the muffled volume of her voice in other parts of the office.

She attached the encryption device to her laptop and followed the instructions. Immediately a screen popped up asking for a password.

Helplessly she stared back at the blinking screen. What if she couldn't figure this out and there was something very important on here?

She tried the code that she and Josh used to access each other's database of passwords for all of their internet and banking accounts.

It worked!

An additional security layer involved facial recognition, and she waited for the computer camera to identify her features. At last a screen opened with three files. She clicked on the first one. It was a brief note from Josh:

Babe:
You know what it means if my cover is blown. If anything happens and the CIA loses track of me, message this number:
202-117-4111
Key in AuCHFOP

You will receive a reply with instructions.

Realize that if you give this number and code name to anyone else, it could result in loss of my job, breach of national security, or even loss of life. The CIA will deny all knowledge of me.

If I am gone for good, I want you to know that I loved you from the first day I saw you and I will love you to my last breath. Tell Atalaya how much I loved her. Raise her right, teach her all you can about God, and coach her to be wise.

With all my heart, Josh

She felt her insides clench and roll. She clutched her mobile with a nervous hand and messaged the number, realizing she was panting. It was a Washington, D.C., number. Was this a person who could help? Who somehow knew what happened to Josh? She waited for it to buzz a reply and re-read the letter as a cold chill crept up the back of her neck. She stared at her mobile for a long while, but there was no response.

She set the mobile down and clicked on the second file. It was a video with background music that Josh had made for Atalaya, telling their daughter his life story in quick, simple language that a child could understand. Josh described falling in love with Chelsea and eloping to London and how Attie was adopted after a tornado killed her grandmother. He must have made the video very soon after he joined the CIA, while Atalaya was a toddler.

The video ended. Chelsea squeezed her eyes shut and felt her eyes well up.

She sniffed and opened her eyes, clicking on the third file. It contained two color photos. One was of a city skyline. The other appeared to be of a ziggurat, or ancient ruins, perched on rock and sand. She stared at the screen, perplexed.

She sat in the conference room chair, still waiting for a response from the text. She rifled through the hardcopy papers in the file. There was a copy of the will they had Kimberly draft when Josh went to work for the CIA. Josh's genealogy notes that he had obtained during one of their stays in the U.K., which traced their family heritage, was in the file with the will. She blew her nose with the available Kleenex, touched up her makeup and then reopened the photo of the skyline with tremendously tall skyscrapers.

At first she wasn't sure what city it might be. It looked familiar, but it was too unconventional to be New York City. It was a foreign city she had seen on television news. Was it Hong Kong? She zoomed into parts of it and spotted tiny palm trees and buildings with distinct Mideast features. Was it Dubai? In the center of the picture was a particularly stunning office building with unbelievable architecture. The lower level curved and bent, with neon colors shimmering and glowing from it.

The second picture left her clueless. Why had Josh left her a picture of a portion of a skyline and a ziggurat? Was there a connection between it and the first picture of the metropolitan skyline? Were the photos personal favorites of his, some unusual places he had visited or projects he had worked on during the course of his work with the CIA? Was he trying to let her know that they were the highlights of his career?

Or were they, in fact, actual clues to his disappearance?

Her first instinct was to call the Agency. But it was a violation of protocol for a case officer to keep personal photographs involving his operations. Regardless, no location Josh had been at would come as any surprise to the CIA. An appalling percentage of his job—the little-discussed mundane aspects of espionage—was filing laboriously and painstakingly detailed after-action reports of every place he had been and every person he had ever talked to.

Outside of the Agency, only Josh's parents and her parents knew his real job, and this was over their paygrade. Kimberly was their lawyer, right? Yet she was afraid to tell Kimberly about the files on the encryption device. What if the CIA figured out that Josh shared classified information with her and she had passed it on to someone else?

She checked the time. Five minutes had passed and still no reply from the mysterious number. She stood up and paced the floor, agonizing over how much to tell Kimberly.

Tired of waiting for a return message from the mysterious text number, she called Kimberly back to the conference room. She would tell Kimberly some things, but not everything, and she would not share with Kimberly how she found out.

"Kimberly, Josh is CIA. He disappeared while on an undercover operation in Iraq. The CIA has a sensitive operation there."

Kimberly did not seem to be surprised at all. Had she suspected? "Well," Kimberly said slowly, "they'll have every resource looking for him. Let's just hope that local authorities there in Iraq are holding him. He won't be subject to that country's court system. He will be expelled from that country."

"No. His status is nonofficial cover. He doesn't have diplomatic immunity."

Kimberly processed this and then muttered, "Oh, no, God help him!" as their eyes locked wordlessly. Chelsea's stomach took yet another plunge as she realized Kimberly would not, and could not, postulate an optimistic outcome for this scenario.

"Chelsea," Kimberly finally collected herself, her voice returned to the normal, loud Kimberly level, "This is very, very serious, but I will do what I can to assist. I will call the State Department on behalf of a missing local citizen and see if there are some back channels that can be worked. I will represent you if the press wants a statement from the family. I will give you a discounted hourly rate."

At supper time a text finally came back from the mysterious number:

Who is this?

Chelsea hesitated. Should she give her full name? *Chelsea*

There was a long pause, then: *what was the special song when you fell in love?*

She stared at the message, confused at first, thought about it, then bit her lip painfully at an old memory and replied with the name of the song: *Beyond What Words Could Ever Say*

She waited. Nothing. She messaged *Help please! Need answers.*

There was no response.

She told Atalaya that night at bedtime that Daddy was missing, but some friends were trying to help find him, and that they would have to pray. Atalaya buried her face in Chelsea's shoulder. It was hard to pray without resentment, knowing that God knew where Josh was.

After Atalaya's bedtime, Chelsea went downstairs and got herself a glass of wine. She turned on the television to the British channel, because it reminded her of their happy times when they lived in London. But she couldn't sit still and began pacing the

171

floor of the house, trying push away the horrible thoughts that stalked her each night when the sun went down and it got dark, sickening images of where Josh might be now, tortured or lying dead.

Did the message recipient have to look up notes or something to verify the name of her and Josh's special song? At one in the morning she poured a drink of tequila. Finally sleepy, she crawled into bed with her mobile pressed to her chest, hoping a more definitive response to the text would come. She imagined holding him close, smelling his aftershave and his cinnamon gum, and running her fingers through the dark, curly hair at the base of his neck.

Chelsea slept restlessly that night, opening her eyes several times to check her phone which was clutched to her chest; but there was no answer from the secret contact.

Good Morning America was on while she and Atalaya ate breakfast together, and Angela Stevens Giordano somberly launched into today's breaking news story. "Last night while America slept, a group of radical Muslim university students blockaded the street in front of the Chinese police headquarters in the southern section of Babylon Metro today. In support of Sharia law, they protested the Chinese directive that prohibits the Muslim practice of beheadings in Iraq. The demonstration got out of hand when one of the students threw a pipe bomb at the entrance of the station. Chinese troops on horseback immediately gunned down several of the students."

Brett Milo smoothly interjected, "Black Lightening claimed responsibility for the attack against the police. The video we have is disturbing and you may wish to send young children out of the room—"

Of course! Duh! Chelsea's mouth dropped open as the camera swept across the skyline of Babylon Metro. The picture was a clue to a specific building Josh was doing undercover work in! He wanted her to know this, in case he ever disappeared! Why hadn't the CIA ever told her about this building?

Chelsea grabbed Atalaya and whisked her away from her bowl of Peppermint Pinkey vitamin-fortified cereal. "Go upstairs and wash up. Now. Brett Milo says you're not supposed to watch this."

Protesting, Atalaya went upstairs. Angela continued. "President Maly is expected to give a speech at 10:00 east coast time, and Hollywood movie star Tyler Tischner is organizing a rally denouncing the human rights abuses by the Chinese…" The perfect-looking morning show hostess continued to read her teleprompter. Chelsea grabbed her tablet and frantically began clicking on the keyboard.

Babylon Metro images.

The tablet blinked and a row of pictures of the skyline appeared on the screen. Most of them contained the building in Josh's photo from one angle or another. Did the CIA refrain from telling her because there were other Americans working there who might be in jeopardy? Was it possible they were evacuating other employees right now?

Outside she heard a horn honk. Kimberly was running the carpool this morning. She sent Atalaya to the car and waved at her friend from the front porch but avoided going to the car window to chat. She hurried back in and sat down at the desk by the television, for the first time ever grateful for a slow, boring job where it didn't matter whether or not she showed up for work. Yappie limped over to the desk and curled up on the dark wood floor by Chelsea's feet while Chelsea called up an online search.

How much could the CIA do to find Josh? If you were a top secret organization that had to deny forever that a covert officer worked for you...A feeling of apprehension gripped her as she thought about all the times he mentioned bureaucratic ineptitude. Was Josh letting her know that she would have to take some responsibility if he was ever to be found?

Babylon Metro Commercial Real Estate. She jumped with surprise so loud that Yappie turned her furry, nearly-deaf head up with curiosity. She was staring at a real estate listing with a photo completely identical to the photo Josh had left for her, the most amazing building of all of them: Tomorrow Globe Financial Center. It was for lease by a Chinese real estate brokerage service. She emailed the real estate ad to Kimberly: *I think this was the building where Josh was last doing work! There may be other co-workers in danger there.*

Kimberly called back immediately with information from an internet search. "It's the tallest tower in the world," Kimberly's voice thundered over the phone and Chelsea had to turn the volume down. "It says here that it will rival Burj Khalifa in Dubai when they construct the final tower on top. Let me pull up a map. I don't know this part of the world very well at all." Chelsea started her own search while Kimberly worked the maps. "I'm zooming in and out of aerials of Babylon Metro. I see the office building. It sits between the downtown and a river. Oh, that's the Euphrates. Did you call the commercial real estate agent in Babylon Metro?"

Call the real estate agent? She shouldn't do that, should she? That might tip someone off and put Josh in danger….

"I'm mapping out a plan for you," Kimberly continued authoritatively. "We're going to be very organized, Chelsea. We'll start a spreadsheet, and then let's do a flowchart of eventualities. Here's what we need on our spreadsheet." Kimberly was large and in charge, throwing out instructions with the rat-a-tat precision of a drill sergeant. "Who are the possible players to help you with this?"

"The CIA, FBI, State Department, Secretary of State, and U.S. negotiators and diplomats."

"Ok, we'll put them down and start contacting them—"

"The problem is," Chelsea said practically, "they're all territorial and egotistical. Any of them might decide to go rogue looking for Josh, and there's no guarantee that they are talking with each other and sharing information. Or they might all think that it's up to the other organization to do something."

She said goodbye to Kimberly and sat and thought for a while. Then she resumed researching on the computer. She felt a surge of adrenaline. She was thinking and planning and actually doing something other than just waiting for Connie the liaison to call her back.

Babylon Metro maps. The city was located about two hours south of Baghdad. She began reading up on it. The fragments of barely recalled international news over recent years, which at the time held little interest for her, suddenly began to come together.

When the Euro had collapsed and America could no longer afford military peacekeeping in Iraq because of crushing deficits, China had stepped in as peacekeeper in exchange for oil well leases. China had started a gold rush when it determined it was going to make an investment in a global trading center that eclipsed Shanghai and rivaled Hong Kong. Before long, every king and emir in the Middle East was leasing land from China and building a monument to himself. But Babylon Metro was also viewed by some as the epitome of corruption, a sellout to both the east and the west; and the Chinese had their hands full keeping resentful insurgent Muslims at bay.

She drove into work late that day. Why had Josh left the pictures for her? Did he simply want her to know where his last operation had been, in case he never came home? Or was there

175

more to it—did he distrust the Agency's ability to search for him and find him?

As she crossed the white-carpeted floor at Mizrahi and Associates, ready with an excuse for the team about a trip to the dentist taking too long and hoping no one noticed her sloppily put-together clothing choices and lack of jewelry, she suddenly halted with surprise.

In spite of the cold January day, the receptionist was wearing a tank top and shorts. The office was very warm. The property manager was dressed in a bright, floral skirt and a sleeveless top. Dane was at the scanner, and he had on his summer golf clothes. His eyes lit up with merriment and he called out her name as she stepped through the reception area. No matter how late she checked in, Dane always had a cheerful, nonjudgmental greeting.

"Why—what is everyone is wearing?" she asked.

"It's South Aucklund Equivalent Hemisphere Day."

"Huh?"

"We're all tired of the cold. So we decided to turn up the heat and celebrate South Aucklund, New Zealand," said the property manager, who was taking a document out of the scanner and shook it.

"They are in our same latitude, only 39.9047 south instead of north, so we're pretending we're them," explained Dane, always the precise CPA with his numbers. "There's some Australian Vanilla Slice for you in the break room."

Chelsea dashed to her office, feeling a bit excluded. No one had bothered to message her about clothes for South Aucklund Equivalent Hemisphere today! And she hadn't brought any food to share with the team!

That afternoon she was grabbing coffee in the first floor terrarium of the Monument Metroplex building when she finally received a text back from the mysterious number: *Meet Thursday 1230 or Friday 1730 park bench across river from Jefferson Memorial. Come alone. No eye contact.*

She sucked in her breath and messaged back without hesitation *Thursday 12:30*

Describe clothes

Quickly she checked the weather forecast. Frigid cold was predicted for Thursday. She answered *Tan parka, black slacks, black boots*

She waited and there was no response, so she added, *What clothes will you wear?*

Once again there was no reply.

Never before had Chelsea summoned inner courage for a meeting the CIA would not approve of—a meeting so awkward and uneasy and one she shouldn't be having in downtown Washington, D.C.

It was with Kelly Dunberry, the CEO of Crestedon, the company that had provided Josh's false cover. The pink-faced executive with thick white hair and shaggy eyebrows shook her hand and ushered her into his private office and shut the door, offering his condolences for her missing spouse. The chief legal counsel was there. These were the only two individuals in the entire international firm who knew that Josh was CIA. The lawyer got to the point immediately. They, too, were uncomfortable with this meeting.

She knew they were fearful of a lawsuit from her, but all she cared about was information in case her worst fear was true: that the CIA was unable to locate Josh. She tried to smooth things over. "Josh was a college intern and a full time employee with you before he went to work for the CIA. He owes his career both then and now to you, Mr. Dunberry. I used to do some commercial real estate work for your firm's offices around the world, and I also want to say thank you. The Agency doesn't know I'm here. I've been unable to get answers from them."

"I will be frank with you, Mrs. Evans. I agreed to cooperate with the CIA and provide a front company solely out of patriotism. I know it's a bad world out there, and I put myself personally at risk doing this. As an incentive, the CIA provided Josh and some other staff for free, and they handle our tax returns relating to this with the IRS. But frankly, from the start it has been a headache, and of course now it's a tragedy, not to mention a looming PR and political nightmare for us if it ever becomes publicly known that Josh is CIA and we are actually a front for espionage." His big, wrinkled hand rested on the conference room table, the hand of an older businessman with age spots and swollen knuckles that indicated arthritis. A businessman who had tried to do good and had it backfire.

She had come to ask them what the suite number was where the offices had been in the Tomorrow Globe Financial Center in

Babylon Metro, and if any Americans were still working there, because Connie had said she did not have any information about Chelsea's question. "After your husband disappeared we immediately shut down the operation," said the lawyer, "but I still don't know if we can tell you the suite number. This may cause problems with the CIA."

They weren't denying it was the Tomorrow Globe Financial Center. Now she knew beyond any doubt it was the building in the picture—the building Josh in fact had been working in when he disappeared. And she wasn't endangering any Americans by asking questions at this point. "Was he doing something with an architectural dig?"

Dunberry looked questioningly at the lawyer from under his shaggy eyebrows.

"We can't discuss the details of what Josh was involved with," the legal counsel said abruptly. "All we can confirm for you is that he has been employed with us on projects in Babylon Metro and various office buildings around the world."

It was as if she had been brought to the brink of further information and then suddenly hauled back. "Please," Chelsea pled. "Josh doesn't have diplomatic immunity and the CIA has to deny he's CIA. It would compromise them if they got caught doing an extensive investigation to find a so-called ordinary citizen. Do you see the situation I'm in?"

The lawyer shook his head. "We need to research the potential repercussions before we agree to give you any information."

She left, wearied by the wall that Crestedon and its attorney had thrown up, but secure in the knowledge that Tomorrow Globe Financial Building was at least the right building. She made her way along the Washington, D.C., sidewalk, noisy with passing vehicles, past the throng of bustling government workers wearing suits, glued to their mobile devices, moving to important meetings with important people so they could accomplish important things. They made her feel small and helpless. She fought against the urge to be resentful at Crestedon's unwillingness to share more information—Mr. Dunberry had tried to be a good citizen, and it had got him and his global firm in trouble. Every day that dragged by meant the chances to find Josh were diminishing. What more could she do?

179

O ver the lunch hour on Thursday, Chelsea sat huddled in her tan parka by the leafless cherry trees that overlooked the Potomac across from the Jefferson Memorial. The McDonald's lunch sat in the bag next to her, cold and barely touched as she jammed her gloved hands in her pockets to keep them warm. Her stomach burned with acid and nervous nausea, and she nearly thought she was going to throw up over the side of the park bench. At last she was going to get some answers.

In her purse was her own registered hand gun. Deep in the folds of the purse, creased into a small square, was a printout of the encrypted note from Josh with the number and password to reach the contact she was meeting with today.

The wind whipped across the waters, making little whitecaps, and she pulled her scarf up tighter around her mouth. She tried to act casual, as if she were simply on her lunch break checking her messages. A little ways down the sidewalk, a man with a dog on a leash wearing a warm dog sweater approached.

Was he the contact?

He passed behind her and he kept on going, his black lab making little clicking sounds with its toenails as it padded down the sidewalk.

A short, very thin woman with a parka and long, auburn spiral curls spilling out of the hood emerged through the trees and onto the sidewalk. She slid into the end of the bench, and Chelsea's heart jumped.

Was this the contact?

She tried to avoid looking directly. The woman was wearing dress pants and dressy boots under her coat. She wore sunglasses, even though the day was cloudy. Unsure of what to do, Chelsea hunched against the cold and tried to fasten her eyes on the stubby white dome in the foggy mists across the water.

"Mrs. Evans?" the voice on the park bench said.

"Yes!" Her heart raced in her chest. She tried not to turn her head towards the voice, but shaking, she put her hand inside her purse and wrapped it around the gun.

Like her, the small woman faced straight ahead, towards the Memorial. "Your husband, he is a very good man. I am sorry he is missing."

"I know. Thank you." Every conceivable question burned in Chelsea's head. Was this a co-worker? A lawyer?

"When he first met me, he performed a kindness for me and I told him I will not forget it." There was the slightest hint of an accent, something formal about the way the woman talked, that suggested a foreign heritage.

Whoever she was, she was a friend of Josh's. Chelsea let go of the cold metal of the gun and took her hand out of her purse, stuffing it into a pocket to stay warm. "Where do you know Josh from?"

"Do not ask, please. It is not safe."

"OK, tell me what you can."

The woman checked around before speaking. Chelsea slipped a quick look at her. She had Asian features behind the large sunglasses. Was the woman in foreign intelligence service?

"Your husband told me, 'If something ever happens to me, my wife will try to figure the thing out to the end, and then she will work the problem until she finds a solution.' He said if it weren't for your child you should be in CIA too, like him."

In spite of herself, Chelsea smiled at Josh's summation of herself. If she were not so preoccupied with Atalaya and worried about her child's safety, she would love helping Josh even more with cases.

"He said to tell you enough that you can try to find a way."

Chelsea felt a twist of nausea. This was her worst anxiety and it was coming to pass. Josh did not ultimately trust the CIA to locate him if he disappeared.

"Here is what you can know. Omar Al Ghamdi went missing and his employees ran off. Crestedon Global Architectural and Engineering took over the engineering operations. Part of his operation was over an ancient ruin near Babylon Metro, restoring an ancient palace."

So Omar had gone missing? A lightbulb went off and the picture became clearer. Somehow, the mutual friend of her boss, Levi Mizrahi, whom Josh had been trying to recruit as a spy, had disappeared. No wonder Josh had asked her on two occasions if she had heard from him or his wife lately!

"Ok," Chelsea said, struggling to remember what Josh might have said about an ancient ruin. He had mentioned the desert. But wasn't everything desert out there? Wasn't everything probably built on top of an ancient ruin, including the whole city of Babylon Metro?

"During the first Gulf war, there were thousands of treasures taken from Iraq's national museum and never returned, and there were many weapons taken."

Treasures. During their internet chat, Josh had said something about gold. Chelsea's neck began to tingle warningly. So Josh was not casually talking about stories from the Quran when he chatted online. He was giving her clues, in case she ever needed to know.

"They were hidden by Saddam Hussein and later by ISIS, all over the country. Your husband was working on a building where some were hidden during the wars. There are Islamic legends and locals don't like it when people are poking around looking for gold."

Her brow furrowed while her mind assimilated pieces, some of which she knew and some of which she didn't. She thought of the picture of the ziggurat. "That's just part of it," the woman hissed. "Wait, here comes somebody."

Some die-hard lunchtime joggers were approaching from a distance equivalent to two blocks away. They were crazy, it was freezing outside. Some geese swooped in across the icy gray water and gobbled up prey, and she found herself vaguely wondering how polluted the Potomac was and if it ever made geese get sick. The feet jogged behind them and down the sidewalk into the foggy distance.

"So what is the other part of his assignment?" Chelsea asked.

"He found out things that helped connect some dots to larger things that are national security. They pose great danger to the U.S. and its assets and the rest of the world. You can find a private detective in Babylon Metro and ask about the local legends about the gold. Maybe some local Iraqis know where your husband is being held."

"Why should I do that? Can't the CIA do that?"

A gust of wind blew, so cold it paralyzed them and stopped them from talking for a moment. They huddled with their chins down in their coats until it subsided.

"Mrs. Evans, an intelligence agency must not get caught by enemies trying to find someone who is non-official cover. This you know. It is called 'plausible deniability'. They have other avenues they can explore. But you can do this part."

"I can do this part," Chelsea echoed, her mind numb with confusion. Was this woman going to take her in circles, give her so little she would still not know what to do? Here was her own personal Deep Throat, but she didn't even know what to do with this information. How was she going to find a detective in Babylon Metro who would believe some wild tale about a missing architect on a treasure hunt for gold from an Iraqi museum?

They sat without speaking for a bit and then Chelsea said, "When did you last see my husband? Please tell me."

"Right before he left. I can tell you, he was very focused, very sure of what he needed to do."

Of course. Josh would always be. "Please, can you tell me anymore? I promise I will tell no one."

"No." Then the Deep Throat added, "He and I, we made an agreement some years ago. If something happens to one of us, the other will give the family a message. You must never talk about me. It could be a danger for me, and danger to him and many people." The sunglasses face remained resolutely fixed on the Jefferson Memorial, never once turning to look at Chelsea, but from slipping peeks at the profile Chelsea could see a taut wistfulness. The woman held a memory of a debt owed, something she wished to repay. "I must go."

"Thank you," Chelsea said, even though she had no idea how to hire a detective in Iraq. "I know that whatever you did to come here and tell me this, it was hard for you."

The Asian-American woman did not answer. She stood and then turned to go. "Good luck, Mrs. Evans."

Chelsea fought the natural instinct to watch; to follow from a distance behind and to observe the woman's car, try to get a license plate.

But what would be gained by taking any kind of risk that could endanger the Deep Throat? Nothing. She could always message again later and see if the woman would help more.

Liu Chen disappeared down the sidewalk.

A *ncient palace near Babylon Metro…*
 Back in the office at Monument Metroplex after the
 lunch meeting with Deep Throat, and with a closed
door which set off a curious buzz among the highly collaborative
Mizrahi & Associates team members, Chelsea completed an
internet search, pulled up the map of Babylon Metro, zoomed out
and began studying the area.

Outside the city the landscape became gradually more rural.
Occasional buildings dotted the sand, surrounded by broken bits of
walls. The map was labeled "Ancient Babylon" in English and
Arabic, and Chelsea zoomed in closer. It appeared to be some sort
of historical site.

She waited a moment and the screen pulled up some
descriptions: Ancient Babylon tourist destination: the site of the
Tower of Babel; the inspiration of Hammurabi and
Nebuchadnezzar's palace…The delusional and bizarre vision of
rebuilding Ancient Babylon by Saddam Hussein went quickly
down the drain when the American Marines and Polish soldiers
occupied it during the Gulf War.

There was a lot to read with various comments and photos
from tourists around the world. She moved on to another search, a
phrase Deep Throat had used: *Iraq's national museum.*

Fourteen thousand artifacts, including gold from Nimrud's
treasure, every one of them precious, taken when Saddam Hussein
was toppled, only one-third recovered…The antiquities increased
in value when ISIS bulldozed the ancient Assyrian settlement of
Nimrud, destroying hundreds of them.

She called Clinton in California. He had not been in touch
lately, and the time had come to let him know that Josh was
missing. Clinton tried to return her message on web chat, but she
made an excuse and then called him back a few minutes later by
phone, because cameras were just not her thing. "Geez, I was
always afraid Bags was going to end up gone for a Burton."
Clinton said in his British accent. "He's my closest chum, Chels,
and I'll underwrite the cost of an investigator. What kind of
computer equipment does private investigators in Iraq have? Is it
Third World?

"I—uh—I don't know."

"I'll talk to some of the chaps in the Pentagon that contracted for the NoitaLever project. I'll make sure your investigator has the best stuff. I'll get spy software that I can use to monitor your device and his, in case you get a ransom request."

"Oh, Clinton, that is amazing," Chelsea caught her breath. How quick he had been to offer help!

After the routine nightly struggle with Atalaya and her homework, she paced the floor of the kitchen. How much should she tell Kimberly? She probably shouldn't tell the part about the personal note Josh had left her with the operation name, "AuCHFOP" and the mysterious number. And she shouldn't tell Kimberly anything specific about the Deep Throat woman that had met her in the park. She would only tell Kimberly what Deep Throat had said.

She messaged Kimberly that she had further information about Josh's disappearance. Even though it was past 10:00 at night, Kimberly immediately called her. The TV was on in the background, so Kimberly's voice was even louder than normal, talking over the volume. "This is pro bono, I'm not charging you tonight. Tell me about this information you have. Did the CIA call you?"

"No, I can't even tell you, my lawyer, how I got this." Chelsea rapidly spelled out the facts and Kimberly asked, "Explain again what the missing engineer had to do with it?"

"That's what's confusing," Chelsea replied. "Josh recruited him to be a spy, but he went MIA, and Josh went there looking for him. Maybe looking for some other things, too, or some sort of intelligence. There's a historic site or archaeological dig nearby where Josh was working. Some hidden gold and stuff. Josh was working for a cover company, and I got the name—"

"What the hell did you just say to me? Did you say hidden gold?" Chelsea could hear her grab the remote and turn off the TV.

"Saddam Hussein concealed some loot from a museum there. Oh, and Josh's best friend Clinton will pay for a private investigator."

"Okay…Okay!" Kimberly was clearly flabbergasted as she practically inhaled the information. "Now we have some pieces of the puzzle. Let me find the names of some private investigators in

Iraq," she mused, doing a search and pulling up a list. "Ugh. Some of these look pretty sleazy and they can't translate to English very well. But let me do some checking tomorrow. Also, on our spreadsheet, which is getting bigger by the moment, we'll put in a column for each clue you received from your source."

Her mind racing and unable to sleep, Chelsea removed the family pictures and decorations off her bedroom wall next to the desk in the television room on first floor where she did the bills and telecommuted. To the wall she taped a physical map of Babylon Metro and a map of Iraq, filling around them with sticky notes, pictures, bits of email messages, and clues, just like police, FBI, and CIA agents on television did.

It was overwhelming. There was no way she could do this. If the CIA couldn't get to Josh, how in the world could she?

She stood back and tried to admire her work, telling herself that she was taking small bites at a time and managing everything as well as she could, and that he needed her to try.

Atalaya's birthday was next week, she suddenly realized. Atalaya would be turning eight years old. Josh would miss it. Chelsea realized guiltily that she had done nothing about planning a party, inviting little friends over, or getting gifts. Feeling like a lousy mom, she got online and looked for the phone number of a birthday party room. Even though it was the middle of the night, she called and left a message.

Connie, the liaison from Headquarters, called Chelsea to let her know she would be receiving a support call from a former Agency wife. The call came the next day.

"Hello, I'm Brittany Dubois," said the friendly, cultured voice on the other end of the line. "My first husband was CIA. He went missing in Pakistan. Would you like to meet?"

Brittany came over to the house on Saturday, a little after lunch. She was trim and diminutive with short, spiky, dark hair. She shook Chelsea's hand warmly. "So nice to meet you," she said genuinely. "Excuse my clothes. I have a yoga studio and I just got done teaching class. I brought this for you," she said with a winning smile, holding out a box of fine chocolates.

"You didn't have to," Chelsea started to say.

"They are wonderful, you will just die for them. They are from a little shop called Choco-La-Ti-Da, do you know the place? Oh, and who do we have here?" she cooed.

From the hallway, Atalaya peeked at Brittany around the corner and quickly ducked her head back. "That is my daughter. She's in first grade. Yappie, stop barking!" Chelsea commanded.

Brittany bent down on one knee until Atalaya stuck her head back around the corner and came over to her, standing before her wonderingly. It was uncharacteristic of Atalaya to warm up to a stranger.

Chelsea showed Brittany to the kitchen. "I have a middle schooler and a high schooler," Brittany said, keeping up a conversation easily as she climbed up on the bar stool by the island. Brittany lived nearby, right here in McLean, and her husband was a private sector defense contractor worker.

Chelsea poured a cup of coffee, listening. There was something about Brittany's sincere, engaging blue eyes and a melodious warmth in her voice that immediately drew a person in. She was extremely likeable and emotive, nothing like the kind of person Chelsea would have somehow expected the CIA to send over.

There was a bit of a pause, and then Brittany delicately cleared her throat and started into her reason for coming. "When I was young, I was married to the Agency." It was the way CIA wives described life with spouses deeply ensconced in a highly secret organization. "My first husband was SAD." SAD was the Special Activities Division, the CIA's version of Special Ops. "He took a tour in Pakistan. He was on a paramilitary security team to bring men home, and they were on horseback in the mountains. There was a skirmish and he and his horse disappeared. His star is on Memorial Wall at Headquarters. As you know, one or two go on that wall about every other year. There was one that just went up a couple of months ago." Her lips pressed together grimly at the memory. "When things like that happen, I volunteer, I meet with the family and tell my story. In your case, there is still hope."

Chelsea studied the lines around Brittany's mouth and tried to get a fix on her age. Was she older than Chelsea? It was hard to tell. She was in excellent shape and attractive. Chelsea felt self-conscious about her own lack of exercise—her flabby arms, as well as the disproportionately full hips and the little tummy pouch that never went completely away, even though she had lost weight lately.

After her first husband's disappearance, the CIA stayed in contact, Brittany said, and she knew that they were working on her husband's case, but they told her very little. She had to construct yet another fiction for friends who didn't know he was CIA to explain why he wasn't coming home. "I was terrified," she said. "Terrified that I would give something away and endanger him if he was captured, sick with not knowing but just imagining what might have happened to him."

"So what happened? Did they find him?" Chelsea said, hanging on to every word.

"No." A year and a half later, she said, the Agency concluded based on various reports of locals fleeing the area that he could not have possibly made it out alive. "I told friends that it was a car accident overseas and that it took a long time to locate and identify the remains."

Chelsea felt her throat tighten, knowing what this meant: the Agency was sending Brittany to warn her. To lower expectations.

"But here's the thing," Brittany said, leaning forward and touching Chelsea on the arm. Her blue eyes were wide and genuine. "I know it looks bad, but you mustn't give up hope. Ever. You must have hope for him until you get final word otherwise.

Even if you never hear for sure, hope is the kindest thing you can do for him. It may be the only thing you can do for him."

"Did you do your own looking? Did you hire a private detective, or go over there yourself and search?" Chelsea asked.

Brittany's hand dropped from Chelsea's arm onto the table and slid back in her lap, and she sat back straight up in the chair, but she didn't lose eye contact. "I was so young and that would have never occurred to me," she said, shaking her head regretfully. "I didn't know. I didn't have any idea what to do. I trusted that they were investigating it. The other Agency wives felt bad, but to them I was bad luck. I was the embodiment of the thing they were most afraid would happen to them."

"My husband is NOC," Chelsea offered, wondering how much she should say. "When it's nonofficial cover, the Agency denies his affiliation with the U.S. government. They do even less for him and tell me less than they would have done for you and your husband, right? Do I need to try to find him myself, as if he were a private citizen that wandered over there and got lost?"

Brittany's voice dropped to a whisper, as if there was someone from Headquarters in the next room that could overhear. "I know the Agency makes you think they know everything there is to know and they're doing all they can. But if that's what you feel—if that's what's in your heart—then you should do it, without doing anything that might endanger him."

Chelsea felt her stomach do a strange flip of apprehension. She refilled her own cup of coffee. With a spoon she stirred it, watching the milk dissolve in pale white swirls into the brown liquid, thinking to herself that the milk was symbolic of a covert officer's life slowly fading away, not to be heard from for years, or maybe even ever. She wondered how much to tell Brittany about Josh. Was the CIA tacitly giving her permission to confide?

"Tell me about yourself," Brittany urged.

Chelsea had a distinct feeling of trust. She began gingerly but found herself telling about her life in as short a time as she could. Brittany was a wonderful listener and it felt cathartic.

When she concluded Brittany said, "I have the benefit of the rear view mirror, Chelsea. You don't. But what I can tell you is, maybe not now, but someday, it will all work together for the good. In hindsight, I see how my story was written. I eventually found someone and remarried, and we are both very happy together.

Terrible things happen now that you and I can't understand—take for example the church that I go to; there was a shooting a few months ago—do you remember that in the news? I think what it has taught us is that there are really bad actors, right here in NOVA, and we can't overlook them, and it's our job to be alert and take action—"

"You go to Fairfax Community Church too?" It was a congregation with thousands of attendees, so random meetings like this between attendees who had never met occasionally occurred, but today it cemented an instant new bond.

"Oh wow!" Brittany clutched Chelsea's hand. "We can pray together about this! So tell me, what can I do for you? If you are going to do your own search, please let me help you with something."

Chelsea omitted the fact that she had not been to church since the shooting. "I've been researching about what other wives of missing spies and covert agents have done, and I have a lawyer. I know that I need someone to help write letters and call—to the United Nations, to the Baghdad embassy, to the head of the prison system in Iraq, to the Foreign Minister..." her voice trailed meekly. "That's kind of hard. I wouldn't expect anyone--"

"I'll volunteer," Brittany set her chin. "I'll help you. I'll work on it while the boys are doing their homework and going to bed. I'll find names and phone numbers, and I'll figure out what time to call people during the day. You tell me exactly what to say and what not to say, and I'll choose one to call, or one to write to, each day!"

Why would Brittany do this? Her own first husband, by her own account, had passed many years ago.

One thing was becoming clear: friends—and even strangers—rose to meet this kind of crisis, ready to help.

When it was time to go, Brittany held her hand and said a prayer for Josh and gave Chelsea a friendly little hug. "Stay positive. Don't give up hope. And Chelsea, thank you for letting me come and for letting me be a part of your story."

In humble amazement Chelsea watched the unlikely visitor drive away, this angel that the CIA had fortuitously sent to help.

52

The Senate Hearing
Room 215
Hart Senate Office Building, Washington, D.C.

Т he Director of the CIA faced the unfriendly Chair of the Senate Select Intelligence Committee, a senator from Louisiana, who commenced the private meeting with him and the other members of the committee. Her eyes were narrowed and her browed furrowed, for she expected obfuscation or even downright obstruction from this presidential appointee testifying before the committee today. Her voice was grim and cautionary.

"On the matter of the missing American case officer, Joshua David Evans, a member the United States Intelligence Community, and Mr. Omar Al Ghamdi, a Saudi spy for the CIA who was gunned down in Babylon Metro, we are here today in closed session to hear their circumstances. Director, go ahead. Please make your statement."

"Members of the committee, thank you for this opportunity to meet in closed hearing."

No one responded because no one believed he was thankful to be there.

"Let me get directly to the point." The CIA Director rustled his notes and began reading. "While on mission for Operation AuCHFOP, Mr. Evans attended a holiday party at the American Embassy on Christmas evening to which all embassy personnel and American workers were invited. During the party, Mr. Evans received a message that there was a security alarm that had been set off in his Babylon Metro office." The Director gave a little cough and took some water, which of course made everyone uncomfortable.

He continued. "Because Mr. Evans was the only employee in the office remaining for the holidays, he went to investigate. During the course of examining the wiring for the alarm, he abruptly messaged Langley that the mission was compromised. Subsequently we lost contact with him, and his communication device has never been recovered."

"Thank you, Director. Did you question Embassy personnel and the attendees of the holiday party that he attended earlier in the evening?"

"We confirmed with the Chief of Station and parking lot security that Officer Evans left two hours prior to his disappearance for Babylon Metro, which is eighty miles away from Baghdad."

"Director, that appears to be insufficient detective work," accused the Chair. The members of the Senate Select Intelligence Committee from the opposite political party who politically supported the Director immediately made irritated, muttering, partisan noises at her denunciation. "Are you telling me that an American citizen spent the evening at a holiday party in the Embassy in Baghdad, and the CIA failed to do an internal investigation and question embassy staff and guests? Without interviewing them, how could you eliminate the possibility that one of them may have had a motive for his disappearance?"

"Madam Chair, I resent your implication." The Director's eyes narrowed. An angry senator and a partisan majority on the Senate Select Intelligence Committee could very well result in budget cuts to the Agency. "There were nearly two hundred nationals at the party that night. We had neither the manpower nor the budget to find them after the party and to question every last one of them."

The Chair made a little huffing noise like a small steam engine. "We'll talk about your continual requests to increase the CIA budget another time. This alarm wiring that you are referring to. Did it relate to security for the office suite? Or to actual intelligence gathering?"

"I would like to emphasize," replied the Director in a bureaucratic monotone, "that this is closed door session and nothing is to be repeated outside of the doors of this room."

"You do not have to remind us. We are well aware of that," bristled the Chair, her voice icicles.

"Mr. Evans was investigating a security alarm that alerted us to a missing micro-drone. It had been installed by Omar Al Ghamdi, our spy from the mechanical engineering firm who was on site prior to Mr. Evans and who abandoned his mission, which we called 'Operation Fly-on-the-Wall.' The purpose of that operation was to monitor the office suite occupied by a

192

neighboring tenant, Iran Central Industries Group, which allegedly procures nuclear assets from supplier nations. We suspect that workers in the space that night saw Mr. Evans, became suspicious, and tipped off Iraqi police."

"So Mr. Evans and Mr. Al Ghamdi were involved in two dangerous missions when they were under your supervision?"

"That is true of Mr. Al Ghamdi. However, Mr. Evans was not directly involved in the investigation of Iran Central Industries Group or Iran's nuclear capabilities. He was only given information about that mission on a need-to-know basis."

"Director, don't you agree that Mr. Evans needed to know that he was chasing an electrical problem relating to a rogue nation secretly developing a nuclear weapon? It seems like maybe you should have told him that!"

"It was an aside to Mr. Evans's main responsibilities. His operation was to oversee a rehabilitation project designed to camouflage our true mission: to as quickly as possible remove antiquities and classified substances from an ancient subterranean passageway that had been stolen from the Iraqi people and smuggled in there by Saddam Hussein's army."

There was a stunned silence as the members of the Committee processed this new information. The Chair did not attempt to disguise her disdain for the man standing before them. "Director, Committee Leadership requests an explanation of why you sent vulnerable members of the Intelligence Community to tamper with local antiquities in a country occupied by China and which has experienced deliberately diminishing American security presence and resources? No matter how noble your intentions of returning valuables stolen by Saddam Hussein's army, this is a trite mission that was clearly a violation of U.N. peace treaty!"

"Let me explain the underlying reasons for Mr. Evans's mission, which cannot be made known to the public without great embarrassment to our country. I will provide you with Exhibit A." The Director passed an exhibit with blurry photos and captions describing the photos to the members of the committee. "We suspected that the antiquities were cached with the classified materials you see in these photographs, the existence of which might prove humiliating to the United States, both politically stateside, as well as diplomatically with China."

193

The papers rustled as the committee members viewed the photos. At first the room was totally hushed with only the rattling of pages. Then, in whispers and low voices punctuated by an occasional hiss, the partisan committee members began quarreling with each other.

Her face pink with fury, the Chair lambasted the Director. "What evidence do you have that this is what these papers claim it is? Reliable intelligence has consistently failed to corroborate the existence of this! Was this mission yet another witch hunt that was politically motivated by CIA operatives?"

"Let me remind Madam Vice Chairman," growled the Vice Chairman, a senator from South Dakota, "that it is unseemly to question the patriotism of our Intelligence Community. It should be obvious that even if the preposterous suggestion that this mission was politically motivated were true, there is no benefit to American-Chinese diplomatic relations for any of this to become public."

"Very well, I will allow the Director to speak to the question of origination of these photos," replied the Chair coldly.

The Director replied, "These photos were taken by Mr. Evans and his team on the day they discovered the antiquities and were immediately sent to Langley. The location of the classified substances was confirmed by our Counter Proliferations Weapons Intelligence team. The mission was turned over to a select group of CIA paramilitary officers, who began making plans to remove them quietly. Unfortunately, Mr. Evans was abducted, and the archeological excavation site above was cordoned off by Chinese authorities before we could send in the paramilitary team."

The Chairman managed, "I would like to state for the record that despite my suspicions and doubts about the nature of the evidence you have presented to us in Exhibit A today, and despite the problems this committee has had with you, Director, I have strong support for the rank and file members of the United States Intelligence community and their service to our country." Her statement left no uncertainty about what she thought of the CIA leadership. "Now, let's move on to a full explanation from you on the assassination of our asset, Omar Al Ghamdi."

53
Going Rogue

It was almost no surprise to Chelsea that Brittany clicked so well. Brittany had magnetism, amiability, and a soft persuasion that perfectly complimented Kimberly's loud assertiveness, wry and dark sense of humor, and general overall ability to suck the air out of the room. They were eating a little Saturday luncheon at Chelsea's house where the three of them met together to talk about the best way to contact government officials for help and figure out how to pick out a private investigator from thousands of miles away.

"You need to take charge of this thing," Kimberly told Chelsea flatly. "I've got nothing. The State Department sends me around all over the place. There's a lot of sympathy but nothing back from our elected representatives. You need to be the one to get out there absolutely everywhere and raise a stink."

"I don't know. I just don't know about this," Chelsea protested. "This is the CIA we're talking about. How rogue should we go? I could get in trouble."

"The CIA is so, so big," Brittany said, the pupils in her pretty blue eyes growing as large as her words. "There are good people there. There are inept people. You know this." Brittany gracefully immersed herself into the conversation in various ways, asking questions, offering to help in whatever way she could.

On Monday Brittany started making phone calls and leaving messages for some of the Washington, D.C., government agencies listed on the spreadsheet, and even some officials in Iraq. Why, Chelsea wondered, was Brittany so interested in helping? Didn't she want to move on with her life? Regardless, the help was very welcome.

Josh's best friend Clinton worked frequently with someone in the Pentagon who knew someone who could do private investigation work in Iraq. He was a retired policeman with a reputable private investigation firm based out of Baghdad. Chelsea and Kimberly interviewed him using web chat. "The Chinese keep the secrets very strong, yes? They hire the young Iraqi men. China pay good money and take them to camps and indoctrinate them, teach them the Chinese, demand loyalty. We can only break their silence if we find a local who wants much money, who takes a bribe."

"Do you know someone we can bribe?" Kimberly did not hesitate for a moment to take the bait.

"This is the challenge. Our firm will make a website and you will raise this money. You need lots of money—a million dollars. We will advertise missing person everywhere."

After the conversation was over, Chelsea sat hunched over in her desk chair, her stomach churning weird gastric juices that burned, her eyes squeezed shut, rubbing her sore head while the voices inside it argued with each other. *A million dollars? There were lots of rich people inside the Beltway, but how was someone like her going to get a million dollars out of them?...*

"The eighty-twenty rule," was Kimberly's virtually unconcerned advice, as if this should be obvious. "One big donor and lots and lots of little ones."

This would be the biggest favor she had ever called in to Josh's best friend, Clinton....

Clinton was still like family, but the fact remained, he wasn't around anymore.

He had always been eccentric, kind of a lone ranger.

What would his new wife think about him putting up most of a million dollars?

Clinton's wife may or may might not approve, but Josh was the person with whom Clinton had the history.

When it came to Josh, the friendship had always meant everything. Everything.

Here goes...

She nervously combed her hair, freshened her lipstick, and logged back onto the web. She really hated cameras of any kind and usually avoided them whenever possible. Clinton popped up onto the screen. "Cheers, Chels. Got some news?"

"Clinton," she said straightforwardly and logically, "Meet my attorney, Kimberly Feldman. We've received the best advice possible from the private investigator you recommended. You're the only person I know that can help me come up with a million dollars for a reward." She felt her heart hammer.

Clinton's expression rarely changed, it was usually stoic, but he blinked in surprise backed away into his office chair. "Uh, how much do you think you could raise from the website or on your own?"

"I—I don't know. A hundred or two hundred thousand, maybe? We'll put out an appeal nationwide but honestly, I don't have any idea how much I can raise. I can take out the equity in the house. Or you can just have our house."

His eyes darted around. A nervous palm rubbed his receding hairline, prominent because it was in a ponytail, and he rubbed his forehead nervously. Then he spoke: "I'm in. Don't worry about the house. I'll figure out a way to contribute the reward money."

It was a victory! Clinton had done what she wanted! She had persuaded him! Maybe since he was remarried and happy once again, he had a burst of open-minded generosity....

The next day, she signed a contract with the private investigator, and she and Kimberly made another conference call to Iraq with all the information they had put together and questions for the investigator. They came to their final point. "Tell us about the Islamic prophecies that refer to gold being discovered in the Euphrates. My husband was there trying to locate and return some antiquities to the Iraqi people that were stolen during the wars by ISIS or Saddam Hussein," Chelsea requested of the investigator.

"Allah's messenger—peace be upon him—said that there will be a fight, and ninety-nine out of a hundred will die! This is very bad!" snapped the P.I. urgently. His voice rose to a high pitch. "Whoever sees it should not take anything from it!"

She and Kimberly had evidently stumbled into some sort of religious and cultural minefield. "Mrs. Evans's husband disappeared in Babylon Metro," Kimberly ventured, taken aback at his tone. "When the Hadith talks about gold in the Euphrates, do the local Iraqis believe it refers to this part of Iraq?"

"Only Allah knows! These are matters belonging to the Unseen Things! We are not to know!" the P.I. scolded over the phone line. "Your husband, he involved in something dangerous!"

Chelsea rolled her eyes. Of course Josh was involved in something dangerous. That was the whole reason for hiring a P.I. The question suggested by Deep Throat had apparently invited a religious rant.

Clinton arranged for brand new state-of-the-art equipment to be shipped to the private investigator. Unbeknownst to the investigator, the new computer had monitoring software on it.

Clinton showed it to Chelsea on webcam. "I can see what's on his screen. I can make sure he's not screwing with you, and I can see the information about Bags that flows to him. I can install this monitoring software on your devices, too, so I can watch messages coming in from people who might try to claim reward money."

They juggled getting approval from the CIA (which seemed impossible; no one said no as long as Josh's association with the Agency remained a secret, but no one seemed to have the power to give a definitive yes). Kimberly located an international publicity firm to create a multi-language website and social media campaign for Josh, one that would track all inquiries and forward any possible leads to the private investigator.

Using the photo of the office mega-plex on the encryption device, and associated real estate records on the property that Chelsea had been able to locate, plus the photo of the ziggurat, the private investigator pinpointed the name of the company Josh had been working for and the exact spot at the archaeological site in Ancient Babylon! "The company called Pyramids and Palaces Architectural Renovation. Is a cover non-profit firm created by the State Department. My informant in building permits say he used to be excavating at Saddam's palace, in the kitchen. But company shut down. No one can go there, the Chinese occupiers have it sealed off." The Tomorrow Globe Financial Center offices were an even more secure fortress—the private investigator could get no information from security, delivery men, or anybody.

Chelsea immediately began searching online again. There wasn't mention of a kitchen in the comments online—probably because it was under excavation—but tourists from many countries had posted many photos and comments about visiting the palace. She printed and cut out the pictures and taped them together, trying to re-create the floor plan of the palace by bits.

She tried to make sense of the clues: Renovating a kitchen in Saddam Hussein's palace. Missing artifacts. A fake business created by the State Department and run by Crestedon.

Slowly the facts emerged more clearly. She wanted to call the Chinese real estate company and ask them about the space vacated by Pyramids and Palaces Architectural Renovation. She wanted to get the private investigator into that office building space to look for clues that the CIA might have missed while hastily closing down the office! But how could she manage something like that?

What if it somehow blew the CIA cover for the remaining employees?

What she needed was help from a commercial real estate company that was impressive enough to crack open a door with the Chinese real estate company. A global firm that could call and make an enquiry about Pyramids and Palaces Architectural Renovation's vacant space and tell them they had a client wanting to view office space. A firm like the one she used to work at when she and Josh first eloped: Goldberger Hewitt!

She dialed an old friend at the London office, her pulse racing and her energy surging once again. She and Priya kept in touch somewhat on social networking but hadn't actually talked to each other in years.

"Chelsea! How are you?" the cultivated, friendly British voice greeted her.

"I'm trying to make connections in Iraq. My husband went missing in Babylon Metro. I need someone to get my private investigator inside his office space, which has been vacated, to look for clues. But Priya, you cannot share this information with anyone."

Priya was shocked and saddened, but reluctant to get involved. "I am not too sure about this," she replied worriedly. "I must consider it tonight. I promise I will call and give you my decision tomorrow."

Chelsea disconnected, discouraged. Who could blame Priya for being reluctant? Priya was an expat who just wanted to do her job and move up in the company.

The next day Priya called her back. "I have taken a decision, Chelsea. I will help you in the best way I can."

Chelsea's heart hammered with excitement. She, an average, a run-of-the-mill CIA wife, was making headway, all by herself, without any help from the Agency. She made a fist and silently and exuberantly punched the air above the desk.

They launched the website, www.FreeJoshEvans.com. The CIA approved the website, which was very simple and gave no more information than what she knew from the very beginning: Josh Evans, an architect at Crestedon Architectural and Engineering, had disappeared in Babylon Metro on Christmas night. It had a couple pictures of him: a professional business photo, and one of him hugging his daughter that didn't show her face.

Immediately she heard from friends in D.C., their hometown, and places around the country. Calls came from the media to Kimberly's office: first, a local television reporter from the ABC affiliate, then Washington, D.C. news organizations. The next day Reuters called, and a few hours later none other than Angela Stevens Giordano from *Good Morning America*, who tracked down Chelsea personally on Chelsea's cell phone.

"I'm very sorry to hear about your husband's disappearance. You and I have some ties, don't we? I remember that you and your husband are from the same hometown as my husband—Governor Tony Giordano—and Vice President Russo," she said in her attack-dog-disguised-as-smooth news reporter voice. "I remember my interview with you nearly a decade ago after the church bombing by the Muslim extremist group in London. I'd like to have you as my guest on *Good Morning America with Milo and Giordano* and help get Josh's story out."

Chelsea's mouth was dry with awe. "Oh!" she gasped. Tony Giordano's wife was calling personally for an interview! Her answer spilled out inelegantly: "I watch *Good Morning America* every day—well, almost every day...I know you and Tony—I mean, I used to know Tony—yes, I remember you...." She felt her face burn with embarrassment.

If Angela Stevens Giordano knew and remembered Chelsea's past with Tony Giordano, she did not acknowledge it. "Hold on, let me get my assistant, and we'll arrange for a flight and transportation for you to our Times Square studios."

Chelsea made choking sounds and managed some words something like, "Let me call you back." Terrified, she called Kimberly.

"Do it," Kimberly urged without any hesitation.

"I can't go through with it. I hate cameras."

"Just do it. You'll be ok."

"Can't you do it for me? They could fly you up there."

"I have to be in court every day this week. You can do it, Chelsea. You have to do it for Josh."

It was like something in a strange dream. Kimberly kept Atalaya at her house overnight and drove the kids to school and back. Chelsea flew non-stop from Ronald Reagan National Airport that evening. As she sat in the plane, she thought about how she used to play NoitaLever whenever she had to sit and wait. She had abruptly stopped when Josh disappeared. Everything about it only served to painfully remind her that Josh had provided Clinton the contacts in order to secure the government contract and develop the game.

GMA put her up in The Chatwal. The sexy movie star, Tyler Tischner and his noisy entourage, were on the same floor. She saw him coming back from the gym in his shorts, accompanied by two security guards, his buff arms wiping the sweat from the back of his neck with a white towel. He carelessly tossed an empty plastic water bottle onto the carpet of the hotel lobby, which was rather strange since he was such an environmentalist advocate. She was too self-conscious and nervous about tomorrow morning's interview to ask him for an autograph. She practiced several potential responses to interview questions and slept poorly, waking up several times in the night.

The studio was surreal with its make-up artists, producers, cords and mics, bright lights, and audience members gawking. She watched Tyler Tischner being escorted down the narrow hall outside her green room, and he and his entourage were placed in the green room next to her. Once again, he and his security guards and staff were very, very loud.

A harried staff member with a clipboard whisked her into the studio. She was so alone! As she sat down on the stiff little interviewee chair, the makeup people touched up Milo and Giordano. The live audience was unnerving. Her stomach burned with fear. She felt like she might pass out from having to do public speaking.

The cameras rolled and the questions began. Out of the corner of her eye, she could see that *GMA* had posted family pictures of her and Josh and Atalaya on the screen.

"So Mr. Evans was an architect with Crestedon Global Architectural and Engineering on a renovation job for a historic site, correct?" Angela questioned.

"Yes." Her mouth was dry and she swallowed and licked her lips.

"It says he was first reported missing the evening of Christmas, yet you waited to create the website and alert the press until now?"

There was a brief flash of shock that she was being thrown a hardball question so soon. She took a deep breath, hoping she was as convincing a liar as Josh often needed to be in order to protect his identity. "Well, when you have a spouse that works overseas a lot, it's not unusual for some time to go by. Then it took us a while to try to work with Iraqi and Chinese authorities and piece together what had happened…language barriers, interpreters…you know how that goes."

There was a slight pause and Angela leaned forward, squinting her eyes reminiscent of a Diane Sawyer-esque way, as if Angela did not, in fact, know how that went. "Help me understand something. I read in another place that your husband worked for a company called Pyramids and Palaces Architectural Renovation. Which one is correct?"

Chelsea felt the back of her neck break into a sweat as she stared back at the composed, heavily made-up face across from her. Angela Stevens Giordano had done her homework! The State Department had done a lousy job of hiding its connections to Pyramids and Palaces Architectural Renovation—not only had Chelsea's own private investigator uncovered it, but so had the press! This was perilously close to CIA secrets! "I don't know, uh, there's some connection there but I really can't say…"

"So are you saying you don't know what company your husband was working for?" The skepticism in Angela's voice was polite.

If only Kimberly had been able to come and help!

This is for Josh. It has nothing to do with me or how nervous I am, Chelsea thought wildly, trying to stay calm. A memory flashed through her mind, a tip she had heard years ago: *pretend you are in a plexi-glass box. No reporter, no camera man, no audience member, can hurt you in there…..*

Chelsea took a deep breath, envisioning the plexi-glass box safely ensconcing her from Angela's dangerous questions. She managed to look straight into the camera, with its frightening red light, and suddenly she felt an adrenalin rush. She pushed forward bravely and forcefully. "Please, we just want Josh to come home! If anyone has any information about my husband, or wishes to contribute to the reward fund, contact our website."

The strength in her appeal made Angela back off to give her the floor. Somehow she made it through the interview and was escorted back to her little green room. A staff person handed her a juice drink, and she sipped it, watching the follow-up interview with Tyler Tischner on the monitor.

"Good morning, Mr. Tischner, your new movie *Avenging Conspiracy* is coming out. Give us a sneak preview."

"Yes! But first, before you play that clip, let me just say that I saw that last segment, and what a wonderful, warm person Mrs. Evans is! When we were backstage, I wished her the best. She is a very lovely and brave person."

Chelsea sat with her mouth hanging open in astonishment. Tyler Tischner never spoke a single word to her, or even looked her way! They weren't even in the same green room! She frantically began messaging Kimberly.

Tyler Tischner barreled on. "As you know, Angela, my activist group, Hollywood for Humanitarianism, is opposed to China's so-called peacekeeping efforts in Iraq."

"It could be that an Iraqi extremist group has Mr. Evans. We don't know for sure that the Chinese—"

"China is a repressive society that is destroying the environment and violating human rights. People disappear in China all the time. I urge them to free Josh Evans. All of the Iraqi people need to break the yoke of the Chinese and set themselves free!"

"Freedom in the Middle East is a broader topic of discussion. Wouldn't you agree, Mr. Tischner, that there really is no economic power other than China with a military large enough to keep a lid on the boiling pot? Wouldn't you agree—" Angela leaned forward on her elbows with that puzzled Diane Sawyer-esque squint— "wouldn't you agree, Mr. Tischner, that the Chinese don't really want to be in the peacekeeping business, but they reluctantly recognize, as do most civilized countries, the threat of Islamic extremism?"

"They could snap their fingers and tell the Iraqis to release him. What do any of them want with a guy like him? Americans and Jews are being fooled. All the Chinese really care about is money and oil."

But Angela, unable to get Tischner to say anything notably stupid in this interview, seemed interested in wrapping up the segment. "Tyler Tischner, spokesman for Hollywood For Humanitarianism, thank you for being with us this morning. And by the way, when does your movie, 'Avenging Conspiracy', open?"

By the time Chelsea got back home, donations—many small, and even a few larger ones, had begun coming in. She scanned through the list of names of donors the publicity company sent over and stopped in surprise at one.

Antonio Giordano Personal Account $5,000.00

Tony Giordano…the husband to Angela Stevens Giordano on *Good Morning America*…A man from her past who Josh personally disliked, but nonetheless, respected. It was neither a large amount nor a small amount, but it was an incredible gesture. What if his media wife, associated with a donation to an interviewee, was accused of being biased?

She stared at the name and the amount for a moment, and then absently looked out the window, thinking and remembering. She pulled up a search. A video loaded, Governor Giordano's most recent speech; it was to some national governor's conference or something. He was wearing a tuxedo and addressing a formal dinner. She studied his face in the video. It was older and heavier with more lines now, of course, and like most ambitious middle-aged politicians he died his hair a more youthful color that didn't cover all the gray; but he was still devastatingly handsome.

"We should not and cannot settle for second place to China on the world stage. We must not resign ourselves to simply managing decline." His voice was controlled, authoritative, ringing out over the room with its clinking glasses and silverware.

His fingers began lightly brushing her shoulder blades. "You and I are a good team. And it would be easier to schedule in this. You would be right there and I could get you whenever I wanted you." His hand moved down her hip and began massaging the inside of her thigh.

A decade later, the memory still made her blush.

"America can and will regain its place at the head table. It begins with each and every city, believing that it is the best and the greatest and the strongest. And then each county, and finally each state, striving to be the best that it can be, and at the same time, working together with other cities and counties and states resolved to be the best they can be." The governor was compelling, persuasive.

"The place you are and the place I'm in are two very different places. I'm in a different stage of life. I'm on an eighteen to twenty hour a day schedule. I can't be what you need right now at this point in your life."

As fast as it had started with Tony Giordano, it had been over....

"We must not stop—we shall not stop!—until the day dawns where once again, the United fifty States are the best, the greatest, and the strongest!"

The governors broke out into applause. Tony Giordano was competent, focused, and forceful. Indeed, he was presidential.

The next morning after the website had been launched, there was a ping in Chelsea's inbox at her offices at Mizrahi & Associates. Curiously she clicked open a message from an old friend in London, Pastor Thorpe.

Joshie messaged me before he went missing. I may have information that could be helpful. Please advise as to a chat time.

There was six hours' time difference. Pastor Thorpe was still working in his church office for the day. She closed her office door (which she knew would send everyone in the friendly, collaborative Mizrahi and Associates office into yet another inquisitive ferment). Rather than chat online and feel self-conscious about how dorky she looked on camera, she called him. A warm feeling settled over her as she heard the familiar friend's British accent—he was the minister at the small Baptist church they attended in London when they eloped.

"I am so sorry, Chelsea," Pastor Thorpe said. "My heart breaks at the thought of Joshie gone missing." Friends in London always called Josh by the nickname. "I'd like to share with you a conversation we had a few weeks ago."

"Where was he when he talked to you?"

"I don't know. But he called to sort out a couple of prophecies in the book of Revelation. He wanted to know if they referred to nuclear assets."

Did Pastor Thorpe know that Josh worked for the CIA? "Which prophecies?" she asked, grabbing a pen to take notes.

"Revelation 9 and Revelation 18. Let me give you a little background. The prophecy states that two hundred thousand troops will gather, and a third of mankind will be killed in the area of the Euphrates River. The city of Babylon is described as violent, in the business of slaughtering people who are religious. It is suddenly and violently destroyed by smoke and burning, and the prophecy says merchants who were some of the world's most important people will mourn because no one will buy their cargoes of goods anymore. From the detailed description and the massive amount of casualties, scholars have assumed for a number of years that the prophecy refers to nuclear war that causes huge economic devastation."

Had Josh been obsessing, overly immersed in the constant barrage of depressing intel coming in from the Middle East?

"Josh wanted my opinion as to whether it might be Iran that will launch such a weapon," Pastor Thorpe told her.

Most ministers did not talk about Biblical prophecies, believing them to be allegorical, or something that had already happened in the past. Clearly, Pastor Thorpe was in a minority camp of theologians who believed the prophecies were literal and would happen in the future.

"So let me get this straight," Chelsea said. "The writings predict a war by the Euphrates River, and they predict the bombing of Babylon, but they don't say which countries are involved?"

"Keep in mind the prophecies were written in the first century A.D. The countries had different names and different borders when it was written," Pastor Thorpe explained. "The prophecy says the Euphrates River will dry up so much that armies from the east could pass through on foot. It's long been thought that to get to those numbers of soldiers, you'd have to have China involved. Also, we do know that the Euphrates flows through three countries: present-day Turkey, Syria, and Iraq. We know this is the general area where the bomb goes off."

She desperately needed maps and instantly regretted she didn't chat online so he could show her what he was talking about. "So you told Josh," she said, taking notes as fast as she could, "that Turkey, Syria, or Iraq might set off a nuclear weapon?"

"The problem, I told Josh, is that ANY country in the world could launch a nuclear weapon. The prophecy doesn't say which one. We just know generally speaking where the nuclear weapon is going to LAND."

Pastor Thorpe told her it had been a brief conversation with little chit-chat. "That's how Joshie's always been. He would ring me up and ask me a cryptic question, and that was that."

Pastor Thorpe wished her the best and prayed with her, but when she disconnected, she was so uneasy and chilled that she left the office and power walked at the hotel shopping center to warm up and reduce her nervous energy.

Did Josh have intel about nuclear weapon development? Passing by racks of clothes and shoes and vendors opening their carts for the day, she shuddered, thinking about what the minister had said, bits and pieces she had picked up from Josh, and what she knew of international news. Why did ancient writers who lived two thousand years ago write something so amazingly specific about something that appeared to be happening today?

Angela Stevens Giordano on Good Morning America often said that Iran, one of the world's largest exporters of terrorism, had been a bad actor for decades, defying treaties. Turkey had become increasingly anti-western. Syria figured prominently in Islamic prophecy. Was Josh now a prisoner in the very land with the prophetic bulls-eye?

She decided to call the P.I. and tell him what she had heard, but he was confused by the Christian prophecy and didn't seem to know what to do with the information, and he went off on her with another rant. "Iran have nuclear capability! North Korea! Pakistan! You name me one country with nuclear capability, I name you one country too. You name me another country, I have another country for you, see? They get supply from other countries who have nuclear development materials...."

She went to her computer and found a map of the Middle East and Asia with the countries that Pastor Thorpe had mentioned. She printed it out and taped it up on the wall with the other clues. She stood back and looked at her work. Her arms fell to her side, physically tired, and her heart felt equally heavy. There were secret burdens that her husband and the other brave CIA employees bore daily that were chilling and massively weighty.

"I—I'm sorry, Chels, I just can't see my way to fund the million." The British accent droned hollowly in Chelsea's ears and the room swayed.

"What do you mean? We've already started advertising the reward!"

"Nobody's found him yet, Chels, there's some time—"

As Clinton Radcliffe pulled the plug on funding for Josh, it was as if the bottom had dropped out of her life and she had plunged to the depths of a pit. How could Josh's best friend and his wife do this to them? Clinton and Jennifer were multi-millionaires; and yes, this was a lot of money, but they had it to spare!

"You can have our house. I'll just turn the title over to you. You can own one house in San Francisco and another house in D.C."

"No, that's ok, Jennifer doesn't want the house, and you have to live somewhere. Talk to some of your rich real estate clients. There's a few venture capitalists I could speak to."

She tried to imagine Clinton pitching a plea for reward money to Californians who hardly knew him, and who could be told nothing more than that Josh was an architect friend missing in Iraq. "I understand, Clinton, you've expended a lot of money on this search for Josh already. I'll—I'll find a way." Somehow she got the words out, unable to hide her shock.

She disconnected and threw her head over her knees, hugging them tightly to her chest. She should have known it had been too easy. You didn't just call a friend and get that kind of money, no matter how close you thought you were.

Somehow, Jennifer, who had never even seen their lovely Georgian-style house, had persuaded Clinton to contribute exactly zero to the reward fund.

What was she going to do? She would have to figure out how to raise the money. Most of a million dollars! She did the math on her assets and started thinking of people.

Mr. Mizrahi and some of his partners and business associates. Josh's parents back in Columbia.

Some of her current and previous clients, such as Dawn Lewis-Garcia in Las Vegas, who owned an international chain of water parks that Josh had helped design. Dawn had always been immensely fond of Josh.

Clinton, and even his mysterious wife, couldn't possibly be so heartless as to offer zero funds towards a reward! Surely she could persuade them to contribute at last some money.

She logged onto the computer and reserved flights to San Francisco, as well as Vegas and Columbia. She reserved flights for two. If it took bringing her child along to convince Clinton and other donors to raise the funds to find Josh, that's exactly what she would do.

"**O**h my goodness!" Levi Mizrahi dabbed his red-rimmed eyes with a handkerchief and blew his nose loudly after hearing Chelsea's presentation. "I am so sorry to hear about our Josh! What are we going to do to find him? Damn those bomb-builder, jacker, whacky Iraqis!"

Chelsea nearly choked on the glass of water she was drinking at fundraising lunch with her boss in the first floor restaurant of the Shangri-La Hotel in Monument Metroplex. "Uh, Mr. Mizrahi, I don't know for sure that it was the Iraqis. The Chinese could have kidnapped Josh."

"Oh, heavens, no. What would the Chinese want with him? He's just an architect out in the desert on an archeological dig! The Chinese don't have time to pay attention to a ghost guy in Haji-land. They're too busy lending me money for low interest so I can invest in malls." Mr. Mizrahi waved his hand dismissively in his usual racially characteristic way of categorizing individuals and nations into stringent categories of either good or evil. "The Chinese are being good to the Jews lately. My best friend in Tel Aviv—you remember Moshe, don't you?—Moshe says they're going to ally with Israel and guarantee military protection!"

"The Chinese claim to be neutral but they're still hacking our computers," Chelsea contended darkly, glancing nervously around to see if anyone dining next to them had heard the thick, East coast accent spouting out its racial epithets. Then she reminded herself that she should not argue when she was fundraising.

"Humph, that's not the Chinese government doing the hacking, those are rogue groups. At any rate, yes dear, I will help you. Let me talk to Miriam. We can cut a few corners here and there. Let me see if she will agree to $50,000.

"Oh, that's wonderful!" Chelsea's eyes shone. "I may need time off here and there to fundraise and to work leads."

"You take all the time off you need, my dear. Don't worry about a thing."

She took another deep breath. "Do you have any business partners with money who would be interested in helping?" she bravely persisted.

"Sure, sure, let me put you in touch," Mr. Mizrahi answered vaguely, and then in a typical streak of attention deficit disorder he got off subject talking about one of his rich business partners whose sailboat had an unfortunate encounter with a hump-backed whale heat run off the coast of Maine.

As he talked on and on, she realized that actually this was the hand of God, and the reason she had not been allowed to get another job with another real estate company. The work relationship with Levi Mizrahi would provide her the money, and perhaps even more importantly, the time, to do what had to be done to find Josh.

Every day she made fundraising calls to their circle of friends in Washington, a few powerful ones who politely dodged her request for large donations, and mostly not-so-powerful ones who could only donate smaller amounts. She called businesses. She called foundations.

Brittany had an idea. "Go to your hometown. Call people that you and Josh knew when you were growing up. Have a rally to raise money for Josh."

Back to Columbia? They hadn't been back there for three years. It was better not to have to dodge questions about Josh's job and the CIA lie they lived. She had evolved over time and it was a place she had tried to move on from and forget about. Sure, she had grown up there. She had met Josh and adopted her child in Columbia. But there were a lot of things she preferred to forget: Columbia's small, parochial attitude and its liberal, college-town quirkiness which was, as Josh put it, "eighty-five square miles of idealism surrounded by reality." It was there she met her first husband, the childish and emotional Scooter, who was eventually killed in a motorcycle accident; after that were years of being unhappily single, and then the scandal with now-Governor Tony Giordano; then a tornado hit the city and changed its skyline and its personality; it was in Columbia she was fired from her job and had to start her own real estate company. Their families were back there, but usually they convinced their families to be tourists and to come to Washington, D.C.

A rally wouldn't be for herself. It would be for Josh. A lot of people from Columbia remembered him and liked him.

She called her sister, Kendra, who was an alderwoman on the town council. Kendra immediately said, "That's an awesome idea, sis! I'll help you with it!"

Each night after work, Chelsea contacted friends in the database from Columbia and invited them to the event. Kendra found a local non-profit that agreed to help organize.

She brought Atalaya with her on the whirlwind fundraising trip with strict instructions that if Atalaya was very, very good on this trip, she would go to Chuck E. Cheese for an entire day when she came back. They flew into Columbia, with its ridiculously tiny airport located in the industrial research park where Clinton had grown his company before he abandoned Columbia for Silicon Valley. It was March but winter had dragged on endlessly. A dusting of fresh snow was falling down, conveniently covering a dirty layer of mud. In the rental car, she and Atalaya wound their way north along the river past downtown, which had rebuilt after the tornado, to the freeway loop with its auto malls; then west past the mall and office park where she used to work; then northwest of town to the Evans acreage, with its picturesque evergreens and its black shutters against white paint and windows with tiny panes of glass.

Visits with Josh's mother were always uncomfortable, and on trips to Columbia, they never stayed at the Evans home overnight. But this trip was different. Chelsea was going to ask them for a tremendous amount of money. In exchange they would get to spend more time with their granddaughter. At the round kitchen table that night, drinking milk and eating cookies with Josh's parents, and large flakes of damp snow slapping against the windows, she laid out the private investigator's recommendations.

"I completely believe," the tiny silvery-auburn haired woman sitting across from her stated ominously, pulling her bathrobe tight around her, "that the CIA knows whether he is dead or if he is alive. They have probably known the answer to this for a long time. If he is alive, they probably know where he is, and they have probably examined alternatives to get him out."

"But he's NOC," Chelsea tried to explain. "They have to deny that he's CIA. They can't—"

Judge Mary Duncan-Evans cut her off, her gaze piercing. "I am questioning the wisdom of mortgaging our home, which is fully

213

paid off, when in fact they may know exactly where he is or was." On Josh's face, freckles were cute; on his mother's face, freckles looked like angry age spots.

Chelsea bristled with irritation and fought back a retort. If the judge was like Clinton's wife, she would stand in the way of raising a large amount of the money needed. If only they weren't staunch Baptists and Chelsea could drink to get through this house visit. "I think I'll go to bed early," she said, and she got up from the kitchen and made her way to the spare bedroom with the twin beds that Josh and Jake slept in when they were little boys, and where Atalaya had already turned in for the night.

Later she heard a soft tapping on the door. Dr. Evans stood in the hallway in a bathrobe, the night light behind him casting a glow against the white paint of the hallway wall. His hair was thatch and more gray than had been on the last trip, and his eyebrows were bushier. "Leave Mary to me. I'll contribute to the reward," he said. "There is value in the house, and there's also value in my businesses."

The next day, a gloomy, gray, windy Saturday, was the noon rally. Atalaya whined about the icy slush and mud. Chelsea didn't want to be in Columbia remembering things she would just as soon forget. But this needed to be done.

The rally was held at the A Pizza Me restaurant and takeout on the Riverfront. A Pizza Me's Thick Crust Pepperoni Pizza was Josh's favorite, and on the rare times they went back to Columbia, he flew pies back to McLean on dry ice. The pizza joint was located just three blocks away from Riverfront Views Plaza, the brownstone where they lived in the first years of their marriage, with its immense windows that overlooked the street and the park along the Riverfront. As the doors to the party room opened to the public that afternoon with its red and white checked tablecloths and kerosene lamps casting a soft glow against the wood walls, and as her old friends blew in with gusts of wind, her reluctance to re-visit her painful past dissolved with the late winter snowflakes.

Atalaya's birth grandfather, Hector, was first in line. The tornado killed Hector's wife and nearly destroyed his business, "but I made it through and I have two restaurants now!" he exclaimed to Chelsea proudly. Atalaya was a lot shyer than she had been when she was younger, and Chelsea could tell it hurt Hector.

214

Surely Hector did not have much to give, and he slipped her a money clip with cash.

Energetic Christopher Durante slapped her on the shoulder. "I brought you a check, Chelsea," he said, handing it to her, two red spots of pride burning on his cheeks. "You sold me your real estate business, and it's doing just great! We're holding our own just fine against the Goldberger Hewitt guys!" Christopher used to work for then-Mayor Tony Giordano in economic development. She had sold her little boutique commercial real estate business to him when Mayor Giordano became Governor Giordano and when Josh graduated from candidate training at The Farm. Steady, reliable Robb Beaver, the former firefighter who had left public service to work in real estate, and property manager Jacqui Wells, who moonlighted as a gospel recording artist, came with Christopher. Chelsea slipped open the envelope from Christopher and peeked. It was for five thousand dollars, from such a tiny little company. She was deeply touched.

She held out her hands to the man next in line. "Aww, Scott Dane!" He was nearly bald now, with little round glasses. He was her first boss at Goldberger Hewitt but eventually became her competitor.

"I miss having you around Columbia, Chelsea," he said sincerely. "Josh was a prince of a guy! I hope you find him over there!"

Not only did Sean Cohen come, her sly, sneaky competitor from Cohen Commercial Brokerage, he also donated generously! Even though they had all been competitors, they set egos and past grudges aside.

And then suddenly with a rustle and a buzz and a great deal of noise a security officer came through the door, announcing that the governor was here. He scoped out the premises and then returned with two other security officers, accompanying the governor through the door.

If Tony Giordano had been magnetic nearly a decade ago when he was running for mayor, he was electrifying now. Tall, assured, and devastatingly handsome with olive skin and silvery-black hair, he worked the room, pumping hands with every person and making his way her direction. As he spoke with the citizens, Chelsea tried to make conversation with the solemn and thoughtful Debra Herzer and her emotional friend Beth McHall from Hope

For Our Future. The non-profit literacy center had been Chelsea's favorite charity, and Debra had made the adoption match for Atalaya. But Chelsea's eyes kept sliding in the direction of Tony Giordano; in fact, like a magnet, every eye in the room kept drifting towards him.

He finally arrived in front of her and took both of her forearms in his hands. "Chelsea. How good to see you again and I'm sorry it's under such unfortunate circumstances."

It had been a decade since she felt his touch, but in an instant it all came back. His deep, resonant voice had always compelled her to listen to him, and he smiled at her once again with those same dimples that had once captivated her and caused her stomach to do flips. She felt as if she were solely the most important person in the universe to him, and it was as if all the noise in the room faded away.

"Thank you," she managed. His jaw line was still strong and handsome. He was thicker and heavier now than he had been but he was still muscular and incredibly self-assured. Why not? His best friend was now the vice president of the United States. "This has been very hard. We've explored every avenue and had so many doors shut. But we're not giving up. We've had some leads come in, and we're going to raise money and we're going to find him. Thank you for the generous donation."

Tony released her forearms, and his black eyes quickly took in something and assessed it, and she had the feeling somehow that he may already know everything, or at the very least that absolutely nothing about Josh being involved in the CIA would come as a surprise to him.

"And how is Atalaya doing?"

He knew her daughter's name? He had, in some way, followed her life? "She does okay. Children are optimistic. They trust adults that everything will turn out right."

His chemistry and power was as raw and compelling as ever. "With your help and your tenacity, Josh will do well. It is only when resolved individuals such as yourself bravely rally its citizens to fight for justice that America regains its prominence once again in the world. I wish you the best of luck in your fundraising, and I wish Josh the speediest return to be with all of us safely."

216

A television news camera shoved its way closer and she was suddenly reminded that it was not just her and Tony standing here in this moment talking alone together after so many years, that there was a roomful of people. Already his eyes had flitted away and he was ready to move onto the next local VIP, the dignified and self-assured Donald Davies, who was no doubt a major contributor to the Tony Giordano for Governor Campaign. Chelsea watched, mesmerized, as the two power brokers conversed with each other. Donald Davies's corporate headquarters for Great Central Bank had been destroyed in the tornado, but he had sold out to China Commerce Bank and was a millionaire. Like Tony's, his carefully gelled black hair was now streaked with silver strands.

Josh's friends in the church band came to the fundraiser, and friends from high school, her friends from Young Professionals who weren't young any more, and a few friends of hers from high school and college. The local media documented the rally, filming and doing interviews.

When the evening was over and she and her sister Kendra were counting the money, she discovered that Donald Davies had brought a twenty-five thousand dollar donation. Over a hundred people attended, and all together they donated nearly fifty thousand dollars.

How could she have been so snobby, so forgetful, so ungrateful for her hometown? They were the people who truly cared and who came out to support her!

That night she came back home with Mom and Dad and Kendra and her brother-in-law Jared and her niece Chloe to the familiar old brick house on Nixon Street with the bay window addition in the front living room window. They watched the segment about the rally on television on the ten o'clock news—the nightly news was always something they did growing up. There was a short interview segment with her, but the real presence in the news clip was Governor Giordano, taking her forearms in his hands, making her feel that nothing else mattered. Did people in Columbia remember? She blushed.

Even with the hard work of the fundraising drive and the short amount of time that she had, she felt herself wind down to the slower pace of the Midwest with all of its genuineness and its simplicity and honesty. She felt comforted, and she felt safe.

217

She slept in her old bed in her old bedroom while the wind slapped sleet on the windows.

From Columbia, she and Atalaya flew to Las Vegas and met Chelsea's favorite former client who built water parks, Dawn Lewis-Garcia, in her beautiful offices with a picture window that overlooked Red Rock Canyon. Chelsea explained the need for funding and a trip to Iraq. Tears welled up in Dawn's leather-worn face. "Yes, we'll put up some of the reward money," Dawn said. "We need to bring this daddy home to be with his little girl! Chelsea, Josh's design of our amusement parks, and of course your work helping us identify the sites, has made us wealthy. Let me talk to the family."

The last stop was a flight to San Francisco. Clinton and his new wife, Jennifer, lived in a fabulous, contemporary six-million dollar home in Menlo Park. Everything about the inside of the house was glass and white, except for random red trim accents around the inside doorways and windows. To the west, the sun slid behind the tall screen of palm trees and landscaping foliage that completely surrounded the yard and obscured the house. A monstrous musical gong, the kind you would see in a Chinese restaurant and probably costing as much as a small car, decorated the corner of the living room.

Clinton could not have married anyone more opposite of his first wife, the shy, frumpy, middle-class Sophie who had self-esteem issues. He had met Jennifer on a technology fundraising trip to Silicon Valley and abandoned their staid hometown of Columbia to move his technology company there. Everything about Jennifer, from her shoes to her teeth, was perfect. Like Clinton, she was at least six feet tall. For a woman in her forties, she had an unbelievably taut, well-toned butt and abs, and she wore expensive designer clothes. Chelsea's co-workers and friends, such as her lawyer friend Kimberly Feldman, were good looking women, but Jennifer was intimidatingly beautiful, like the people in Hollywood. She wasn't warm or hospitable. She stood too close to you, invading your personal space and making you take back one step. Chelsea found herself nervously running her fingers through her own hair. She felt short, chubby and terribly self-conscious about potentially messy hair and makeup that she had forgotten to touch up.

"Attie, I have something for Peppermint Pinkey doll," Clinton said. This time the gift was an aesthetician set. It had a fold-up inflatable chair and a small microdermabrasion machine on little wheels so that Peppermint Pinkey could enjoy a spa facial and rejuvenate her doll skin. How would they ever get this on the plane home? Clinton seemed to enjoy torturing her and Josh with these Peppermint Pinkey gifts.

Jennifer, and Clinton sat down across from her on beautiful white leather couches. There didn't seem like a polite way to ask that Jennifer not be present. This was a different side of Clinton than she had ever seen—his long legs and arms and hands draped all over Jennifer, like an octopus. Jennifer had her hand on the inside of his thigh, so high it was almost to his crotch.

Atalaya had the doll and the microdermabrasion equipment spread out all over the floor and had turned on the tiny little motor. "Atalaya, honey, the grownups are trying to talk," Chelsea said, attempting to launch into the fundraising plea. This trip had been trying.

"What nationality is she?" Jennifer asked. "Is she yours?"

Chelsea stiffened. It seemed crude to say this right in front of the child, as if she couldn't hear.

"I'm adopted," Atalaya replied proudly. "Mommy and Daddy picked me to be in their family."

"That's right, we loved you and chose you to live with us." Chelsea quickly reassured her." She explained to Jennifer, "Atalaya's Hispanic grandmother, who took care of her, died in a tornado that hit our hometown." Chelsea tried to get the subject back on track and began a little earlier in the disappearance to fill Jennifer in. "Josh was kidnapped and taken to an Iraqi prison while working for Crestedon Architects and—"

"I know you're CIA. Clinton told me."

Chelsea glanced at Atalaya in alarm. Quickly she caught Jennifer's eyes and pressed a finger against her lips. "Atalaya," she said sweetly, "don't you have to go to the bathroom?"

"No."

"Just go. Take Peppermint Pinkey. Tell her it might be a long time before she has a chance to go potty again."

Atalaya looked puzzled but got up from her chair and headed into the hallway with the doll under her arm. In a low voice, Chelsea said, "You aren't supposed to know. *She* isn't either. You shouldn't talk about it. It could blow Josh's cover and put him in danger. Most of our family members don't even know what Josh does."

"Don't worry about it," Clinton said unconcernedly. "Jennifer's a venture capitalist. She's used to keeping trade secrets. You can trust her completely.

"Clinton. Why did you tell her?" Chelsea chided him.

Clinton replied calmly, "I can't spill any national secrets. I have no idea how Bags went about recruiting spies all day."

Jennifer didn't say anything, and it was almost as if she wasn't even listening; it was as if she were floating above the drama, patiently waiting for it to run its course.

Chelsea tried to recover her composure. Clinton had betrayed their confidentiality, but it was important to press on with her presentation. She laid out her new, alternative plan to the Radcliffes. "Put up whatever money you can, Clinton and Jennifer. Tell me what you can do. A half million? A quarter million? I've been working so hard to raise money; see all these names?"

Jennifer made a noise to protest. But Clinton cut her off. "I'll put up two hundred thousand. I'll at least do that for Bags."

Jennifer looked neither irked nor pleased, and she said very little the rest of the conversation. Chelsea tried to think of it as a win, rather than a humiliation to have to beg, but it was hard.

Unlike Clinton's visits to Washington, D.C., Clinton had not reciprocated with an offer for Chelsea to stay at his own house. She and Atalaya would have to go find a hotel. She gathered up her things and prepared to leave. "I haven't heard anything from you about the spy software, Clinton. Any legitimate leads at all lately? Have you been monitoring what's been coming into my computer and the leads on the private investigator's computer?"

"No, not lately, there just hasn't been anything much of it." He saw Chelsea's barely-concealed look of frustration. "I know, I know," he conceded lazily as they stood up from the chairs. "I've been, well, distracted the last few months." Jennifer laughed, and as they stood up she pressed close to Clinton and kissed him. He kissed her back and she grabbed him in the near vicinity of his jeans zipper. He gave a low, throaty laugh and Chelsea quickly averted her eyes. It sometimes took a few years for that honeymoon thing to wear off, right? Jennifer had certainly injected soul into Clinton's robotic computer engineering existence.

"Where's my little Attie girl?" Clinton called. Atalaya could be heard somewhere near the kitchen exfoliating Peppermint Pinkey's skin. Atalaya called back brightly, and Clinton made a growling sound like a bear and went to collect her.

Jennifer remained standing in the living room, waiting for Clinton. She stared down from her high boots unblinkingly at Chelsea. "You and Clinton are extremely close. It's kind of weird."

It was abrupt and almost accusatory, and Chelsea felt for some reason she had to justify the friendship. "To tell you the truth, when I first met Clinton in London about ten years ago, I didn't even like him. He monopolized Josh's time. Clinton was a partier and a bad influence, and I thought he was kind of geeky. He got all of us in danger with his strange government technology prototype experiments. Then we moved out to the East Coast, and I missed my family. I never had a brother, and over time, I guess he became one to me."

The Jennifer factor changed the dynamic of the meeting and the friendship. She felt lucky tonight to have any help from Clinton at all. She and Atalaya went to the rental car out on the driveway, where she sat in the driver's seat hunting online for a hotel. She couldn't shrug it off; Clinton had been nonchalant, almost reckless, about the software. No matter how newlywed someone like that was and distracted with a life change, surely at least once on the private investigator's computer Clinton would have seen something unusual, something to question, something to merit further investigation. Wouldn't he?

T he radical mufti from Saudi Arabia, the head of "Black Lightening", abruptly cancelled his tour of Iraq.

Believed to be secretly transporting weapons and recruiting military insurgents under the guise of teaching, he was in the crosshairs of not only the United States and China but multiple intelligence operations around the world. He went into hiding in an undisclosed location, thought to be somewhere in the United Arab Emirates. He sent his video instructions to the faithful online.

No longer did the housemates joke lightheartedly about being Hillah Hillbillies or play pranks. Ali, always bossy, insisted that the three housemates watch the Black Lightening recordings together in the trailer with the blinds closed when they were all off duty from the prison. Hakim protested mildly, suspecting that he was not going to like either the messenger or the message. Yazen was too frightened of Ali not to watch the lesson.

"Praise be to Allah and to the messenger of Allah." The mufti appeared to be sitting cross legged in a dimly lit cave with a lantern flickering behind him. "You say that you believe the Quran. But have you strayed from believing its every word? Do you only believe what you choose?" The video did not stay fixed in one place, it wavered. Someone was apparently holding the camera, rather than setting it on a tripod, and it was shaky and difficult to discern the mufti's features in the dingy light.

"The Almighty Allah has sent me to tell you that the playing of music will be *haram*. It is a pastime which is wasteful. Music is the gateway to fornication, intoxicants, and tragic consequences. It leads to the elevated stress hormone adrenaline, which can cripple one's nervous system. Remember the words the prophet's apostle has said in the Hadith." The reference, Bukhari number 5590, rolled across the bottom of the screen. 'From among my followers there will be some people who will consider illegal sexual intercourse, the wearing of silk, the drinking of alcoholic drinks and the use of musical instruments, as lawful.' If you turn your ear away from music in this world, it will be allowed to hear the most melodious of sounds in heaven, which words cannot describe."

Irritation and rebellion flashed across Hakim's face. There was not agreement in Islam on the matter of music! Ali was captivated, nodding his head vigorously. Yazen's expression, on the other hand, reflected uncertain stress.

"Also, I have been sent to tell you that you are prohibited from playing computer games. They glorify the western *Kafir* and present our Arab countries as weak, or even as countries to be destroyed."

Hakim cringed guiltily, thinking of the Eagle in NoitaLever which represented the Americans and was always dropping help to the "weak" in their hour of need.

"The games ruin your eyes and ears and do damage to your nervous system. They cause you to miss your prayers and your Islamic responsibilities. Even our enemies, the Chinese, agree that the game and the advertisements are addictive like alcohol and lure you with dreams of western riches. Know this, sin can hurt you; but Allah is most merciful if you do your best to avoid sinful ways."

The video went on for an excruciatingly long time about the need to establish the caliphate, and Hakim's eyes glazed over as he stared at the woolly eyebrows that bounced up and down, up and down. "You know the saying, 'After Saturday comes Sunday!' On Saturday, we overthrow the Jews! On Sunday, we overthrow the Christians and the West! Then we must overthrow the East, the Chinese!" With a final exhortation, Black Lightening called for jihad from the entire global Muslim community.

The minute it was over, Ali went on a rampage, storming around the tiny living room, throwing up his arms. "We have been dishonored! NoitaLever has tainted us and enticed us to evil luxuries and Western thinking! We have dishonored our parents by working in this city, Babylon Metro, and allowing it to change our ways. We must go through this trailer and clean out all things that are *haram*!" He bounded across the floor to the tiny rusty refrigerator and began to pull out the unclean Faridas and food items that were not specifically *halal*. "Hakim, you must rid yourself of the tight Western clothes that cause you to stumble and fall! Throw away the hair gels! Yazen, you must discard the ear buds and erase the music from your phone! Have you been making up the prayers that you have missed?"

Hakim sat sullenly on the couch, regarding Ali with resentment. Yazen looked frightened.

"Don't just sit there and stare like goats. Go to your rooms and begin to clean."

Hakim snarled. "Who are you, a *marja,* to treat me like a pupil? Where is your advanced training from the clerics? What seminary did you attend?"

"You know the path of uprightness!" shot back Ali angrily, pumping a fist in Hakim's direction from the kitchen. "You have led us in the way of sin, serving us beer and taking us to Babylon Metro with the beautiful girls who refuse to wear the *hajib* on their heads!"

Yazen interrupted hesitantly in his halting voice. "Hakim, we are all weak; we…were all playing NoitaLever… before we moved here. Perhaps our brother is right and…we should consider throwing away a few things…*inshallah.*" Allah willing.

"Ali never cared about being right before my promotion!" Hakim's voice rose accusatorily. "Now that I got one and he didn't, he must make himself to appear more righteous than you and me!"

In a fit of rage, Ali threw all the prohibited *harem* foods and beverages in the trash can and burst out the front door of the trailer, slamming it shut so hard that the whole flimsy structure shook.

There was a long, uncomfortable silence and Yazen went to his room. He came back miserably with his earbuds clutched tightly in his hand, holding them uncertainly over the trash can. "We cannot make Ali angry. We must be good Muslims…in his presence."

Hakim's heart clenched. Yazen adored music of all types and listened to it constantly, bobbing his head and tapping and drumming with his fingers to the beat, even though he knew all the Islamic cautions. "Hide them in your pillow," Hakim hissed.

Yazen considered this, the war with his conscience battling on his face, then went to the bedroom to hide his beloved earbuds.

Hakim pushed the furniture around in a different position in the living room. With the clerics and imams clamping down, it would not do to have the television, especially with the NoitaLever game, on in Ali's absence, in a position so that it could peered at from the outside window through the drapes.

He knew Yazen was right. It could be very dangerous to cross Ali, even more dangerous than to cross Commander Yang

Chunying. The commander did not live in the trailer and know everything that went on, but Ali did. Ali had turned into a fundamentalist and would bring the wrath of the extremist brothers down on them if he and Yazen did not comply.

Josh could hear Hakim's familiar footsteps outside the row of cells and the familiar pinging of the NoitaLever video game at a very low volume. No other guards were around. Whistling, Hakim walked down the row, the mobile between his hands and his security card dangling between two fingers. It was a blatant violation of protocol, but it was an incredibly quiet and dull week at the prison, and staff had been very lax lately.

All of a sudden behind Hakim the door buzzed and flew open and Commander Yang Chungying burst in. Hakim jolted and whirled around in surprise, hitting the bars with his elbow. "Sir!" He scrambled to keep hold of the security card, but the mobile flew through the bars and landed on the floor inside Josh's cell, face up.

The commander burst a rapid-fire question to Hakim in a mixture of Arabic and Chinese, and Josh surmised it was something about Hakim's order of supplies from Baghdad that had not yet arrived.

Hakim's mobile did not break when it landed on the floor. The NoitaLever game he had been playing still danced on the screen with its images of a tank approaching a very real-looking Chinese village, ready to fire at a weapons munitions facility. Josh quickly and stealthily stepped his foot on the phone, hiding it under his foot and muffling the sound.

Flustered, Hakim managed an answer about the Baghdad order. The commander spun on his foot and stormed out in frustration, miraculously not hearing the beeping of the game.

Panicked, Hakim scrambled to get the pass card into the door slot and enter into the cell, fully prepared to give Josh a beating if he attempted to use the phone.

Josh thought quickly, weighing possible consequences. He swept up the mobile and handed it back through the bars before Hakim could even get the door all the way open. With a wild lunge, Hakim grabbed it, stuffing it into his pocket.

"NoitaLever." Josh said aloud in English.

Hakim froze. He thought he had the volume turned down enough, but the American had recognized the game! Had he heard the discussions about it being forbidden?

A Way of Escape

Josh said to Hakim, "When the game is done, when your soldiers are all gone and you give up, when you think it is time for *Istishhad*, you do not have to kill yourself or die. You can call for help from the Eagle. You must look for the way out. It is a ladder, or a rope, or a green button." He repeated the words with a mixture of Chinese and Arabic.

Hakim backed up a few steps, shocked, understanding everything, and muttering, "*Masha'Allah*." May God reward you. The prisoner could speak multiple languages! Hakim's face flamed red with confusion. "Why you give me back my phone?" he demanded, struggling to regain his composure. The American prisoner could have smashed the phone; or worse, tried to message the outside for help before Hakim made it into the cell.

"No job for you if the Commander knows you play NoitaLever."

Frightened, Hakim stormed out of the corridor and through the door, slamming it shut behind him, and hurried down the corridor where he hung over a small, dirty sink, trembling.

He had achieved one of the highest levels of the game that very few gamers achieved, the Insurgent level, where the Chinese were attacked. It was only due to the favor of Allah that the commander had not seen it. He was pretty sure he knew why the American didn't try to hold onto the phone: he knew he would be overcome. But the problem was, now the prisoner had far more on Hakim than Hakim had on the prisoner.

The prisoner might try to bribe him.

Hakim tried to force it all out of his mind but was faced with it once he got back to the trailer after work.

To keep the peace, Hakim and Yazen complied with every Sharia law to the best of their ability, particularly when Ali was present. But one evening Ali was on duty at the prison and not at home, and Hakim was aching to feed his NoitaLever addiction during Ali's absence. Yazen hovered by the television uncertainly, drawn in by the game, but afraid to log in on the big screen where a record of his own playing time and scores could be discovered by Ali. Yazen wanted to kick the addiction but couldn't, so he played NoitaLever on his own mobile at night under the covers.

What was it the American prisoner had said in the fragments of English, Chinese, and Arabic? No more *Istishhad* if you were having a losing game? There were three things to give you a way out so you did not have to commit martyrdom and log off?

Hakim studied the screen. Tonight he was a Fighter Pilot, manning a plane and preparing to bomb India. He got up from the mat on the floor and studied the television screen at closer range.

Suddenly he spotted something off to the right. "Yazen!" he said sharply, putting his finger to the spot on the television screen where a noticeably green button was to the right of the airplane navigation system. It was a tone of the color green that was brighter than the other greens in the picture, a little more noticeable. "What's this?" He hovered the lever over it and clicked to see if anything happened. The green button pulsed, and up popped a screen in Arabic: "New Identity: Where would you like to live?" Hakim's profile picture began to morph, his face took on slight Indonesian characteristics, bouncing happily on a boat with the Samaya Bali resort in the background.

"What…what is that? It is new!" Yazen exclaimed. "Let me try that!"

They tried the different options and let out such a loud, excited whoop that they clasped their hands over their mouths, laughing, and then peered out the window of the trailer to see if anyone could see what was happening inside. "Who knows of this?" Yazen asked in awe. "Who has discovered this? Does anyone know? It must have happened…with the new update!"

Hakim nearly blurted out, "The American prisoner" but thought better of it. He was uncomfortably reminded of what the American had over him and decided for now to keep the source of his knowledge to himself until he had time to think how to deal with his new problem.

"You and I can be the first to know," he said evasively. "Maybe around here we will be the only to know."

Tomorrow he needed to do something to bribe the prisoner into quiet. There was one thing he could think of that he could do. He would get extra food to the prisoner.

The jolting phone call came to Hakim while he was at work, the broken sound of his father crying inconsolably. "Son, you must come home. Your baby sister has been killed!"

It was as if Hakim were in a trance. In a daze he went to the Chinese commander's office and was informed that he could leave immediately and go to the funeral. Yazen, pitying him, embraced him. Yazen called a friend who drove a truck to see if a way could be provided to get Hakim back to his hometown immediately. Even Ali, with whom relations had been frosty lately, murmured his sympathies and insisted on handing over his own bottled water and sack lunch for Hakim to take on his trip. "Your sister has died for the cause of Allah," he proclaimed. "My sacrifice is nothing compared to hers."

Three hours later, the beat-up truck dropped him off at his father's house where the neighbors had gathered, weeping. He handed Yazen's friend some money and jumped out.

The old Shiite woman in the dusty village who performed the ritual washing of the body was just leaving the house with her bag smelling of olive oil soaps, berry leaves, and camphor, and with a wail she dropped the bag and took Hakim in her arms before leaving.

Inside the home the relatives were making final preparations for the funeral, which would be held just before sundown. He pushed his way through those who were loudly sobbing to the sad little shroud, the box with the funeral white cloth. He lay the beads he had purchased from the roadside stand onto his sister's slight body.

His beautiful mother clung to his neck, crying, as his father poured out the story of the youth in their village recruited by Black Lightening who drove a truck with explosives. The Chinese had responded with gunfire. His dear sister Rukiya, seven years younger than him, with her black curls and long, baby-doll eyelashes that once fluttered over eyes identical to his mother's, crumpled in the street never to arise again! Tears spilled down his cheeks. He remembered comforting Rukiya when she was a hungry baby, when the terrorists attacked and held the village siege. He remembered creating little toys out of strange odds and ends, which caused her to laugh. He remembered holding her up on his shoulders above the crowd to see the parade that the Chinese peacekeeping troops put on to celebrate the restoration of the village.

And now, ironically, the very ones who had come to keep her safe, the Chinese, had killed her.

Black Lightening.

The words were whispered throughout the village with a mixture of fear and awe.

He stayed for three days.

The village men gathered in the house of Hakim's parents late into the night, arguing vigorously. "Black Lightening will avenge the death of our sister Rukiya. They will set up a caliphate for Allah!" one of Hakim's uncles exclaimed.

"We should stay out of this. We are Shiites, and our family tribe will endure! We are not Sunni or Wahhabi, and we disagree with their violent ways to interpret the Quran. Only Allah can set up a caliphate!" Hakim's father rebuked the uncle.

"But the Sunnis and Wahhabis speak truth. We Shiites have taken no action. We Shiites have failed to follow the words of the Quran to fight unbelievers. We must join the Sunnis and Wahhabis to fight the Chinese and preserve Iraq! The Chinese have first taken Iraq, what follows soon is Saudi Arabia!" argued one of Hakim's cousins.

"If the Chinese are building Iraq and bringing prosperity to people without stealing, then peace with China is permitted," the next door neighbor reminded them all.

"But do you believe that there is not one Chinese occupier who steals? Do you believe that there is not one Chinese occupier who is corrupt? Yes, they have invested great sums into Babylon Metro, but do not they take what they wish that belongs to us, and deliver to us what is left, and tell us they are generous?"

Hakim knew the answer to this, but he was afraid to enter into the conversation.

His parents did not accept his decision to go back to Babylon Metro. "The Chinese are not our friends. They are pawns of the United Nations and all they care about is our oil. You are on their payroll and you are betraying the country," his father warned as they sat cross legged on mats drinking tea the night before he left.

"I must go back. I have invested much time to learn Chinese. I have a new promotion. They did not mean for this to happen to our Rukiya," Hakim found himself giving lip service to the occupiers, the godless unbelievers who now controlled security in the country of Iraq and who provided his paycheck. If only his father knew that while he sat in the large room listening to the uncles and cousins and brothers, he had already been involved in Black Lightening, he had accomplished the initiations, and his friends were pressing him to join the insurgency....

His father urged, "*Inshalla,* stay in this village." If Allah wills. "Go into business for yourself. You can be a salesman, set up a tent in the bazaar, offer clothes for sale. We will have a settlement from the Chinese for your sister's death."

In some ways the thought was appealing, but the local village was too small to support the affluent lifestyle Hakim envisioned for himself. Babylon Metro offered limitless possibilities, a passport to money, status, and the world.

"You are so handsome and charming," his mother persisted. "But your thoughts are too much on fancy hair and tight clothes and Western ways. Try to be yourself, my son. Cease trying to be something that you are not! Why have you not found yourself a wife yet? You have your future before you. Let us select for you a nice girl and you can settle down and get married. Give us another daughter to comfort us in our old age after the death of our dear Rukiya."

A pang went through his heart. How he longed for the love of a woman, the feel of her in his arms. He was increasingly enticed towards the temptation presented by seeing the women in Babylon Metro and on the computer, and like every young man, he wanted a wife and a family. But he always thought that would come later, when he had money and was weary of fun.

He lay on his little bed in the darkness that night, tossing and turning, his heart hardened and bitter against his Chinese employers. The image of the commander's ugly faced floated up in his mind, the one who had given him a promotion but who took corrupt bribes from vendors and prisoners' families.

His housemates were not Shiite, but they had shown him kindness and they were willing to stand against the Chinese.

Perhaps he should leave his job and join the Black Lightening resistance and fight. The Quran demanded it, they had shown him its verses.

He longed to speak to someone in the village he could trust about the decision to join Black Lightening. But every Black Lightening meeting ended with an oath not to divulge the identity of its adherents or the discussion of the meetings, on the pain of death. And his clan was in disagreement on Black Lightening.

He wanted a normal life. A life of peace and prosperity with respect from the community and a wife and children.

He twisted and writhed. There was no solution. He reached for his own earbuds and escaped into Western music.

Josh waited until exercise time and he could not be heard by others before he asked Hakim about his absence from Governorate of Babil prison. "You were gone for a while. You look sad."

It was against the rules to engage in personal conversation with the prisoners, but Hakim answered him anyway. "The funeral of my sister. She had seven years," he replied, struggling to keep his voice devoid of emotion.

"Seven years old?" A memory of a little girl with long curls and Peppermint Pinkey dolls caused Josh to swallow. He studied the young man for a brief moment. "Was she your favorite?" he guessed.

Hakim nodded, sensing empathy. "Yes. She was my baby sister. I saved her life when terrorists came to our village many years ago when I went to find her food. But this she did not survive last week."

"I am sorry. I would like to hear the story."

Hakim's eyes widened in surprise for a moment. The American prisoner may be *kafir*, an infidel; but nonetheless he seemed to have a sympathetic heart. "She walked to the market place for my mother. A jihadist in the village crashed a truck with a bomb behind the police station where the Chinese officers were smoking. The Chinese hear the truck and shoot their guns. Then the smoke is clear and they find my sister."

Across the courtyard, some of the prisoners kicked a soccer ball, and everyone ran to the far side. "You always ask me questions about America," Josh challenged him. "Now it is my turn to ask you questions. Ok?"

"Maybe I will answer. Maybe I will not." Actually, Hakim didn't mind at all. He liked talking to the American. Not only was it a chance to improve his English, there was always something unusual and interesting about the conversation.

"The suicide bomber that killed your sister. The jihadist. Will he go to Paradise since his actions caused her to die?"

"My sister and the jihadist both die for the cause of Allah," Hakim replied.

"What if the suicide bomber committed a sin before he killed for the jihad? What if he committed adultery just before he strapped on the bomb, or told a lie, or stole? Then will he go to Paradise?"

"If he is ignorant," Hakim started to answer, thinking with huge discomfiture of the words of the Quran—and the clerics' constant warning about sin: *'And of no effect is the repentance of those who continue to do evil deeds until death faces them and he says: Now I repent.'*

"If he repents before death," Hakim stumbled uncertainly and then he snapped, "Who is to know? Allah knows best. Allah is merciful."

But he walked away, disturbed. What if both the jihadist and his little sister had done sinful deeds before their deaths? What fate would befall them? The prisoner's questions were a trap, causing him to doubt. And Muslims had faith. They did not doubt.

63
The Housemates

Once the grief of the funeral had subsided, the tension between Hakim and Ali over Ali's promotion escalated and set off a chill into the trailer that no desert heat could warm. In an obvious power move, Ali—who always had the strongest opinions about everything anyway—took charge of all decisions ranging from what could be purchased at the market (*halal* only) to what could be viewed on television (no Chinese or western influences). And he began to use the death of Hakim's sister in his tirades about joining the mujahedin for jihad against their China occupiers.

Hakim slid into silence more and more often, coldly ignoring Ali or retorting with brief, angry answers. When they were home in the trailer, Ali's dark, wary eyes followed Hakim under thick eyebrows and heavy, primate-like forehead. They began to fight about money. Yazen tried to keep the peace, outwardly compliant with Ali but clearly alarmed by the extremist brand of fundamentalism that Ali was embracing.

Hakim grew more and more nervous. He did not want trouble with Ali and the clerics. He kept up outward appearances, doing his prayers, going to the mosque, eating *halal*, and not playing NoitaLever in Ali's presence. Whenever Ali was home, he turned on an instruction from the mufti and played it at a slightly high volume.

The idea of marriage became more appealing, as a possible escape from the trailer. The face of his old school chum in chemistry class floated up in his memory.

Yasmeenah.

He had been a good student, when he applied himself. Yasmeenah had an oversized nose, but other than that she was an acceptable looking girl and definitely very smart; they had competed for grades. He had excelled over her in English class. She had excelled over him in chemistry class. She was studying at Baghdad University now, and a marriage to Yasmeenah would improve his status.

But wives always wanted babies, housing in Babylon Metro was expensive, and there goes your money. He tried to work it out in his head. He should find a second job. There were some possibilities.

If he improved his English or his Chinese, maybe he could be a translator. He could barter lessons from a fellow Chinese prison guard. The English seemed more problematic. The English they learned in school seemed different than the English that the American prisoner spoke.

He was charismatic and able to persuade. He could sell, like his father, who owned a small shop. Perhaps he could have a cart on Wangfujing Avenue at night or on his day off, but it was a huge sum to rent a stall and purchase the inventory.

Bored with the problem, he picked up his mobile and logged into the NoitaLever game, missing the nights when the three housemates gathered around the large screen of the television for a tournament. He remembered an animation ad he had seen on NoitaLever and clicked on it.

A military figure in combat boots with an assault weapon raced through a village that had been attacked by snipers. Tufts of smoke and debris wafted to the sky. Everywhere the military figure ran, the smoke cleared away from a marquis or a bus advertisement or a billboard. All of them had plain background with an eagle emblem. They all said the same thing in white letters:

www.cia/careers.gov

Careers in Military Intelligence

He clicked onto the website, thinking about what the prisoner had said about opportunities in America. He began to daydream about escaping to America. In the daydream, there was a wife who went with him, and they had a nice American house to live in with a swimming pool, and a car, just like the European immigrants to America who invented the NoitaLever game.

The next break he had from work would not be taken in the arcade in the mall in Babylon Metro. It would be taken at Baghdad University. He hunted and finally found the email address for his old high school friend, Yasmeenah.

64

The Humiliation

Baghdad University, where Yasmeenah attended, sat on the curve of the Tigris River in the center of Iraq. A massive, extremely narrow arch straddled the street at the entrance, and the arch was flanked by trees. The campus, with its curving sidewalks and carefully groomed grounds, was beautiful in an intimidating and imposing way. Baghdad University might not be Hakim's life path, and he was not in its social class, but it was certainly his age group.

He paid money to the trucker he'd hitch-hiked a ride from, grabbed the small bouquet of flowers laying by his side on the seat, hopped out of the truck, and nervously primped his carefully gelled hair, wishing he had a mirror.

He made his way to the reflecting pond with backless concrete benches surrounded by low rising concrete buildings. Yasmeenah appeared with two girlfriends, standing up from the bench to meet him, timorously saying hello. She thanked him for the flowers, tucking her nose into them. "Would you like to see some of the campus?" she asked him.

She led the way, and he and the two girlfriends followed. The boxy university buildings had mostly been designed in the middle part of the last century and showed the strain of time and local conflict. She pointed out some of the notable buildings, and they walked past the vast track field with its athletes in training. Attendance at the university fluctuated between 10,000 and 80,000 students, she said, depending on whether Iraq was engaged in war. The two girlfriends gradually drifted a slight distance behind them.

She wasn't her old self. She didn't make humorous, sarcastic comments about annoying teachers and dumb pupils like she had when they were in school together. "I am applying myself to my college work," she said seriously. She was interested in engineering, but other than that, she did not say a whole lot. So mostly he talked about himself, the classes he had taken to learn Chinese and the prison system. He also tried being funny.

"You must eat before you go back," she said, evidently putting a time limit to their meeting. The four of them went to the cafeteria and ate a snack of kiwi fruit, apples, and tomatoes.

"May I visit you again next week?" Hakim asked at the end of the visit.

"I think yes," Yasmeenah said.

The second weekend they sat on another backless bench in a grassy courtyard. Still she did not laugh very much. She just was not the same carefree Yasmeenah who played jokes on him in school with the chemistry test tubes. He tried to ask her about the future.

"Finish school, get a good job as an engineer, *inshallah*," she said elusively.

He kept glancing at her two girlfriends nearby, sitting on the grass checking their mobiles and talking softly, but frequently casting sideways looks at them. He wished the girlfriends would put more distance between them. If only Yasmeenah could see Babylon Metro, where couples interacted all the time without escorts! He imagined her walking with him along Wangfujing Avenue, where all the merchandise and spices were sold. "I want to be a respected businessman," he told her.

"If Allah wills," she reminded him.

"Yes, *inshalla*. I want to invent things on the computer, such as computer games. You can sell to Americans and make a lot of money. They like the games. You know the game NoitaLever? That is invented by Americans. I know the person from America who made it." It was a wild overstatement meant to impress her. Her girlfriend heard him and looked up in surprise.

"You would invent games? You must have a talent with the computers," she stated.

Clearly, he had ignited her admiration. "Maybe someday I will go to America," he said pointedly, watching carefully for her reaction.

"You must study in school to be good at computers. I must get back to the library to my studies," Yasmeenah suddenly concluded the meeting.

In his mind drifted a vision of a swimming pool in back of a mansion in the United States, and sharing the mansion with her and smart little children with black hair and hazel eyes.

The third weekend, he resolved that he needed talk to Yasmeenah alone. He did not make an appointment. He chose to show up at the campus. Again he took flowers.

He remembered the name of one of her classes and hunted online until he found the building and the time the class was offered. He waited until he saw her on the sidewalk and then he ran up to her, jumped and dropped down on one knee, and offered the flowers to her with a little charming flourish.

"Hakim!" She gave a slight little screech of astonishment. "What are you doing here? You did not make a date!"

"I wished to surprise you. Come and sit with me on the grass under the tree."

She took the flowers and once again hid her nose in them, standing still on the sidewalk. "Well, would you like to walk?" he asked.

Yasmeenah's face was red. "Let us step over here," she said in a pinched voice, moving a few feet away from the young men and women with backpacks passing along the sidewalk. "It is inappropriate for you to meet me without a chaperone," she scolded. "You know the teachings of the Prophet! Whenever a man and a woman are alone, the third person with them is Satan! You say that you believe the Quran. But do you follow its every word, or do you only obey what you choose?"

Everyone, it seemed, was adopting the strict teachings of the mufti, Abu al-Qummi of Black Lightening! Why could not people make up their own minds what they wanted to believe? "I wanted you to be the old Yasmeenah, like we were in school," he began helplessly.

"We are not children. I am a woman now!"

"I know, I know. I wanted to talk to you more of the future. Of marriage."

"Babylon Metro is corrupt. The United States is corrupt. I do not want to marry. I want to complete my studies," she said.

The rejection startled him. "But—you can complete your studies," he managed. "You can finish them online. Or perhaps I could be transferred to a prison in Baghdad."

"No. I do not want to marry you," she snapped definitively.

"But you agreed to meet with me these two times…."

"I will not change my mind," she said resolutely, and he saw from the shake of her head and the look in her eyes that it was final.

239

Stung and humiliated, he said his goodbyes and left the University of Baghdad, wondering if he had frightened her with his forward behavior or his dreams of a prosperous life in Babylon Metro and in the United States; or even worse, if she looked down on him because of his lack of schooling.

Once the wound of being rejected by Yasmeenah had subsided a bit, Hakim approached his mother by telephone about the business of selecting a wife. Choosing one on his own had not worked out so well. It was perfectly okay, he concluded, to fall back on tradition and let his parents bring him some choices.

His mother and father were quite pleased with his request for help, and after a vibrant and noisy family discussion that included the critical point that the new wife would have to move to the Babylon Metro/Hillah metropolitan area, they settled on Farah, his second cousin. She had been at the funeral for his sister. She was prettier than Yasmeenah, if a few years younger than himself. His parents made the pitch to him. "She is smart in the school, pretty and funny and daredevil. You would be a good match." They did not speak much of the trouble the seventeen-year-old had caused her parents; they all knew that marriage would tame the wild spirit. Intrigued by this description of a younger girl he simply remembered as constantly giggling, he agreed to date her.

His mother made the approach to Farah's mother. Farah accepted the invitation to see if it was a match. There would be two or three weekends of dates, and assuming all went well—as it usually did when the parents did the choosing—he would issue the invitation to marriage.

He traveled back to his hometown on his day off. His mother went with him to the house where Farah lived with her rambunctious brothers and sisters. It was a humble house of concrete block and peeling paint, but no shabbier than the home of anyone else in the village. It was a life he was glad he had escaped. Their first date went well. Farah's parents let them sit alone in a room and talk. She was not shy, as most Arab girls were, but absorbed, staring at him with beautiful brown eyes behind fluttery, coquettish lashes. He importantly told her the story of being accepted into the Chinese security training academy.

The idea of living in a large city was an adventure. She was willing to try it, she said. Unlike Yasmeenah, Farah laughed at his jokes, and this appealed immensely to his vanity. She had a brother close to her age—her favorite brother, she said—who hovered nearby curiously with a bold wink in his eye.

Hakim suggested a date the following weekend. Farah agreed eagerly and the parents gave their approval.

His male cousin, who was a couple years older and had recently been married, met up with him the second weekend. Farah's favorite brother and a younger sister also accompanied them to a tea shop in the village. Hakim told Farah somewhat embellished tales of security training and incidents with prisoners. When the cousin and the brother were so deep in a loud conversation about cars that they were no longer paying attention to them anymore, and when the little sister was distracted, he said to her, "I will tell you a secret."

"What?" she asked curiously.

He leaned in towards her head and lowered his voice, and she leaned in to listen. "If it is the will of Allah, I want to invent things on the computer, such as computer games. Americans like the games. You can sell to Americans and make a lot of money."

Farah's eyes shone. "Iraqis do not make many of these games. You are very smart to think of that idea," she said decidedly.

"You know the game NoitaLever?"

"The imam in the village has forbidden it to keep the peace with the Chinese. He also says it is Western and corrupts us." She glanced at the table where her brother and cousin were and lowered her voice conspiratorially. "But my brother ignores the fatwa and still plays the game."

The favorite brother at the next table who was pounding his fist about quality carburetors suddenly shot up several notches in Hakim's value and estimation. "I know the person from America who made the NoitaLever game." It was a flagrant exaggeration, if not an outright lie, meant to impress her, because as far as Hakim knew, the American prisoner had nothing to do with the actual invention of the game.

"How you know this person?"

He deflected the question. "Business people who sell games in America are rich. They have mansions with swimming pools."

Her eyes grew large. Clearly, he had secured her curiosity and admiration. Now was the moment of truth, the test. "Maybe someday I will go to America," he ventured carefully. "You can be anything you want in America."

He held his breath. Had he given away too much? Would she reject him? If he had gone too far, would she tell her family and friends? Would they chastise and ridicule him for his admiration for the riches of the West?

“The Americans will think you are handsome. You are clever and will advance quickly! I would like to still know you when you are rich in America! Ok, you have shared a secret with me. Now I will share one with you. I want to learn how to play the NoitaLever game on my phone with you and my brother. I don't care what the imams and the Chinese say!”

Farah was adventurous, just like him!

Hakim's ego bubbled up and nearly burst. He had quickly become fond of her, she seemed enchanted by his attention, and it would grow to true love for both of them, he knew. Just like it had for his recently married cousin, who, like his mother and father, had been encouraging throughout the process.

On his way back home the truck on which he had hitchhiked a ride creaked and swayed, and he stared longingly at the mall on the edge of Babylon Metro as they rolled by on the freeway. No more would he be able to indulge himself in the NoitaLever booth. After the fatwa from Black Lightening, and when the rumblings about the insurgency started, the NoitaLever booth had been scheduled for removal from the arcade.

When he arrived back in Babylon Metro, he rode his bike to Hillah, the old, original part of the city that had been there before Babylon Metro had been built. The housing prices were far cheaper than Babylon Metro, but rent for a decent apartment was still out of reach. He put down a deposit on a shabby room on the third floor in a densely populated and less than safe neighborhood, but it was the best he could find.

At work he walked the halls of the prison, studying his Iraqi co-workers when they weren't looking back at him. How much did they know? Were they a part of the insurgency? And he imagined they studied his face for clues as well.

When he got back to the trailer, he heard of the plot.

Yazen told him, in halting whispers, with the television turned up loud. There was to be a Black Lightening operation in Babylon Metro very soon, targeted against the Chinese. They were to await instructions from a video, which would only be made available to the most highly trusted followers, and from there, insurgents would be recruited at the last moment by word of mouth.

Hakim felt his hands and feet go cold. The mufti was calling them to jihad! He wanted to avenge the death of his sister but he did not want to have to choose! He was hoping to be married and now was not the time to join an insurgency! "What are you going to do?" he whispered to Yazen.

Yazen's eyes were round with fear. "But we have to! You know the mufti's….reminder. Did you not watch…his most recent devotional message?"

Hakim shook his head guiltily. There had been a new message, but Hakim had avoided viewing it. He went to the computer and called up the video from a couple days ago.

Abu al-Qummi was in hiding and his message had been filmed in a cave. A lecture to his closest disciples had been posted on the internet as a message to Muslims throughout the Middle East. The strange light cast long, eerie shadows behind the mufti as he spoke. "You say that you believe the Quran. But do you believe every word, or do you only believe what you choose? The time has come for a caliphate which will rule the world. Listen now to the words of Allah's messenger—peace be upon him! 'Fighting is prescribed for you, and ye dislike it. But it is possible that ye dislike a thing which is *good* for you, and that ye love a thing which is *bad* for you.'" Underneath the picture, the Arabic reference in the Quran, Al-Baqara 2:216, floated on the bottom of the screen.

Hakim squirmed uneasily. He wanted to honor the memory of his baby sister Rukiya, but how much he disliked the idea of fighting! How very much he wanted a peaceful life, a life of prosperity! The Quran was right—Hakim disliked something that was good for him and loved something that wasn't….He felt pulled into opposite pieces with guilt. He was such a bad Muslim!

Off camera, one of the disciples in the cave asked a question that was so obviously scripted it was almost comical. "But Teacher, are not some called by Allah to stay, to guard our women, to protect our hospitals, to work the crops, and to study for the future?"

"These are the beliefs of many," conceded the mufti. "But what are the words of the Quran? 'Not equal are those believers who sit at home and receive no hurt, and those who strive and fight in the cause of Allah with their goods and their persons. Allah hath granted a grade higher to those who strive and fight with their goods and persons than to those who sit at home.'" He looked up from the scriptures, his eyes flashing. "There is great reward for all who give up everything they have to fight, who give up all of the comforts and all of the pleasures of this life. 'Let those fight in the way of Allah who are willing to sell the life of this world for the other. Whoso fighteth in the way of Allah, be he slain or be he victorious, on him we shall bestow a vast reward.' Allah knows best. Peace be to you."

A grade higher! Great reward! That's what Hakim wanted! An uprising against Chinese security forces was sure to have only one outcome: death and the rewards of the Hereafter.

But he wasn't as sure that he wanted to die, as the rest of the brothers seemed to be sure.

He met Yazen's eyes, but both young men were afraid to voice their true feelings aloud. Any success would only be temporary. It had been drilled into the staff at Governorate of Babil prison that China had millions of active, reserve, and paramilitary troops at their disposal that could be called to the Middle East in hours to quell rebellions!

Yazen read his thoughts. "Brother…they said they could sell us…some drugs for a good price. They said it would give us…the courage to do this thing."

"Allah knows best," Hakim finally croaked. He turned away. He went into the room and threw himself on the bed, losing himself in thought, trying to evaluate his options.

To leak the secret to Commander Yang Chunying would purchase protection for a while. But that was unthinkable treason. He would lose his life, if not immediately, certainly later, at the hands of his own countrymen. He ground his fist into his thigh in frustration. The last few years, at least he had felt safe, and he had thought of death very little. But now his baby sister was dead. Once again he entered the dark, cold tunnel that he had walked as a child—that odd paradox of feeling young and invincible and lucky, believing that you were going to make it out of the tunnel safely; yet somehow, at the exact same time, knowing in your heart that violent death was inevitable.

That night in bed he wrapped himself around his thin pillow, the fantasies swirling in his head from the forbidden websites he had secretly watched online. He vowed that he would not leave this life a virgin. He resolved to have a woman before the insurgency.

If there was an insurgency, and if he survived but had no job, how would he pay for the new apartment?

No, he couldn't even think of staying after the insurgency. He needed to leave Babylon Metro, now! But where should he go? Should he go back to his hometown? There was no work there. There was hardly time now to make application to transfer to a different prison in another city; such things ran through layers of Chinese bureaucracy and took forever.

There is always a way of escape.

He thought of the latest version of the NoitaLever game. He began to daydream about changing his look and moving to an exotic location, like you could in the game. But where? As he made his rounds, his mind was a million miles away. Should he flee to a tropical island? As always, his thoughts came back to one place: the United States.

In the imagination, he carried pretty little Farah in his arms as he dashed across the border to freedom.

He called Farah and his parents and told them the parties and the wedding need to be carried out quickly because of his work assignments. At the engagement party they exchanged rings, and Farah and her sisters and girlfriends peered at him from behind things and giggled. A cleric in the village legalized their marriage in court and the families had a party. Farah was beautiful in white. He made the money pledge. He missed several days of work due to a series of parties, which was the custom.

He got to be friends with Farah's favorite brother, who he used to think of as a younger boy; but the brother was nearly grown up now and was an energetic, outgoing youth with an interesting streak of rebellion, quick to drink a Farida and smoke as well as make jokes about imams and clerics.

And then they finally had the actual wedding with the joyous wedding dance, the beautiful cake, and the delicious dinner.

Farah became quieter, speaking less and less as the transport brought them closer and closer to Babylon Metro, her eyes as wide as saucers at the skyscrapers spinning and shimmering over the river in the setting desert sun.

"You will get used to it. You will like it here," Hakim tried to encourage her. "There are many opportunities to be successful here and go different places around the world for opportunity."

By the time they arrived at the apartment in the older part of Hillah with its bullet holes and chunks of wall torn out by shells, and when they carried the worn suitcases inside, Farah had no words and her face was pale. She feigned confidence as she squatted on the edge of the mattress on the floor, but then she suddenly began to cry. He wasn't sure what to do. He lay down on the bed. Eventually she crawled into the mattress with her back to him, and they did not touch.

Where was the courageous daredevil, the rebellious little Farah he thought he had married?

He did his best to comfort her and then left her alone while they both fell into an uneasy sleep. Sometime during the night he awoke, rolled over, took her into his arms, and made love to her. But it was clumsy and awkward and it wasn't anything like the steamy, sexy movies on the internet that he had secretly watched.

The Abused Prisoners

They had been brought in by bus, this new group of five men, to the Governorate of Babil prison. They were treated badly by both the Chinese and Iraqi guards. The prisoners were pathetically humble, accepting punches and kicks and other types of mistreatment without retaliation or anger. The guards smacked them on the heads with the butts of their rifles if they attempted to talk to each other. Josh overheard what sounded like the word "Assyrian" spoken by the guards in a derogatory manner and tried to guess what their offense might be.

He studied the new prisoners, intrigued by their meek behavior. At first it was a suspicion, and then it grew, and finally enough clues developed that Josh was fairly certain what they were probably "guilty" of.

One prisoner seemed to be rapidly losing weight, and Josh squirreled away some of Hakim's extra food for him. He waited until a lazy moment in the exercise yard when the guards were not paying much attention and offered it to the gaunt inmate, making the sign of the cross in a tiny, subtle motion. Then he turned and walked away.

Two days later he did the same thing again.

The next day after that, the prisoner reciprocated, bringing him a bit of his own food this time. Then the prisoner, after taking a quick look around, grabbed Josh's arm. He said something in a rush of whispered language that Josh could not understand.

Alarmed, Josh took a step back. The prisoner let go; then he made a hand signal that Josh understood with a fair degree of certainty.

The gaunt man made a subtle sign of the cross, then pinched his thumb and index finger of his right hand into an oval. With his left hand, he criss-crossed his index and third fingers. He touched them to the bottom tip of the oval. Then he pressed his finger to his lips and looked around. It was as if he was saying, "our little secret."

Josh tried this new signal with one of the thin inmate's colleagues, and that prisoner reciprocated with the same new hand signal, with a hint of a smile, then looked away. And Josh knew for sure.

It was the sign of the fish, the universal symbol for Christians, less obvious than bringing attention to oneself by making the sign of the cross. No doubt the new inmates were facing capital punishment for their ethnicity and belief. Only the recent Chinese stay on executions was prolonging their lives.

By this point Josh didn't care which brand of Christian they were–Catholic, Lutheran, Eastern Orthodox, or Coptic. He no longer felt alone. In fact, he was injected with hope at the thought of other Christians being in the prison, sharing his experience.

And he knew if he were discovered by his captors, he would probably be in even more trouble than he already was.

He put the new fellow prisoners on his mental list for his wife and daughter, one more story he would tell them when he was able to go home.

Back at work, Hakim brought a pile of invoices to Commander Yang Chungying's in-basket on his desk and nearly dropped them on the floor in surprise. A hard copy of an internet ad—a screenshot from the commander's computer—had fallen out of the commander's printer onto the floor with a picture of the American prisoner in Arabic, Chinese, and English. There was a phone number to call, and a reward of $500,000 American dollars!

He knew without a doubt that he was not meant to see it, nor was anyone else on staff. He ran out of the office and froze in the hallway for a moment, listening. No one was coming. He stepped back into the office, gingerly picked it up, and took a photo of the flier with the website address. Five hundred thousand dollars! Listening for noises in the hall outside the door, he tried to put it back on the floor the way he found it.

He thought he would burst inside. He could finally be rich! This could be his way of escape from joining the mujahedin!

The unscrupulous commander was probably planning to turn over the prisoner and pocket the money. He stopped outside the cell and stared at the American, who was stretched out on the sleeping mat in boredom, and tried to formulate questions to ask once they could get a moment alone together. But there was always someone around in the prison cells or prison yard, or some problem with an order that kept him on the phone with vendors and away from the prisoner.

That night he lay awake, talking with Farah about all of the things they would do if he were to be rich someday. She eagerly played the fantasy game with him, although he did not tell her about the prisoner with the reward. No one must know. Farah drifted to sleep by his side as he fantasized about riches that could be his if only he could figure how to get the prisoner under his control. He agonized over what to do. Could he share the information with someone else, kidnap the prisoner, and split the reward? The only person he came close to trusting was Yazen. Yazen was heavy and looked more intimidating than he really was. In a group setting he could kick and fight hard as he had been trained; but actually he was a somewhat timid person, mostly interested in keeping the peace.

The next morning he woke up, determined. He was going to beat the commander to it. Somehow he needed to send proof that the prisoner was alive, today! Photographing a prisoner was prohibited. He would have to find a way to do it covertly.

A daring plan came to mind. He climbed out of bed, reached for his phone, headed to the bathroom in the trailer with a wadded up stack of laundry, shut the door, and silently practiced in front of the bathroom mirror.

Once he arrived at work, he visited the American's cell with an armload of clean laundry. The mobile was underneath it, set to video, and filming the prisoner was actually an easy matter. "Here, you have good behavior this week. You receive clean blankets," he said, perching the mobile strategically under the bottom blanket.

Acclimated somewhat to special treatment lately, ever since the dropped mobile phone incident, the prisoner approached him and reached through the bars and pulled the clean bedding into the cell. Hakim slid the mobile into his back pocket before it could be noticed.

And then he waited until the commander was sure to be gone and went into the office with another pile of invoices.

He waited until no one was in the hallway. As soon he came into the office, he closed the door. His eyes fastened on the pink Talky Watch that had belonged to the American that was gathering dust on top of the filing cabinet. He snatched it up, making his way to the commander's computer.

"AHLAN," he told it to turn on. The screen blinked, waiting for him to enter the commander's password.

He was disappointed but not surprised. The computer was set to require the commander's password every single time. He would have to resort to Plan B.

He unbuckled his belt, unzipped his jeans, and stuffed the Talky Watch in his underwear. He opened the door of the commander's office and hurried towards his locker to gather up his things for the day. Scurrying down the hallways towards the Exit, he called the commander's voicemail. The ugly Chinese voice answered and Hakim left his superior a message: "I am very sick today with the diarrhea and request the commander to leave work."

He made his way to employee security checkout, doubled over, and feigned a horrible stomach ache, telling the same story about being ill with diarrhea. He was let out with a minimal, hurried pat-down and took off on his bike for the old city, Hillah.

Farah was in the shabby apartment, watching an Iraqi soap opera. Her phone was next to her and she was set to resume the banned NoitaLever game during a commercial. If she wasn't playing the game these days, she was on the phone with her silly sisters and friends back at home. "Go to the store, buy medicine for the diarrhea," he ordered her roughly, shoving money at her. Startled, she scurried up from the couch, throwing her hajib on her head and wrapping it around. She muttered a stream of Arabic swear words and scampered out of the apartment before he could scold her.

He sighed. Marriage had not been what he dreamed or hoped for. His married cousin had not told him it would present such difficulties! They were always short of money. Farah was bored and lonely by day, constantly begging him to take her someplace interesting and even talking about finding a job. It was becoming evident why her parents were eager to get her married off. She had a defiant streak and was prone to go exploring without a chaperone and strike up conversation with strangers. She went out in public without her hijab the other day.

He turned on his computer and set the Talky Watch next to it. He pulled out his mobile, set the time and date stamp, and began recording a video. The watch turned on, showing the date and time on its little screen (apparently American time, because it was several hours wrong) and jabbering questions at its imaginary little American friend. He shut off both devices and then saved the first video of the American prisoner on the computer, edited down to a short snippet, showing only the blurry image of the prisoner as he walked towards the bars to reach for the linens.

Tomorrow he would return the Talky Watch to the commander's office. He would make it appear to have fallen on the floor next to the filing cabinet. If he were lucky, no one would even notice.

But if he were caught, he would be accused of stealing and maybe even of being a traitor. He could be fired, or brutally punished.

253

Hakim makes plans

Hakim's former housemate, Yazen, wanted to be a good Muslim. However, Yazen fundamentally loathed anything riskier than a soft life of computers and basic necessities, so getting him to go along with a plot to get the $500,000 reward did not prove to be as difficult as Hakim had anticipated. For one thing, Hakim had some things on him—the earbuds, playing NoitaLever under his pillow at night, and Yazen's confession that he did not want to join the mujahedin.

"We are not betraying...our Muslim brothers by...abandoning them," Yazen rationalized breathlessly. "What we are doing...is stealing the American away from the Chinese... so they cannot claim the reward, yes? If we have money...we can pay the mujahedin not to join....like the sons of the rich sheiks!" Yazen immediately set to work and secretly located an intermediary who would take a percentage in exchange for setting up a Swiss bank account.

"I know a place we can take the prisoner and keep him until we get the money," Hakim said, holding up the key he had found in the prison cell in the basement of Saddam's palace on their initiation trip up the river. Yazen's eyebrows shot up in admiration. Suddenly Hakim got an alert on his mobile. He read it and stuffed it hurriedly back into his pocket.

"Who is that?" Yazen asked suspiciously. They were on a tightrope with each other. They had a blood oath not to tell anyone else what they were doing.

"Farah." Using her NoitaLever online identity, Farah had sent Hakim an invitation to play a round. He rolled his eyes. She was constantly doing that. He usually accepted her requests, but his current decisions and responsibilities were great. Farah should just send a request to her favorite brother instead.

"She still does not...guess?" Yazen pressed.

"No. She is curious. She asks many questions."

"What are you going to...do about her?"

"We will call her after we get across the border. We will find a way to get her to us," Hakim retorted agitatedly. It was a monumental problem, but not as imminently monumental as their present tasks.

Spiriting the American out of Governorate of Babil Prison would be difficult, but not impossible. The window of time was small, but they knew the intervals of lax attention and vulnerable points of exit. The biggest challenge would be to actually transport a live, uncooperative human being. Neither one of them owned a vehicle. They argued over nearly a half-dozen possibilities but came to a barrier at every turn. Without a vehicle, how would they get the prisoner to Saddam's palace, and how would they go to him each night with food and water? How would they get out of the country quickly? And what country would they escape to?

"We could go to America," Hakim broached the subject.

"Oh, no!" exclaimed Yazen, appalled and stuttering. "Brother, the Quran…leaves us no doubt! *'Let not the believers…take the disbelievers for friends…rather than believers. And whoever does this…has no connection with Allah.'* We must go to a…Muslim country!"

America was where Hakim was determined to end up. But that did not matter for now. He would talk Yazen into America later. The first thing they would have to figure out was how to get past Chinese troops and across the Iraqi border.

"**S**o, you have chatter about an American prisoner being held in a prison in the vicinity of Babylon Metro? These," said the tech, unrolling long rolls of paper the size of blueprints, "are your two possible detention facilities."

Liu Chen, the analyst from National Clandestine Services, and The Farm classmate of Josh Evans, a/k/a Ryan Taylor, was in Springfield, Virginia, nineteen miles south of CIA headquarters. She pored over amazing GEOINT photos of two different prisons, including one prison in Babylon Metro, along with a tech team member of the National Geospatial Intelligence Agency, known as NGA. Liu sucked in her breath. The photos were incredible in their detail. Several shots had been cropped together to form a large aerial picture, an overlay of each prison's outer areas.

"We are looking among these individuals for a prisoner who does not appear to be native," she explained to the tech. A photo of Josh Evans, prior to his kidnapping, was posted on the bulletin board over the work table, and she pointed to it. "He is short, approximately five-foot-seven inches."

Some of the photos had high enough resolution to view the prisoners at various times a day in the prison courtyards or working in enclosed gardens. One photo was quite detailed and showed a long line of prisoners lined up in chains to enter a van. "If this is north, then based on the shadows, this is probably early morning," the tech observed. One by one, they studied each prisoner, and even individuals they were not sure were prisoners. "It would be hard to keep something like this quiet for very long, wouldn't it? An American prisoner being held without the media finding out, or at least the consulate, or the Foreign Minister, or the Chief of Station?"

"It is Iraq," Liu shrugged uncomfortably at the question, not quite sure which was worse—for an American to disappear, particularly a close colleague; or for another branch of the government to find out that the CIA did not have information until now where he might be held.

"My guess is," the tech continued, pointing to the vans, "that they would not take him off site—that he is probably kept in the compound 24-7. Maybe even inside where he cannot be detected. You may not be able to get a trace on him visually. Can't you send in one of your CIA micro-drones for a DNA sample?"

"That's an older technology we purchased, about seven years ago," Liu replied. "The Chinese developed anti-drone detection for those. Wait, look at this. Can you zoom in?" She circled a figure standing in one of the prison courtyards next to a second figure. It was difficult to tell, but there was something different about the height and the build of that prisoner than the other prisoners. The second figure appeared to be a little taller and to be armed.

"No, but we can work with the shadows and try to reconstruct a close-up. It looks like many of the prisoners have beards. It won't be great but it will still be a little better than this."

"Can you get more satellite photos of the prison?"

"I don't know. It's expensive. That's above my paygrade. We can get you an estimate and you can try to make a budget request from your department."

Liu continued to study the aerial shots, chewing on a fingernail and thinking about drones. It would definitely take some more creative accounting to fulfill another expensive budget request on the search for Josh Evans, a/k/a Ryan Taylor. She tried to think of a workaround of the system, feeling her stomach churn anxiously. Until recently, Analyst Liu Chen had never been anything but the most loyal of team players, always playing by the book. Lately she had stretched and broken the rules in her research on the disappearance of Ryan. She had some clearance designators by her name that allowed her to read traffic and cables, but they were well outside of the scope of her daily job, and she had gone beyond the boundaries. Her nights were sleepless and her job was on the line.

"You've got yourself a clusterfuck," the tech said, shaking his head, also studying Liu's photos. "This is the kind of thing that lands the CIA in a hearing across the river with the Senate Select Committee on Intelligence."

They may be working together, but at the end of the day he was from another agency, one that fought for its own turf and competed for its own budget. She did not answer him.

257

It was late morning at Monument Metroplex. The Mizrahi and Associates team had improvised a putt-putt golf course that ran around the cubicles. The associates cheered and high-fived each other whenever the golf ball rolled into the tin can taped to the carpet.

Chelsea ducked into her office to head out to visit a client on Chain Bridge Road who wanted to meet her with his executive committee and lawyers about an office lease. While they were all playing putt-putt golf, a message for the www.FreeJoshEvans website had popped into her inbox. She squinted at the clunky translation: *"I have American. Money required in US dollars wire to bank..."*

Her immediate instinct was that it was a scam. Several other messages had come, preceded by a surge of hope and followed by disappointment. She clicked on the attachments, squinting at the screen.

It was a video of a Talky Watch. She blinked at the video in shock as it chattered, trying to comprehend what she was seeing.

Then she clicked on the other attachment, a second video.

A scream tore from her throat at the image of her husband, barely recognizable, as he advanced towards the camera, clearly behind bars. His hair was wild and long, and he had grown a beard. This was for real!

Dimly she heard the rush of feet as her concerned team members ran to her office door. She sat frozen in shock, and her golf ball dropped out of her hand into the thick white carpet with a thud. In seconds every employee crowded by her side as well, their golf clubs down at their sides, gaping at the screen, jabbering in apprehensive voices and pointing and asking questions.

The room swam as they shouted. She couldn't deal with this here. She needed to talk to the CIA immediately! She needed to talk to Kimberly! "I—I need to take this to my lawyer's office. Now." She stood up on wobbly legs, teetering at the desk and fumbling for her purse and keys. "We need to figure out what to do, call the proper authorities, follow protocols," she mumbled, staggering around the side of the desk and bumping her hip hard on the corner. "OW!"

"No, Chelsea, you shouldn't drive. Let one of us take you to your lawyer's office."

Chelsea faced all of them bravely, her face white, grateful for their empathy. "I'll be ok."

"No, you won't. You can't drive with a shock like that. You need someone with you. Accounting duties and golf can wait. I'll take you in my car," Dane said firmly.

She staggered alongside him to the door and the elevators, her hands clammy, her stomach like ice, and her ears ringing. Vaguely she felt him holding her left arm, supporting her. As they went down to the garage, she tried to process it while he opened the door and helped her into the car.

Josh was alive!

Somehow, the captors knew that Josh was connected with Peppermint Pinkey toys!

Later, she could not remember much about the drive to Kimberly's office, only that Dane tried to ask her some questions and finally gave up. In a blurred daze she made her way from the car in the warm June sun to Kimberly's office, Dane holding her elbow. She barely heard her own quavering voice ask the receptionist for Kimberly. The receptionist, startled by the ghastly pale and trembling figure standing before her, lost no time frantically messaging Kimberly to come back to the office as fast as possible.

As she and Dane sat in the waiting room, his face nearly as white as hers, the thought flitted through her mind that in an awful way Dane must certainly be reliving his own missing wife's death in Africa.

She had the presence of mind to call her client and cancel the appointment, giving the excuse that she "suddenly got sick and had to get a ride from work." She called the summer nanny with instructions not to leave the house with Atalaya.

She tried to calm her thinking and analyze, watching the video over and over. Josh was in a prison, the kind with bars and concrete block where prisoners wore uniforms…at least he was not in a cave or a vacant house…and he wasn't tied or chained. Dane peered at it over her arm, trying to offer helpful observations. How long, she wondered, could she keep it a secret from people that Josh was CIA? Somehow she had to get rid of Dane so he didn't overhear something he shouldn't….

The old-fashioned clock across from the receptionist in the corner of the waiting room ticked slowly, its hands crawling, an ironic juxtaposition to the modern Talky Watch in the photo and the traffic zooming by on the busy street outside. Atalaya had not played with Peppermint Pinkey much lately. She definitely had not played with the Talky Watches. With a sudden jolt, a memory flashed back.

She recalled standing at the sink, washing the dirty Peppermint Pinkey doll the day Atalaya ran away to The Hole. Behind her, out in the hallway just off the kitchen, she remembered Josh's reproachful voice speaking to Atalaya before they left for the reception with the architectural and construction lobbyists:

I am going to take away the Peppermint Pinkey Talky Watch. You can have it back when you've shown me that you are a big girl and you will play with the other children at recess and not run away to The Hole. Don't keep asking me and Mommy to have your Talky Watch back. You are going to have to show us first that you will follow the rules."

Did Josh tell someone there that he had a daughter who liked Talky Watches? Come to think of it, what had Josh done with the watch? Had he actually taken it to Iraq, as some kind of memento?

THE TALKY WATCH HAD GPS!

The thought exploded into her mind so hard she jumped in her chair and Dane jerked sideways towards her, his face alarmed, his Adam's apple throbbing with wordless questions.

Frantically she fumbled with her mobile device, looking for the Talky Watch password Clinton had sent her. Her hands shook so hard she could hardly hold it. She logged in and entered the password.

A pulsing light appeared.

She zoomed out slowly. It was a residential neighborhood in a city. There were locations in Arabic!

Hillah, Iraq.

She zoomed in and out and studied the street level view. It was shabby and old and crowded and looked residential. She was confused. Josh had looked like he was behind prison bars. She needed to report this to Headquarters! But Dane remained steadfastly seated next to her. She asked to use the conference room with the door closed while they waited, and the receptionist obliged. She called Clinton, got no answer, frantically messaged him, and got a brief "I haven't checked the spy software lately, I'll look into it." Then she called CIA headquarters in a low, shaky voice, hoping the door between her and Dane was soundproof.

While she was talking, the door suddenly flew open. Kimberly, sweating from rushing back to the office in the summer humidity and who had not even bothered to put down her heavy brief case, burst into the room, her mouth a huge round "O" of shock.

Τhe cave where the brothers were meeting in the dark of night was along the river south of Hillah and where Hakim and his friends had disposed of the dead body required by their second initiation into the group. The recruits had begun arriving over an elongated period of time, parking some distance away and walking so that they would not bring attention to themselves, carefully watching for the cloth strips that provided a safe route through mines. A satellite dish and generator were running outside of the cave, and cords snaked into the interior to provide power and a minimal amount of light for the would-be insurgent fighters.

What if the Chinese had a spy in their midst? And what if the brothers read their mind and determined that Hakim and Yazen were planning a way of escape from the mujahedin?

They all shushed each other and came to attention for the introductory slide presentation. Ominous music played in the devotional video, the kind of music that portended doom. Photo after photo floated across the screen of construction cranes assembling the spectacular tower buildings in Babylon Metro against the blue desert sky. "The prophecy in the Hadith has come true," intoned the narrator's voice. "Hundreds of years ago the Hadith prophesized that at the end of the world, 'People will compete in the construction of very tall buildings.' The enemy lives in your presence!"

Hakim felt a chill creep up his arms as the music swelled. If he ever doubted the Muslim faith, the doubts were swept away when he heard prophecies like this which had actually come to pass. Then the screen turned blue and zig-zagged, and the face of Abu al-Qummi emerged. This time he was live, talking to them via satellite from what appeared to be a safe house. *"Salaam alaikum."* Peace be upon you.

"Alaikum salaam," the group responded.

"In the name of Allah, most gracious, most merciful. There is no power and no might save in Allah…" The fatwa against the Chinese, the Jews, and the Crusader tyrants, their offenses, and the measures that must be taken went on and on and on for an hour and a half. The cave grew stuffy and uncomfortable.

At the end the mufti told them to wait for the day that their imam would instruct them to lift up arms. "You are not to ask; just wait," he said. "Praise be to Allah, the lord of the worlds! May he be exalted! Now I am ready to take your questions."

A young man raised his hand. "When we were children, there was famine, and the people of Iraq were butchered in the streets by ISIS and terrorists. Will we and our families receive food and health care to join the fight against the Chinese?"

Hakim knew the youth that was speaking out. His tent, one which sold shoes, was just down the way in the marketplace, and it was from him Hakim had procured the American sneakers.

The mufti's tone was harsh. "You say that you believe the Quran. But do you follow its every word, or do you only obey what you choose? You must banish weakness and fear! The time is not right yet but we are raising the money to fight. I will ask you this: have you given of your money for the cause of weapons?"

The mufti was just as corrupt as anybody, flashed the disloyal thought through Hakim's mind.

Then the mufti's tone softened into a cajoling one. "But your reward is greater than any money we can raise for you. Let me ask you a question. How far are you from the Euphrates River?"

They looked at each other and snickered. A chorus of voices rang out in a jumbled answer. If you meant the main Euphrates, it was just a few miles to the west. The river that ran by their settlement, Al-Hillah, was a branch of the Euphrates. Basically, you couldn't be any closer to it.

The mufti stuck his hands out in front of him, parallel. "Quiet, now, quiet. Listen. Consider the promise of Allah's messenger in the Hadith about the future, the end of time, before the Madhi and Jesus come again: 'The Last Hour would not come before the Euphrates uncovers a mountain of gold, for which people would fight. Ninety-nine out of each one hundred would die but every man amongst them would say that perhaps he would be the one who would be saved and thus possess this gold.' Now just imagine if you obey the call to fight, and drive out the Chinese, and we are in the last days, and *you* are the one to preserve the mountain of gold in the Euphrates! You will go to victory, or you will ascend to those who never die!"

A roar went up around the cave at the idea of this particular prophecy coupled with a call to jihad against the Chinese. Hakim felt his neck prickle as energy surged around the room and he heard the familiar words. A mountain of gold!

"Your attention! Please!" the mufti said severely. "What if the gold is the oil pipeline, and you are the one meant to preserve the oil for the Iraqi people? These are the Unseen Things! Allah knows best!"

The men in the cave muttered among themselves. Certainly Iraq's oil, while plentiful, was slowly and surely being controlled by the Chinese. The Americans were about to lose another oil field lease because they could not repay their national debt to the Chinese. Thus far, the Chinese had been generous towards the Iraqi people with the oil splits. Food and medical care in Iraq were more available than ever before.

A shout went up in the cave. Hakim looked nervously towards the exit. The prophecy of gold in the Euphrates…Hakim's mind began to wander. He had not thought much about the prophecy in recent years. As a boy, it had captured his imagination. He drifted off into a daydream, briefly forgetting his plan to get rich holding the American hostage. He imagined that the gold was close by, right near Babylon Metro, and that he, Hakim, would find it.

The imams had always held a general consensus that the prophecy warned of greed. People would die while trying to find the treasure.

The Analysts

The analysts at the CPD in the basement of CIA headquarters in Langley were very, very busy. The email with the Talky Watch video, sent to the www.FreeJoshEvans.com website, was tracked via its domain. The email had come from Iraq from a server in the ghetto part of Hillah outside of Babylon Metro. A bevy of CIA personnel went to work scrutinizing every detail for every possible clue, painstakingly analysing the video frame by frame. Another team identified the type of phone device and home computer and began a search to determine what store it was purchased in and who the buyer was.

The origination of the email with the photo of the Talky Watch, however, did not correlate with Talky Watch GPS location. That location clearly indicated that the hostage was at Governorate of Babylon prison. Liu Chen was called in. She placed prints of the GEOINT photos of the prison on the conference table, and a swarm of investigators hovered over them.

The taker of the photo, they finally concluded, may have taken it in at the prison but sent the email from the apartment house.

A second email, a different account, with demands to wire five hundred thousand dollars to a bank account in Switzerland, tracked from the same area.

There were many meetings involving many divisions and departments and numerous personnel to determine exactly how to respond to the emails.

A plan was drawn up to establish contact to verify that Josh Evans was alive. There would be full audio contact involving a parabolic mic, video feeds, security feeds, and a horde of operatives to man all of the technology.

After that would be a series of reports on possible evacuation of the target by a Special Forces team. It would involve a drone, satellite feeds, and translators tracking chatter. But first, of course, they would need the go-ahead from the Baghdad Agency office to double check that they did not intrude on Baghdad's organizational turf or upset a sensitive political situation between either the Chinese or the Iraqis.

There needed to be a strategy for each and every detail, approved by multiple departments and layers of bureaucracy. And it must be done while denying that Josh Evans was a clandestine officer and simply treating him like a normal citizen.

Liu Chen, with her soft, meek voice, expressed concern to her immediate supervisor about the delays. There was chatter about local unrest and a possible terrorist plot or plots. Was there a way to expedite this rescue operation in case violence broke out in the region?

Her supervisor said he would request an analysis from Homeland Security on the potential for regional conflicts in the area and send it on to his immediate supervisor for review, who would then pass it on to his director.

The phone call to Jihad, spoken in cryptic code words, "Black Lightening" with brief instructions, came in the middle of the night.

Nothing about this was a surprise, but nevertheless, Hakim dropped back onto his pillow and beads of sweat popped out on his forehead, staring at the dark ceiling. Outside the shoddy, pitted walls of the apartment complex, a vehicle rumbled past, its headlights casting spooky shadows on the bedroom wall.

"What is it?" Farah mumbled in sleepy alarm, stirring on the pillow next to him.

"Nothing, my pretty one, a disturbance at work." he said, touching her petite body lying next to him. Oh well, at least he had experienced the pleasures of a woman before he died or left the country. His hand stroked the tangle of her hair. "Do you not get tired of the disturbances? Do you also tire of the Chinese and their rule over us?"

Somewhere under the long, curly hair was a small sound. Was it an agreeable acknowledgement?

"We would always be safe if we lived in America," he continued. "They do not have all the travails that Iraq has."

"Mmmhmm."

"If anything happens to me," he pressed, "You should try to go to America. Do you understand me?"

"I would adore to have an adventure," she rolled halfway over and yawned. "Shall we go this very afternoon, my husband?" Her voice was a dry, croaky whisper, but even in her sleepy state there was a coquettish recklessness about her.

"Don't ever tell anyone we discuss America!" he snapped worriedly in the dark. "I must go now."

"Where are you going?" she stirred and sat up as he rose from the mattress.

"I have a meeting at work."

"No you don't. You do not get ever called to work this suddenly at night. I want to come with you. I am tired of this place."

It was ridiculous. "Stay!" he ordered savagely. "It may be long hours at work tomorrow for me."

With an angry huff she rolled over, her back to him. He could not help but admire her spirited sense of adventure. Would he ever see her again?

He put on his shoes and clothes in the dark, ducked out of the apartment without any more speaking between them, and headed on his bike towards Ali's trailer where a particular group of employees—Iraqi resisters, of course—were to receive more specific instructions for the jihad. He and Yazen would play the part to the end; they would try to fool the brothers.

From his father, who was expecting the settlement from the Chinese government for his sister's death, Hakim had borrowed money for transport of the prisoner. Farah's favorite brother had quickly helped locate an old, inexpensive white Volvo truck to buy and even brought it down to Hillah for them before catching a ride back to the village with a local farmer. Hakim admired his young brother-in-law's bravado and enthusiasm and nearly took him into his confidence, but then he reconsidered and decided it was too dangerous. No one should know of their plot.

Yazen and Hakim would head north towards Mosul and the Turkish border. From there they would escape to Switzerland and collect the money. But the call to insurgency came too soon; they were not quite ready—somehow, they had yet to work out exactly how they would cross the border. Hakim wished to make a plan for Farah, and hopefully her brother also—to join them.

The meeting was over just before the light of dawn. Hakim went home and washed and shaved himself and said his prayers.

"Fighting is prescribed for you, and ye dislike it. But it is possible that ye dislike a thing which is good for you, and that ye love a thing which is bad for you."

The prophecies said that two thirds of the world's population needed to die before the Mahdi—Islam's savior—would come and rule the world. Jihad was necessitated in order to bring on the end times! On the other hand, if he was successful in getting the American out of prison and receiving the ransom, he could go far, far away with the money....

The resistance employees at Governorate of Babil Prison were tense and alert, barely speaking, watching the clock tick, waiting for the signal. He and Yazen huddled together in a storage closet for several minutes, sweating and listening in the hall for footsteps, making last-minute plans and contingencies.

The opportunity to spirit the American out came when the others were chained and loaded up to go to the vans to do farm work. The American prisoner was left to scrub the latrines. Hakim stepped in and closed the door and locked it, pulling out a pistol and throwing women's clothing on the floor. "Stop! Take off your clothes. Wear this. We take you away from here! You will go home!"

The prisoner jerked back in surprise, clutching his only possible weapon, the brush. His eyes flitted to the bucket of soap. "Don't touch that," Hakim snapped, pointing the pistol towards the prisoner's foot. "Take off your clothes! Put this on so you can hide!"

The prisoner stared at him suspiciously. Hakim repeated the request in Arabic. He threw his mobile and Yazen's mobile in the toilet. They had new mobiles, the cheap kind without tracking devices.

As he held the gun on the prisoner, he was thankful for his Chinese military security training which gave him the courage to do this, but his heart thumped so wildly he was sure it would jump out of his chest.

The prisoner warily accepted the dress and slowly began to take his prison uniform off, eyes darting behind Hakim, looking for a chance to escape. Hakim smacked his arm with the butt of the pistol. "Hurry! We take you now!"

When the prisoner got the woman's dress on, Hakim clamped his wrists in handcuffs in front, tied a gag around his mouth, and covered the dress with an abayah and shoved a niqaab over his head so that only the slits of his eyes showed.

"March!" he ordered, gesturing down a tiled hallway.

All of a sudden they heard the sound of an explosion down at the other end of the building. The structure vibrated and shook.

"Run! Run!" Hakim shoved the prisoner towards the exit door. He flung it open. Outside acrid smoke and debris poured out of a gaping hole in the wall by the road.

"HURRY! GET IN!" bellowed Yazen.

The prisoner stumbled and started to fall, unable to catch himself with his hands. Hakim picked him up and bodily threw him into the back seat of Yazen's white Volvo truck and jumped in. "Go! Go!"

Jeeps with mujahedin pulled off the road, cut through the barbed-wire fencing, and streamed into the bombed-out section of the prison wall. Inside the prison, pandemonium ruled as Iraqi staff and insurgents opened gunfire on the Chinese personnel, chanting, "Death to China!"

In his office, Commander Yang Chunying frantically clicked on his keyboard, trying to get the close-circuit images to re-appear on the screen. He was simultaneously on the phone shouting to the control room when the door burst open.

An Iraqi resistance fighter pulled a pistol and shot him dead in the head. Blood and brains splattered against the wall, dripping down onto the filing cabinet with the Talky Watch, which just yesterday the commander had noticed had fallen to the floor and had returned it to its place on top of the files.

In the loading area in the other part of the compound where the vans were lined up to transport inmates to work duty, mujahedin seized the five Assyrian Christian prisoners, unchained them, and dragged them at gunpoint to the far end of the prison exercise yard. "On your knees!" they screamed.

Insurgents surrounded the vans and more gunshots sounded, then an ear-shattering explosion went off. A grenade created an instant barrier between the rioting crowd at one end of the prison courtyard and the group of Christian prisoners and their captors at the other end. The prisoners cried out in plaintive prayer. A hooded figure with a butcher knife approached the first prisoner. "Allahu Akbar!"

And with a slash, he began the decapitations.

75

The White Volvo Truck

At CIA headquarters in Langley, alarmed team members from the CIA Middle East Division, the State Department, as well as the Deputy Director of the National Clandestine Service, Technical Services Unit of Nonofficial Cover supervisor Rich Novak, and Analyst Liu Chen studied the replays of video feed from multiple sources with dismayed incredulity. Other screens around the room showed live footage from the news agencies and AWAC's live-action satellite feed. Billows of smoke puffed into the sky and obscured the concrete cinderblock prison structure. Chinese troops completely encircled the building, returning fire at the insurgents remaining inside.

"Get the National Action Center on the phone ASAP to re-task the satellite. How soon can we get verification if the target was decapitated?"

"It's also possible that he was taken out in gun battle inside the complex...."

"Operational goal for Operation AuCHFOP is modified from divert-disable to containing collateral...."

"It's going to require a United Nations resolution to put pressure on the Chinese to allow us in to verify the dead. The Chinese will never release casualty figures...."

"Black Lightening has claimed responsibility for the insurgency...."

Liu noticed something in the replay just before the first explosion. The next time it looped, she pointed her red laser beam to the screen. "Look, this is very strange, it appears a truck is leaving the prison, not arriving," she said in puzzlement. "It's white."

But no one listened to her. Unfortunately, Liu was short and slight and had a voice that was very soft and timid. There were other red lasers zooming around and pointing at various details on multiple screens, and far too much mayhem for anyone to hear what she said.

Richard Novak, Josh's supervisor, punched his fist on the countertop, shaking his head and muttering. "And we were just twenty-four hours away from a targeted drone strike on the prison and rescue…Twenty-four damned hours! Operation AuCHFOP," he grumbled sourly, "is FUBAR." He leaned over the counter, supporting himself with his arms, shaking his head. Sweat beads popped out on his forehead and stains encircled the armpit area of his white dress shirt.

FUBAR. The military and CIA term for 'fucked up beyond all recognition.'

76

Saddam's Palace Prison

J osh finally realized after the blindfold was taken off where he was, and a bitter, choked laugh escaped from his throat.

What irony!

He had been bound and gagged again and taken by gunpoint by the two prison guards, Hakim and Yazen, in a truck that was a recipient of gunshots as it skidded crazily out of the prison. Then he had been blindfolded and dragged onto a boat in the dark of night in the stinky Euphrates River. After that they had taken off the blindfold, handcuffed his hands in front of him and forced him to stumble up a riverbank and to the top of a rocky hill on hands and knees in the dark and crawl through a hole in a wall.

They shoved him through a hall and down stairs into the small below-ground prison underneath the kitchen that Crestedon, doing business under the front name of Pyramids and Palaces Architectural Renovation, had never finished restoring. Hakim drew a key out of his pocket and unlocked a cell, pointing a Russian-made sniper rifle at Josh's head as Yazen pushed him inside and undid his restraints.

These kids were crazy, Josh thought to himself. Yazen might have some sort of speech impediment, but he was large and heavy, and when teamed up with someone else, unafraid to inflict pain. Hakim was wildly greedy. If only they knew what might be down underneath the prison floor, if they had any earthly idea what could happen once they invited the attention of the Chinese military.

As soon as the gag was off, he said, "Give me some water. Hakim, you know the legends, about Babylon don't you?"

"What?" Hakim handed him a bottled water.

Josh took gulps of water, eyeing his captor with wide, innocent brown eyes. "Superstitions. Bad luck. Evil. You know the legends. The curse of Babylon. It is in the ancient writings! They say, 'Babylon will never be inhabited or lived in from generation to generation; nor will the Arab pitch his tent there, nor will shepherds make their flocks lie down there. But desert creatures will lie down there, and their houses will be full of owls; ostriches also will live there.'"

"Ah, yes, curse of Babylon." Hakim shrugged. Most visitors learned about it; it provided intriguing mystique for the tourism industry. He had certainly escaped the so-called curse himself. "Now I am going to tell you what will happen. You will be rescued and you will go home as soon as we get the money. I need you to talk to the camera to your wife. Chel-sea."

Josh's heart thudded. Chelsea must know he was alive, must have arranged a reward. On the extremely razor thin chance that this might actually happen, Josh calculated that his odds were better if he cooperated as much as possible while always looking for a way to escape. There was a moral ambiguity to confront, his own personal Stockholm Syndrome—the possibility that he may have to kill the very captor he was trying to recruit as an asset.

He followed instructions, posing for the camera and saying exactly what was instructed, meanwhile trying to concoct a scheme to get a weapon and get away alive from the two juveniles and nearby Chinese soldiers; and even more importantly, away from what might be below the prison floor.

77

The Smugglers

Hakim and Yazen took turns around the clock sitting guard and sleeping in the small basement prison with their backs against the cinderblock corridor wall and their guns on their laps pointed at the American prisoner behind the bars. The hours crept by and none of them slept much. There was no cell phone reception for their disposable phones down in this part of the palace. The yellow Caution tape still remained in place upstairs on the ground level, and tour guides always steered visitors to the other end of the palace away from the re-construction, so they were isolated. Yazen left while it was still dark to sneak out and steal some paint in order to cover their white Volvo truck with camouflage.

It was easier, Hakim thought, to converse with the prisoner in the night when they could not see each other's faces. They were restless and bored. What harm was there in robust discussion? He plied Josh with questions about the United States. Why do the Americans follow their fleshly desires? Why do the women show their skin? If there is plenty in America, why do Americans steal and kill each other?

The prisoner listened carefully in the darkness and answered Hakim's questions thoughtfully. "There is freedom and plenty in America, but just because there is freedom and plenty does not mean that you have to do as some of the Americans do. You are right, you should never steal and kill. Freedom means that as long as you do not break the law, you are free to live as a Muslim. Your women do not have to show their skin." Then he said, "You asked me questions. Now I will ask you questions. Where is the reward money? When will I be going back to America?"

"We are waiting," was Hakim's only response. To tell the truth, things were not going well. Skeptical mediators for the American wife were trying to negotiate a payment plan over time and demanding to talk to her husband live on camera. He and Yazen had the distinct feeling that time was running out.

They fell into silence. Hakim was wary, but clearly the American was attempting to assist. Earlier, the prisoner had heard Hakim and Yazen discussing crossing the border and pointed out some flaws in their plan and suggested an alternative. Hakim was thinking by now that in spite of all the problems they seemed to be having with the Americans in this negotiation, America was still their best option, if they could just get out of Iraq undetected.

"I have a question about Islam, about Black Lightening," came the prisoner's voice through the darkness. It was sudden, and the tone was challenging.

"Ask it to me."

"You had a job at the prison with Allah's enemy, the Chinese. You helped them oppress your fellow Iraqis. Will Allah allow you to go to Paradise?"

"I say my prayers and give money to the poor," Hakim answered defensively.

"Do you ever forget? Do you ever miss?"

"Allah will judge." Hakim was grateful for the darkness that hid his face. He thought guiltily of the countless times in his life he had ducked prayers, especially with the upheaval in his schedule and living conditions lately. He'd been real sloppy recently about giving to the poor because he was saving all of his money to escape.

"So you do not ever really know if you have forgiveness, then, right?" the American observed. "Because you will always make some errors."

Hakim sputtered and stumbled over words at first. "Of course I don't know. But anyone who lays down their life in service of Allah will go to Paradise!" he proclaimed.

"You really think you have to lay down your life to be guaranteed of Paradise? Then why did you run away from the prison uprising?"

Hakim bristled defensively, but he thought for a moment and then answered in the darkness in a low voice, "I am young. There will be plenty of chances to join the jihad later."

"You always have to worry where your soul will go, unless you die in jihad?"

"Good Muslims do not doubt!" retorted Hakim, but he bit his lip.

"I believe that I don't have to die for God. God died for me, so I never have to worry. See, that is the difference between you and me," the prisoner calmly pointed out.

"You are wrong! It is presumptuous and arrogant to assume that one is forgiven! Your stupid Bible is corrupted!

The American was unruffled. "So that means there is no way to know if you are forgiven and whether you will really go to Paradise, even if you die in jihad. That would be presumptuous, right?"

"Yes—no—" Hakim had never thought it all the way through like this before.

"The Quran came after the Bible, not before it. How do you know for sure which one is corrupted?"

"It is not about which one come first! It is about the tremendous miracles the Quran has, the science facts revealed to prophet Mohammed one thousand four hundred years ago, and the Quran doesn't contradict itself, ever. Not even one letter. Allah gave us one final chance to be correct with the Quran!" bellowed Hakim angrily, slamming a fist against the prison bars. When he was a little boy in the mosque, he had posed this very question to the imam and received the exact same emotional response. It had frightened him so much he had been afraid to ask any more questions.

Hakim jumped up and fled to the kitchen above, leaving the American alone in the stuffy, desolate jail cell.

Hakim returned as the early morning sun beamed a stream of fresh daylight down the steps of the prison cellar. He pointed his weapon as he delivered Josh some breakfast—an MRI that he and Yazen had stolen from their place of employment. He tried not to think about the troubling questions the prisoner had asked him earlier. The prisoner was toying with his mind. "You have a girl," he said harshly.

The American looked up from the meal briefly and then resumed digging hungrily into it.

"I know you have a girl. We have the Talky Watch of the girl."

There was a long pause but the prisoner did not meet his eyes. Finally he said, "I used to."

"What is this meaning? If man fathers a daughter, she is always his daughter."

The prisoner shrugged, and he dug further into the MRI with the flimsy plastic spoon without replying.

"Did she die?" Suddenly Hakim felt guilty for throwing the one emotional weapon he had back in the American's face. Did the girl get sick and die? He had never considered the possibility that the daughter may not be alive. No wonder the prisoner had been compassionate when his own baby sister died….

The prisoner still did not reply.

"What did she die of?" Hakim pressed.

The prisoner did not answer. Hakim plopped himself down on the concrete floor outside the cell with a grunt and took his weapon apart, polishing it and putting it together. He paused in his polishing, suddenly noticing for the first time the pile of cinderblocks that hid the opening that led to the sub-basement, the ancient secret passageway the sultans had constructed in order to reach their concubines. The American watched with increasing anxiety as Hakim crawled over and beamed his light on them. Hakim examined the loose blocks, scraped and pried, dragging them back with grunts, and finally scrambled through the hole in the wall.

Hakim was gone for thirty or forty minutes, during which time Josh was left alone. The ambiguous, dark, vague response he had given to Hakim was a calculation. If Hakim thought Atalaya was no longer a part of his life, or dead, so much the better. Atalaya could not be used as an emotional sledgehammer, or worse, tracked and kidnapped and held hostage.

When early morning sunlight began to stream down the stairwell, Josh examined every hinge of the door and every bar to the cell for some means of escape, though to no avail. Then Hakim emerged through the sub-basement door, clutching some artifacts in his hand, and ran through the small corridor past him and continued upstairs.

"Hakim! What are you doing? You are stupid if you don't take precautions!"

But Hakim ignored Josh. Sometime later, Hakim and Yazen returned together, conversing rapidly in Arabic. Together they ran back down below, carrying some empty gunny sack bags. After a time there were bumps, rattling, and knocking about. When they emerged, Hakim was euphoric, and Yazen's eyes were wild with terror, but they had filled the gunny sacks and began hauling them out.

"Hakim! HAKIM! Stop! You are a crazy man! Do you know how dangerous it might be down there?" Josh insisted urgently.

Hakim huffed and puffed as he lugged a huge box towards the exit. "There are weapons everywhere in Iraq," he retorted unconcernedly.

Josh was running out of diplomatic patience. He rattled the bars of the cell hard with his hands. "Are you getting your reward for finding me? When do I get to go back to America?"

Hakim ignored him and exited the prison.

Josh slammed an angry hand into the bar of the prison cage, panic sweeping over him at the thought that Hakim and Yazen may very well abandon him to starve and dehydrate. Whatever was cached in the basement probably had more monetary value than himself. The two captors had taken a break from stealing the antiquities and hauling them off to who knew where.

Keep calm, he told himself firmly. They were being stupid, they would come back for more and would be caught, someone would discover them all, he tried to assure himself. But even if that happened, if his suspicion was correct, a confrontation involving the sub-basement of the prison could possibly result in consequences that were disastrous beyond measure.

Hakim did finally return, bringing more water and food. "When am I going to go home?" Josh persisted. He was afraid to touch anything they had touched, or eat the food they brought.

"When the time is right, praise be to Allah." Hakim sat on the floor outside of Josh's cell with his back against the concrete block wall, cleaning and re-loading his Russian-made sniper rifle. It was an intimidation tactic, designed to fray Josh's nerves with the worry that it could go off at any time.

Was Chelsea working with Langley on a plan?

Yazen, Hakim finally said, had sneaked out to a tent in the desert along Route 8 where he would not be recognized to pick up a supply of water bottles for the prisoner. Taking advantage of their minutes alone, Josh played to Hakim's superstitious fears. "You know it is not safe to be here in Ancient Babylon. You know it has an ancient curse. You know that no one who has tried to live here has survived. Look what happened to Saddam Hussein, and he was the ruler. You and I could die at any minute." Josh was a good actor and actually it wasn't all that difficult to convince anybody of the curse at all, considering the last twenty-seven centuries of Ancient Babylon history in Iraq.

Hakim rotated his rifle over and over in his hands. Hakim had been trained to hide emotion, but Josh could tell that the emotions were just below the surface. Hakim was definitely more jumpy, constantly checking the time, and a bit irritable. Something about their plan was not moving fast enough, presumably the transfer of funds.

Josh suspected that what he was saying about the ancient curse was in fact making Hakim even more nervous. He followed his instincts and pressed his captor. "You could ask for safe passage to America if you turn me back to the Americans."

"Muslims are required to live in a place with Sharia law, for mere mortals cannot make laws." Hakim's words sounded mechanical, memorized; as if he had not really internalized them.

"In America there is always food, a place to live, a car for people who need it. If you want respect and admiration, all you have to do is work hard. In America there is a job somewhere for everyone. If you have a dream, you can live it in America. Your future is up to you."

"Allah knows our destiny. It has all been decided," Hakim replied weakly. "We are all grains of sand in Allah's plan."

"You hope it is Allah's plan for you to go to the United States, don't you? But Yazen does not want to go there," Josh intuited.

Hakim shrugged, dropped his eyes, and set the rifle on his lap. Josh knew in an instant he had made a connection.

Josh continued. "You don't want fighting. You want a job that you can enjoy and you want a family. You want to be safe. You just want to live your life, don't you?"

Hakim did not reply.

"Perhaps Allah is putting the desire to go to the United States in your heart. Perhaps he has a plan for your life. Perhaps if you go there, a whole new opportunity awaits you. You know this, and you want to go there."

The statement shattered a crack in Hakim's emotional wall. The vain, good-looking youth looked up from the floor where he was sitting and confessed to his prisoner urgently, "We cannot tell Yazen of these things. I would like to go to America."

That single sentence, *"We cannot tell Yazen of these things. I would like to go to America"* was the one hundred-percent breakthrough, an unexpected success and the hoped-for triumph. The blood pounded in Josh's ears and head but he kept his demeanor calm. "There are many things you could do, you know," he spoke calmly to the Iraqi youth. "You could be a translator. You could start your own business and sell things. You could go to college. If you could go to America, Hakim, what would you want to do? What is your greatest wish?"

"I want to be an inventor of video games."

"You can do that. There are many companies who like to try to invent new things with computers." Josh kept talking in a placid but persuasive voice. Hakim was still a ways from solid recruitment. That would take time. But he was ready to be pitched.

Ten miles away, at the little roadside tent on Route 8, the tangerine sun drifted down behind the desert sand, casting a beautiful rosy glow across the tan desert. Yazen, with a baseball cap pulled low on his head, asked to buy the rest of the bottled water. He had come as late as he dared. The proprietor of the water bottle and trinkets business was grumpy, for he wanted to close down for the evening and have a good supper. Bedouin goats that were tied to the back of the truck trailer bleated, and the small children of the owner of the tent peered around the corner and giggled, then ran away. Yazen could hear their mother call them inside.

"No, I sell you some cases of the water! Not all!" the proprietor of the little water business haggled with Yazen. "I do not have time to go into town before the morning and get more!"

Yazen paid the price and took away as many cases as the man would let him take.

The man watched him drive off, then went into the curtained off back area. There was a bulletin board set up, with various license numbers and descriptions. He unpinned the freshly delivered photocopy of wanted individuals by the Chinese police and stared at the picture.

The young man who had just bought the water had a new beard but could most certainly be one of them.

The proprietor dialed the phone number. "I want to report a criminal," he said.

In the dark of the night, Iraqi police with weapons drawn advanced on a dilapidated three-story apartment building in Hillah. The street lamp in front of the building had been shot out earlier in the day by a bribed Iraqi youth who escaped detection by Chinese security.

"Breaker switched off in hallways and stairwells. Proceed," came the instructions in their ear pieces in Arabic.

The police crept into the structure both from the back door and from the front and up the stairs to the third floor, meeting in the hallway, listening. There was no sound inside. Across the hall the dim blue light and the sound of a TV filtered out of the cracks around the front door.

One of the officers stepped back and kicked the targeted door so violently that wood splintered and flew. They stormed inside the threadbare studio apartment. The young female occupant lay in bed sleeping, and with a leap two of them made it to her just as she began screaming. A hand slapped over her face, but fierce little teeth bit into it, and the officer stifled his own yell and broke into a fiery curse. They restrained her, binding and gagging her. She continued to resist vigorously, kicking her legs and writhing.

The third and fourth officers searched the apartment while the first two hauled the struggling and thrashing female teenager out into the hallway, down the stairs, and into the waiting van.

"This is it!" The first officer inside the apartment announced jubilantly. He shone a light over a laptop bag hidden under the mattress and pulled out a computer. The second officer continued to rifle through the contents of the small apartment, gathering receipts for expenditures, a "REWARD" flier for the missing American, and the teenage girl's cell phone, dropping them in an evidence bag. "Let's go!"

The occupant down the hallway with the television on had shut it off and was shrouded in darkness. There was not a sound to be heard. Any resident in the building that had heard the noise was hiding silently in the dark shadows of their bathrooms and inside closets.

With a noisy clatter and banging, the police made their way down the stairwell and to the van outside, throwing the teenager into the back onto the floor.

The van took off, keeping a close eye out for fellow Chinese police officers in the neighborhood. It would not do for the Chinese to intercept the young female witness.

One of the officers violently ripped off the gag and began interrogating the terrified girl. "Where is your husband, Hakim Al-Obaidi?" he demanded angrily in Arabic.

"I do not know!" Farah sobbed. She had urinated on herself and the odor permeated the van. Terrified spittle drizzled out of the corners of her mouth "He has not called me and he has not come home these three days!"

Another day dragged by. As a matter of security, Yazen and Hakim usually tended to Josh in pairs, but whenever Yazen left, with calculated patience, Josh would launch into more information about escaping to America. No doubt there would be multiple people who would offer Hakim a reward for Josh's safe return, he told the Iraqi youth. Hakim could go to an American Embassy. Additionally, there was a website where he could share information about Iraq and about the Governorate prison to the CIA. The government would pay money for computer secrets!

Hakim listened without commenting. He seemed to have another plan that involved Switzerland which he and Yazen no longer discussed in front of Josh. So another day passed that was largely endless hours of solitary boredom punctuated with the rustling noises of Hakim and Yazen taking turns down in the dangerous below, doing whatever they were doing, carrying their gunny sacks of artifacts past him along the little corridor and up the stairs at all hours.

On the following morning, a noise caused Josh to stir. The door to the basement opened and no sunlight filtered in yet, so it must be before daylight. Hakim was bringing his breakfast unusually early, cold kebabs; and he was alone. Hakim unlocked the cell door and thinking Josh was sleeping, propped the rifle so it rested against the outside bars as he pushed open the door, rather than slinging it over his shoulder like he usually did.

In an instant, the providential opportunity that Josh had waited on for months fired his synapses awake and shot up his adrenaline.

In a flash he scrambled to his feet, and charged Hakim, smashing him against the concrete block wall just beyond the cell door. The breakfast went flying and Hakim let out a fearful, strangled yell, the Russian rifle clattering to the concrete floor. Josh delivered a kick in the general direction of the groin which took the inside of Hakim's thigh, cracked his head against the wall as hard as he could, and grabbed the weapon. He took off running, pointing it up the stairs in case Yazen was coming down, but there was no Yazen; he ran into the shadows along the wall of the palace with one thought in mind: to get to the river, which would get him to Route 8, which would get him to the railroad. He needed to make his way to the American Embassy in Baghdad….

He knew this building and he knew the ruins, but he also assumed the Chinese doing security for the ruins did, too. It was difficult to see in the dim morning light. He lurched over a pile of rubble, dislodging it with thumps that echoed on the palace walls. He sprinted through an archway decorated with a stone carving of Saddam's profile over a pair of eagle's wings.

The black of night had turned to the purple color of dawn. Just outside the palace near a driveway he could hear the surprised shouts of a Chinese guard who had heard the noise or spotted movement and was stumbling his way in the semi-light through the palace ruins. There was a gunshot as the officer discharged his weapon slightly behind Josh and closer to the kitchen.

Despite the ill-fitting sandals Hakim had dispensed to him, Josh zig-zagged his way through the palace, finally stopping to hide under a bed in an ornate bedroom with luxurious carpets. He slithered under and waited, panting and sweating. He was shocked at how weak he was, how heavy the weapon felt, and how quickly he ran out of breath, despite his attempts to stay in shape in prison.

He had the rifle, he just had to figure out how many bullets it had and get the feel of it. Should he stay in the palace and hide?

No! Even if the guards left, they would be calling reinforcements. Daylight was emerging. Later this morning a tour group might come through down at this end of the palace! Water would be an urgent need; dehydration could easily set in within an hour or two.

He stumbled through the maze of dark rooms, some restored and others dusty with vandalized rubble, and past a courtyard. The low sky in the east was turning pinkish-yellow. He heard vehicle engines and he scrambled through a first-floor window that was missing its glass and dropped into the scrub and sand below. Down at the bottom of the steep embankment of Saddam Hill, he could see occasional lights along the Al-Hillah River that snaked its way past Babylon Metro and merged somewhere northwest with the Euphrates. But the problem was, the ring road looped two circles up the hill around the palace, and an extremely steep expanse of sand and rock only occasionally interrupted by miniature palms and short, scratchy rose bushes separated him from the river.

He slid down on his back down Saddam Hill, the sand and rock scraping at him and the heavy rifle bumping against him, following the line of shrubbery that was inadequate to cover him; and then with a loud, painful grunt he skidded to a halt under some landscape bushes near a street lamp at the edge of the ring road. His palms and the backs of his legs were raw and stinging. Coming around the curve were headlights, no doubt the Chinese security looking for himself or headed to the palace where they would find Hakim dazed and injured. A military vehicle approached, and Josh pressed his body to the ground, praying that he would not be spotted.

The vehicle passed, and then another. He felt his heart hammering and his breath nearly stop, but when they were gone he made a break for it, crouching and running across the road and leaping down the second embankment. The sky was pink and blue now, and the sun was emerging out of the silhouette of Nebuchadnezzar's palace to the east. This part of Saddam's Hill, fortuitously, had rocks with little crannies. It would provide him a good hiding place, except for the problem of water....

He waited for what seemed like an eternity. The vehicles disappeared in the distance and quiet fell. Then he heard voices. He crawled out and peeked around the rock.

"Damned early morning sunshine tourists," he cussed bitterly. The tourists were cheerfully hiking his direction, clutching their water bottles, which only plagued his thirst worse.

He ran back and ducked under the little outcropping of rock, feeling its coolness, listening and strategizing. The tourists clambered over the rocks within thirty feet of him, speaking a European language he couldn't make out enough to recognize, and they paused to take happy photographs of themselves in the sunrise before they moved on. He curled into a tight ball, pressing himself against the wall of the little cave as they passed on without incident, one last fifty-something man dawdling along behind the rest to take pictures of the sunrise.

As this tourist passed him, Josh jumped from under the rock into the pathway, silently grabbing him and brandishing the weapon, then clapping a rough hand over the tourist's mouth. Deftly he wrenched the water bottle from the tourist's hands and then let him go, shoving him forcefully in the direction of his buddies.

With a garbled cry, the tourist threw his hands up in the air and ran. Josh tore off in the opposite direction.

The sun was up now, casting revealing light over the yellow sand, rocks, and himself. He scrambled on down the hill, angry at the vehemence of his own panting as he maneuvered his body from rock formation to rock formation and headed towards a shady area that covered the second, outer ring of the ring road. The frightened cries of the tourists in the distance echoed faintly against the rocks. Once he got to the road, again, he made a break for it, running across and leaping into a dark, little forest of date palms planted by Saddam's horticulturalists. Disappearing gratefully into the foliage, he fell down on the ground gasping for breath. All the pushups and jump squats he had tried to do in prison were no substitute for climbing and running, and lack of nutrition had taken a toll.

He drank some of the water, then located a coconut in the shadows, smashed it against the sharp roughness of the palm tree, and drank greedily, pouring more on himself than he got in his mouth. Then he found another and did the same.

It may be his only meal for a long time. He found a piece of gravel and dug out pieces of coconut, hungrily devouring them, wishing there had been time to collect Hakim's cold gyro off the prison floor. Mentally he outlined multiple options for how he was going to get from the Al-Hillah River at Babylon Metro to the U.S. Embassy in Baghdad seventy miles away. He had been trained by the CIA to create a flowchart of eventualities, and he thought rapidly through each of them as he ate the coconut. He had no money but he had a gun. Did he dare go into Babylon Metro for help, or would he be recognized by potential captors? Could he jump a train? Should he wade along the marshy edge of the river beyond Babylon Metro, then make his way to Route 8 and hitchhike to Baghdad?

He wasn't far from the river now, and the bugs were thicker. Infection and disease from a bite was an imminent danger. He heard another military vehicle pass on the ring road and the sound of a dog barking, and fear suddenly gripped him. The Iraqis didn't like to use police dogs because they were unclean, but the Chinese sometimes did, even though it caused offense. They might be combing the area, and he had a finite amount of bullets.

He had better keep on the move. He thought about his training at The Farm and the field manuals. He needed to get more water and stay out of the sun.

He moved in the direction of the river knowing dogs would lose his scent at that point, but his progress was interrupted by a fence encircling a warehouse. It forced him to explore a long, circuitous route.

The sun was soon fully up, which helped him locate an open area that contained a narrow path to the river. The foliage was denser closer to the water, but it wasn't very tall and it didn't offer the kind of hidden protection that the thick grove of palm trees had. He felt exposed and vulnerable, and he dropped to his hands and knees, crawling. Someone working in the nearby warehouses might notice him, and his movement could probably be spotted from Saddam's Hill.

And then he heard the whirr of a helicopter.

"Oh, hell, there's a sand storm every other day in this country, why can't we have one right about now and make that thing go away?" he muttered dismally. He threw himself down onto his stomach. The river was only a few yards ahead. If he could get down to it and see if any traffic was going up and down, maybe he hitch a ride....

The helicopter banked to the east away from him, circling to the other side of Saddam's palace. Was it coincidence, or was it looking for him? He scrambled to the riverbank and reached down into the dirty, smelly, muddy bottom, scooping up fistfuls of mud and covering his skin to protect himself from the bugs.

The helicopter was circling back!

This time it was flying low, very low; there was no doubt now that it was a search helicopter investigating the entire area. He shrank into the marsh, hoping that the reeds were hiding him.

Then the copter swung out directly over the river.

He covered his ears at the loud noise and froze in place. It was hovering so low he could see the pilot as it came towards him. The waters churned whitecaps, and birds with startled cries flew out of the marsh. His heart hammered in time with the rotators, and every blood vessel in his body pulsed with fear. He slunk down into the mud, but the filthy, marshy water was not deep enough at this point to cover him, and he didn't dare move....

Suddenly gunshots burst from the helicopter, and a garbled cry tore out of his lungs when a shot barely missed him.

With a surge of adrenaline he pointed Hakim's weapon in the air and concentrated on the front sight. Locking his wrist, he fired back at the helicopter, but it was ineffective at this range.

He was going to die, or he could throw himself at the mercy of the Chinese.

He threw the rifle on the shore, tore off his shirt, hoisted it high, and waved both arms in the air in surrender as he waded out of the reeds.

82

The Arrest

The Chinese, of course, could have gunned down Hakim and Yazen instantly when they were apprehended in the kitchen of Saddam's palace up above the little jail where the American hostage had been held. Or the fate of Hakim and Yazen could have been to disappear to a Chinese labor camp in Iraq, or even somewhere deep in China, for the rest of their lives.

Instead, in a political move, Hakim and Yazen were brought before the interim commander of the prison. He was fresh from Beijing, a commander in the China Marine Corps who had been quickly installed to restore order after the murder of Yang Chunying. "I have no use for them. They are traitors. Turn them over to the Iraqis. They will deal with them equally as harshly, if not more," decreed the commander.

Upon hearing it, Hakim, already bruised, nauseous, and suffering the effects of the concussion he suffered when the prisoner smashed his head against the wall, felt his internal organs go cold. The Chinese were throwing fresh meat to the Iraqis in an attempt to appease them. With the UN pressure not to use capital punishment, the outcome was going to be torture. Death would be far more merciful.

Yazen was pale, his forehead dotted with beads of nervous sweat. They were delivered over to a contingent of Iraqi soldiers and herded into a van to his former place of employment, the Governorate of Babil prison, where they were separated from each other.

Farah bravely came to visit in the prison. Prisoner's families were allowed to come once per month and to bring some food only on the first visit; after that, gifts would be confiscated. Rarely did women ever come. Her favorite brother escorted her. An Iraqi guard inspected her package for Hakim comprised of grapes, olives, and meat. The guard stood close by, listening to every word of their conversation, and they could not talk freely.

Farah was frightened but defiant. She held her head high, as if she was not ashamed that her husband had been accused of treason. She had scratches on her face and a bruise near her left eye, and Hakim's heart writhed with guilt. He longed to ask her what intimidation tactics had been used on her and her family, but she did not speak of them. He cast about frantically for a way to message her and her brother to leave the country, a hint he could drop.

"Will you move back to the home of your parents?" he asked.

"I will stay by your side," she answered resolutely, her pretty, determined little chin jutting.

"I always said that if something happened to me, you should go away. Go far away. You know that," he snapped. Her shoulders slumped but her face was stubborn. The Iraqi guard moved in closer to listen.

Did she remember what he had said about America? Did she realize that was what he meant? Would she seek a better life? Or would she choose to remain a proud Iraqi, residing in the birthplace of civilization with its millennia of unending wars and political unrest?

83

Caught

Josh went back into solitary confinement in the Babylon Metro prison for one night. He did not know any of the staff—they were all Chinese, and they were all new. Processing him, cleaning the mud from the river off him, and getting him food and clothing was very slow.

The next morning they blindfolded him and hustled him into a prison van. It rained heavily outside, a rare occurrence; the excitement of the prison staff was similar to Americans in the South experiencing a snow storm. A van with three guards transported him to some sort of air field; he could hear the shouts of workers and the whirr of engines as raindrops pounded on the pavement. His captors removed him from the van and carried into some sort of aircraft without ever removing his blindfold. They heaved him onto the floor with a thump.

An engine started, and with great noise and shaking, the helicopter rose up in the air.

He tried to guess the direction which it was going, but he was completely disoriented. Surely the helicopter must be going to Baghdad, he thought. They were probably transferring him to a Baghdad prison. No, think positively! Perhaps they really planned to release him to the American Embassy! The thought gave him hope and he rolled slightly in the floor, stretching and flexing his legs bit by bit, slowly and carefully, hoping a guard would not strike him.

A copter ride to Baghdad should only take—what, thirty minutes? An hour? But time seemed to drag on. The helicopter must be flying high because the temperature dropped, which actually felt good at first but quickly became chilly. Surely an hour had passed.

Maybe even two hours.

He was thirsty again and had to go to the bathroom, and with a raspy voice he asked aloud for water and a blanket. He heard a rustle, and a Chinese soldier roughly removed the hood and the gag and gave him a thermos with bad-tasting water. The pilot and co-pilot manning the helicopter behind sunglasses were Chinese, also. The soldier reapplied the gag and hood.

He was downright chilled now, shaking. He began to face the strong possibility that he was leaving the country and that no one would ever know.

Was there any dignity left when you had sinned and stood before your brothers in judgment? Hakim was herded in shackles to a van and driven to a court room for his trial. In the audience he recognized some of the brothers who lived around Hillah and some who worked in the prison. An Islamic cleric presided as judge.

He tried to hold his head up, but he could not. He was a thief and a kidnapper, and he had betrayed his brothers; and by doing that, he had betrayed Islam. He felt he could not bear the shame. His mother and father had driven into Hillah from the village, and they sat with his child bride, Farah, who was openly sobbing. Farah's favorite brother sat on her other side, his face taut and bitter. How his mother's heart must be breaking at the news of what he had done.

Ali was called to the witness stand. His thick, protruding forehead and narrow, accusing eyes reminded Hakim of an enraged baboon. He hurled out accusations against Hakim, most of which were true and some which were not true. "He say that he believe the Quran. But he does not follow its every word, and he only obeys what he choose! Our television has been seized and you can see for yourself: he played NoitaLever even after it was banned! I saw with my own eyes that he engaged in lustful viewing of that which is indecent on the computer. He listened to music that was forbidden! He used more of the food than was his fair share, and I found many things missing in our trailer."

Hakim looked up from his humiliation long enough to glare at his former housemate and betrayer, and then returned his gaze to his knees while a computer IT expert—a supervisor of Yazen's in the prison system—recounted how Hakim had sent email bribes to America, taken the American prisoner from his work duties just before the uprising, dressed him in women's clothes, spirited him away, and then Hakim was found in possession of gold antiquities from the Iraqi National Museum.

There was no mention or accusation of Yazen. Where was Yazen? Why wasn't Yazen also blamed for the crimes of thievery, kidnapping and desertion? Left all alone with no support, had he confessed and turned into a betrayer?

The men in the room stood, and Hakim was yanked to his feet and brought in front. They turned him to face the brothers as the cleric pronounced him guilty and read the edict from the Quran.

"The recompense of those who wage war against Allah and His Messenger and do mischief in the land is only that they shall be killed or crucified or their hands and their feet be cut off from opposite sides, or be exiled from the land. That is their disgrace in this world, and a great torment is theirs in the Hereafter."

He heard his father's agonized groaning. His mother and Farah wailed loudly. His brother-in-law glared at the clerics. Hakim felt his knees buckle. His mind could not accept the words.

Liu Chen felt the back of her neck sweat with nervousness as once again the tech team member at the National Geospatial Intelligence Agency unrolled more long rolls of paper the size of blueprints. Permissions had not been secured through the channels. She wasn't authorized to be in Springfield, which was a half hour south of CIA headquarters.

The second round of GEOINT satellite photos the tech had procured for her had been shot forty-five seconds apart, so there were few to see. "The angle isn't great, there's a lot of smoke, and there's too many shadows because of the time of day," the tech explained. "But it appears that two guards and a women are evacuating the prison facility. In this shot you can see the long robe and the head covering with slits for eyes."

"But this is a detention facility for men, and it is run by men," she pointed out.

"I don't know, maybe a visitor to the prison? Someone's wife or daughter? They certainly would try to get a civilian out of the prison as fast as possible if there was an uprising, at least I would think," the tech conjectured.

A woman visitor to a Muslim prison probably would go to lengths to thoroughly cover herself. Disappointment stole over Liu as her personal theory appeared to crumple. She studied the next picture, which showed the three in blurred movement—apparently running—to a truck parked in a loading area. A final picture showed what appeared to be the same truck on the road just outside the prison, though it was partially obscured by smoke. Judging from the time stamp on the satellite pictures, they had evacuated quickly.

"Any other questions?" the tech asked, handing her a tablet with an authorization and billing form to fill out.

The sweat dripped from her neck down to her back. Nervously she scratched her initials in what she hoped was unintelligible writing. Eyes flitting around the room nervously, she caught sight of a screen on the wall that seemed busy with activity. "What is going on there?" she asked, pointing to the monitor, momentarily distracting him from the form she was supposed to be filling out.

She scrolled the tablet screen to the top of the document so that the signature line was no longer visible.

He launched into a technical explanation with a certain degree of pride, and she handed the tablet with the incomplete form back to him, feigning interest but slowly edging her way towards the door. She threw out one more question at him to keep him distracted, then cut him off: "Oh sorry, didn't see the time," she called over her shoulder.

"Good luck getting your spook back," the tech called back to her as she hastily scurried down the hall, though it was clear from his voice he did not think her odds were good.

In the car on the way back to her cubicle at Langley, she bit her lip in frustration. Then a thought occurred to her. Why was the vehicle where it was? Was it a planned escape, or a lucky accident? Was it their own vehicle? If they stole it, how did they get in it, get the vehicle started, and get moving so fast?

Was there any scenario where Ryan Taylor, a/k/a Josh Ryan, might be one of the three?

She got back to Headquarters and to her desk, and sure enough the phone rang. The caller ID was the NGA, and she picked it up with dread.

"Hey, I tried to input this form just now, and you didn't finish filling it out," the tech advised her.

"Oh, sorry." She could hardly keep her voice normal. "Uh, I'm late. I'll come back and fix it tomorrow," she hedged. She hung up and stuck her hands under her thighs. They were shaking.

With the void of leadership in the top, everything at the CIA was uneasy and this would be just one more thing. But going rogue was definitely not a part of her DNA. Her career was hanging by a thread.

The Laogai.

It was China's system of over a thousand detention centers, prisons, and slave labor camps, although with some reshuffling and rebranding they were represented to the United Nations to be no longer slave labor camps but employment centers. Josh's prison was located outside of Beijing, and he was now an invisible resident in one of the most dangerous counterintelligence states in the world.

The prisoners sat cross legged on the floor with clear plastic bags of electrical components next to them. Josh's quota of miniature plastic Peppermint Pinkey night lights that needed to be assembled for shipment to an international retailer leered at him mockingly. If he ever escaped and made it back alive to America, a hope that was fading to fantasy, he would personally hand-paint over those pink walls in Atalaya's bedroom and hurl every shred of Peppermint Pinkey doll, bedcover, watch, towel, and tea set into the Potomac River.

Josh had been here for thirty-eight days. There had been one meeting—a very brief one—with a Chinese lawyer who spoke heavily accented English and advised him to plead guilty.

The newer Babylon Metro Chinese prison was a five-star hotel compared to this one. The bullies in this prison made prison guard Ali seem like a school teacher. They walked the room to monitor production, using the electrical strings of Halloween lights from an old assembly job as whips, effecting punishment by proxy for the Chinese administration, who looked the other way. The mentally disabled man who sat in the row in front of Josh had red welts all over his skin. Some of the most brutalized prisoners were the religious dissidents, particularly the Falon Gung, who were considered a cult and suffered torture at the hands of Chinese authorities.

As in Babylon Metro, an American prisoner was a curiosity and the recipient of less brutality, although that was certainly relative. The guards rarely struck Josh, but they did cut his meager food rations ten percent for consistent failure to meet his quota; he was not as fast at assembly as some of the prisoners that had been there longer. The food was also worse than Babylon Metro. There was rice and cabbage, and meat once per month. He craved milk and cheese, the kinds you could get in America and Western Europe. Cheese had been rare in the Iraq prison—occasionally goat cheese; it was non-existent in this prison. His face was gaunt and even his feet were becoming thin and bony. He brutally disciplined himself to never, ever think about American pepperoni pizza or chocolate chip cookies.

The hours were excruciatingly long, particularly when there was a rush order of decorative lights to fill. Sitting on the floor for hours with no support was painful to the back. The routine was broken by toilet scrubbing duties, meditation, and two daily rounds of exercise in the courtyard. He only exercised when they ordered him to, in order to conserve his strength. It was summer and though the average temperature was about thirty degrees cooler than Iraq and punctuated by an occasional thunderstorm, it was wretchedly humid.

At the end of the day they were herded into cells that fit twenty-five people. They slept on thin mats on the floor with only a small blanket and no pillow. It was so crowded that Josh usually slept on his side. There was a cold shower available once a day but you had to earn your soap and shampoo with higher production, and the room stunk of human odor.

Seven thousand miles from home.

He ached with crowded loneliness. The days dragged endlessly on. Devoid of music, beauty, and hope, the barren colorlessness of the prison camp sucked the life out of his soul, and his strength and morale began to seep away.

Deep Throat Speaks Again

Chelsea stopped in the middle of doing her makeup to run from the bathroom into the bedroom and stare at the television. She stood holding her mascara wand as Angela Stevens Giordano on *Good Morning America* made the report. "The president accepted the resignation last night of the CIA Director, but White House sources say he was asked to resign."

The CIA Director resigned? How would that impact the investigation on Josh?

Her mobile rang and she realized that her towel had dropped to the floor and she stood before the television naked. Atalaya was right across the hall getting dressed for school. She grabbed the towel and answered, trying to wrap it around herself while she listened to the voice from Langley on the other end of the line.

Her own voice was incredulous in response, rising to shrill levels on the phone. "I told you everything my private investigator knows! I immediately turned over the video and pictures to you in good faith, just like you said to, and I let you completely run with this operation! Yet you're telling me you knew where Josh was being held all along and you didn't disclose it to me? And you were planning a rescue operation, and you didn't tell me that, either? *Now* you've completely lost communication with him and his captors for this long?" she scolded.

Connie, her liaison from the CIA, replied, "I want you to know that we know exactly how you feel, Chelsea. Others in your situation have felt the same way. We have found that sharing your concerns helps us understand each other, and we are here to support you in this uncertain time. We are requesting verification from the United Nations, and we continue to investigate whether or not he was moved from the facility before or after the uprising and if there is proof of life."

Proof of life? Her blood went cold.

Completely unable to speak, somehow she got Atalaya out the door and into Kimberly's carpool for school. She grabbed a pair of sneakers and jumped into the car and headed to the mall where elderly McLean, Virginia, residents power walked each morning.

At the mall she donned the sneakers and joined their queue, trying to think. Passing the various shops with the metal security gates still pulled down for the night, conflicting emotions overwhelmed her.

Euphoria. There had been news. Josh had been alive.

Grief. The grim knowledge that perhaps he may have suffered a sudden, violent death.

Death was better than torture, wasn't it?

And anger! She burned with resentment at the Agency, that they had told her nothing sooner. Her trust with them was damaged. What was the point of liaisons? Was the only reason they called her because they were afraid she would hear about his rescue—or his death—on television?

She called work to tell them where she was, then the private investigator, then Kimberly, and then Josh's parents and her parents.

For two days, Connie was unreachable by phone. The Washington, D.C., news speculated endlessly on who the appointee would be to replace the CIA Director and whether or not the Senate would confirm the new appointment. Chelsea scoured CNN, Reuters, and BBC, viewing everything she could find on a prison riot in Babylon Metro. There were only eyewitness videos from outside the prison, and there was lots of smoke. The Chinese had immediately crushed the resistance.

On the third day after the update from the Agency, she finally reached Connie at about ten thirty in the morning. Connie's voice was thick and sleepy sounding. "Did I wake you up?" Chelsea asked, wondering if the woman had been sick.

"No, no, I'm…heading back to my…desk," Connie answered. Suddenly Chelsea thought of a story Josh had told her, a few months after he started working for the CIA. *"I had to go in to Langley today for a meeting, and I went to a supply closet to look for a power cord. I opened the door and Dudley was sleeping in there. That's the perfect embodiment of government for you. You can work your ass off and still be paid the same as the slacker in the next cubicle."*

Groggily, Connie informed her that the Chinese had allowed no information to be released about casualties, but the CIA was examining a graphic internet video posted by a mujahedin who was bragging about restoring capital punishment—the beheadings of religious dissidents in the prison. The CIA was authenticating it. They could not confirm whether or not Josh had been one of the executed.

Unable to stand the suspense, Chelsea messaged the mysterious number that Josh had left her, hoping to find more information from Deep Throat. Once again, in a cryptic voice, the mysterious Deep Throat returned the phone call twenty-four hours later and told Chelsea to meet her at the bench along the Potomac again, this time in a slightly different place, under a tree.

It was very muggy and windy, and the Potomac did not really smell nice. She brought Yappie this time and regretted it as soon as she brought the dog out of the car. It was just too hot and humid and the poor old Sheltie panted and moved so slow that Chelsea ended up carrying her and setting her underneath the bench on the grass.

As before, Deep Throat arrived, this time wearing a ball cap and sunglasses that mostly hid her Asian features. Looking around to see that no one was close by, she sat on the far end of the bench without a greeting and took a bite of a sandwich. And once again, she did not look at Chelsea but stared across the road to the other side of the river as she spoke.

"There are three possibilities," Deep Throat opened the conversation without a greeting. Her voice that was so low that Chelsea had to struggle to hear. "Your husband could have been killed in the gunfire. He could still be there in the part of the prison that was not damaged, but the humanitarian groups and our intelligence do not believe that he is. The third possibility is that he was moved."

Well, duh! She and the private investigator and Kimberly and Josh's parents had already discussed the obvious. The P.I. was practically camping outside the gate of the prison (or as close as the Chinese would let him come) but was unable to find any indication that Josh was there. "What I want to know from you is, what does the CIA *believe* happened to him? My liaison will not tell me."

"It would be bad for the captors to know what the CIA thinks."

Impatience overcame Chelsea. Everything with the CIA was so slow, or late. "You dragged me all the way out here on a ninety-degree day to tell me nothing? Why didn't you just say so on the phone?"

Yappie, at her feet, heard the anger in her voice and gave a little whine, shuffling anxiously under the bench.

Deep Throat ignored Chelsea's irritation. "When the dead are confirmed, possibilities will be eliminated. Hopefully there will be an opportunity for optimism."

"An opportunity for optimism," Chelsea echoed bitterly. "How long will that take? Weeks? Months?"

"There is a possibility, a very small one. There was a truck that left the facility with three people during the gun battle. Two appeared to have weapons. They forced a third person into the car. It was either a woman or maybe it was someone impersonating a woman. It is small odds that it is proof of life, but perhaps he was an important prisoner and moved by the Chinese to a different facility."

It was a small spark of hope, and the spark caught on fire and leaped up into a flame in Chelsea's heart. "What kind of truck was it?"

Deep Throat studied the activity around them. A couple of lovers were approaching. They clung to each other's waists and ambled along the sidewalk slowly, and Deep Throat waited to speak until they passed. Chelsea fed Yappie a cold French fry under the bench.

"It was white, probably a used Volvo, about fifteen years old." Deep Throat stood up from the bench. "I must go. Again, no one must know about this conversation. It would completely end our communication and I would not be able to help Ryan."

She knows his real name but she's referring to him by his covert identity. She's either CIA, or a spy for a foreign intelligence…

"I'm sorry, I didn't mean to get mad. Please tell me more." Chelsea said, suddenly gripped with fear. Josh might be alive after all, but with her big mouth, talking without thinking, she had jeopardized her link to any useful information! If this woman worked with Josh at the CIA, she could be fired if it were ever discovered that she had passed information onto Chelsea. If she was a foreign spy, she could be killed.

"I must go," Deep Throat repeated.

305

Liu Chen arose from the bench without accepting or rejecting Chelsea's apology. She melted into the stream of joggers and walkers on the Mount Vernon Trail.

That night Chelsea was so shaken by the meeting with Deep Throat she could hardly sleep. Who was the woman? Chelsea went over and over various possibilities, wondering how to proceed without compromising the woman's identity, wondering if they would have contact again. All of a sudden she remembered Clinton's hacking software. She jumped out of bed and messaged him, leaving him the woman's phone number. Why hadn't she thought of that before?

The private investigator in Iraq went to work obtaining information on the ownership of used, white, 15-year-old Volvos. Clinton did not get back to her on the number for mysterious Deep Throat. There was no word from the Agency for two weeks, and whenever Chelsea tried to call, she was told that "the resignation of the CIA Director resulted in changes in internal organizational structure and someone will get right back to you." And there was no word back from Clinton on Deep Throat's phone number.

She decided to complain to the Family Advisory Board on the CIA website that her liaison was not remaining in touch. This, however, appeared to be the wrong department. The Family Advisory Board assisted with relocations. After a series of phone calls with transfers and left messages, finally Chelsea received a call back from a new liaison.

There was no explanation for what had happened to the first liaison, Connie. The second liaison came for a home visit. The liaison's name was Brick. Brick was stocky with a military buzz cut, a thick, square waist, a wide belt and pants, and heavy shoes that thumped on the wood floors. Yappie slunk away timidly to the cool floor of the kitchen. Brick set down a briefcase on the wood floor of the living room with a heavy thump. It was another hot, muggy day in NOVA. Brick wore a pit-stained white dress-shirt, and just under the edges of the short-sleeved dress shirt peeked faded tattoos with pink hearts. Brick had a voice that sounded like an early adolescent: "I'll be your contact throughout this and will provide you with information and updates. You are experiencing what we refer to as ambiguous loss. There is no answer for you about your loved one and no certainty. You do not fit into a grieving program and there is no closure. We have many resources available to our CIA family. The Employee Assistance Program and the Family Advisory Board can be found on the Benefits page of the Agency website. The Office of Medical Services has psychiatrists and psychologists available who are well-integrated into our overall objectives."

Chelsea ignored the cryptic reference to 'ambiguous loss' and support groups and launched hopefully into the information she had found on her own. "My private investigator found a possible clue," she fudged the truth to protect Deep Throat. "A fifteen-year-old white Volvo truck left the prison after the riots with three people. One of them could have been my husband. In subsequent days the truck was seen driven by an Iraqi youth near some tent vendors on Route 8 outside Babylon Metro." She presented Brick with another long list of questions and ideas about searching for proof of life. She found her eyes drifting frequently to Brick's large, hairless hands as Brick slowly logged questions and comments onto the Agency-issued notebook.

"I don't know the answers. I'm sure you feel frustrated. Others in your situation have felt the same way. They have found that if they give us the questions and requests, and if they give us an opportunity, we can research their questions and ideas and get back to them."

It was the standard Agency answer in a procedures manual somewhere in the event that this happened. How reliable was the Agency if all she could see from the outside was constant turnover and lack of communication? Deep Throat's original advice had been sound. She was better off relying on her own private investigator and her own means of trying to find Josh.

A crazy, wildly impulsive thought entered her head. Maybe she should go to Iraq herself and implore the local authorities for help! No one would look for him as hard as she! Perhaps if she could be in the places Josh had been, she could better sense what to do and maybe she would be guided towards him....

There had been a spy once a few years back who disappeared. His wife and family had traveled to the Middle East and talked to local authorities and looked for him. His cover had been blown and it had received a lot of publicity. She logged onto the computer and pulled up news articles to read how the family went about it.

She chewed a fingernail nervously and then angrily shut down the computer. What in the world was she thinking? She was just an average, plain person from the Midwest with a seven-year-old daughter whose husband worked for the most secretive agency in government. She could never travel to the Mideast and look for him, much less find him!

The Chinese put Josh on the box.

He had learned how to navigate lie detector tests passably at Langley. But they knew something, and they were harsh. The MSS were closing in on the truth. He sat shackled and chained across the desk from his MSS interrogator, he could see it in the corner of the interrogation room, the horse trough with the water, sitting on the concrete floor. He tried to block it, to not think of it. Behind the desk, the wall was ugly with layers of peeling pale yellow and pale blue paint.

His accuser faced him from across the desk. "You an American spy! Name Josh Evans. You have alias, Ryan Taylor. You live in Washington, D.C. You used to be partner in company that create the NoitaLever game that has been banned by Chinese government. You an architect for the CIA. You an assassin for the CIA. We know this. You gun down Muslim extremist in Washington, D.C., church. You try shoot down Chinese security helicopter."

His career as a non-official cover case officer was officially over.

The two MSS officers on either side of him grabbed him and hauled him towards the trough.

Surely they won't do that. Countries don't kill each other's spies! They imprison, torture, or trade them, but outright killing would open floodgates of retribution!

He struggled violently but they smacked him hard across the head with the butt of his Russian-made sniper rifle. Pain seared his head as they shoved his face down into the water.

Remember my training. Remember the hellish exercises at The Farm.

He managed to gasp for a deep breath but quickly his chest was in pain from lack of air. He writhed and twisted. Rough hands shoved him deeper into the water.

I am doing my duty to my country.

Agony. His lungs felt like they might burst.

If I die, state secrets will die with me.

His mouth and nose exhaled, then took in water. Everything went black.

Chelsea, Kimberly, and Brittany sat cross-legged on the floor by the study with their laptops and tablets. The map of the Middle East taped to the wall was covered with sticky posts. Prints of aerial maps of Babylon Metro were strewn about the floor. Kimberly ran the meeting, and they each reported the progress—and lack of progress—that had been made contacting numerous government agencies, as well as the sporadic tips that had been collected on the FreeJoshEvans website, most of which came from posers trying to get money.

"Chelsea," Kimberly rattled off instructions like a drill sergeant, "You need to speak to any families of CIA agents who have had their loved one disappear, and get detailed information about what they did and didn't do, so we'll start a new section of the spreadsheet for that."

"I did. I called and talked to one of the CIA spy families. They went to Iran and held a press conference…."

"That's what we need to do."

A jolt went through Chelsea's body. Kimberly was thinking exactly the same thing she had thought.

"Here's what I think. We should fly out to Babylon Metro and do a press conference and appeal to both the Chinese and the Iraqis for more information. We need to meet personally with the private investigator. We need to go talk to someone at that prison."

"I—I don't know. I've thought of it, but I wonder if the CIA would even let me do something like that."

Brittany eagerly jumped in. "If they allowed another family to go to a hostile state and do a press conference, then of course Chelsea should go to Iraq. Once she's there, she can see the places where Josh was. Chelsea, maybe you will feel him there! Maybe you will be able to intuit something once you see where he has been!"

Excitement crept over Chelsea. She turned to Kimberly. "Would you really go with me? To Iraq?"

"What did I start my own law firm for, if I can't take off on a special case for a best friend? And who wouldn't want to see

Babylon Metro? It's had the most amazing growth of any city in modern history. Besides," Kimberly added with a touch of bitterness, "My ex can take a break from humping that younger model he dumped me for, and he can take care of his own kids for a change." She picked up the wine glass on Chelsea's kitchen island, downed a swallow, set the glass down with a little thump, and smacked her lips.

Chelsea grinned. Kimberly was not at all bad looking with her strong cheekbones and thick lips; she was somewhat tall, kept control of her weight, and always dressed well with a professional hairstyle. But her ex-husband had called her "knobby" and had always made fun of her long, hooked nose and her little tummy pouch. He eventually ran off with a woman fifteen years younger. Now a single mom dealing with visitation squabbles, Kimberly was finished, she claimed, with men.

"Remember how the bathroom looked when you and I went on the shopping trip to New York last summer?" Chelsea teased Kimberly. "Every time we walked into the bathroom, more bottles of lotion and makeup would appear, and then they would tip over and it was like dominoes—"

"And remember the porter on the train?"

"No. I don't want to remember and I don't want you to remember, either—" They burst into giggles.

"So both of you are going to fly to Babylon Metro to search for Josh?" Brittany's blue eyes widened incredulously. "Oh," she added wistfully, "I would like to be a part of the picture, too, of what this could look like! Just think what an impression it would make on these foreign dignitaries for you to be escorted by a team! And I've been so curious about Babylon Metro, too. It has such a—a wild reputation."

"Uh, that's really nice of you to offer and it would be fun if you came, but it isn't much notice to go on an overseas trip," Chelsea managed.

"Seriously. I mean it."

Chelsea and Kim glanced at each other in surprise. "It's kind of expensive," Chelsea said carefully, not exactly knowing Brittany's financial situation. "This is a lot to ask of someone who is a new friend."

"Really, you don't think your hubby would mind?" Kimberly asked.

"Let me talk to him. A lasagna in the freezer and peanut butter and jelly, and he and the boys can manage just fine." Brittany held up a well-manicured little finger in the air, jumped down from the bar stool and zipped into the living room. They could hear a prolonged, vigorous discussion on the cell phone.

"She's really into this," Chelsea whispered to Kimberly in puzzlement. "She doesn't even know us all that well. I know her first husband died in service to the CIA, but that was an awfully long time ago. Why do you suppose she wants to do this?"

"I don't know," Kimberly whispered back, "but we will take whatever help we can get. Or I should say, your husband will take whatever help we can get."

Brittany came back into the kitchen, her blue eyes lit up with excitement. "Ok, ladies, he's going to have to process this. But I can talk him into it. Don't worry," she said with a confident wave of her hand. "Now, listen. Even though Babylon Metro is supposedly more progressive than the rest of Iraq, I have a feeling that we'll be better accepted if we also come with male escorts."

They considered this insight. "Maybe I could invite Clinton Radcliffe to come along," Chelsea contemplated. "Maybe Josh's father might agree to come!" The thought occurred to Chelsea that perhaps Clinton Radcliffe might agree to sponsor Brittany's costs.

"Well, I'm all in!" Brittany's face was excited.

"I'm in," said Kimberly. "Ok, here's what we do next. Chelsea, call the CIA tomorrow and tell them you want to go to Babylon Metro for a press conference and to make a personal appeal to local authorities. Then tell them you want to go on a sentimental visit to the last places Josh was seen and—I don't know—make up something about how you want to drop rose petals in his memory and leave a tribute to him. In the meantime, Brittany and I will work some of these back channels and see if we can get actual interviews with officials over there. If the CIA doesn't prohibit you from going over there, the next step is to call your friend Clinton, and Josh's father, and see if they will go with us. Got it?"

"Got it!" All of a sudden Chelsea was distracted by a text alert on her mobile from USA Today. "Oh, wow. They just appointed a brand new CIA Director…." She opened the news article, scanning it quickly. Brittany and Chelsea dashed around to her side of the table, peering over her shoulder, reading the article along with her.

"Hmm. Do you know anything about him?" Kimberly asked eagerly. "Will he be better than the last one? Do you suppose this will help Josh's case?"

"I don't know. I never heard of him," Chelsea responded.

"Think positively, now." Brittany urged. "See what the article says? '*President Maly desires a CIA Director who is more hands-on and more in touch with the daily operations of the organization.*' This is good. It has to be good, it can only be good! There will be new leadership at the Agency now. Somebody will do something about Josh."

"Do you guys want to stay for another drink?" Chelsea offered.

They shook their heads. "I need to get home," Brittany said. "My first yoga class tomorrow is at 5:30 in the morning. Chelsea honey," she stood up and reached her strong, slender little arms around Chelsea in an embrace, "thank you for allowing me to be a part of your story."

Touched by their kindheartedness and zeal, Chelsea saw them out the door and went back to the kitchen island to clean up. She picked up the wineglasses. Brittany and Kimberly had hardly touched their drinks.

What a waste to just dump it, and besides, this had been an unbelievable week. She picked Brittany's glass up, twisted it around to the other side opposite the delicate lipstick mark, and downed it.

In shackles, Hakim was led outside of the courtyard and taken to the main city square of Hillah behind one of the mosques, Saddam Square. When Hakim was growing up, his grandfather had told the story of how Saddam's army gunned down sixty Shiite boys and men in the square. The army shot over one hundred fifty a few days later, and subsequently more were thrown to the ground from the top of Hillah Hospital, or drowned in the river with weights tied to their feet. In recent months, a Saudi traitor to Islam on business in Babylon Metro had ended up shot and in an oil drum in the bottom of the Euphrates. And now Hakim, a Shiite, would be tortured by his former friends, Sunnis and Wahhabis.

Because the Chinese would not allow a legal execution or hanging, the brothers who were secret members of Black Lightening had chosen the alternative method that would end his life more slowly and result in excruciating pain. He would eventually bleed to death or die of infection. An even worse outcome would be that he might recover somewhat; and if his stumps actually healed, he would be consigned to the group of beggars at the outside of a city or village. The starvation, exposure to the elements, and disease would eventually kill him.

At the realization of what was really going to happen to him, he burst into terrified tears, and with nearly superhuman strength struggled with all his might to tear himself away. He was twenty years old! He had a new bride! He had his whole life ahead of him! How had it come to this?

His captors slammed him in the head and threw him to the ground, beating him for missing his prayers. The taunting cries of his fellowmen rang in his ears. Roughly they yanked him up to his feet and dragged him across the courtyard. Chinese security stood by, rifles poised, ensuring that the demonstration did not get out of hand. Plywood planks were placed in the shape of a cross. They lashed his feet up with ropes and shoved his back to the plywood. His captors spread his arms out and suspended straps across both wrists, then they brought out a staple gun and stapled tops and bottoms of the straps into the wood and raised the cross up in the courtyard.

If only their torture was brutal enough that he would die quickly! How he would have preferred to be beheaded like the unfortunate Assyrian Christians and the Falon Gung in the prison courtyard!

When he finally died, would he suffer torment in the Hereafter? He was so filled with terror that his limbs were as weak as oil. He felt bile rise up in his stomach and he vomited and lost control of his bodily functions; the stench dribbled down him and onto the tiles below. It was the ultimate degradation: he who had been so vain in this life, who had examined himself in the mirror to make sure every hair was in place and had venerated the image that gazed back at him. His cries and sobs came out in hulking breaths as he begged forgiveness of Allah and everyone around him.

He hung there while they recited his crimes, and through his minds flashed the memory of the American prisoner who believed that men were always imperfect, no matter how hard they tried to be good Muslims.

"Do you ever forget? Do you ever miss? Allah is perfect and you are not. You do not ever really know if you have forgiveness, then, right?"

The American prisoner presumed on Allah's forgiveness, took it for granted. But he was wrong, wasn't he? There was no way to know for sure if you were forgiven and if you would really go to Paradise unless you died in jihad.

"I don't have to die for God. God died for me." The American had not seemed to care if it was presumptuous and blasphemous. As a matter of fact, he had seemed quite sure.

Hakim watched them gather up the axes and shout, "Praise be to Allah!" He fervently wished that Islam was wrong and American infidels were correct: that Allah would not torment a young man who lived a life of vanity and pride and fantasies and who made a terrible mistake, but who begged forgiveness in the final moment! *Inshallah! Inshallah! Inshallah!* Allah willing!

"When the game is done, when your soldiers are all gone and you give up, when you think it is time for Istishhad, you can call for help from the Eagle. You must look for the way out."

"Allah knows best! Save me!" Hakim croaked the words out loud, clinging to hope for absolution. The two Iraqi security guards stood on either side of him and raised their axes.

315

A shop keeper across the way turned his head and went back inside his shop.

With a great slash, they simultaneously slammed the axes into his wrists. Blood gushed out, splashing on him and on the tiles below. It took a minute, but then the nerves at the ends of his arms felt the searing, unendurable pain. His screams tore through the courtyard, echoing across the stone walls of the mosque.

"**O**h my gosh, that wind is unbelievably hot! Ugh, sand just blew in my mouth!" Brittany clamped her sunglasses onto her face, struggling to hurry with her carry-on bags as they exited the stairs down from the plane and walked the tarmac the short distance to the inside of the airport. Hot gusts of wind blew at high speed, causing trash and sand to billow everywhere.

"That isn't hot wind, it's airplane exhaust," Kimberly said.

"It's hot wind," Clinton informed them. In fact, a sand storm was coming up suddenly. The flight attendants onboard had urged them to hurry inside as fast as possible and take shelter. As they ran inside the airport, dark, tan-colored billows of clouds rolled in. The street lights flickered on, and when the sand storm hit, ghostly and rapidly-fading yellow spots of light on the tarmac were nearly obliterated by sheer blackness.

Inside the darkening building, the West fused with the East, with Middle Eastern men in suits and thawbs, women in low-cut shirts and jeans and burkas, and throngs of Chinese tourists. An attaché from the American Embassy met them, the CIA's way of micromanaging the press conference. Dr. Evans, who had arrived a few hours prior, also met them inside. His back had been bowed with anxiety and burden when Chelsea made the trip to Columbia, but today he stood tall, energetic and hopeful. He slapped Clinton on the back, squeezed Chelsea's shoulders warmly, and shook hands with her friends. "Thank you for coming along to help out this daughter-in-law of mine," he said gratefully.

The attaché pointed towards a wing of the building. "There is a van waiting for us to take to Babylon Metro when this is over." Just as with the passing of a thunderstorm, the skies had cleared and the sun was out again. They made their way to the loading area where a van driver opened the doors for them. "Peace be upon you," he said.

"*Alikum salaam*," they murmured, uncertain about their accent and pronunciation. And upon you, peace.

Inside the van they stared at the strange sights outside the window—desert with occasional near-forests of trees and date palms, sand and houses, odd shaped temples and minarets. The van rolled past a bizarre electronic billboard at the entrance of the city that pronounced *"Welcome to Babylon Metro, Forever a Happy Place!"* featuring a gaudy, iridescent cartoon-character queen holding a scepter in her hand, and seven exploding stars in a kaleidoscope of color.

"So. This is the result when local Chambers of Commerce run amok," Kimberly noted wryly. With her authoritative, confident voice and her aptitude for immediately getting down to the bottom of pretty much everything, what Kimberly thought naturally dictated the opinions of most everyone else.

The attaché pointed out some of the significant landmarks in the skyline. "The city is stunning. It's like Las Vegas-meets-Third-World," Brittany replied in an awed voice. The van moved into the futuristic skyline with its angles and baubles and skyscraper after skyscraper pointing to heaven; but right next to the freeway, Bedouins herded goats through the sand to slaughter for Ramadan. As they pulled into the central business district, Chelsea rolled down the window and craned her neck, gawking in stupefied amazement at the massive office towers that reached to the sky.

If it was like looking for a needle in a haystack to find a lost seven-year-old in McLean, Virginia, she thought to herself with a sense of helplessness slamming into her with sudden impact, *finding a missing man in all of that will be like searching for a gnat in a sandstorm!*

She shook off the rising panic and firmly set the thought away. The CIA had, with reluctance, finally approved this trip to make an appeal to Iraqi authorities, with Kimberly understating and even omitting parts of their itinerary. But the little search team had a plan. They would start with what they knew. One little piece at a time....

At the edge of the river, graced by date palms and eucalyptus trees, was the casino and mall at the base of the breathtakingly spectacular high-rise office structure. "Look at that. It won international awards from architectural and shopping center associations," Chelsea said. "It's mind blowing."

Just outside of the massive mall and hotel complex, Chinese guards with AK-74Ms lined up on horses, providing protection with an aura of pageantry. "Actually makes me homesick for London," Clinton mused. "It's quite a bit like the chaps with the bearskins hats, horses and Royal Mews at Buckingham."

Clinton, Chelsea thought to herself, had not referred to England as 'home' in recent years. Iraq had once been a British territory. Occasional British-tinged accents and other remnants of British heritage reminded her somewhat of the place she, Josh, and Clinton had once lived.

The mall and casino were as much of a melting pot as the airport had been. They arrived at the entrance with its roar of traffic from the nearby freeway and passed through weapons detection security, where the Chinese guards separated the men and women and patted them down. Everywhere they looked there were directional signs in multiple languages: Arabic, Chinese, English, Mandarin, Japanese, and more.

The attaché led them to a pre-arranged meeting place for the press conference. A small group of four international reporters, cameras pointed, met them at the urban eatery with its exotic aromas of multi-ethnic foods wafting delicious odors.

Chelsea felt her stomach do flips and tried to remind herself, *You've done this before.*

It really was less intimidating than being interviewed by Angela Stevens Giordano in America. She stood in an alcove just outside the eatery and read the prepared statement, carefully crafted by the CIA Public Affairs division, as curious shoppers hurried by and then stopped, straining to see and hear what was going on. "We received visas to travel to Iraq and we look forward to visiting with government officials," she read. "Our private investigator has discovered that a white Volvo truck with three occupants left the prison during the uprising, and we cling to the slim hope that Josh Evans may have been one of them. We appreciate the support of all of you in our endeavor to find our loved one."

The cameras snapped and flashed. The press conference was mercifully short. The reporters quickly melted away, hauling their equipment with them. The passersby moved on. But one reporter from Reuters remained, a local who was the chief correspondent for Iraq, asking a few questions as Chelsea handed him some REWARD flyers with information about Josh.

"I covered the insurgency right after it happened," he told her.

"You did?" she asked in surprise.

The search team and the embassy attaché listened intently. Chelsea's heart jumped into her throat. "Please," she begged, grabbing eagerly at opportunity to befriend someone in the press who may possibly be an ally, "tell us everything you know about people involved in the prison uprising!"

The entire search team stood breathlessly, hoping for an eyewitness account and additional information from the Reuters newsman about the disappearance of Josh. "There is little I can say. I could not get inside. The royal guard had its guns, and the soldiers were shooting to kill. All I could do was interview witnesses on the highway outside the prison. The officials of the prison and the employees refused to be interviewed, and Chinese officials only released prepared statements to the press."

"Did you interview anyone who escaped?"

The reporter paused carefully before answering her. "Let's go over here and sit down." He pointed to a table at the urban eatery, and they followed him over to it, pulling up chairs around him as he sat down and turned on his tablet and began doing a search. "A number of people were killed. We have not found any escapees to interview. But I will show you my article with the name of a witness outside the prison that I spoke to."

Chelsea beamed at her friends, who hung expectantly to every word. The reporter scrolled through his tablet, located the article, and forwarded it to her. "This is the witness. He lives in the old city, in Hillah." He checked the time. "It's probably of little value but I wish you the best. I must be on my way. Thank you, Mrs. Evans." He stood up from the eatery table to leave.

"We're hoping for a miracle," she called after him optimistically as he turned to walk away.

The interpreter read the article and made a phone call, speaking rapidly in Arabic. "We can discover the address of this boy," he reported confidently.

Just a few hours and they were onto their first clue! How glad Chelsea was that she had taken charge of the situation and come to Iraq herself!

Brittany, always fascinated by religious practices, paused to snap a photo of one particular sign as they made their way outside the urban eatery: BABYLON METRO IS RELIGION NEUTRAL ZONE. She and Chelsea cast knowing looks at each other. Inside the zone, the Chinese didn't license mosques, synagogues, churches, or religion of any kind. The Chinese described Babylon

Metro as "an experiment in neutrality," but it was understood by everyone that "religion neutral" was no experiment; it was actually a polite euphemism for a strict policy of "religion-free."

A cold feeling gripped her. If it was the Chinese who had Josh in captivity and found out about his religious beliefs, he may be in as much trouble as he would be with the Iraqis.

The attaché went back to Baghdad and the search team checked into the hotel. The women shared a suite on one of the upper floors with two bedrooms and a common living area and bar, although the view was of an ugly salinization plant by the Al-Hillah branch of the Euphrates. They asked to be moved and obtained a suite with a much better view: one that overlooked Ancient Babylon, with Saddam's palace a pinpoint on a hill, and in the distance the blocks of ruins of King Nebuchadnezzar and the blue speck in the sand called Ishtar Gate. From their expansive view high up in the hotel, the desert sand dotted with palms was beautiful. Clinton and Dr. Evans, who had known each other since Clinton's and Josh's college days, also shared a suite.

It was a nice hotel—that is, until you looked closely, Chelsea thought. The pipes in the new bathroom were naked of insulation, and covers were missing on some of the electrical outlets. She took over a wall of the suite and unpacked her clues she had taken down from her house—the maps of Babylon Metro, Iraq, Asia, and all of the notes and photos. She taped them up and stood back to study them. There was a hairline crack forming in the wall, even though this was a relatively new hotel. She had the sense that the construction was shoddy.

Her mobile buzzed, and it was Clinton. "Chels, want to go back down to the arcade? They have our NoitaLever game in a 3-D booth complete with odours!"

When her life had dramatically altered, the NoitaLever game had been dropped, lost among all the other preoccupations. She met Clinton at the elevator and they took off at a brisk pace, following multi-language signage directions on an endless walk through the immense complex to the blinking, twinkling, singing games located outside the urban eatery with its mixture of ethnic aromas. People from all over the world with every kind of garb passed them—businessmen in suits on cell phones, women in native dress carrying shopping bags.

"You could spend a week in this place alone just finding your way around," Chelsea panted, wondering how she would ever find Josh in this massive city.

But when they reached the interior of the arcade, they skidded to a stop in disappointment. The NoitaLever game was being dismantled! There were construction sawhorses around it, and a huge ventilation coil dangling down from the upper deck, its end cut off. A yellow banner was suspended from the ceiling that said in English, Chinese, and Arabic, "COMING SOON" with a black silhouette of a Middle East young woman in a burka charging forward with a sub-machine gun.

"Damn!" Clinton growled. "The bloody Chinese stole our game and replaced it with Jihadi Janna!" Pink crept up his face to his pale hairline.

"What is Jihadi Janna?"

"It's a game with a Middle East female hero who guns down terrorists and turns over the territory to the Chinese. The villages earn points for food, a bank, health care, and education. It's the same benevolent propaganda NoitaLever has, only it's Chinese." Clinton seemed disturbed, as if perhaps he were for the first time accepting Jihadi Janna as an actuality. Then he shrugged. "You can go ahead and go back to the hotel. I'm going to stay in the casino."

She tried to mask a look of disapproval at her benefactor. There was money for gambling, but he had cut back on the reward money funds for Josh.

Their interpreter and the private investigator met them and the rest of the team for a delicious supper of grilled lamb, vegetables, rice, hummus, and flatbread. Neither the investigator nor the interpreter was impressive in person. The investigator, whom they had talked to many times online, was a heavy-jowled, pot-bellied former Iraqi military officer with stains on his shirt who smelled and whose eyes darted constantly. He seemed to have a chip on his shoulder about absolutely everything. The scrawny male interpreter was a student, skinny with clothes that hung on his slight frame. He seemed horribly ill at ease with the hotel china and flatware. Chelsea, desperately craving a drink, weighed the social consequences of ingesting alcohol in front of her tee-totaling Baptist father-in-law who was a major donor to Josh's cause. She elected to wait until she got to the hotel room.

The next morning the team met for breakfast in the hotel lobby. The strategy for Day 1 was to hit Ancient Babylon.

Their interpreter doubled as their tour guide, and he loaded them up in two vans and took them outside the city for a tour of the dusty, sandy tourist attraction. The private investigator jabbered in Arabic on the phone, trying to reach the family of the boy interviewed by Reuters news and finalize the meeting. Chelsea's heart beat furiously as they arrived. It was a vast area, with occasional ruins dotting the barren landscape. Somewhere here, Josh's feet had walked! For the first time in months, she felt close to him.

Even though it was morning and the desert sunrise was beautiful with its rosy pink glow, the desert was heating up as they pulled up to the striking blue Ishtar Gate, clumsily re-created by Saddam Hussein. A local, yelling in three languages, "Antiquities!" tried to hawk a piece of broken pottery. Dr. Evans walked around mesmerized, pointing here and there but speechless at the garishness. "Tacky, over-rated shameless tourist trap," Clinton summarized the ruins.

The private investigator moved up next to Chelsea and spoke in a low voice. "We are being followed everywhere. Do not look now but a Jeep has been doing the following."

It was creepy, the thought of traveling in a country where every move they made was being watched.

The interpreter led the caravan to the ziggurat known as Saddam's palace. They made their way into the fortress that covered an area as vast as five football fields with its strange towers, arched doors, a basketball hoop, and vaulted ceilings. A part of the palace held the remains of a movie theater, pool, former offices and bedrooms, some of which had been refurbished and other parts that were damaged by the American and Polish military and were open to the elements. He led them towards a commercial kitchen which had been restored, near the southeast corner of the structure. "Your private investigator say this is where your husband work," he said. "In ancient times, conquerors build on top of old buildings. Many layers built over each other. Sometimes at the bottom are tunnels. The sultans want to secretly visit concubines, you see?"

A hot gust of wind kicked up, and sand coated everything. "How anyone can work and live in this searing cauldron of heat is beyond my freaking imagination," Kimberly complained bitterly, fanning herself, "much less romp around in an airless underground tunnel with a prostitute when you're covered in desert sand."

"Maybe it's knowing Saddam Hussein committed horrible atrocities, but something about this place is just creepy. It has bad karma," Brittany said portentously.

"This the spot," the interpreter said to Chelsea, pointing.

But the abandoned construction area with its scaffolding was cordoned off with yellow warning tape, and no matter how hard they pleaded with their interpreter, he would not let them past the tape. "Stop! Do not advance! We are not supposed to be here! See those?" he said, pointing to Chinese and Arabic signs. "This cause many argument between the Chinese security and the Iraqis! No good, no good."

"That's a load of cobblers," Clinton protested. Clinton had pulled back his receding hair into a ponytail, and his fair skin was already burning from the sun.

"Sir, we came all this way—" Dr. Evans protested, feigning patience.

Chelsea flat out argued with the tour guide. "We depended on you to get us inside the place where my husband used to work!" she chastised the young Iraqi.

But the interpreter would not budge. He did not want to create an international incident, he said.

"Then give me my fee back!"

He refused. She was so angry she wanted to throw something.

The Euphrates River

Pouting, Chelsea stormed away, walking to the far west wall that overlooked the Al-Hillah branch of the Euphrates. It snaked and curved its way along, meandering at the bottom of the cliff past the ancient site, between agricultural farms, and towards the sparkling high-rise towers of Babylon Metro in the smoggy haze in the distance. She could hear Brittany running to catch up, calling, "Chelsea, are you ok?" but she almost didn't hear because she was staring down at the muddy waters.

The Euphrates River.

So the gold that Saddam Hussein or ISIS had hidden was somewhere around here? From this height, it was a massive area, immense miles of winding branches and tributaries. But certainly Josh must have narrowed it down, and there had to be a clue. She needed to work this through, figure it out and follow to the end of the thing....

Brittany caught up to her and stood at her elbow. "I want to go down there," Chelsea pointed to the river below. "It was important to Josh. There had to have been something going on there that had to do with his job."

Brittany called back to their interpreter, her feminine voice surprisingly strong and insistent. "Sir? Sir! Come here! If you won't take us inside the excavation area, Mrs. Evans would at least like for you to take us down to the river."

The interpreter shrugged and stumbled down the steep hill towards them. A movement suddenly caught their attention. "Look!" Brittany pointed with an amazed expression. "Is that what I think it is?" On the south edge of Saddam Hill, a pair of large, clumsy white birds ran down the bank, loping along around the rocks and sand. A flock of huge vultures feeding on carrion were startled and fluttered up in alarm, their caws screeching eerily against the blue sky.

"This is ostriches. They escape from the zoo," the interpreter explained, panting and sweating from the heat radiating from the rocks and archaeological rubble. "Very big, nice zoo outside of Babylon Metro. The Chinese bring back many unclean animals that used to live in this country but die out. Black Lightening burn the zoo down because of unclean animals. Some of them escape. You see them? They run around like crazy out here. Watch out, do not step in this jackal dung. Very nasty."

Brittany turned to Chelsea with a strange, haunted look. "Wait a second. Didn't—didn't Pastor Rouch say something about Babylon being destroyed, and a prophecy about ostriches and jackals living in it?"

Chelsea turned to stare at her friend, remembering.

"Yes, he did, I know he did!" Brittany insisted, locking eyes with Chelsea. "That was the exact same day of the church shooter…."

Of course he had. The skin on Chelsea's arms prickled with goosebumps and the little hairs stood up, even in the desert heat.

They returned up the steep hill, loaded up the van, and took the road flanked by miniature palm and rose gardens and which spiraled all the way down Saddam Hill. They exited the van and the interpreter led them past a warehouse and to a small, abandoned boat dock by the river.

"So this is it?" Chelsea almost felt disappointed. The shallow river was muddy and had pools of algae in spots and smelled like diesel fuel. It wasn't mystic, it was just a boring agricultural area amid occasional clumps of distribution warehouses and ancient ruins.

The private investigator told them about the river, launching into a political tirade. "Boats keep getting stuck on sand bars," he explained, pointing to a rusty fishing boat that was half-way overturned and stuck in the middle of the water. "The Euphrates start in Turkey, and Turkey take some of our water for irrigation. It is why we hate Turkey and have talks of war. Iraqis take their own water, too, for crops. But Chinese take the water for Babylon Metro. Is so very, very foolish. In a few years, it will be so shallow we will not be able to navigate boats at all. It will be the fault of Babylon Metro."

The private investigator certainly left no doubt about his personal feelings about Babylon Metro, thought Chelsea in amusement. Dr. Evans was tapping furiously on his mobile and doing an online search. "Listen to this," he exclaimed, his voice filled with awe. "I think we may be standing in ground zero for a future nuclear war. 'A sixth angel poured out his bowl on the great river Euphrates, and its water was dried up to prepare the way for the kings from the East...Then they gathered the kings together to the place that in Hebrew is called Armageddon.'"

Islam and Christianity had little in common, but amazingly their ancient prophecies portended a similar ending: an epic battle involving the banks of the Euphrates. "Josh said there is a Muslim prophecy, too. That there will be a fight over gold in the Euphrates River at the end of times and ninety-nine out of a hundred people will die." Chelsea told them.

"It gives me the creepy crawlies." Brittany shuddered. "Just think, someone wrote that thousands of years ago, and we might be standing right where it's going to happen."

"Something about Josh's job must have involved weapons. But he never said anything about it," Chelsea said.

Up the river a few miles away, the skyline of Babylon Metro gleamed and shimmered, a layer of smog hovering over it. They could hear its distant sounds of roads and traffic rumbles. Chelsea remembered one piece of paper with notes from Pastor Thorpe's web chat that were tacked up on the wall by her maps of the Middle East. She had even looked up the verses for herself in the two-thousand-year-old prophecies late one sleepless night at home. The scriptures referred to 'Babylon the Great,' and the merchants of the earth 'growing rich from her excessive luxuries'. But then there was a prophecy about the city being violently 'thrown down, never to be found again,' in a great ball of smoke, and all of a sudden the 'glittering of gold, precious stones, and pearls' were brought to ruin 'in a single hour'.

"Sorry, peeps. No gold to see here," Kimberly impatiently interrupted Chelsea's thoughts.

Everyone was tired and getting sunburned, even with sunscreen. The bugs were strange and large and icky. Clinton seemed detached and spent an inordinate time online everywhere he walked or rode, and it annoyed Chelsea. Why not keep his eyes open at all times looking for clues to Josh's disappearance, instead of constantly looking at his myriad of electronic devices! And besides, how many times did anyone get a chance to tour the Middle East?

Unused to desert climate—especially Dr. Evans—they were too hot and exhausted from the sun, the wind, and the intense heat to do anything but go back and rest at the hotel, eat a bleary-eyed supper of grilled salmon and rice and vegetables, and get caught up with sleep due to jet lag. But for Chelsea, it was a restless sleep, with dreams about gold and oil and wars and fighting; and every time she rolled over, she woke up thinking of all the things they ought to be doing to look for Josh.

Chelsea was up an hour before the alarm. Today was the most significant meeting of the trip: They were to meet the commander of Governorate of Babil Prison. Getting admission had been extremely difficult, even with the private investigator's police connections. While waiting for the others to wake and come to breakfast, she trudged through the hotel and casino, locating smiling and nodding staff people who would take a MISSING flyer from her with information about a reward.

But when they all met for breakfast, Dr. Evans scanned the room and asked, "Where's our interpreter?"

The Iraqi boy was nowhere to be found! The private investigator said that another tourist probably offered the interpreter more money.

They all knew the real reason. It was because Chelsea had lost her temper with him. If there was any day to garner sympathy with local authorities, if there was any day to uncover clues, it was today. She nearly panicked. She stalked down the hotel manager and begged for help, but it was going to take some time, time they could not waste.

She came back to the breakfast table and pronounced firmly, "A flyer with a picture is a flyer with a picture. We'll use pantomime. They can look at a picture and call the phone number. Our private investigator knows a little Chinese." She was trying to reassure not only them but herself.

Was the prison where Josh had been held any different than anywhere else in the world, with its concrete and barbed wire structure on the outside and gray and institutional and claustrophobic inside? The only unusual thing about this one was that the far south end was under re-construction. There were heaps of coils of barbed wire, and Chinese troops milled around on horses, guarding the construction entrance fiercely with a faux veneer of pageantry.

At security they were searched two times. They were allowed to take no items with them at all—no purses, passports, tablets or mobile devices, which Chelsea had planned to use to show the video of Josh and a picture of the model of truck that had purportedly left during the riots. The guard indicated that their personal items would be locked up in a locker. "I'll stay in the waiting area with our things," Clinton quickly offered. "I'm sure you'll be back in two ticks."

Clinton, Chelsea thought dully, would sooner have his arm amputated than be without his personal electronic devices.

Once the rest of them were inside, they were locked into a desultory meeting room with a folding table and metal chairs and Chinese and Arabic paper posters on the wall advertising Coke. Chelsea breathed a quick prayer to God, asking for success in their most important meeting.

But no one came to meet them! Time crawled by: fifteen minutes past their meeting time with the commander, then thirty, then forty-five. They got impatient and stood and paced, stopping frequently to stand on tiptoe and look out the tiny square window in the door with chicken wire glass to see if anyone was coming down the hall.

A prison matron finally came in and set down a tray with a tarnished silver teapot and cups along with slightly stale cardamom cookies with an almond pressed in the center.

Another twenty minutes went by and finally the commander arrived. They cleared their throats and stood up at the table deferentially and alertly. Thank goodness, the commander had a translator! The translator abruptly asked them what it was they wanted.

"We have come all the way from America to try to find news," Kimberly solemnly began to make her client's case in her resonant, authoritative voice; but about half-way through her speech the commander held up his hand and interrupted her with a torrent of Chinese.

"He say he the interim commander. He not know where your husband be, or his body," explained the prison interpreter.

"*Interim* commander?" Chelsea felt panic. Where was the permanent commander? "We need to talk to the top commander that was here when my husband disappeared. How can we find him?"

After a slight pause: "He on vacation. Do not know when he will come back," lied the interim commander via the translator.

331

"Surely you must have some information on my son," said Dr. Evans. "We had a report that he may have been taken away in a white Volvo truck."

There was no need for a translator to interpret the defensive, abrupt response of the interim commander. "We have no confirmation one way or the other."

"Please, sir," Brittany's little voice was soft but strong, her face plaintive and beseeching but her jaw firm. "This man has lost his child." She gently touched Dr. Evan's forearm across the folding table. "This woman has lost her husband." Brittany's hand slid over Chelsea's shoulder. "Certainly you must have some information."

There was another exchange in Chinese and then the interpreter replied, "No information. The Iraqis bury corpses immediately according to Muslim tradition. It is too late to locate your husband."

Chelsea could not help but gasp as the words cut to her heart like a knife. Next to her, Dr. Evans recoiled as if he had been slapped. "No, you don't understand. We don't believe he was killed. We heard that there was a white Volvo truck with three people who escaped during the riots."

The interim commander stood up and let out of stream of robotic, unemotional Chinese words. "He is sorry," the interpreter translated rapidly, "for the loss of your dear one and that there is no further information on this unfortunate event that occurred prior to his arrival at this prison."

"Please, sir, let us talk to someone who was working here when it happened!" Kimberly started to demand, but even her resonant, authoritative voice was impotent; the interim commander ignored her and stood up from the table. Stiffly he shook their hands, maintaining but the briefest of eye contact, and then he quickly turned away and walked out of the room, his interpreter scrambling to keep up with him.

Chelsea froze. Brittany jumped to her feet clutching Chelsea's shoulders. A guard motioned them to leave the room and escorted them down the concrete floors of the hallway, and she and Dr. Evans clung to each other, shaking, as they made their way to checkout, and they walked without a word until they reached the parking lot.

"He was hiding something, hiding everything!" Brittany snapped in righteous indignation after they met up with Clinton, her soft voice filled with a surprising venom.

"Every one of you is as white as a sheet," Clinton observed.

"It was just like interviewing a patient with lung cancer who won't admit to me that he smokes," Dr. Evans said, shaking his head and recounting what the interim commander had said.

Chelsea's mind reeled, and she refused to accept the fateful words that burned in her ears. "There is no proof that Josh died," she told the team. "They would be humiliated if he escaped, wouldn't they? They wouldn't want us to find out."

"Of course they would," Brittany agreed stoutly. "We have to keep hope. Our hope is all that Josh has."

Kimberly and Clinton looked confused and uncertain.

That night after supper they loaded back up into the van and went into the old city, Hillah, to meet the witness who had been interviewed by Reuters outside of the prison. Because they were departing the insulated western bubble of Babylon Metro and did not want to bring unnecessary attention to themselves, the private investigator advised the women to dress in hijab. ("It's like tossing a space heater to a burn victim," complained Kimberly, fumbling messily with hers.)

Even though it abutted Babylon Metro, Hillah was such a stark contrast from Babylon Metro, a weird mix of cranes and new construction in some parts of the city but mostly centuries of unchanged poverty. The small house they went to was in a neighborhood with graffiti, metal gates on the doors and windows, and laundry strewn across the fences. There was an electricity shortage in this part of Hillah, and the power was shut down for a few hours, so the little house was dark. The family spoke very little English but offered them tea and apples. They weren't hungry but it was rude to refuse.

The father of the family did the majority of the speaking to the P.I., and they went back and forth in rapid fire with occasional comments inserted by a young boy who looked to be about age twelve who had routinely watched the Chinese horse-mounted security that regularly patrolled the outside of the prison. Chelsea desperately wanted the interview to be solely with the boy, but the P.I. ignored her request. Was it considered improper?

"There were three people who left the prison gates in great haste," the P.I. tersely relayed bits of information. "The truck was white and very old with lots of rust." Then ensued what appeared to be a family argument about the three people. Were there three men? No, replied the pre-adolescent boy, there had been two men who worked every day at the prison and one woman. However, this did not make sense to the Iraqi parents. Their son was most surely wrong; there were three men because it was a men's prison, they insisted in loud voices.

"Where did they go?"

There was more discussion; the truck had apparently disappeared in the cloud of explosives smoke onto Route 8. "Sometimes they go to caves and talk and hide," was the vague and inconclusive answer of the boy.

Then followed some sort of argument between the private investigator and the parents. The P.I. stood up abruptly and announced angrily in English they would leave immediately.

Confused, the search team gave their thanks to the mother, who refused eye contact. They filed out to the van, and once inside the P.I. exploded with wrath. "They are tired of people asking questions about this. They want money for this information. I say to them that there is no reward for them unless we find husband of this lady! But they do not like this answer."

Chelsea would have been fine with giving the family some money, but didn't the P.I. know the customs of his own city far better than she? In a Third World country, you were probably constantly open to extortion. "What is this about caves?" she asked. "Can we go look for these caves nearby?"

"This he does not know to be true. It is impossible! Who knows where is a cave? There are many, many caves by Euphrates! There are many rocks. Any rock is a cave, you see? Is dangerous. There are land mines and explosives." The P.I. seemed to be working himself up into an angry tirade.

"We are giving up too easily," Chelsea patiently tried to point out, attempting to calm the P.I. down.

"I think that family was bullcrapping us," Kimberly defended the P.I. "If that kid hangs around all day staring at the decorated guard, he probably knows who regularly drives trucks in and out of there. If he can't give us any better description of trucks and caves and people than that, the family is probably just trying to bribe us."

Their hijab head coverings itched and were horribly hot. Chelsea scratched and then rebelliously yanked it off.

Lying in bed in the darkness of the hotel room, she tried to wrap her head around everything that had happened today. The full impact of the words of the interim prisoner commander thumped away at her with brutal, almost physical force.

The Iraqis bury corpses immediately according to Muslim tradition. It is too late to locate your husband.

What if it was, in fact, the truth? Was the clue from Deep Throat and the twelve-year-old boy about a white Volvo a wild goose chase, a fantasy hope? Maybe the Chief of Station of the Baghdad CIA would have some answer, some clue.

She hugged a pillow close to herself in the darkness, wishing that they were successful and found Josh and that she could feel his hard muscles of his shoulders, his arms around her, his body on hers, his brown, curly hair between her fingers, and the smell of aftershave and cinnamon gum.

On Day 3, they were able to hire an alternate translator-tour guide. She was an adorable local, a college student with heavy eye makeup who did not seem to know quite as much Chinese as the first tour guide but apparently she made up for it with sincerity and extensive, energetic pantomime.

They visited the massively, unbelievably huge Tomorrow Globe Financial Center where Josh's Crestedon office—otherwise known as Pyramids and Palaces Architectural and Engineering—had been located. On the outside it was surrounded by a large reflecting pond with goldfish and a vast concrete oval of highly secure driveway. Many of the world's most famous banks and oil companies had set up headquarters in the new, competitive environment, implications that impacted Dubai, Switzerland, Cayman, and beyond. The office, hotel, and casino complex was breathtaking.

Chelsea's commercial real estate friend from London, Priya, was only able to discover the name of the investment group that owned the building. Priya could not get any information about what part of the building Pyramids and Palaces had been located in. However, Priya had a cover story all ready for the Chinese leasing company and had even sent over a curriculum vitae and fake business plan, telling the listing agent that Chelsea was setting up a new real estate office and these were her co-workers.

In whispers, Chelsea hurriedly instructed her friends to "accidentally" get separated in the bathrooms so that they could each case the building and try to discover where Josh's so-called non-profit office had been and hopefully question the neighbors and pass out REWARD flyers.

But the task was overwhelming! The tight elevator security, locked off corridors, and the sheer, unbelievably immense size of the compound made it utterly impossible. Chelsea tied up the Chinese real estate agent's time for as long as she could, asking to see innumerable spaces and posing endless questions about the building and the type of tenants and where they were located. The Chinese real estate agent's accent was difficult to understand. The rest of the group wandered around unsuccessfully, largely unable to get to most areas of the complex, much less identify where Josh's office had been. When Chelsea asked straight out where it had been, the agent did not know. Eventually the agent dropped her veneer of politeness and said to Chelsea bluntly, "This taking too long. I have other appointment. We must find your friends and leave."

After they had been summarily ushered outside of the building, with no better idea of where Josh's office might have been than when they started, Chelsea fussed and fretted. "How are we going to get back and search the building and pass out flyers to the neighboring tenants?"

The others shook their heads. "The simple answer: we aren't. It's impossible. Let's go back to the hotel," Kimberly stated firmly.

"Bullocks," Clinton complained. "The whole thing was a spectacular waste of time."

As tired as she was, she still wanted to go out and pass out REWARD flyers after supper. No one else wanted to. Kimberly claimed planta fasciitis from too much walking, Clinton said he had work for CRAJE Technologies to do in his hotel room, Brittany wanted to chat online with her family, and Dr. Evans said he needed to lay down. Chelsea called home and talked to her mother and Atalaya. The sun was setting over the desert. It was beautiful, casting a rosy glow and dark shadows on the tan-colored sand, and it reflected against the ancient buildings in the distance. Brittany practiced her yoga and some type of elegant dance moves against the wall of the suite. Kimberly had her foot elevated on ice and did her nails while watching Arabic television.

"Anyone want a drink?" Chelsea asked, reaching into the refrigerator and pouring herself a glass, and then another. She let it burn down to her toes.

There was something different about Kimberly tonight, a shift in mood. It was true of the men, too. This was hard work, and things were not looking good.

Early the next morning, Josh's superior at the American Embassy postponed their appointment in Baghdad until tomorrow. It catapulted the fourth day into uncertainty. Chelsea decided to split the team in two groups to pass out REWARD flyers, with half the team scouring the casino, mall, and hotel and the other half of the team outside walking Wangfujing Avenue tourist district.

Clinton and Kimberly drifted off together into the casino and mall area to pass out fliers—they seemed to have developed a rapport during this trip. The private investigator went off to question casino and hotel security.

Chelsea, Dr. Evans, Brittany, and the cute little interpreter hit Wangfujing Avenue with the fliers and water bottles. The interpreter admonished them not to wander off alone. "The tourist district is safe, but the other streets need specific consideration, especially the woman," she advised.

They sweated their way up and down the busy tourist areas with the open markets and their smells of herbs and spices. Two different vendors seemed to indicate they may have seen Josh. They wanted a reward. The interpreter plied them with Chelsea's barrage of questions. But the vendors contradicted themselves on when they had seen him and what he was doing. Most of the vendors just shook their heads and turned away.

Brittany was fairly good about passing out flyers, but she was frequently distracted by the carts in the bazaar, and she stopped to browse items and attempted to converse with the locals. Chelsea chafed with impatience. They needed to find Josh.

By eleven o'clock, the heat was already suffocating. As pre-arranged, at noon they returned to the urban eatery at the hotel and casino to meet Clinton and Kimberly. Kimberly was leaning back in her chair with her feet up on the table, people-watching. "Thanks to the universal language of shopping, we can get by just fine without Chinese and Arabic interpreters in this mall," Kimberly joked. The armload of "REWARD" flyers was sitting on the table. It looked like virtually untouched.

Clinton, Kimberly told them, had to go back to his hotel room and do some work. Chelsea was flummoxed. He had donated money and came all this way to help find his best friend and he was sitting in a hotel room! She fidgeted impatiently until he arrived at the urban eatery. She asked in what she hoped was a bright and enthusiastic voice, "You're not having any luck in this building? No one here has identified Josh's photo, have they? How about we go to some of the other tourist areas in the city?"

"Our feet are killing us," Kimberly replied unenthusiastically.

"You know the difference between an American podiatrist and an English podiatrist don't you, Kimmy?" Clinton asked in his droll way.

"No."

"They are arch rivals."

Kimberly snorted and Chelsea found herself snapping. "C'mon you guys. Get serious. We're here for a limited window of time. Don't you know that every minute looking for Josh counts?"

Clinton pulled out his mobile to check messages. Kimberly also refused to meet her gaze and replied coldly, "This is a bigger city and a bigger country than we realized. We're doing an excellent job getting the word out as well as five people can who are in this country without the protection of either the U.S. or the Iraqi government, Chelsea. But this is your show. You can do what you want."

She was taken aback at this comment. In a lot of ways, this trip had been Kimberly's show. She felt the burden squarely on her shoulders. Even Dr. Evans seemed disheartened, telling her, "It's just too hot. I'm an old man and I can't be out in that anymore. Chelsea, you have to realize, we are looking for a needle in a haystack, and we have to remember that the needle was out here working undercover, trying to dress and look like a piece of hay."

She took the flyers all by herself and walked as much of the hotel, casino, and shopping center as she could. With her senses heightened and desperate because time was running out, she began imagining that she saw Josh out of the corner of her eye—here, a slight male; there, a man with dark curly hair—but then when she would turn to look fully, his skin was too olive, or he was too tall or too short, or he was just a European tourist.

At supper back at the hotel that night, Clinton arrived at the table carrying his travel bags and rolling his suitcase under the table. Chelsea stared at him in shock.

"I have to go back home," Clinton informed her flatly. "Jennifer said one of our funds is having a call for capital. I can't stay in Babylon Metro any longer. I'm going to catch a flight out tonight. Sorry, I know it's been swings and roundabouts for you on this trip."

She hated it when Clinton went Brit on her. It either meant he was making fun of her or it meant he was trying to patronize her. Bottom line, he was abandoning her! With shock and mounting bitterness, she watched Clinton turn his back and walk away from them to his cab, rolling his suitcase behind him with his laptop slung over his shoulder, the glass doors of the lobby sliding shut behind him. She stormed after him through the glass doors.

"Clinton! Clinton!" she challenged him. "How can you do this? Just walk out on us like this, right in the middle?"

Clinton glanced back over his shoulder but continued to head resolutely towards the taxi stand. "I can't help you with this, Chels. I regret it."

"You were too helping! You researched some things on line for us! You funded us! We found out some things!"

"Sorry, I can't do this. I can't live in this dual world you live in, where one minute Bags is here somewhere and the next minute he's gone for good. He's long gone, Chels. Accept it." He held up his hand to motion the valet that he was ready for the next cab.

The words struck her violently, almost with a physical force, and tears filled her eyes. She whirled around and stomped back into the hotel.

All the rest of the evening and the next morning she tried to pull herself together and present a normal appearance to the others, but she felt the team was giving up.

The Embassy

They got up early the next day, Day 5, to go into Baghdad to meet with the American Embassy. "When we leave the city," explained the cute little interpreter, "we need to take in our eyes special precautionary procedures."

Once they left the sparkling enclave of Babylon Metro and traveled to Baghdad, the poverty and Third World conditions became more apparent. Baghdad was run down, not only from decades of constant warfare with Saddam Hussein and ISIS, but most recently from losing industry to Babylon Metro. The roads were in poor condition. Chinese soldiers were on guard at various points, rifles ready. Most drivers of vehicles had long sticks with mirrors attached to them which they sent out the window in order to keep constantly on the lookout for danger. Laundry hung on clothes lines right next to the dirty street, suspended by wooden clothes pins. Locals pushed carts containing all of their earthly belongings, and they saw occasional beggars, old women with no teeth who held out their hands. They heard the surreal and seemingly atonal wailing sound of the Muzzin's call to prayer.

The American embassy was in the Green Zone, a much nicer part of Baghdad jointly controlled by Chinese and Americans. The staff, including the Chief of Station who had worked with Josh, were polite and sympathetic but extremely cautious about every statement they made, choosing their words carefully.

"The last we heard from Josh was when he was here for the holiday party the evening he disappeared," the COS gingerly responded to Chelsea's question regarding the last conversation with Josh. There was something about him she didn't like. He was the type that looked the women in the party up and down, particularly Brittany. He was slick, evasive, and self-protective.

"Holiday party? Here in Baghdad?" she exclaimed in surprise. The Agency had never mentioned a holiday party.

"He was unable to stay for the event. He had a security emergency call and had to turn around and drive back to his office building in Babylon Metro, which, as you know, was where he disappeared."

Chelsea wrinkled her forehead and tried to process the significance of this. "No one told me this," she said, her voice quavering.

"Had it been significant," the COS said smoothly, "Headquarters in Langley would have mentioned it to you. He was last heard from while working in the Globe Financial Center down in Babylon Metro later that night."

He was obviously covering up for Langley, but for now Chelsea decided to let it go. "Do you have any leads on Omar Al Ghamdi? Please tell me. I believe he is a suspect in my husband's disappearance."

For the first time, a flicker of surprise and confusion flickered over the face of the COS. "Omar Al Ghamdi? I don't have any reason to think he was responsible for Josh's disappearance. He was gunned down by Black Lightening shortly after Josh arrived in Babylon Metro. His body was found in a barrel in the Euphrates River. If Al Ghamdi was cooperating with the uprising, they certainly wouldn't have gunned him down."

Wait a minute. Omar was dead? Killed by extremists before Josh disappeared? He didn't have anything to do with Josh being betrayed? She caught Kimberly's glance and they both shook their heads disbelievingly. It simply did not compute! Omar was a foreign spy for the CIA who went off the rails and turned, wasn't he? It happened with more frequency than the CIA ever wanted to admit—and it had to be the reason why Josh asked her if she had heard from Omar's wife, right?

Thank goodness she had hired her own private investigator rather than waiting for the CIA to figure all of this out....

The advice the COS offered for the search seemed benign, if not downright ineffective, and he made it clear that the State Department and the CIA disapproved of Chelsea's search efforts. "It's one thing to pay tribute to him, but you are walking a fine line between looking for a missing family member and interfering with a government investigation," the COS told her. "You realize that if the Agency determines that you did anything to jeopardize the government's investigation of the whereabouts of your husband, you could be facing civil penalties or even jail time, don't you?"

It was practically a threat! Her eyes narrowed. "I'm on your side, sir," she snapped. "I'm the one that turned over the information about the location of the Talky Watch to the CIA." How dare he be so territorial when she had been so resourceful?

But the intimidation shook her and Kimberly and upset the others in the group as well. From that point the conversation with the COS was chilled, and there seemed little reason to continue the visit at the Embassy.

They loaded in the van to go home. Chelsea stared out the window as the vehicle rolled back to Babylon Metro, thinking how slow and ineffective the COS was, to believe that Omar Al Ghamdi had nothing to do with Josh's disappearance!

"Let's talk through this, now," Dr. Evans said as the van made its way back to Babylon Metro. "We have spent five days here and really learned nothing new except for one thing." He began to grille the private investigator as the van sat stuck on the hot freeway in commuter traffic. "Why didn't anybody say until now that Josh went to a holiday party in Baghdad? Did you know this?"

Chelsea was grateful to Dr. Evans. For once someone besides herself who cared deeply about Josh was taking the lead.

"It was never told to me," replied the P.I. defensively, his voice racing faster and faster and turning into another one of his rants. "Everyone in Baghdad hate Babylon Metro! They do not wish to help. People in Baghdad and Babylon Metro, they do not like to talk to each other, you see? The business people don't like, because Babylon Metro steal all the business. The sheiks don't like, because Babylon Metro steal all the tenants in the buildings. The imams don't like because of the greed and the prostitutes and because the prayers are not allowed. The soccer teams don't like, nobody like. Everyone is jealous of Babylon Metro, you understand?"

Chelsea queried Josh's father, "Should we pay our P.I. to go to Baghdad again and spend some time questioning the people that worked at the Embassy that day?"

"Surely that was the first thing Langley did," argued Kimberly. "The Chief of Station said they talked to all the people at the Embassy that they could."

"But why didn't the CIA say anything to *me* about Josh being in Baghdad?" Chelsea demanded.

Kimberly replied, "Because at the end of the day, it does not matter, Chelsea. Josh wasn't seized in Baghdad. He was seized in

Babylon Metro, right in or near his own office, which we couldn't get even close to."

They were no further ahead for having visited the prison, Josh's office building, his dig site, or the American embassy, Chelsea thought dismally. She may as well have stayed home and done her research online and continued to work with the private investigator.

They still had one more day to hit the Route 8, where a couple of witnesses had observed the white Volvo truck, and pass out flyers. She stared out the window at the sand and the desert. It wasn't beautiful. She analyzed all the factors that made a country a depressing Third World country. There was that contrast of low, flat-roofed, dilapidated mud brick homes juxtaposed directly next to villas and expensive, walled enclaves for the wealthy. There were also many little things. The lack of curb and gutter. Light poles, electric lines, and telephone lines with swoops of electric wires—something she hadn't seen very much since she was a child, because in America utilities were now mostly buried underground. Drainage areas filled with standing, fetid pools of water and junk cars at the edge, right in the middle of the city. An old, shabby train with a worn depot with peeling paint that took commuters from north Iraq to southern Iraq and the Gulf.

Chelsea pointed to a high rise building protected by scaffolding and construction netting and surrounded by caution tape and danger signs. There were no lights or people and it appeared to be deserted. "What is going on there?" she asked the interpreter.

"That building engineered wrong in the sand. It have faulty foundation. Many lawsuits. It will be torn down."

"*Welcome to Babylon Metro, Forever a Happy Place!*" The strange cartoon-character queen holding a scepter in her hand with the seven exploding kaleidoscope of stars representing prosperity danced mockingly before her on the digital billboard as they drove into the glimmering, shimmering city. It was a phantasmagoria, a jarring distinction from the real poverty in the rest of Iraq.

Babylon Metro was a hastily constructed, carelessly built illusion.

At supper, she ordered drinks for herself, the tee-totaling Baptist Dr. Evans notwithstanding. The liquor fortified her courage.

Abreakfast the next morning, on behalf of the rest of the search team, Kimberly raised doubts about that search they had planned along Route 8. The private investigator had arranged a route for their van to stop by security booths along the freeway and pass out flyers to the vendors in the little white tents along the highway outside of the villages. "Couldn't we change our flights once again and fly out today, after all?" she concluded.

Chelsea stared at her food, numb. They believed Josh was dead. They didn't say it, but Chelsea knew it was what they thought.

She felt her nerves beginning to fray. She pleaded with all of them. This was the last day to look for Josh! Some small clue might emerge, or at least they would know they had done all they could to find what happened to him in his last hours of life....

Guiltily, the team agreed to make one more try. They waited for morning rush hour traffic to die down. Even though it was still early, the heat was miserable as they moved towards the freeway and the security checkpoints out of town, handing out REWARD flyers at each security booth. The high temperature was expected to be one hundred twenty-two degrees. The freeway eventually narrowed to Route 8, and the traffic crept along slowly in the heat. They passed a dead donkey along the side of the road with flies buzzing over it. There was not enough bottled water and they stopped at a group of vendor tents to purchase more bottles to drink. The hajibs they wore around their heads were suffocating. They stopped at a few more vendor tents, but no one claimed to have seen Josh or a white Volvo truck.

"They don't come same place every day," the private investigator said for the first time. "Sometimes they move vendor tent to different place to get more business." When he said that, Chelsea distinctly felt reproach of the entire group at her and the P.I. for not having done enough homework ahead of time.

"We cannot go much further," said the cute little interpreter. "This is not allowable for my job, to go this far from Babylon Metro." She spoke to the taxi driver in Arabic. He pulled off the next freeway exit, circled around, and merged back in the traffic heading into Babylon Metro.

Kimberly pointed out the window. "There is something absolutely weird about that tour bus." A bus with no identification and heavily tinted windows slid into the lane beside them. It was almost impossible to see inside, but it appeared to be a bus full of young women who pressed their faces to the tinted glass, gaping at the towers of Babylon Metro. Some of them were snapping pictures with cameras.

"They are the prostitutes, and the Chinese mail order brides," the little interpreter said reproachfully. "They come to Babylon Metro from eastern Europe for the men."

Brittany gave a soft little wince. Wide-eyed, she craned her neck to stare out the windows at them and snapped a picture.

Chelsea's mobile buzzed; it was Dane calling from the office. She frowned. They had agreed to use email, and there had been very little communication with the office on this trip. She answered it.

"Chelsea, I'm giving you a heads up. There were some strange guys that came into the office to see you today. They said they understood you were going to be back by now. We told them your trip had been extended. Something didn't seem right about them. We didn't think they seemed like clients, and we weren't sure we should have told them that, so we decided to call you."

"What did they look like, Dane?"

"Let me ask." Another call was coming in at the same time. She ignored the second call and waited while he put her on hold. He came back on the line. "There were two of them." He described them, but they could have been anybody or nobody that she knew, and they did not leave their names or a phone number. They just questioned why Chelsea wasn't back yet and when she was expected.

"I've got to go, Dane, there's another call coming in."

"Call back when you can talk a little longer. We miss you."

She disconnected, trying to decide whether she should be worried or annoyed. There was a message, the call that she just missed. It appeared to be one of the CIA internal numbers. She listened; it was Internal Investigations. "We are requesting that you report to our offices immediately upon your return to the United States to provide a full accounting of your activities in Iraq."

She sat unmoving in the van seat and replayed the message, feeling somehow guilty and ashamed, but at the same time, unwitting of what it was she had done wrong.

And then clouds formed and another sandstorm came up. They had to wait it out while the sun battled the darkness, a hazy ball of pink-orange occasionally peeking through sandy black whirls of dust. Brittany, usually the most positive, went silent, weary of the whole thing. Kimberly became downright sour and short-tempered.

The storm subsided and traffic began to move again. The mysterious-looking bus full of prostitutes in the lane beside them passed them, moving on ahead. "Kimberly," Chelsea said hesitantly, "I don't know what to think of this. A representative from Internal Investigations in the CIA wants to talk to me immediately upon re-entry into the United States."

"What? What NOW?" Kimberly asked with frustration. "Did that jerk at the Embassy prompt that?"

"Probably," Chelsea answered in a low, timid voice.

"You are not going in there and talking to them without me with you," Kimberly admonished.

All of a sudden there was a screech of tires slightly behind them. A black pickup truck accelerated past them, its dark color sending out blinding glints of reflected sunshine. Almost without comprehending what they were viewing, they witnessed it hurtle into top speed; and with huge force, it slammed ferociously into the back of the bus. The bus swerved into their lane, crashing into the car in front of them.

Metal ripped, pieces of bus and glass flew everywhere, and then there was a great explosion and a ball of fire. Screams of pain from the bus tore through the air as upholstery, bodies, and body parts littered the freeway and a thick plume of smoke shot up into the air.

The Confrontation

Their van driver swore in Arabic, completely panicked. "What the hell is happening?" Dr. Evans shouted, but the driver and the frightened little interpreter were too busy pointing and exchanging frantic Arabic conversation to answer. A cacophony of horns beeped from vehicles all over the freeway and vehicles skidded to a stop with several rear ending each other. The driver maneuvered out of the line of vehicles, steering the van off the freeway and onto the sandy shoulder. The van rocked dangerously as it bumped down into the median, kicking up a cloud of dust. They jounced along, straddling the desert scrub.

"It's a suicide bomber," the little interpreter panted in English, trembling and hugging her body as they passed the flaming wreckage. The sudden, intense heat was so hot they could feel it inside the van. Smoke billowed into the sky and grew like a storm cloud over suitcases, bits of cloth, and debris strewn on the road.

"We have to stop and help," insisted Dr. Evans. "There are casualties." He began to reach for the door handle.

"No!" barked the van driver, reaching over with one arm and roughly snatching the doctor's collar. "We go back to the hotel! Now!" He maneuvered the van up the bank and back onto the shoulder to merge into the traffic.

"I didn't see that, I can't believe I saw that." Brittany sobbed, clutching Chelsea's arm, her fingers digging into Chelsea's skin. Chelsea squeezed her eyes shut and pressed her hands over her eyes, trying to block the horrific images.

"For the love of Muhammad and everything that is holy," Kimberly snarled through clenched teeth as the van careened back to Babylon Metro, "if we get out of this Oz alive and get back home, I will never—I repeat, never—set foot on anything or any place resembling sand again."

"Look what's coming towards us!" Chelsea pointed ahead in a strangled voice. Vehicles on the freeway ahead of them pulled to a stop as Chinese equestrian guards from just outside Babylon Metro deftly galloped their sweaty horses on the shoulder of the freeway through the traffic gridlock and to the chaos, their AK-

74Ms pointed, arriving far ahead of emergency responders whose sirens blared a distance away.

When they got back to the hotel, they practically threw tip money at the van driver and ran inside for the elevators, panting. Once inside the double-room suite, Kimberly and Brittany flung themselves on the couches in front of the TV, trembling and shaking. "Should I send my picture of the bus before it blew up to anybody?" Brittany fretted. "The embassy? The CIA?"

Chelsea went straight for the bar, downing a glass of scotch. She felt Kimberly and Brittany staring at her. Out of the corner of her eye, she saw them give knowing looks to each other.

When it was time to go downstairs to dinner, she could barely walk a straight line.

They were all sick during the night. It was something they ate or drank in the last day or two. Chelsea thrashed and tossed uncomfortably all night, plagued with replays of the suicide bombing and the smell of burning fuel, plus guilt over work undone to find Josh. The worrisome call from the CIA demanding a meeting only added to her sickness. Thanks to the kind ministrations of the hotel bell desk, Dr. Evans was able to obtain medications from a nearby pharmacist, but Chelsea ached for her daughter and her dog. It was the lowest point ever for all of them, a time of total discouragement and defeat.

They had no choice but to get up the next morning in order to pack and catch their planes. Getting up and moving around the hotel room in the daylight made her feel improved. They were due to fly out this afternoon.

According to the local news reports, a jihadist for Black Lightening had blown up the bus of prostitutes. An alert came from the airline: The State Department had issued a travel warning to tourists in Babylon Metro. It was as if the State Department itself was deliberately trying to put a note of finality to her unfinished and ambiguous trip.

She ordered a Bloody Mary to be brought up and broached the subject with Kimberly and Brittany in their hotel room.

"I—I know we haven't made much progress, you guys. I want to get out of this stinking city as fast as I can, but I need to go back to Baghdad and talk to some of the employees who saw Josh at the holiday party. I think that was a mistake not to pursue that tip."

Kimberly stood stock still. "You have got to be kidding me."

"I need to do more research on Omar Al Ghamdi and what happened to him. I still think he had something to do with Josh's death."

"First of all," said Kimberly firmly, "you need to get out of this entire country as fast as you can, because the State Department has issued a travel warning. Second of all, there's no point in your going to Baghdad. We know where Josh was when he disappeared. It was here and it's no surprise. Did Omar Al Ghandi figure out Josh was CIA and betray him? Maybe, but I doubt it. The CIA Chief of Station said that Omar was shot to death long before Josh was kidnapped. Anyway, whoever kidnapped him, they had inside information and knew how to get around in that building. When he went to his office, they seized him."

"Maybe he said something to someone at the party about what he was doing next—"

Kimberly cut her off abruptly, enunciating her words decisively. "No, Chels. The Baghdad station isn't going to help you. You're out here on your own with no diplomatic protection in this godforsaken Third World pit." Kimberly began throwing clothes into her suitcase.

"I'm not asking you to go with me. You could call the State Department again and request a meeting for me and then I'll call you from Baghdad. And then there's this clue from the boy in Hillah who thinks Josh was taken to a cave somewhere around here, it was a mistake not to follow up on that—"

"Are you out of your mind, going to those places alone with landmines ready to detonate at any minute? I'm sick and I'm hot and I'm done with this. And besides, I have other clients!" Kimberly snapped. She shook out a shirt she was trying to pack, cussing when sand dropped on the carpet.

Chelsea stared at Kimberly in shock. They had never had a disagreement before. Brittany sat weakly on the bed watching the interchange, her blue eyes widening with alarm as their voices rose.

"I'm your biggest client—" Chelsea started to pull out the last bit of leverage that she had.

"You are not my only client," Kimberly spat back angrily. "I've given you a good billing rate. I've thrown in pro bono work. I have to keep prospecting and keep clients coming into my firm,

351

because at some point, for better or for worse, we will be done, and my world does not revolve around you and your alcohol problem!" She stormed into the bathroom and slammed the door shut, turning on the shower angrily.

Chelsea slunk with her back to the wall and slid down onto her butt with the Bloody Mary in her hands between her knees, shaking. Brittany slowly climbed off the bed and came to where Chelsea was. She put her hand on Chelsea's shoulder. "She's sick. We're all sick. She didn't mean to say those things. And this has been very hard." A damp sheen misted in Brittany's pretty blue eyes.

Tears dripped down Chelsea's cheeks. "We raised all this money. We spent all of this time and energy. What if he's still out there somewhere? I can't just turn my back and leave him when I'm this close."

Brittany slowly slid weakly onto the floor beside Chelsea and touched her shoulder. "What you are experiencing is ambiguous loss, Chelsea. You are living life in a gray zone. There is no black and white, no right or wrong, no answer, no closure. He may come back and he may not. God knows where he is. I think maybe it's time to let go and let God. You have done all you can. What other woman would do what you've done to get her husband back?"

A stab went through Chelsea's heart. Brittany had always told her to follow her heart, to keep believing; but even Brittany had given up.

"Kimberly is right—" Brittany paused and said in a quiet but firm voice—"Chelsea, you have a drinking problem. You need to get ahold of it before it gets ahold of you."

"I do not. It's for my stomach." Chelsea yanked her hands away.

"Chelsea. Listen to me." Brittany grabbed her wrists back. "You're a single mom with a missing husband. You are thousands of miles away from home. Of course you want a drink. But here's the thing: if it's not a problem, you should be able to give up drinking for a month—"

"Why should I give up something I enjoy? I never asked you or Kimberly to give up TV or social networking for a month." Chelsea continued with denials but Brittany raised her feminine voice and talked over her.

"Chelsea, if you can't give it up for thirty days, it's a problem. You know I wouldn't just say something like that."

Chelsea let out an angry sound, rolling her eyes and banging the back of her head against the wall.

"Please! Just be quiet for a moment," Brittany said in a sharp voice, and then in a quieter tone: "Let me pray for you and Josh,"

Chelsea let Brittany hold her hand and shoulder and Brittany prayed a prayer that God would keep Josh in his safekeeping, no matter whether he was in this world or the next, and that Chelsea would be able to accept an ambiguous answer to her questions.

"Brittany," Chelsea asked, her voice low-pitched from the vodka, "Why did you get so interested in me? Why did you want to help so much and to come on this trip? It was so long ago when your husband died. You're remarried and you have kids now that are nearly grown."

Britany stood up from where she had been squatting on the floor. She perched on the edge of the bed, her feet dangling, her eyes boring straight into Chelsea's. "Because there's something I always regretted," she said softly. "I was so young when Jason was killed. I didn't know what to do. If only I had tried harder. If only I had pressed for more answers from the Senate Select Investigation Committee. If only I had gone to Pakistan and talked to some of the officials. I didn't know what to do. I completely trusted the Agency. I wanted—" She hesitated a moment, tears welling up in her eyes. She swallowed, and then pushed on. "I wanted to do this for Jason, Chelsea. I felt I owed it to him, that he would be pleased in some way that I tried to help find another member of the Agency family."

It was the first time Brittany had ever used her first husband's name: Jason. He was a CIA paramilitary officer who was recognized only by an anonymous star on the Headquarters Memorial Wall, and by a blank entry next to a date of death in the Book of Honor that rested behind plated glass underneath the star.

Many of the victims on that wall and in that book were from Josh's arm of the CIA.

Her friends had given up, but Chelsea couldn't. Even if it was too late, she had to continue trying to determine what happened to Josh.

She left the P.I. with specific guidance: to search for new clues about Josh leaving the Holiday party early, and the youth who had seen the white truck.

If Josh were ever found and she needed to come back, it would be an expensive, lengthy fifteen-hour plane trip.

She thought about potential trouble with American authorities that might come as a result of her actions. What if the Agency did determine, as the Chief of Station had warned, that she was impeding their investigation? Would she really face fines and penalties? Jail time? The thought of being detained when she got back home made her feel ill again.

She began to question her patriotism to a country that would leave its service man adrift, lost in a bureaucratic shuffle and possibly dead; a country that refused to negotiate for the precious lives of its hostages. For the first time she resented the United States of America. How dare they detain her and question her like some sort of criminal? Genuine terrorists with true intent to harm were making their way into America via boats, busses, and planes all the time!

Suddenly she wanted to talk to Pastor Thorpe, Josh's favorite pastor in London. Pastor Thorpe had such a sensible outlook on justice. She briefly considered web chat—she had pretty much lost her horror of cameras lately—and then suddenly an idea popped into her head.

She could go to U.K. She could talk to him in person.

She could change her flight home to a London stopover. And wouldn't it be nice to see the places she and Josh had once lived? To visit some of the people they had known? Somehow it seemed to her that Josh would be pleased, and honored, if she did. More importantly, she could procrastinate on the dreaded re-entry interview with the CIA!

She got on the phone to call her mother.

"Well, I guess I could give a few more days, Chels, but I do have to get back to Columbia before too long. I'm hosting the Retired Women Accountants' luncheon this month."

Mom never complained. Chelsea felt guilty, making her care for Atalaya for so long.

"There's something else. It's your dog, honey. Yappie is not doing well. I took her to the vet."

Chelsea's stomach clenched. "What did he say?"

"He said it's old age." Mom was neither discouraging nor encouraging, just factual.

Well, at least it wasn't urgent. Nonetheless, she felt remorseful; embarrassed that she had left her child for so long, regretful that she had disrupted the routine of her beloved old dog. Nonetheless, she changed her flight destination, grimacing at the cost to divert her travel destination from Washington, D.C., to London. She booked a trip home for a week later.

The rest of the search team's suitcases were ready to go and checked in with the bellhop. Brittany tried to act as if everything were normal, even though it wasn't; Kimberly refused to make eye contact or speak in any more than monotones. "She still feels a little queasy," Brittany the peacemaker covered for Kimberly.

Chelsea thanked them for everything they had done. Kimberly dodged her, but Brittany gave her a hug. Chelsea announced that she would be changing her flight to London and outlined her reasons. Thank goodness Kimberly and Brittany's flight for Washington, D.C., via Istanbul, left right away. There was no more awkwardness and it was a relief. Dr. Evans's flight to Columbia, via Dubai and Chicago, did not leave for two more hours. He wanted to spend most of the time in the lobby getting caught up with his partnership business on his computer.

She stayed with him to keep him company. Dr. Evans watched the footage about the suicide bomber on the television, shaking his head sadly. "I feel badly that I did not stay and help," he said. "Lives could have been saved."

Sometimes she didn't really understand her father-in-law. They were just prostitutes. There could have been explosives that hadn't been detonated. He could have been killed if he had tried to stop and help.

Curled up in a comfortable leather chair in the hotel lobby, she left a phone message for her old boss at Goldberger Hewitt

London and for the friendly Pastor Thorpe from Josh's old church in London. She poked around on apps, comparing hotels. Pastor Thorpe messaged back not very long after she left her contact information. *"Come stay with my wife and me whilst you look for accommodations, or more so, just make your visit with us for the entire time."*

She stretched and yawned, grateful. Outside it had clouded up and started raining, and the local news television station was capturing not only the rare rain event but also footage of flooding in the streets in Babylon Metro, which had hurriedly and abysmally designed drainage systems.

Her father in-law gingerly brought up the unspeakable topic. "Did you and Josh ever talk with each other about what you would do if he were gone and couldn't be found? Was it the kind of thing Josh would discuss? Or was he too sure of himself and confident to bring it up with you?"

"We pre-planned, but you're right, he was confident," she said. "He said several times when we were working on estate planning not to worry, that he was a cat and that he would land on his feet."

The doctor was silent for a moment and bowed his graying head, looking down at his hands, turning them over to inspect them. His once tall, straight back was bent with age and the new burden he carried. "He was always the kind of child we had to— to let go," he said heavily. "He wanted a 'life experience' and decided to go to university in London. He lived with a girl who was a bad influence on him, something that really upset us. Then he was terribly shaken up in the Tube bombing by the group of Chinese militant Muslims that killed his co-workers. He went through a depression but we were far away and couldn't help him. Pastor Thorpe brought him back from the brink."

She had heard some of this story from Clinton. She let her father-in-law remember, let him talk, let him mourn.

"We had to let him go again when we deduced that he was involved in espionage in London, back when the two of you eloped. By the time he decided to officially join the CIA, I guess we had resigned ourselves to the fact that..." he cleared his throat but gave her smile and a sad little wink, "we were pretty sure that settling down in Columbia like a normal American couple wasn't going to happen."

No, Josh was never really wired to live a quiet life in the suburbs of the Midwest. She felt sorry for her father-in-law's sadness and knew that he was looking for something to grasp onto, something for comfort. "He's going to pop back up," she said with confidence that she wasn't quite sure that she felt.

"God knows when a sparrow falls to the ground, and he knows what happened to Josh," Dr. Evans responded. "But God isn't some sort of servant boy obligated to cater to my wishes. The truth is, no father ever really imagines that he will outlive his boy. It's a hard thing to contemplate."

His words made her feel guilty because she had certainly made her own bargains with God, demanding that he give her what she wanted in exchange for being a good person. A sudden impulse seized her, a desire to ease her father-in-law's pain. She opened her purse, looking for the carefully creased final letter from Josh tucked deep in the folds, the letter with the name Operation AuCHFOP and the number for the mysterious Deep Throat. She pulled it out and handed it to him. "No one has seen this," she said. "I've been saving this for Atalaya to have. It's—it's very personal," she said apologetically, "but I think I want you to read it."

He took the letter and smoothed it out. A mist appeared in his eyes. "That was my boy," he said, a catch in his throat. "He was a loner and a risk taker, but he had a heart full of love for the people closest to him."

Dr. Evans was speaking in past tense. He stroked the letter with his finger, the most recent link to his son. A noisy group of Chinese tourists wheeled their luggage past on the way to the taxi stand. Momentarily distracted, she watched them while he re-read the letter.

"AuCHFOP," Dr. Evans talked to himself. He began repeating the word.

Worriedly, she glanced around the hotel lobby. A staff person was within hearing distance, cleaning the carpet with a little carpet sweeper. "Sh-h-h-h, don't say it aloud. I'm not supposed to know it. We're not supposed to know!" Hurriedly she snatched the paper back from him.

He lowered his voice. "AuCHFOP," he mused again, then began spelling the individual letters out loud, quietly enough to avoid being overheard. "It has to be a clue in and of itself about his mission!"

AuCHFOP is Unraveled

"The CIA uses nicknames for projects that make sense later when you hear about them publicly, like Bay of Pigs. Bay meant Caribbean Ocean. Pigs meant communists, of course. And there was also Project Stargate. Remember Project Stargate, Chelsea?"

Chelsea shook her head. Project Stargate was not anything she remembered.

"Oh, you're too young, I suppose, that was in the '90s. The CIA was running experiments with psychics and telepaths who claimed to have ESP. It was a waste of money and it got shut down. Psychics, astrologers, thus the code name Stargate."

"Ok, so what do you suppose is an 'AuCHFOP'?" Chelsea queried the doctor. "It sounds like someone sneezed. Or something flopped, failed. Maybe it was a mission designed to nosedive all along," she added bitterly.

On the brink of solving the puzzle, he was sitting up straighter now, alert and invigorated, his brown eyes flashing with excitement. "Remember *Au* from high school chemistry? That's the chemical element for gold."

A lightbulb came on. Of course! The antiquities! She read his mind. "So if we knew what C-H-F-O-P was, we might have a new clue…" She turned on her tablet and eagerly began a search.

Dr. Evans was doing his own search on his own device, more slowly than her, of course, squinting at it because of his older eyes. "C-H-F-O-P. I'm trying to think, what chemical element is that, or is that similar to? There is something about it on the edge of my memory, but I don't think it's a chemical element. Not exactly."

But they were stuck. The internet results were a confusing mix. Patents? Elements? They couldn't quite put together any clues and they had been sitting a long time. They decided to power walk around the mall.

They stopped at the urban eatery for a final meal of lamb kebab without much conversation. Then suddenly Dr. Evans leaned over and grabbed her arm.

"I figured it out," he said in a low, grave voice. "My dear, C-H-F-O-P is the molecular formula for sarin."

She froze as the doctor, in the clinical manner of a person with a scientific mind, quickly outlined the properties and risks of the liquid compound.

Colorless, odorless nerve agent.

Partial doses could cause paralysis and permanent nerve damage.

Lethal, with suffocation within ten minutes.

Something Josh had been doing involved the chemical weapon, sarin gas!

Fear welled up in her. "If Josh was investigating nuclear or biological weapons, it would explain why he could not get by on his cover story as an architect repairing a building and stumbling upon a few antiquities. If the Chinese or the Iraqis found out what he was really doing, he got in over his head. What do we do?" she asked.

"Call Deep Throat again. Tell her you figured it out."

In the Analyst division of the National Clandestine Services of the CIA headquarters in Langley, Liu Chen was called in by her immediate supervisor for an official warning. Liu remained outwardly calm but her head was so light she felt she might faint as she faced him from the other side of his desk. What had been discovered in the back halls of Langley? Did they whisper that she had passed information on to Chelsea?

"I keep getting messages from NGA," complained her supervisor. "They have an undocumented billing for some aerial shots." He flipped his computer screen around towards her direction and showed her the invoice evidence. "This signature is illegible. But it's yours, isn't it?"

Liu came clean immediately. "That is for close-ups of the escape vehicle when we were looking for Ryan Taylor during the prison uprising."

"But I did not authorize you to do this, Liu. This was never run up the channels. Look how much they're billing us!" he stated accusatorily. "And it wasn't even supportive. It turned out to be inconclusive."

It was the CIA's job to analyze every potential outcome, even the most remote. The team had viewed the unauthorized shots, but of course there were endless interpretations of what the photographs could potentially indicate or not indicate. There was little to go on; no consensus and no conclusion.

"This messes up our departmental budget," he rebuked her.

She knew she had not been a team player. She had gone rogue, and it was just the tip of the iceberg. Was this just the ramp up? She forced her voice to be flat and factual, without a trace of emotion, belying the turmoil going on inside her. "If it helps us to locate him someday, then all of a sudden we do not mind paying the bill," she answered.

"You were out of line. I am going to have to write you up for this. It will remain in your team member file." He flipped the monitor back towards himself, touched the screen and began inputting something. She waited for what would come next, the additional evidence and accusations.

He glanced up at her with annoyance. "Go. You can go now." He raised his hand and pointed towards the door.

There was a stop in Beirut and then Chelsea arrived in Heathrow airport. She was so grateful to be back in a First World country. No dead donkeys on the side of the road, no beggars, no streets with horrendous pot holes the size of trucks, no peeling drywall, no chipped and filthy flooring, no graffiti, no Chinese signs and hastily constructed buildings.

Heathrow was bigger and more crowded with international travelers than ever, but she remembered the way to the subway station and managed her luggage alone onto the Tube and towards OxTower Hill where Pastor Thorpe lived. She checked her messages. No word back from Deep Throat.

A few years ago the OxTower Hill neighborhood had been aging, dangerous, and a habitat for rogue minority groups and Chinese Muslim terrorists, one of whom had tracked Clinton and marked him for death. It was the reason she and Josh could not move back to London sooner. In recent years, OxTower Hill had seen a struggling shift for the better during the government crackdown of the Prime Minister Evans era. A few of the Chinese Muslims still lived in the borough, but only remnants of unrest remained. Compared to most of Iraq, OxTower Hill was pristine. A data security firm bringing jobs had located in an old shipbuilding industrial center and rehabilitated it. Here and there were new shops and brownstones with fresh paint.

Pastor Thorpe and his wife met her at their parsonage, welcoming her with British courtesy. She resisted the impetuous American desire to throw her arms around them, which would probably seem a bit overbearing; really, they had been closer to Josh. The Thorpes were well into their fifties, empty nesters. Pastor Thorpe's hair was much grayer. Mrs. Thorpe, motherly with ruddy cheeks and blond hair streaked with white, made sandwiches while they talked lightly about the flight from Iraq. They rarely drank alcohol. That was fine with Chelsea. She would prove to Brittany that she didn't have a drinking problem.

As the evening went on, the friendship rekindled and quickly they became more at home with each other. The Thorpes seemed rather pleased to have an interesting house guest to talk to. "We've had our share of extremist violence here, as you know," Pastor

Thorpe said empathetically. It was true—Pastor Thorpe's church had once been bombed by Chinese Muslim Uyghur extremists. She had been there when it happened.

She told them about the discouraging trip to Iraq, including the wrenching conversation with the Chinese prison commander who assumed her husband was dead. "We made an appointment with the prison and we came all that way. He didn't pretend to try," Chelsea bemoaned. "He did nothing for us."

"To the Eastern and Middle East cultures, conformity with the group and unity is paramount. Those of us independent types in Western culture, with our striving to be individualistic, our search for truth, and our propensity to whistle-blow, find it incomprehensible," Pastor Thorpe thoughtfully observed.

"Josh was—um, acquainted with—a structural engineer who was Saudi. I used to think that Omar was a friend, but now I think he was the one who betrayed Josh. And I think about Omar, my gut twists around inside, Pastor Thorpe. I know God doesn't like it, but I loathe him."

His forehead creased sadly. "It's hard for us to understand what life is like under a harsh regime, where freedoms are restricted and where destruction is valued more than life. Try not to think of Joshie's associate as an enemy, but instead, think of him as a victim of the enemy," he counseled wisely.

How much she needed Pastor Thorpe! More than anyone, he understood what she was going through. Why didn't she reach out to him sooner?

"I need to stay positive, because if I don't stay positive, I won't find Josh. Right?"

There was an awkward silence, and then Pastor Thorpe cleared his throat. "Chelsea, there is One who knows exactly where Joshie is, and he knows the number of hairs on Joshie's head."

"Actually, there are fewer of those than there used to be," Chelsea quipped, trying to break the ice.

Mrs. Thorpe smiled sadly.

Ian Clarke, the polite, aloof, prosperous branch manager at Goldberger Hewitt's London office, was too busy the next morning to take much time, but he visited with her briefly in the reception area on the way to a meeting with a client. "I remember that you hastily left the U.K. under startlingly mysterious circumstances. We received a visit from the MI6 shortly after, telling us it was necessary due to terrorism, and to give you a good recommendation," he told her.

She saw a few co-workers that she remembered, including her friend Priya! Priya greeted her professionally, shaking her hand just like the Thorpes and asking politely about the visit to Babylon Metro. Priya was happy to go for a coffee at the balcony level of the Starbucks on Bond Street and listened with dignified sympathy to the story of Chelsea's unsuccessful attempt at piercing the veil of security in Tomorrow Globe Financial Center.

It was exhilarating to be in London once again and to visit the busy, successful office she had once worked in.

It took several attempts but at last she got in contact by phone with Deep Throat. Without any pleasantries, Chelsea jumped immediately to the point. "C-H-F-O-P. It means sarin gas, doesn't it? Chemical weapons? Did the Agency have Josh working on something with chemical weapons?" she accused.

There was such a long silence on the other end that Chelsea thought Deep Throat had disconnected. Finally Deep Throat replied, "I am sorry. I have no more information for you."

Chelsea persisted. "One other thing. Josh was in Baghdad the day he disappeared, at a holiday party at the American embassy. Why didn't anyone ever tell me? Did embassy staff get questioned?"

"Do not contact me again." Then Deep Throat really did disconnect. Chelsea shivered, endless unimaginable scenarios going through her mind. Had Josh been exposed to sarin gas? Was he lying somewhere, sick or brain damaged? Had it killed him in a horrible, tortuous way?

She tried her best to block it from her mind, which of course made her feel guilty, but what else could she do?

That afternoon, Chelsea made a sentimental journey to Finchley, the borough where she and Josh and Clinton and his ex-wife had lived when they were first married. It had not changed very much. It still retained its somewhat suburban character with golf courses along the Tube and its long, pragmatic retail corridor ("If it isn't available in Finchley, you can probably cope without it," Josh had always said). The doors of the Tube opened, and she stepped into the quaint, early 1900s train station that she and Josh had frequently utilized. Nostalgia overcame her as she walked the tree-lined Woodside Park Road, past the Jewish boys' school where the students lingered outside in their little black caps, and past the stately Victorian guest house with its tea room and beautiful garden where they had lived when they first eloped.

The next day she took the Tube to Marylebone. When they were newlyweds in London, moving to Marylebone had been Josh's financial career goal. It didn't have the greenery that Finchley had, but she was fascinated by its rows and rows of stately brick flats, and its proximity to the famous sites and government embassies. There was a cute little primary school and two pretty parks, and everything you could need in walking distance.

A plan began to evolve in her mind, a plan to put the resentment towards the CIA behind her. A plan that would have her within eight hours' proximity to Josh, rather than fifteen, if there were more clues or if he were finally found....

Josh had always wanted his little Attie to live in London someday. Maybe she could get work at Goldberger Hewitt or another London commercial real estate firm!

There would be a $2.5 million tax-free annuity from the U.S. government for her and Atalaya.

She could rent out the house in McLean until she decided how long to stay.

In London she wouldn't need a car.

School had always been challenging for Atalaya. Could the cute little primary school in Marylebone handle her?

What about Yappie? The Sheltie had been with Chelsea since the loss of her first husband. Yappie had been with her through some of the most poignant stages of life: remarriage, miscarriage, adoption, job changes. A move would be traumatic for a senior dog.

Could she create a support system in a new city? Would Pastor Thorpe and new friends at work be adequate for life's ups and downs?

She just wasn't sure. Maybe it wasn't very realistic. Moving would be very hard.

Going without alcohol was like being on a diet and craving fat and sugar. She cheated when she stopped into a pub for lunch. Just one glass! It didn't even have a calming effect, she had been drinking so much in recent months. She walked out knowing she had failed.

And then she received another call from Internal Investigations. "You had originally indicated that you would arrive back home by now. Your passport and travel records indicate that you changed your plans and flew to London. We are reminding you that you are summoned to our offices upon re-entry into the United States."

"I'm flying back on Monday. And I will not speak to you without my lawyer present," she snapped. But fear gripped her, that they would call her on a Saturday.

Making things worse, she noticed that like Dr. Evans, Pastor Thorpe and his wife talked about Josh in the past tense. When she spoke of searching for him, or what he would think of her moving back to his favorite city, London, it was almost as if they knew something she did not know, something grim and final; and she knew that they believed she could not accept the truth.

Chelsea called Brittany, Atalaya, and her mother on Saturday night to report what was happening. She hung up, feeling inordinately homesick for them—especially her daughter—yet somehow convinced in her mind of what she needed to do.

The next morning she dressed and went to church. It had been the better part of a decade since Chelsea had been to Oxford Hill Baptist Church on a Sunday. When a Chinese Uyghur Muslim extremist group bombed the Tube and Josh alone escaped, he had become suicidal from depression; Pastor Thorpe had pulled him back from the brink. The church had grown and was much larger since she had last visited. It was now housed in an ancient Anglican church with soaring ceilings. She spotted some familiar faces who remembered her and Josh and who said 'hello'—the guitar player in the church band, the family from Somalia, and the woman who fell down the fire escape at the church bombing. They were older now, of course, with sprinkles of gray hair and evidence of wrinkles. They had all been so young once!

"We heard. We've been following the news stories."

"We're so sorry Joshie is missing."

"He was a good bloke." They murmured their regrets and patted her on the shoulder.

She slid into the wooden pew, recalling the metal folding chairs and cheap, improvised surroundings in the other building seven years ago. Oxford Hill Baptist Church hadn't reached the affluence of an American mega-church by any stretch, but it was in better shape now than it had been.

There was a choir accompanied by a small orchestra. The choir performed the closing piece by Handel from The Messiah, its voices reverberating up to the once-beautiful arched ceiling:

Worthy is the lamb that was slain

Was Josh still suffering somewhere? Or was he long gone, to a better place? Because if he was gone, there was no use living any longer in the prison of pain she had created for herself.

Forever. And Ever.

The choir began to softly sing Handel's "Amen" and Pastor Thorpe stepped up to the mic, talking over the music. "The greatest teacher that ever lived said to love our enemies and pray for them. He did this in the Garden. I'll admit, the love part is the hard part. But we can follow his example. We can start by praying. Feelings follow action." He stepped away and the "Amen's" of the piece increased in volume.

How exactly did God love the unlovable? How could he love someone like Omar Al Ghamdi, who lured Josh into danger and perhaps even betrayed him? And how in the world could God possibly love the Black Lightening Group or the Chinese who probably executed him? She could probably also add to the list the hopelessly underwhelming CIA liaisons, Connie and Brick and the people at the agency who failed her husband.

Yet God did love them all.

She doubted she could ever love any of them. She supposed she ought to at least work on forgiving. It was like facing a high cliff that must be climbed, one with sharp rocks that would pierce her knees and her hands if she tried to ascend.

The room swelled as the choir sang the final, triumphant "Amen" of Handel's chorus, and she allowed the timeless piece to stir her emotions. She had lived for music when she was younger. Music used to cut to the core of her soul and propel her into the jagged jaws of emotion, especially when she was a teenager. But now she had passed forty years old and life got in the way, and it seemed as she got older that music lost more and more of its power. It was as if you were sitting in a car when you first left town for vacation and you had your window open and you got to feel and hear every bit of air and wind and sound; but as the trip dragged on, you realized that the glass had somehow raised up, the noises and odors and sounds were muffled, and your window was cloudy with dirt and dust and dead bugs.

The tenor line chased the alto line, the sopranos echoed the basses, and the musical fugue interwove and encircled like water swirling in a warm pond on a summer day, and she allowed it to enfold her completely.

She closed her eyes in prayer, elevated by the vision of that which the choir sang; and the music raised her above the earth to a different place outside of space and time into the future, an immortal place of reunification and healing where, not today, but someday, there would be justice.

Was Josh watching her from the other side, waiting for her to let go and to move on?

The tympani reverberated, vibrating throughout the auditorium. She felt shivers and goose bumps shudder throughout her whole body, from the top of her scalp to the base of her feet, as the music cascaded to a glorious finale.

After church she helped Mrs. Thorpe set the dining room table for lunch and then went and stood in the kitchen while the pastor's wife pulled out the traditional Sunday shepherd's pie from the oven. Chelsea fidgeted at the counter, hearing her own words ring hollowly across the kitchen floor.

"I—I want to have a little memorial service for Josh," she said hesitantly. "Something very short and informal. Do you think the old band friends from the church would come over this evening for a little while and tell stories and remember? Then could Pastor Thorpe say a few words?"

"Oh my." Mrs. Thorpe nearly dropped the dish on the counter. She caught it with the hot pads, corrected her balance, and stood still for a moment.

Then she turned to face Chelsea, her face full of relief and her eyes glistening with tears. "Of course, love. Of course."

"MOMMY!"

Atalaya shrieked with excitement and ran to the front of the house as Chelsea dragged the heavy suitcase in. She enveloped her daughter in her arms. "How was your first day of school? Did Grandma take you to your new class?"

Atalaya nodded excitedly, and then she dropped her gaze down to the floor. "I'm sorry you could not find Daddy. I know you did your best. It will be you and me together, Mommy. We will be a team." Atalaya took her hand and lifted her gaze from her feet to her mother with a young girl's innocent brown eyes and empathetic expression. Chelsea's mom appeared through the doorway, and Chelsea met her eyes gratefully. Atalaya had obviously rehearsed the speech with her grandmother, but that didn't mean it wasn't heartfelt. Out of the corner of her eye, she saw Yappie in the living room, tail wagging weakly, trying to get up on her haunches.

"That's right, honey. As far as we know, it's just you and me. God is taking care of Daddy somewhere." It was Chelsea's own rehearsed speech back, one that Pastor Thorpe had suggested, to prepare Atalaya for the eventuality that Daddy would probably never come back.

Atalaya dropped her hand and began to tug at Chelsea's suitcase. Chelsea's mother stepped forward and embraced her. "I'm sorry it has happened to you twice now," Mom finally managed. Her eyes were wet and she wiped her nose with a tissue.

"I know, Mom. I guess it shows the kind of guys I pick," Chelsea replied with a rueful smile.

There was a thumping sound. It was Yappie, struggling across the floor. Chelsea sucked in her breath. The dog had declined, fast, and could hardly drag her back end across the carpet. Chelsea hurried over to the old Sheltie. The furry tail still wagged, but the gloss was gone from Yappie's coat, and the sable fur was matted and dirty. She held her pet for a while. Yappie had lost weight. "What happened to my girl?" Chelsea managed with a whisper. The dog licked her hand.

"She hasn't eaten since yesterday morning," Chelsea's mother said in a hesitant voice.

"She will, now that I'm home," Chelsea said reassuringly. She offered Yappie a kibble of food. Yappie licked it off her hand and crunched it slowly.

They ate dinner with Mom and saw her off. Left alone in the silence of the large house, they started the laundry. Atalaya helped happily, getting the majority (though not all) of the pieces of clothing into the laundry instead of on the floor. Atalaya jabbered about school and television and her time with her favorite grandmother. Chelsea dreaded tomorrow, the phone call to schedule the interview with Internal Investigations.

But Yappie stayed in the living room. Chelsea carried the dog outside to go to the bathroom, but when she set her pet in the grass, Yappie fell to the ground. Chelsea felt her throat tighten and tried to hold the Sheltie up, but to no avail.

Yappie was suffering. She would never make a trip to England. A hard decision would have to be made, and very fast.

She carried Yappie back into the house, to the favorite spot in the living room, and sat back down on the floor beside her with a handful of food, petting the graying, golden head. Yappie gave a weak lick of her hand and rested a chin on her knee, and Chelsea stroked the white stripe on her forehead, thinking sadly back to the time she adopted the Sheltie puppy. It was after her first husband died in a freak motorcycle accident. Yappie had been through some of the most momentous highlights of Chelsea's life—widowhood, dating, remarriage, miscarriage, motherhood, career changes and relocation.

The old dog gave a wheeze and a shudder and became still, and Chelsea continued to stroke the sable fur, remembering once when Yappie was poisoned and nearly died, and the time she thought she was giving Yappie up for good to her parents when she and Josh moved to London.

And then she noticed the dog remained still.

"Yappie?" She shook the animal, but the furry little chin dropped limply to the floor. She felt the dog's chest.

There was no breath.

"You stayed alive until I got home, old girl, didn't you?" She remained in place next to her dog, tears leaking from her eyes, petting the soft, sable fur and saying goodbye.

The employees at Mizrahi and Associates dropped everything and huddled in the lunch room listening to Chelsea's tale of searching for Josh and the suicide bombing (or at least the highly abridged parts she felt she could tell them.) Twenty-five minutes into the story, the receptionist, who had to run up front to catch the phones, interrupted her with an urgent call.

It was from Internal Investigations in the CIA. "You are hereby in violation. You have been back in the country since last evening and you have not yet contacted us. We are requesting that you report to our offices in two hours to provide a full accounting of your activities in Iraq. You may have your lawyer present. This is an investigation to determine if you have interfered with due process of law and hampered an agency operation and mission."

"What?—" Chelsea was dumfounded. "I can't! I have another appointment then! I was going to call you and schedule something for this afternoon or tomorrow—"

The officer cut her off. "If you do not appear, you can be arrested and possibly jailed. You are entitled to an attorney as due process of law."

Add to the list another person to detest and thus require God's forgiveness: the turf-protecting Chief of Station in Baghdad, who was probably responsible for this. Shaking with sick nervousness, she called Kimberly. It was their first conversation since leaving Iraq. Despite the recent altercation they had, Kimberly responded with professional reassurance. "I will be there for the meeting. This is going to be ok. This is a bunch of crap. You had every right as a citizen to hire your own private P.I. and go look for your husband."

They met at the bland government building where the Inspector General for Internal Affairs was located, and they were led into a cubicle meeting room. Two investigators recorded the interview. "Depending on the answers you provide today, this may satisfy the Agency's request for information. If the answers you supply do not satisfy the Agency's request for information, you could be summoned back for a Congressional inquiry."

The interviewers asked many questions about how they gained access to local authorities and what information they gave to the private investigator, and what the investigator found out. Kimberly was forthright and clear in her answers. There was little to hide. If their local contacts had bribed anyone, they had no knowledge. However, Chelsea and Kimberly were very careful to release no information that might give away Deep Throat.

"During your time in Iraq, did you make any inquiries about chemical or nuclear weapons?" asked one of the officers.

"No," answered Kimberly, taking charge of the meeting with her resonant voice.

"We suspect my husband was investigating chemical weapons," Chelsea piped up. "Like, maybe sarin gas or something."

Kimberly kicked her foot. Immediately the interviewers began furiously taking notes. Kimberly smiled wanly. "What my client is saying is, she researched chemical weapons in Iraq on open sources. It's something you can find on the internet in five minutes. However, it wasn't anything Mr. Evans ever discussed with my client."

One officer hurriedly left the room, muttering "Let me get someone with Special Weapons." The barrage of questions continued. "Did your husband ever express frustration with the United States government and express sympathy with the Iraqis? Did he suggest that the Iraqis should be the ones to recover the antiquities?"

"No!" Chelsea answered, shocked. "I told you over and over. I didn't even understand at first what he was doing!"

Kimberly faced the officer squarely and narrowed her eyes, every word enunciated and her voice cutting and accusing. "You mean—are you insinuating, sir, that my client's husband was disloyal to the U.S. government? Because if that's what you are saying, that's pretty heavy, and you sure better not run around accusing loyal CIA employees of treason—"

The door opened and the second officer came back with the Special Weapons officer into the room and asked them a long series of repetitive questions. Three-and-a-half hours had already passed. Chelsea was impatient. There was simply nothing else to add. It was the same question being asked five, ten, fifteen different ways.

The interviewers read a list of chemical weapons with frightening names—nerve agents, uranium, mustard gas. "While he was working at the Agency, were you ever exposed by your husband to secret information?" they asked.

Irritation swept over her, and outright resentment. Suddenly in an emotional outburst she exclaimed, "What kind of country is this? I thought this was the United States of America!"

"The whole time she was in Iraq," interjected Kimberly, "what Mrs. Evans was trying to do was to find her husband so her child can have a father as she grows up. That is all Mrs. Evans wanted!"

Chelsea sat ramrod straight in her chair, awash with a sense of wounded disillusionment and anger. "I'm a good citizen! I don't cheat the IRS and I pay taxes on time! I've been in service with my husband to the CIA off and on for years!" Her voice rose; Kimberly kicked her foot warningly again under the table, but she ignored it. "We've given up a normal life for a dangerous, secretive life. We've missed holidays and anniversaries and birthdays. My own sister doesn't even know where my husband really works. Now I feel like my country has dropped the ball on my husband, one of the most loyal and hardworking undercover officers in the CIA, and they've treated me like a common criminal!"

"I think," Kimberly interrupted again in an equally loud voice, "My client just told you all she knows."

Chelsea stood up from her chair. "No, Attorney Feldman, as a matter of fact, I'm not finished telling them things." She leaned over the table to the investigators, whose faces were slowly turning red. "This whole meeting today is a bunch of bullshit. You CIA people sit at your comfortable little computers filling out your comfortable little after-action reports, looking for someone else to blame, and casting judgment on me. I went and got my OWN reward money and my OWN funds to get on a plane and go to Disneyland-in-a-desert, the Las Vegas of the Middle East, to look for my child's father. A father, who is probably dead, by the way, because of something dumb YOU did!"

Kimberly sat unmoving, poker-faced with the pen in her hand poised on her notes paper, witnessing the tirade.

"I feel betrayed by my own country!" Chelsea was injured to the core. Her voice rang shrilly through the little room, louder than Kimberly's voice could ever be. She wagged her finger at the men sitting across from her. "Since I couldn't find proof of life and since my husband is probably dead, likely due to something that is YOUR FAULT, guess what? I am ready to accept that he is dead! Go ahead, bring me the papers to sign. You know what I think? I think you should proceed with a memorial service for him. Let me know, and I will be there, and I and my little eight-year-old girl will PERSONALLY drape a flag over a casket, or over an empty vase, or whatever you want me to do, if that's what it takes to put this ridiculous CHARADE of blame shifting to an end! You can write him up in the book of Honor and carve a star on Memorial Wall, for him, okay? C'mon," she snapped her fingers. "Where's the papers? Where do I sign?"

There was an awful silence and the interviewers stared at their pens. An old, yellowed, battery-operated clock on the wall ticked.

"Ok, you may leave now," one of them finally said.

They stood up and Chelsea stomped to the door and down the hall. She heard Kimberly behind her query them authoritatively, "Just one final question, gentlemen. Will we be summoned to a congressional hearing?"

They cleared their throats and looked at each other. "We doubt it."

When she got home with Atalaya, no dog barked at her entrance. She was so shaken with grief and anger that she could barely speak, and she raced to the kitchen for crackers, cheese, and a bottle of wine while she microwaved a frozen gourmet entrée of Country French Chicken. She gulped down a glass of wine, feeling it burn to her toes and the wonderful feeling of relaxation.

During supper she poured a second glass and drank most of it. Every shadow or glimmer of light that crossed the floor momentarily seemed to be Yappie, but Yappie was gone. She felt like a failure for drinking. She had done fairly well since leaving Iraq!

After supper, she set up Atalaya with her homework, told her she could watch the television, and told her that she couldn't go near the outside doors of the house. Stepping out of the home, Chelsea drove to Chain Bridge Road to the red brick Presbyterian church with traditional white steeple that hosted the neighborhood Alcoholics Anonymous meetings.

When it came to her turn, she said, "Hello, I am a single mom with a child. I don't know for sure if I'm an alcoholic yet, but I do know one thing: I don't want to ever be one."

The group applauded.

On the way home, she did not notice a dark blue or black sedan that pulled out behind her when she was a block away from the church parking lot.

The next morning, Mr. Mizrahi, who was in Tel Aviv, returned her call immediately to the offices of Mizrahi and Associates. It was the fastest he had ever returned a call to her. She told him what she could about the trip and explained her reasons for resigning. "I think Josh is probably gone for good, Mr. Mizrahi. But he always liked living in London. He wanted Atalaya to see Europe and to have an opportunity to live there. If he is ever found, I can fly quicker to get to him. If he doesn't come back—well, I've started a new life that he hoped we could have someday."

"My dear Chelsea," sighed Mr. Mizrahi. "We have to do what we have to do…" his voice faded sadly.

The employees reacted to the news regretfully. Turnover was extremely rare at Mizrahi & Associates. Dane Schwartz was obviously dejected. He stayed in her office for a long time, longer than anyone else.

There was a message from the school in McLean. Atalaya had been distracted and inattentive lately. Could Chelsea come in and talk about her school work? There had been a discipline problem last week….Once again, she was wracked with mom guilt.

She noticed that since her trip to Iraq the trees outside had turned from green to a softer yellow green and the nights were a little cooler and less humid. Dane Schwartz often brought coffee to her desk. For at least a little while each day, and other times for long periods, he hung out in her office, hearing how her plans to relocate overseas were coming along. Just as she had done with him when his wife died, he made sure that she didn't isolate herself and coaxed her to come along to lunch with the others. He was a rock, a good friend; less and less she noticed his plain looks and corny jokes and more and more she simply appreciated him for himself.

Thank goodness Dane still did not connect the dots and suspect that Josh was involved in espionage. "I never had to live with the lack of closure you've been living with," he explained. "I guess I don't know what I would do if I were you. When my wife was killed in Sudan, we knew right away. It was just—over. I've thought about moving the kids closer to home, but I'd never get the pay in Wyoming that I'm getting here. Europe wasn't something I ever considered," he concluded with a rueful grin. It was a soft rebuke. He did not seem to share her enthusiasm about starting life over in a foreign city. It made Chelsea doubt herself and gave her second thoughts.

His face fell the day she told him it looked like Goldberger Hewitt London would be able to work out a position for her. "But it's a good opportunity! It's for a broker who does hotels!" she said brightly. "Ian Clark says the broker is 'overcome,' and my experience here with the Shangri-La provides a good background!" It was clear that Dane wasn't happy for her. He was profoundly disappointed that she would be leaving.

Searching online for a flat was fun; she and Atalaya would wait until time to leave, then they would identify a few to view and 'let' when they arrived in London. But finding a primary school was another drama. "The school system in London is totally unlike America," she explained to Dane one slow afternoon at work as she was poking around on the internet trying to fill out applications. "Yes, there are primary schools; but apparently you can't just get into them. You have to be admitted, and that is if there is even any space available." The cute little primary school that Chelsea had seen in Marylebone had a poor inspection report from the government. "Here's the most appalling thing," she told him. "The religious schools—and that appears to be the majority of them!—require verification of your local church attendance!"

She began taking Atalaya to Sunday School and sitting in on Pastor Rouch's sermons again, though not just because the British schools preferred it. It was also because the ancient prophecies that appeared to be coming true in Iraq gripped her. She did not realize how much she had missed church.

She wasn't sure when she first became aware of the sub-conscious signals, but some movement in the rear view mirror, or some glint in the side windows, caused her to know she was being followed. A chilling thought seized her. Had someone in Iraq targeted her for surveillance?

Josh had talked about how to watch for surveillance. The first step, he had said, was knowing the cars in your neighborhood and your place of work, so you could eliminate the possibility that someone got a new vehicle. Josh had said that if you thought someone was following, you should turn left quickly and circle back to see what happened. The first time she did that, the dark navy or black sedan kept going straight. The windows were too tinted to identify a driver. She took note of it, and it was what Josh called a "repeat", a vehicle that appeared a second time.

And then one morning when she was telecommuting from home and turned on her computer, something seemed different about it. It was running slow. One of the little virus protection icons briefly flashed as if it was scanning a potential problem and sending her an alert, but then it dissipated. She felt a chill. Josh had warned her about things like this. Was someone trying to hack her? Was Clinton's spy software that had been installed on her computer and the private investigator's computer picking up on a virus? She called Clinton but he didn't answer his phone, and so she messaged him cryptically: *concerned about a breach. Contact me on a secure line.* Clinton did not call and he did not ask any questions, he just tersely messaged back that he would look into it. She was bewildered. Why didn't Clinton call and ask her for details?

She called her father-in-law, Dr. Evans, and asked him to watch for unusual activity, electing not to frighten the others in the search team unless he noted something. She made a formal request for security protection to Headquarters, but she was denied. Offended and frightened, she still remained convinced that she was being followed; and each time she drove somewhere, she took her handgun from the bedroom and stored it in the little metal box wedged under the car seat.

She quit seeing the black or dark blue sedan, and she had just started to believe that the Agency might be correct; and then one day she observed a suspicious dark brown Ford pickup truck. She noted it coming out of her subdivision and then was quite sure she saw it again in the rear-view mirror on the way to Sam's Club, a full forty-five miles away, when she took a trek with Atalaya out of their comfort zone one weekend in order to get out of their rut and away from the monotony and traffic of McLean.

Sam's Club was north of Dulles Airport. Was someone from the CIA following her? Did they think she was leaving town without notifying them?

380

Anger overtook her, as well as bravado reinforced by bright sunlight. How dare the CIA (or more likely, they had farmed out the job to the FBI) refuse to offer security to her, and then possibly even follow her and treat her like a criminal! Were they also tapping her phones and computers? "I hate you guys!" she growled through clenched teeth.

"Mommy, who do you hate?" Atalaya asked worriedly from the back booster seat.

"Nobody, honey." With a sudden impulse she changed her route and darted south on Sully Road, closer to the airport, past the motels, watching the dark brown truck turn behind her, keeping itself to a pinpoint in the distance. The stretch of road was just long enough that the truck could not exit; it would have to stay behind her. There were no vehicles on this road right now.

A frightened thought occurred to her. What if his intention was to run her off the road? What was she going to do on this remote stretch?

It was completely up to her. No cop could ever get here fast enough. She had a helpless child to protect!

With a cautionary warning to Atalaya to duck her head down and squeeze her knees and be totally quiet, she tapped on the brakes and swerved the car slightly, flipped on the emergency blinkers, and quickly pulled off the road. Heart thudding, she reached under the seat, pulled out the gun, and rolled down the window, crouching down as low as possible with the gun in her hands, pointed out the window.

She couldn't do this! She HAD to do this!

The brown Ford truck behind her slowed down.

And then with a squeal of tires, it accelerated, no doubt approaching something like eighty miles an hour, and zoomed passed her, causing tiny bits of gravel to fly up and hit her and her car. She caught glimpse of a male in sunglasses and a baseball cap. Hands sweating, she fired a round towards his tires. The noise was deafening and she let out a yell. "Damn you!" she screamed after him. "Leave me alone, do you hear me?"

The bullet missed his vehicle, deflecting on the asphalt. Quickly she fired again and this time she heard the sound of metal.

With a screech of tires began to tail him, holding the gun out the window with one arm pointed at the back of the truck. She tried to read the license plate number, but she was too terrified and the numbers wouldn't stick in her head.

In the back seat, Atalaya frantically asked. "Mommy, why did you yell a naughty word at that truck? Why did you shoot your gun?"

"It's ok, honey," she shouted back to her daughter, suddenly feeling a surge of bravery. "Mommy is taking out bad guys in order to protect you!"

Whatever she had hit with her gun was causing the brown Ford pickup to leak fluid. Adrenaline pumped in her. She felt a thrill and flirted with the idea of getting close enough to take one last shot at the vehicle tires. On the other hand, if fuel was leaking, the vehicle might explode!

With a sudden squeal of tires, the pickup lost her at the cloverleaf, briefly banging its side against the guardrail. There was no way she was going to take the exit at the speed he took! She shot past the cloverleaf. She turned the car back in the direction of Sam's Club. Her heart was thumping and blood pounded furiously in her ears.

She called Brick's phone number and left a message in a furious but triumphant voice. "Brick, this is Chelsea. Chelsea Evans, in case you've forgotten me, because I sure haven't heard any news about my husband from you lately. If that was Chinese or Iraqi intelligence tailing me just now with a brown Ford pickup truck, you guys are total failures. I had to use my own gun to protect myself and my kid because you assholes failed to provide me security! And if it wasn't them, and it was you guys following me, give your stupid spooks a message, would you? Tell them to spend their time harassing the bad guys, instead of citizen wives who are taking their child to Sam's Club!" Wrathfully she disconnected.

But as she arrived at Sam's Club, worry crept over her like cat's feet, a sensation of growing doom. *What have I done? I just pissed off the only people left who might attempt to help Josh.* And as she pushed the cart through the aisles, *What if the people tailing me weren't Americans? What if it was the Iraqi National Intelligence Service? Or the Chinese MSS?*

She began to tremble so hard that she could hardly hold her purse. What if her actions compelled them to engage in an all-out assault on her way home?

Somehow Chelsea checked out of the store and fled to the parking lot. Sitting in the car with Atalaya and the packages and boxes, she thought what to do. If they were still following her in broad daylight, where would she be the safest?

Chuck E. Cheese! No foreign assets would seriously stalk a mother and a child there, would they?

Brick called back two hours later, denying any knowledge of surveillance on Chelsea.

Chelsea begged Brick for personal protection. Brick was unable to authorize the request but promised to stop by on Monday. For the rest of the weekend Chelsea jumped at every sound, fanatically locking doors and securing windows.

She called Dane to tell him she would be working from home on Monday. "It's just not the same without you on Monday Morning Weekend Roundup," he said with a delicate touch of humorous irony. The young Mizrahi & Associates McLean team members always spent an inordinate amount of time on Monday morning re-living their weekends, a weekly conversation to which Chelsea rarely contributed much of anything (because how much weekend entertainment did a working mom alone with an eight-year-old child have?), and she usually cut out early.

The first thing on Monday morning, Brick and a team of Agency personnel visited her house, trying to talk calmly and rationally to her. They checked her computer but could not conclusively conclude there had been a security breach.

"But isn't the point of a security breach that you aren't supposed to know you've been breached?" Chelsea insisted.

They suggested some self-calming techniques, hinting that she had over-reacted. She was insulted. They said they would make a request for home security. The CIA family was here to support her, they said soothingly. But that didn't make her feel any better—she was a misfit in the 'family' because she was not sure if she was a widow, or if she still had a husband in the service of the Agency.

They left the house. A growing suspicion began to creep over her.

Brick hadn't denied that the CIA was involved. Brick had denied *knowledge* of any activity on the part of the CIA. And Chelsea's general sense of the way things worked at the CIA was that personnel were only told things on a need-to-know basis.

She had heard nothing back from Clinton, who was supposedly also monitoring her devices for malware and suspicious messages. Both Clinton and the CIA were treating a stalker, and what she believed was a computer security breach, lightly.

Whose side was Clinton on?

All of a sudden, slowly growing suspicions burst to the surface of her emotions. Was Clinton really acting independently to try to find out what had happened with Josh? Or was he somehow actually working against her?

Her pulse raced. Was he aligned with the CIA, for some reason helping them in surveillance against herself?

Or worse, had Clinton been compromised somehow? Had he inadvertently done something to endanger Josh? Had Clinton or his wife accidentally talked too much in public, or done something online, that had put Josh in danger and caused him to disappear? Clinton's technology background was shrouded with dark, shadowy characters who had a vendetta against him.

Chelsea paced the floors of the house, reviewing in her mind everything Clinton had said and done, or more precisely, hadn't done, in recent months. How his spy software never produced any leads. How he never talked about the data on the private investigator's computer which supposedly he was able to hack and observe. How detached and disinterested he was when they went to Iraq. As the minutes and hours crept by, she became clear. She was sure. She knew what she needed to do.

The line Clinton wouldn't cross was harming his own goddaughter. Atalaya was her insurance policy. But Chelsea would take no chances. She picked up her handgun and turned it over slowly, trying to think. There was a ten-day waiting period in California. What should she do? Overnight it? Yes. There were procedures for mailing a gun to another state. She could pick it up after she landed in San Francisco.

She called up the airline schedule online, grimacing at the price, but went ahead and bought two tickets to San Francisco International Airport, then went into the bedrooms to collect clothes and pack an overnight suitcase for two.

She called Dane at the office from the stopover at O'Hare. "I need to tell somebody where I'm going." She didn't tell Kimberly, because Kimberly would stop her. "I'm headed to San Francisco," she said. "Menlo Park. I'm meeting with Clinton Radcliffe—you've heard me talk about him. I brought Atalaya with me."

"Chelsea! Why? Why didn't you say you were leaving?" Dane's voice was confused, concerned.

"It's—it's about my husband. Don't get excited, there isn't any news or anything.

"If there's no news then what's going on? Tell me."

"It's just—there's something I need to check into."

"Chelsea. This isn't good. We missed you on Monday already this week," Dane replied soberly. "What address in Menlo Park?" He took notes.

Was Dane reproving her for leaving without giving her co-workers advanced notice? Or was it just that he missed her when she left town? She pushed that thought out of her mind. She couldn't deal with Dane and his feelings at this time.

That evening she sat in the living room of the fabulous contemporary six million dollar home of Clinton and Jennifer Radcliffe in Menlo Park with its glass and white and its occasional red accents around doorways and windows. Chelsea was too overcome with apprehension to tell Atalaya to stay away from the expensive ten-foot gong, and sure enough Atalaya picked up the mallet and hit it, sending tremors throughout the house and shudders through her body that vibrated with the thumping of her heart. Could she go through with this? She had to go through with this....

"Do you want a drink?" Jennifer asked. It was easy to forget how tall and imposing Jennifer was.

"No. I'm an alcoholic. I quit drinking. Soda is fine," Chelsea replied.

There was an awkward silence and then Jennifer walked back to the bar, her heels clicking loudly on the light colored wood floor, and poured a Coke. Atalaya soothed the moment by running back to the couches and climbing into Clinton's lap. "You surprised me with your visit, Attie, or I would have gotten something for Peppermint Pinkey," he said, awkwardly rumpling her head.

Jennifer handed the Coke to Chelsea and sat down on the luxurious white couch next to Clinton. She wished Jennifer would leave. Having her here would make it much harder.

"So, you have some news about Bags? Is that why you came?" Clinton got to the point. Clearly he expected bad news.

She felt her heart pound and her face turn pink. For courage, she slipped her hand into the pocket of her jacket and grasped the gun. She swallowed, feeling sick in her own mouth. "Jennifer, can you leave? I need to talk to Clinton alone. It's about Agency business."

Jennifer looked pointedly at Atalaya as if to ask why she was remaining but stood up from the couch without a word and walked out of the room. Chelsea waited until her footsteps faded into the back of the house.

"No news. But someone has been following me. Attie and I were tailed by a man in a brown pickup truck all the way to a Sam's Club. That's close to an hour's drive. I pulled off the road and took a shot at him with my gun and he got away. Someone also hacked into my computer, didn't they?" She faced Clinton and stared him down, feeling her heart hammer.

His looked confused. "Hacked your computer? I said there was no sign of a breach. What do you mean?"

She had a sequence of questions to ask him that were designed to lead him into a trap, but a rushing sound of blood filled her ears that sounded almost like wind as she tried to remember the order. "You never got back to me about the hacking. You were vague." Her mouth felt dry as the accusation rolled out.

"I have firewalls around firewalls," Clinton replied in an offended tone.

In her nervousness she could hardly remember the next question on the mental list, and it came out with sort of a half-squeak. "Who is it, Clinton? Is it the CIA or the FBI that's tailing me and hacking me? Or the same people who came and kidnapped Josh? I came here to find out who it is."

There was a stunned silence. Clinton's veins in his forehead pulsed, and the skin reddened under his thin blond ponytail. "What are you saying? Are you accusing me?"

"Josh and I warned you never to talk about his CIA service to Jennifer, or in public. It was you or Jennifer, wasn't it? One of you blew his cover, didn't you! You said too much and someone nefarious overheard you and passed on the information. You knew, and you felt guilty, and that's why you felt you had to help."

Alarmed at the tension between the adults, Atalaya slid off Clinton's lap and onto to the floor. Clinton's mild, gray eyes filled with an animosity she had never seen in her life as the realization swept him. He began wordlessly shaking his head. "Oh, no, you don't. Don't dare you have a go at me with a load of horseshit like that!" he growled. "I'm not even allowed to tell my own wife what Bags does for a living, but it's ok for you to tell all your girl chums and haul them along on your stupid mission?" His cultured but angry British voice reverberated in the room.

"Girl chums? Kim is my attorney! The CIA liaison referred Brittany to me! I didn't…" Chelsea struggled.

"What the bloody hell are you talking about? You've gone nutters!" His face overcome with disgust, Clinton stood up from the couch and stomped over to her. Surely he would not attack her right in front of Atalaya! Fearfully she gripped the gun, ready to pull it out in an instant.

Clinton looked so utterly shocked that she felt doubt. But she reached down with her free hand to grasp her child's hand, bravely persisting with her questions, because maybe he was shocked that he had been caught. "You didn't really want to help. You never wanted to go to Iraq. Did the Chinese Muslim Uyghurs who put a bounty on you when you lived in London track you down? Are you a double agent for some kind of rogue group? Have Josh's captors been blackmailing you this whole time?"

His voice was ice. "Are you kidding? Those miserable Third World agitators trying to exist in a Second or First World? They'd trip over their dresses trying to find the end of a computer plug, they could never locate me, and why would they…this thing has made you a paranoid bitch, Chels!" His face was pulsing with rage. Every bit of emotion Chelsea thought had been buried along with the marriage to his first wife had risen to the surface.

"So tell me what really happened, Clinton." Her voice was so near breaking, it wasn't even her voice any more. "Did the CIA put you up to going to Iraq to shadow me? Or was it somebody else?"

"Mommy. Uncle Clinton, please stop fighting," Atalaya pleaded miserably.

The shock on his face was so transparent it was easy to believe that he might be innocent. "How dare you!" Clinton spat. "Get! Out!" He pointed a shaking finger towards the front door of the house. "Get out of my house and Jen's house! Now!"

She swept up her purse and began backing up in the direction of the front door. Atalaya let out a strangled little whimper. "Please, Clinton, just tell me the truth. You need to tell the truth to someone. Are you working for somebody?"

Clinton's arm dropped and he stared at her with incredulity. All of a sudden a film appeared in his eyes and he blinked rapidly.

"Bags was my very best chum in the world," he said, and there was a catch in his voice. "He was like a brother to me." He shoved an angry palm up at his wet eyes. "How can you possibly think…how could the thought ever cross your tiny, suspicious pea brain…"

Her own accusations roiled around the room like a boiling cauldron. Clinton's angry retort, and his accusation that she was a paranoid nut job echoed from the glass walls of the house. "Clinton," she managed, "of *course* it is possible that I'm right! Of *course* you or Jennifer could have carelessly mentioned to someone—anyone—that your best friend was undercover with the CIA!"

"Like Jen has time to call terrorists on her day off, or in between venture capital meetings, and chat or let something drop—"

"Ok, fine, but how in the world could I ever know with certainty that you'll never be tracked by one of your past targets? How can you know?" She held on to the thin reed of courage deep inside but she was shaking so hard she could barely hold Atalaya's hand. "This, Clinton, is the paranoia that every single CIA covert officer and every partner worries about, every single day and night of our lives! Don't you realize how dangerous his work was? To not get this is to be naïve!"

Wordlessly he shook his head at her with undisguised astonishment and brokenness at her words. His mild gray eyes had widened so big they looked as if they would pop out of his pink forehead. "Never!" he swore to her in a cracked voice. "Never, ever!"

389

They stood facing off with each other. "You promise me this?" She managed, nearly unable to breathe. "You aren't working for anyone but yourself? Not anyone?"

"No one."

A numb, horrible, awful silence filled the room. She let go of the gun in her pocket. She turned and walked with Atalaya out the door and to the rental car.

How had she seen this so wrong?

She had irreparably ruined the friendship. And as she drove to the hotel, she wondered: Even worse, what if Clinton refused to pay the bills for the trip when they came in?

What Clinton said made sense. Even if Jennifer or Clinton did let it slip to a co-worker, or a best friend, or restaurant server, would anyone in San Francisco know who Josh was, much less care?

She was seized with fear. She needed to give him a little time, but somehow she was going to have to apologize, try to smooth it over and patch it up.

B ack in McLean, even though she was confused as to whether Omar or Clinton or someone else had blown Josh's cover, she needed to make sure the expenses for the trip got paid, so she composed an apology note to Clinton and sent it by email. He did not reply.

She had an audit performed of their home security. She met prospects at their office first before she would agree to show them vacant space at Monument Metroplex. She followed every principle Josh had ever taught her about surveillance.

But she had no more encounters with suspicious individuals, and no more vehicles appeared to tail her anymore. Nothing unusual happened to her computer. As time went on, she began to believe that American law enforcement had been behind the surveillance. She felt betrayed and abandoned by the country she loved. She just wanted to leave. She sent a second email to Clinton and told him this because she was too humiliated to call him. He did not answer.

Fall set in, and the stifling humidity in D.C. turned to dryer, cooler air. Bits of color began to touch the trees. It was taking an awfully long time to arrange the move to London. At work, Dane sat in the visitor chair across from her desk nearly every day, listening patiently as she maneuvered endless obstacles: the paperwork involved in relocating to another country; finally locating a school and gaining acceptance; cleaning out the house in McLean; the process of putting it up for rent, and the very difficult decision of what to do with Josh's possessions, in case he came back. ("Don't feel too guilty about getting rid of it, we guys just think that stuff is stuff. We can always buy more," was Dane's advice). Frequently he walked with her to the parking garage as darkness set in earlier and earlier.

Colder air gradually set into northern Virginia, and the leaves dropped off the trees. And then as the last of them fell to the ground and the cold and chill of Thanksgiving and Christmas weather began to set in, a message came from Clinton.

Found these emails. Received your regrets. Bags was the best thing that ever happened to me besides my wife. Hopefully you'll sort out some answers on things. Good luck in Old Blighty and give my love to Atalaya and to all the parents.

Of course he hadn't just found the emails, but at least he had acknowledged them. Was Clinton suddenly sentimental about the years he spent the holidays with her and Josh and their families because his ex-wife and children wanted nothing to do with him?

She put on her big girl pants and called him. He was the same Clinton as always: non-emotional, methodical, and slightly formal and taciturn in his British manner. No, he would not be coming to either Washington D.C. or Columbia for the holidays, he'd be spending Christmas with Jen and her family at Grand Cayman Island again this year. He asked how Atalaya was doing.

And then she received her karma for going to Iraq and then losing her temper with Brick and the CIA investigators who had interrogated her after her trip to Babylon Metro. She discovered that her visa had been blocked.

There was one unused chip left that she could try to play. It was a chip from long, long ago, back when she and Josh lived in Columbia, and Vice President Russo was a state senator. Would the vice president remember her?

At lunchtime she resisted the expectation that she should join the others for the daily catered lunch, making the excuse that she had some personal things to take care of and needed to get outside for some fresh air. She stayed in her office and composed a letter on her computer:

Dear Vice President Russo:

You may remember me and my husband, Josh Evans, from our days in Columbia. I don't know if you knew, but my sister and I volunteered for your senatorial campaigns. You were with presidential candidate Maly and you both met my husband and me in the airport with Governor Giordano when we moved back to America after a terrorism incident in London. At the time, my husband was running a spy operation for the MI6 and the CIA.

After that, he went through training and was officially entered as a covert officer with the CIA. As you know, he disappeared in Iraq eleven months ago and is believed to have been killed in a prison uprising. However, we have been unable to confirm his whereabouts.

If new information surfaces and there is any chance that he is still alive and in the custody of the Iraqis or the Chinese, or if his body is located, I feel that I can come quickly to him if I am located in Europe.

Also, it was always his wish to return to London to live someday. It was an opportunity he hoped our daughter could have. He had requested a transfer.

I am writing to ask for a favor: My visa is blocked. Can you assist me in obtaining quick clearance to residency and work in London?

She paused, not sure exactly how to end the letter. Outside the window, a hard, cold wind blew and the first miniscule, icy snowflakes of the season swirled. They stung the windows and clung to the professional holiday decorations installed by the company in October on those trucks with extra high lifts.

Thank you for your service to our country.

She printed it off and put it in an old-fashioned letter with a stamp. Probably nothing would happen. Her visa might be blocked for months on end. She may as well focus her attention on Mom and Dad coming out for the holidays. Christmas Day would mark 365 days since Josh went missing.

Dane, presuming that no normal human would want to go outside for lunch on a raw day like this, came into her office afterwards to ask if everything was okay. She went into a rant about her visa being blocked, but she decided not to tell him she had written Vice President Russo a letter. It almost seemed silly and she was already starting to regret that. Dane sat in the visitor chair, his Adam's apple bobbing up and down noiselessly, clasping and unclasping his hands, blushing clear to the roots of his thinning blond hair, as if there was something else he wanted to talk about. She felt uncomfortable drawing him out. Mercifully, the front desk buzzed her that her 1:30 appointment had arrived early. Chelsea took off for the conference room hastily, leaving Dane alone in the visitor chair.

The next week the phone at her office desk rang, and when she picked it up, the young receptionist was nearly screeching. "CHELSEA! It's a call from the WHITE HOUSE! O, M, G! They want to know if you can take a call from the VICE PRESIDENT!" The receptionist's voice turned into an indistinguishable squeal.

Chelsea's eyes nearly popped out of her head and her mouth went dry. She had not really expected Vice President Russo to reply! Dazedly she connected to the line. Why was he calling her at work? And then her own stupidity hit her like a thunderbolt: she probably had forgotten to put a private, secure number in the letter!

"Chelsea Steele Evans. I remember you!" said a familiar voice on the other end of the line. "You were Tony Giordano's little lady."

She felt her face flame. That wasn't the highlight she had hoped the vice president would recall when he got her letter....

"It's great to talk to someone from back home. I remember when you escaped London and came back. We were running for office."

It was a presidential campaign she would never forget as long as she lived. She and her sister, a volunteer campaign worker, had followed it every day. All of a sudden she felt completely shy, asking for the favor.

But Vice President Russo was kind and courteous. He asked her a number of questions and then told her that the West Wing would offer its assistance to expedite her visa and work permit as soon as possible and try to help arrange her entry into England through channels with the British government.

She hung up the phone, grateful, and shaking with emotion and breathless.

It was real. It was almost time to go. Now she could rent out the house. She was going to cut off ties and start a new life.

Outside the office she heard a noise. The receptionist's face popped around the corner, her mouth round and her eyes popping out of her head. The others appeared, and then Dane; and she felt uncomfortable as they all peered at her in astonishment through the doorway and she realized they had heard.

"What did he say?"

"Do they know where Josh is?"

"Did you have any idea he was going to call?"

"Chelsea! Is Josh okay? Was it bad news?"

She struggled not to bite her lip, and she froze a smile in place on her face. "There's no word," she croaked. "They don't know anymore. He just promised to—to help with my visa. He said he's going to help."

They chattered crazily. For the workers at Mizrahi & Associates, it was the highlight of a boring afternoon treacherously close to holiday vacations. Dane broke away from the group first and went back to work. He had end-of-year accounting tasks to perform, he said.

She sat down and wrote Vice President Russo an old-fashioned thank-you note on paper and envelope.

Chelsea continued to purge and pack. No one was interested in looking for a house to rent over the holidays. In January, a military family with the Navy came for a viewing. They agreed to lease it, furniture and all.

On a cold, icy Thursday in February, a few days before Valentine's Day, she announced to her co-workers that her work visa had come through. They immediately arranged for a good-bye party. On Friday when she came to work, she found her office completely full of black balloons. They had been filled up with helium and delivered by truck the night before, and it had taken four elevator trips to deliver them. The Mizrahi & Associates team members shut down the office at 3 p.m. for the day and went to the Just the Fax '80s retro vape bar and lounge in the lobby of the Shangri-La hotel in Monument Metroplex. All the team members dressed in black from head to toe, and the lounge staff stared at them oddly when they filed in.

By 4:00 in the afternoon, the after-work crowd filled the lounge, and the Mizrahi & Associates team members exited hastily in order to beat the traffic. Dane remained behind and walked her out of the hotel, clasping his hands together and rubbing them nervously, his Adam's apple bobbing in his throat. "Sometime before you leave for Europe, would you like to go for dinner? We've both been through a lot. It would be good to go out."

Instantaneously she felt a rush of conflicting thoughts. Dane had been attracted to her for a while. He was lonely and ready to find someone else. He had been so nice. Maybe she should go out with him…after all, when she was growing up, Mom had always told her to date people from work or church or the grocery store. How could one date possibly hurt?

That weekend they both got babysitters and he picked her up at her house. She wanted something more casual and fun, so they went to an upscale bar in downtown D.C. on U Street with superb food and tons of TVs. "Now, if you think this place only does burgers, that means you've only been here rarely," Dane quipped. "You know, when I worked for the CPA firm in Wyoming, before I went to work for Levi Mizrahi, we had a lot of restaurant clients. We were always worried that they were cooking the books."

The Capitals hockey game was on. The team was doing well against Detroit and every once in a while the room erupted with noise. Dane talked a lot about his three children, ages nine, seven, and four. You weren't really supposed to talk constantly about your kids on a first date, were you? She realized she didn't know the rules. "The four-year-old is, I don't know, jacked on sugar or something. He never stops. If he's not playing loud, he's talking non-stop. It starts in the morning before the rest of us are up and goes until bedtime. I tell him to be quiet all the time. Then he asks me who's sleeping."

"Have you had him tested for ADHD?" Chelsea suggested.

"I suppose I should take him to the doctor or something." Dane grimaced. Then he said brightly, "With the older two kids, I'm working on the Ten Commandments. You know, the one about 'Thou Shalt Not Kill,' because they're almost getting big enough to kill each other."

They must take after their mother, who had been in the military.

"You'll have to meet them. They're great kids. Really, they are," he asserted.

Chelsea smiled and made a vague answer. She had met one or two of the kids when he brought them into work on the weekends. She would never forget what they did to the office scanner. "What do you want to do next?" he asked. "Should we let the babysitters loose, go over to my house for popcorn and a movie with the kids?"

She hesitated, feeling uncomfortable. She had envisioned a night of cutting loose and having some fun, even if she had a resolution not to drink. Immediately an image rose in her mind of three wiggly children, clamoring all over their father noisily during a movie, spilling popcorn on the carpet. If Josh was gone for good, this was the what she was in for if she jumped back into the dating game: an endless, ongoing series of nights and weekends with wiggly kids; and how would you ever get to know somebody, much less be romantic with, a person in America or in Britain or anywhere who had three children under the age of ten, or even under the age of eighteen?

"I have an idea," she said brightly. "How about we go to a night club and go dancing?" She and Josh had always tried to make a priority to go dancing every so often, and they had even taken lessons once or twice. How she missed it.

Dane was uncertain, but he agreed. They bundled up in their winter coats and walked to a club a couple blocks away that was loud, and they danced to the thumping vibrations of the music. Dane was not a good dancer. He wasn't heavy or anything, it was just that nothing about him reminded her of Josh with his lithe, graceful body. She gave up and they sat down and ordered non-alcoholic drinks. It was just too awkward.

But he liked being with her, she could tell. He touched her and dialogued easily with her as they went back to his car and during the drive her back to her house. They stood on the front door step by the tall, white graceful columns as she fished for the key in the dark.

"Thank you for this evening, Dane. It was fun."

"I wish we had done this a long time ago. And I want to do this again." He put a hand on her shoulder, and leaned towards her. She neither responded nor resisted, and he took it as a yes, putting the other hand on her other shoulder and moving in awkwardly towards her face. As he touched her lips, his mouth was nervous but eager, warm but unfamiliar. She knew he wanted more, much more.

It was like testing the water in a swimming pool, to see if it was warm enough to wade in, and for a moment or two she was suspended in uncertainty, a million thoughts flashing through her mind. He wasn't hot like Josh, but this could be a relationship of convenience. He was low risk. He was a person she could trust. She could put her plans to leave America on hold for a while and see what happened.

But there wasn't really any chemistry. Could she eventually fall in love him?

Two marriages was one thing, but three?

He felt the sudden rigidness in her as she pulled away, and he took a small, surprised step back. They both coughed nervously.

"We have a lot in common, Dane. But you need to know that you're looking over the edge of the Grand Canyon when it comes to me," she said quietly. "As you stand there and look down, you see two bodies in the ravine below. Are you really sure," she said, turning a half-smile up to him filled with pain, "that you want to hike down that trail?"

"I—I don't understand."

"I'm probably a widow, for the second time. I've had two turns. I'm—probably finished when it comes to relationships. But I will always, always be your friend."

There was a long, painful silence. He swallowed and his Adam's apple worked up and down in his throat. She felt sorrowful for him; it was probably the only date he had been on since his wife died, and even though they were close friends, it had still taken courage to ask her out.

"Keep your options open," he finally said.

She didn't answer. He gave her shoulders a final squeeze, closed his eyes and kissed her forehead, and then turned and walked down the porch steps and into the night.

"It's so pretty, Mommy!"

Atalaya clasped her hands in delight as she spun around the room looking at the London flat. Little cars zoomed past on the wrong side of the road outside the towering bay windows flanked by long drapes that soared to the ceiling. The floors were wood and the flat was painted white with sleek, square, contemporary plumbing fixtures. It was an old building, and every room had an original fireplace. Their moving boxes were piled high in the corner of the small living room.

The journey to London had taken six months. It was late February. The days were becoming noticeably longer and the weather in London was milder than Washington, D.C. The weekend of Valentine's Day, on a frigid and windy evening, Brittany had thrown a "We Love Chelsea" goodbye party for her at Brittany's house. Kimberly had helped host, and the three of them took a picture together which was now the cover photo for Chelsea's computer screen. There were a few other school moms that had come with their children, although Atalaya just didn't have a lot of friends. One of the neighbors and the three coffee servers from church who had taken refuge with her during the church shooting came. Kimberly had not apologized for her outburst in Babylon Metro nor had she ever mentioned it again. She had simply carried on as if everything was normal. That was just Kimberly—she was almost like a guy and she didn't hold grudges. She had given Chelsea a hug at the end of the evening and said, "Keep in touch, girlfriend." Brittany held Chelsea close and sniffled, wishing her nothing but happiness and the brightest of futures.

She and Atalaya had flown to London and stayed with the Thorpes. They had picked out the flat on York Street in Marylebone and placed a bid. It was a two-bedroom in a four-story brick building with a black iron fence. There was no grass, just a single topiary tree perched on a stanchion. It was walking distance from everything they needed: the Edgeware and Baker Street stations, a small grocery store, a fitness center, a drug store, a McDonald's. Chelsea tried to ignore the absence of greenery and trees and the acres of brick and high-rise concrete—the flat was near Paddington Park and one Tube stop away from Hyde Park and Regent's Park. When they were young entrepreneurs just starting out, it was the neighborhood Josh and Clinton had always dreamed of living in.

Tomorrow would be the first day at a new school, a huge hurdle to get through.

It was so exciting to be back at Goldberger Hewitt the next day! A couple of the team members actually remembered Chelsea from her brief summer assignment a decade ago. Her managing broker, Ian Clarke, had authorized a cubicle for her. It was nothing like the spacious office with a window that she had at Monument Metroplex. After all, overhead on Bond Street was five to ten times higher than at home, and in a huge international company like this, Chelsea would be starting at the bottom of the food chain.

She worked out a time to web chat with her friends at Mizrahi and Associates and show them the offices. They eagerly crowded their faces around except for Dane who stayed in the background, half-way off the camera. They politely ooh'd and ahh'd as she gave a video tour and showed off the view out the window of Bond street. "We miss you so much already!" they assured her. "Good luck with your new job in London!"

It made her feel sad and guilty for leaving, after all of the money Mr. Mizrahi had spent to help find Josh. No co-workers could have been more supporting during a trying time. Most of all her conscience panged for disappointing Dane. A flash of apprehension gripped her: had she made a horrible mistake?

No. It would be best, she knew, not to do anymore video chats with them. The decision had been made. She needed to forge on ahead.

Until she developed her own clients, she would be an assistant to another very busy, extremely successful, harried and stressed sales agent on the hotel investments team who represented hotel investors all over the world. Ian said that being around the development of Monument Metroplex and the Shangri-La Hotel gave her a good background. The hotel sales agent had no time to train her—she would have to learn as she went! There were lots of spreadsheets to evaluate and packets of information to get to potential buyers, but it seemed like interesting, fast-paced work, yet another twist in the commercial real estate journey she had traveled most of her adult life. She called Mr. Mizrahi and told him she knew of some good hotel properties for sale.

Ⅰn the nightmare, the water was covering his head. No longer could he hold his breath. His lungs gasped for air but took in liquid.

With a start, Josh woke up in the night. For a week, he had had a cough and it was worsening. The illness was spreading through the cell rapidly. Many of the prisoners hacked throughout the night. Medical care and doctors appeared to be available only for suicide attempts or those so sick that they never returned.

The prisoner laying on the mat behind him, who was not yet sick, landed him a hard kick in the shins. Josh lay sideways on the mat, trying to muffle his cough, afraid to go back to sleep.

He had always been a survivor. Twice in London he had escaped death, and he'd thought he was invincible. His entire life he had a sense of destiny about himself, an aura of purpose and a sense of responsibility, imparted to him by his religious mother. Had he come this far, for it to end here, like this? Utterly abandoned and forgotten, nothing but a serial number in the Chinese prison system? Even if your life counted for little else, the ultimate tragedy was to be cheated by death without the chance to raise your child.

As time had dragged on and hope had faded away, living became an equivalent option to dying.

He thought back to a night, three decades ago, at home.

"Ok, boys, into bed now. Time for your verse." Their mother's voice floated from the living room where she and his father sat, recounting the day's events with each other.

He and his twin brother Jake rolled their eyes at each other. They hated weekly verse time, but protest, they knew, was futile.

They put their toys down reluctantly. Compliantly they went to the bedroom bureau and took their old-fashioned recipe cards their mother had written out for them. They sat down on the side of their twin beds facing each other, reviewing the words, lips moving, trying to get the verses in their heads before she came into the room. They heard her footsteps coming down the hall.

Judge Mary Duncan-Evans entered the room and held out her hand. Grudgingly they turned the notecards over to her. "You first, Josh." His mother still had her work clothes on, and she looked tired. She had worked this evening on an emergency hearing down at the county court, but she wasn't too tired to forget verse time.

Josh's feet dangled over the carpet while he struggled to repeat the words that had been written on the recipe card. Josh was smart enough to keep a bland countenance, clever enough to not let his mother know how much he disliked verse time. Jake was not always so smart.

Josh spit out the first part fast—that was the part he had memorized fairly well. "If I go up to the heavens, you are there, if I make my bed in the depths, you are there—" He paused, struggling to remember. Was the part about the sea next? "If I settle on the sea—"

"No," his mother interrupted, prompting him with a hint. "Think of a bird."

"If I rise on the wings of the dawn," he fidgeted.

"Go on."

"If I settle on the sea, you will guide me; even there..." he faltered, then raced to the end of the verse: "your hand will guide me."

"It's 'if I settle on the FAR side of the sea, even there your hand will guide me," she corrected. "The verse is making the point it doesn't matter how far away you go, God is still there. Reference?"

"Psalm, um—" he absolutely hated references for verses! They were just random numbers—ridiculous! Who cared about a bunch of numbers?

"Psalms 139:7 through 10. Someday you might be in trouble and you will want to look it up. Jake, your turn now."

On the prison mat, Josh drew his knees up to his painful chest, praying inside his head without moving his lips. If other prisoners or guards discovered he was religious, he may be subject to brainwashing techniques.

"I'm on the far side of the sea now, so if there really is a God, if you are really there..."

Liu Chen's assignment tonight was an unusually momentous one, especially in light of the fact that she was on probation with the National Clandestine Services of the CIA for ordering aerial shots from GEOINT without authorization. The atmosphere was bristly. Egos occasionally flared. Each agency had its own turf, its own piece of the Federal budget. The high-ceilinged, soundproof control room in the FBI headquarters in the sprawling fifty-acre campus, two miles from Interstate 495, was packed with team members from multiple agencies: the Middle East Division, the State Department, Homeland Security, the NSA, and various other members of government alphabet soup on hand to watch and offer assistance.

The new hands-on director of the CIA, with the approval of President Maly, had given the provocative order to violate the tacit agreement long held between countries: to arrest a spy.

Because it was on United States ground, the FEEBs were taking a lead on this assignment. Multiple monitors filled the wall and various satellite and CCTV images leaped up onto the flat screens. It was 2145 hours and the sun was setting. The Washington, D.C., buildings cast long shadows. "The live feed is up," one of the operatives announced over the PA system. "Do we have full audio contact?"

"Can't we capture a clearer image?" an FBI agent snapped critically to Liu, who was helping to man the visual tech.

Liu obligingly clicked more keys on the keyboard and brought up another focused satellite image from Atlas V, the clandestine communications satellite. The screen momentarily flickered, and then the details of the car, a black Mercedes, became clearer as it exited the gates of the Chinese Embassy in the darkness of night. The rented Mercedes had caught the attention of the CIA, confirmed suspicions, and helped create a more detailed profile of the target. It was far too rich for a low-level diplomat from China.

Liu made a click on her computer and a red dot hovered over the car. "Target headed east on International Place..." Liu said. "Right turn on Van Ness...Connecticut Avenue." On another video monitor, the unmarked FBI surveillance vehicle tailed the target, and the red taillights could be seen in a distance from the dashboard camera.

"Target took a hard left and is off the grid at 18th Street," radioed the operator of the FBI surveillance vehicle.

"Unit 5, can you take the tail?" queried one of the controllers.

The target made his way along L Street to Chinatown. He meandered around Chinatown, doubling back on his path several times, finally parking the Mercedes on a dark residential street lined with trees. The other FBI units began to close around the area, opening doors to let agents jump out of the vehicle.

Suddenly an operative frantically barked directions. "Proceed to 8th Street! Target northbound, approaching I Street intersection....Unit 3, target is at your nine o'clock!"

"Got it," said one of the techs manning one of the other videos. The screen blipped to a view of the target through a night camera attached to the collar of an undercover FBI agent. The subject was slight of figure, in his mid-thirties, was dressed in clothes of a college student, and carried a backpack. He had donned a wig with longer, nearly shoulder-length hair. Even in the darkness his Asian features were apparent, and he certainly blended in with the occasional Asian restaurant workers or American bar customers who were still meandering through the district late at night.

Perhaps he suspected he was being followed, because he suddenly darted into an alley. The control room rustled with anxiety, but after a long wait he finally emerged, sans the wig and the backpack, crossing the street several times and making strides in the general direction of the tree-lined Mount Vernon Square. The site of the genteel old Carnegie Library, it was the closest thing resembling a park near Chinatown.

"Unit 4, search the area for the wig and the backpack and bring it in as evidence. All remaining units in position. He's about to make the drop," came the voice over the radio. The target became visible on the multiple flat screens, each screen recording his image from different distances and at different angles.

The room fell into suspenseful silence as the target shuffled casually along a pathway through the trees and to a park bench and trash can. He stopped one more time and did a three-sixty, checking for aberrations in the environment, then knelt down and pulled out a piece of chalk from his backpack, making a mark on the bottom of the trash can. Then he slipped around behind the can and slid a package underneath.

"I'll begin the countdown," said the operative on the radio as the Chinese spy stood up to walk away. "Ten.........nine........."

The room was breathless. Did he see any approaching figures partially obscured by trees and benches?

"Three.......Two......One........launch!"

The various units began to rush the target. "HANDS IN THE AIR! FBI!"

In a split second, it seemed, the target whirled around back into the direction of the trash can, nearly colliding with it, then zig-zagged to the left and to the right.

"FBI! HALT OR WE WILL SHOOT!" This was from a different direction, a different unit. A shot rang out in the night, carefully calculated to hit a tree just ahead of the target as he ran.

The spy dropped low and continued to stagger forward, covering his head. All of a sudden it seemed that there were dozens of agents swarming the park. In an instant one, and then two, reached the subject and tackled him to the ground. "You are under arrest for espionage against the United States of America. Anything you say may be used against you....."

The control room burst into applause, cheers, whistles and high-fives. Egos, turf wars and battles for the Federal budget were temporarily forgotten.

Liu Chen smiled with satisfaction. The mission had required the cooperation of multiple agencies, including the CIA and herself. The public would probably never know, and likely all the agencies would never receive credit; but that was of no consequence. It was controversial, risky, and an aberration of global protocol. A top-level mole by the name of Hua Kalkai—an MSS agent living in the United States and working for the Chinese as an undercover spy—had been captured. He would be held and interrogated.

In the security holding area in the lower level of the U.S. Navy ship at sea, the interrogator turned off the loud rap music, which had run non-stop in the holding cell for twenty-four hours. The Chinese detainee being held in the black detention site sprawled contorted on the floor, arms covering his head and ears.

"Get up and come with me," the interrogator said in Mandarin Chinese. He grabbed Hua Kalkai's arms, snapped handcuffs on his wrists, and escorted the wobbly prisoner into the office where the second interrogator was sitting. They showed the detainee into a chair, where he swayed slightly and sat down. His skin was sallow. Dark circles had embedded themselves under his eyes.

"I will give you a break from the noise," the first interrogator said with phony benevolence, "if you will answer more questions for me."

Interrogators shot out the questions in tag team fashion. The method of holding and questioning the detainee was advised in the Army Field Manual and in full compliance with the Geneva Convention. The questions were planned in advance and volleyed rapid-fire at the prisoner in order to trap him into inconsistent statements.

The queries started with some of the same from yesterday, which the detainee either avoided or answered consistently, giving up no secrets. Then abruptly they changed tactics. The first interrogator flashed a series of four large photographs onto the wall. The second interrogator asked. "Do you know any of these men?"

"No."

But they both observed that the detainee's eyes rested briefly on one of the particular individuals. Without missing a beat the first interrogator abruptly jumped up and slapped his hand on the single photograph, a middle-aged man with dark curly hair and brown eyes. "Do not lie," he screamed and pounded the table. The prisoner reflexively backed away. "You know this man. Who is he?"

Despite the fog of pain and fear, the detainee was now quite sure what information the Americans wanted. "American CIA."

"What is his name?"

"Josh Evans. He has alias. It is Ryan Taylor."

"Where is Josh Evans?"

There was a pause. The detainee licked his lips nervously. "He was taken by MSS in Beijing."

The interrogators glanced at each other and then the second one shot out the question, "Is he alive?"

"Yes." Hua Kalkai, of course, had no way to know this for sure, but this was a slim chance to barter for his own release.

"Is he in service to the MSS?" It was necessary for the CIA to find out if Josh had turned.

Hua Kalkai replied, "This you must discover. My life for his life."

Ever since the capture and information from Hua Kalkai, Liu Chen and the other analysts had been busy, scouring intelligence reports of Americans known to be in the Beijing area.

The team compared databases and ran algorithms that attempted to analyze Chinese intel from spies and case officers in the Beijing area. State Department personnel cross-checked records and eliminated legitimate students and American workers from suspicious Americans with shadowy connections. Queries were set up on open sources, which supplied hundreds of computer hits, which were perused by analysts.

One report uncovered an interesting American social media post made by the friend of a couple living and working in Beijing. The friend had copied and pasted a portion of a personal email into a social media site called "Americans for Free Speech in China."

"Nick's pneumonia got so bad that he was hospitalized and I sat with him in the hospital out of concern for the level of care. A few beds down I heard a patient with an American accent ask, "Are you Chiefs fans?" I went over to talk to him. He was trying desperately to talk but he was terribly thin and weak and kept coughing. I tried to brighten his day, took a selfie with him and wished him well. Immediately security and a nurse ran in and took away my phone. I started yelling and demanded my phone back, and they ordered me to leave the hospital. I contacted the American Consulate. My phone was returned the next day but the picture was deleted. So now I'm working with an identity theft company because who knows what other information was taken off my phone…"

A few days later, on the seventh floor at Headquarters in Langley at 1100 hours, the conference room was packed as personnel from Counterintelligence, Nonofficial Cover, Asia Analysis, Counter proliferation Division, Community HUMINT, Support Medical Services, and Science and Technology squeezed into the room. The Deputy Director of National Clandestine Services was on hand. Down the hall the Executive Dining Room was preparing lunch, and the aroma of food wafted in. Nonofficial

Cover Supervisor Rich Novak was about to make an important announcement and lead a brainstorming session. Suddenly there was a noise in the hallway and a rustle as an important group appeared at the door, causing a nervous buzz. The new Director of the CIA, just appointed by the president and Congress, stepped into the room.

"Welcome, everybody, on the matter of a tip received about missing Case Officer Ryan Taylor, also known as Josh Evans." Rich Novak, Josh's supervisor, found that his mouth had gone dry upon the entrance of the top commander of the CIA. "The State Department and Justice Department report that the Chinese spy, Hua Kalkai, has turned some credible information. We suspect that Case Officer Taylor has been held in a labor camp in Beijing."

A rumble made a wave across the room. Rumors had circulated in the halls of some of the departments, and there had been attempts to get intelligence to confirm it.

Rich was terribly nervous in front of the deputy director, who was his superior, and he was absolutely terrified in the presence of the brand new, micromanaging Director of the CIA. He swallowed hard, abandoned his presentation and elected to punt to Liu Chen. "First we have a report from our Analyst Liu Chen. Uh, go ahead."

Liu looked startled to have the ball thrown to her so suddenly in front of the highest officer of the Agency. "Um, thank you to all the team members for being here today. Uh, the word from the American Consulate in Beijing is that they have confirmed that an American prisoner has been hospitalized. This an aerial satellite photo of the hospital." She flashed a picture up on the screen. "It's been verified by a national that works at the hospital, and we believe it is Ryan Taylor." Her normally placid expression was animated with anticipation that was rarely evident on the part of someone usually so reserved. Internally her pulse was hammering.

A torrent of questions was unleashed. "How reliable is the intel of a source who is being subjected to interrogation techniques?" "Did Taylor give up information?"

Liu tried to talk over them in her thin little voice. "We're studying these high resolution images. We think he's in this part of the hospital complex, but there may not be enough time to cultivate a source inside the hospital before he gets released."

"How much more intel can we get out of Hua Kalkai?"

411

"We could request that the State Department contact the Israelis and see if they would mediate—"

"Let's try to get a humanitarian organization to work this—"

"If we have Hua Kalkai, and we've only gotten extremely limited amounts of intel from him, we can negotiate—"

"I'll tell you one thing we don't want," Rich interrupted loudly. "What we need is to prevent is Ryan's spouse—I mean, Mrs. Evans—from hiring a private investigator or a lawyer and running over to China to try and find him."

"Well, if that's the case, we'll just block her visa again like we did last time."

"Unless the West Wing interferes again."

The new director of the CIA cleared his throat impatiently and shuffled his feet. The rest of the conversation in the room dropped and all eyes turned to him. He strode over to the electronic whiteboard and wrapped his knuckles on it, sucking the air out of the entire room. "Focus, everyone. This is no way to run a meeting. We have an American who's been in captivity for five hundred fifty-four days. Let's get some organization to this."

The Deputy Director of National Clandestine Services turned solid red at the way his new superior was stepping in and usurping the briefing. Rich Novak was mortified.

"The State Department and the National Director of Intelligence are waiting for a report and recommendation. The highest levels will receive private briefings as soon as possible." This meant the Senate Select Committee on Intelligence, the National Security Council, President Maly were waiting....

"Let's get some ideas down." The CIA Director began to write on the electronic whiteboard:

Infiltration
Israelis
Humanitarian organization
Swap

He listed several sub-points, crossed one item off, and then hit the button under the board with his thumb. A printout rolled out and he handed it to the Deputy Director, who like the other bureaucrats in the room remained outwardly stoic but inwardly seethed at the commandeering of the Agency by their newly appointed superior, their turf being stepped on.

The CIA Director's voice rattled like a machine gun. "We aren't going to eliminate the options with risks, pick the least risky option, and just hope that it works. We are going to take an aggressive, simultaneous, three-pronged approach. Here's what we're going to do."

Senate Select Intelligence Committee
Room 215
Hart Senate Office Building, Washington, D.C.

The Chair of the Senate Select Intelligence Committee virtually slurped over the new CIA Director, who was abundantly more to her liking than the old one. "Thank you for appearing before us today to share your thoughts about the fine men and women working for the CIA, most particularly Case Officer Josh Evans, who has now been missing five hundred sixty-one days and is being detained in prison in Beijing. In your opinion, Director, was Mr. Evans imprisoned because the Chinese discovered the weapons that were identified by the Operation AuCHFOP mission in Babylon Metro?"

The new Director faced his questioners with straight posture and wide-eyed forthrightness. "Madam Chair, in answer to your question, initially the Chinese believed Iraqi police brought him in on bogus, trumped-up charges. But as they examined the evidence, they came to believe that Mr. Evans was involved with a non-profit attempting to smuggle Iraqi antiquities out of the country. We don't think that the Chinese discovered the existence of the weapons cached with the antiquities until later."

"Director," queried the Chair, "Are you implying that the Chinese extracted information about the weapons from Mr. Evans?"

The Director was careful and measured in his response. "Mr. Evans was trained to resist interrogation. He also had, at best, marginal information and training on identifying these particular kinds of weapons."

"I'm confused. Are you saying he is being detained simply for smuggling antiques? Why would they spirit him all the way to China, unless they suspected the part about the weapons? Why not just deport him?"

"The Chinese alleged that he was a CIA assassin because of the shooting incident at Fairfax Community Church. I'm not trying to accuse anyone here, but it's conceivable that he may have given up intelligence about the weapons stashed with the antiquities. We'll have to debrief him when he gets back."

"I see." The Chair furrowed her brow.

"There's another possibility," continued the Director. "Some of the antiquities turned up at a flea market sale on Route 8 just outside of Babylon Metro. At least one Iraqi was hawking the antiquities for money. Since Mr. Evans ran, rather than turn himself over to the Chinese authorities, the Chinese may have assumed he was not a prisoner of, but actually an accomplice with, the Iraqi thief. We have to concede the possibility that they were correct."

"Hmm." The Chair briefly chewed on her pen. It was embarrassing enough to the United States that an ops officer had his cover blown. It was worse if he turned.

The Chair tapped her pen on the desk and continued, "Yet there is still the practical issue of getting our officer back on home soil. Regardless of whether he turned or not, we are also convened today at the request of Mr. Evans's wife, Chelsea Evans. Mrs. Evans cannot be here today. She relocated to London after a series of unproductive contacts, and ultimately a hostile encounter with, Agency personnel. She reached out to me about the problems she experienced attempting to communicate with Agency personnel, which I have outlined to you in a previous memo."

"As you know, Vice Chairman, we have taken steps to rectify—"

"Yes, I'm aware and I appreciate your effort. Mrs. Evans also shared with me some information obtained by a private investigator. She believes the information was ignored by Agency personnel. At the start of the Governorate of Babil Prison riots, a white Volvo truck was observed by witnesses to be leaving the area. Mrs. Evans hypothesizes that this was how her husband was removed from the prison. She questions why these witnesses and the truck were never investigated by the CIA?"

"Madam Chair, my heart goes out to Mrs. Evans, but let me paint a picture of the events on that day. There was an immense amount of pandemonium and casualties, not to mention smoke. Yes, there was a white Volvo truck observed in some of our satellite photography. However, Mrs. Evans could not possibly have any personal knowledge of how thoroughly our experts examined it. They did eventually examine it, and quite frankly, our various analysts disagreed on its significance. There were two prison personnel and a woman that left in that truck."

The Chair snapped, "Quite frankly sir, the previous director's investigation of this case seemed to be characterized by incomplete inquiries and poor communication with the victim's family. This has cost the Agency time and money, not to mention untold suffering for the detainee and his family. Please proceed with your report to us on your attempts to free Mr. Evans. Hopefully your negotiations will go better than your predecessor's investigations."

"I have a plan, Madam Chair. And it is going to be successful…."

T yler Tischner, the sexy Hollywood movie star with the feathered-back hair, lounged in a chair in the white hotel bathrobe next to the double doors of white-paned patio glass topped with palladium windows. On the bed lay Tischner's clothes. Two men sat across from him in wing-backed chairs on the tile floor in front of the fireplace. Outside on the patio of the Bel-Air Hotel, palm leaves swayed softly in the afternoon breeze. Tischner's agent took notes on the clandestine meeting at the small table across the room.

"So you're CIA?" Tischner repeated with awe. He leaned forward to reach for his drink, not taking his eyes off the two men across from him. The bathrobe gapped open, exposing broad, rippling chest muscles underneath a tan. A large bamboo fan circled overhead, and its gentle circulation caused bits of his hair to rise.

"No one can ever know that. We want the reward money that we are offering to flow through your organization, Hollywood for Humanitarianism. The Chinese can never know where it came from," said Rich Novak.

"Interesting." Tischner nodded.

Rich stood up walked over to Tischner's agent, who had been taking notes on the conversation, and held out his hand. "I'm sorry, but you'll have to relinquish those notes to me."

The agent made a small sound of protest and looked at Tischner. Tischner nodded; the agent reluctantly handed the notes over.

"Sir, it's a unique opportunity for you to be in service for your country," added the Contracting Officer from the Support Division.

Tischner picked up the drink and stood up, turning around and walking to look out the French doors onto the foliage outside the room. He nodded his head. "I like it."

"Here is the series of appeals that we would propose that you do." The Contracting Officer took a paper proposal from his briefcase and handed it to Rich. Tischner turned around and came and took it from Rich, scanning the page.

Rich explained, "The initial approach would be non-threatening, but if they don't cooperate, the information you would release would be successively more and more embarrassing to the Chinese. We think the third appeal, coupled with a public march or demonstration, could be sufficient to privately compel the Chinese to release him."

"What if it doesn't work?"

Rich and the Contracting Officer glanced at each other.

The huge ceiling fan circled, providing cool relief from the outside heat.

"That's our problem, not yours. You and your organization are paid, either way."

The new Director of the CIA stood in his office with the Deputy Director of the National Clandestine Service and a couple of his staff, his arms crossed over his chest and one thumb cupped under his chin, watching. Tyler Tischner's interview was today on *Good Morning America with Milo and Giordano* on the television on the wall.

Tischner's shirt was unbuttoned halfway down, baring his sexy chest, and he flopped casually and self-assuredly in the visitor chair facing his interviewer. "Angela, human rights are a topmost priority of my non-profit organization, Hollywood For Humanitarianism, and we are prepared to offer a reward for five million dollars to the Chinese to bring home Josh Evans safely."

Angela Giordano was leaning forward on her elbows, squinting carefully at him in a very Diane Sawyer-esque way. "That's very generous, but would you say, Mr. Tischner, that your non-profit is in effect bribing the Chinese government?"

"Mr. Evans has been missing for five hundred seventy-five days, with no communication with his loved ones since one hundred sixty days into his captivity. We ask the Chinese government to put pressure on Mr. Evans's captors to disclose his location."

The Director of the CIA nodded his head. So far, so good; Tischner was following instructions.

"We also ask that they consider human rights violations of all their prisoners, including the sex trafficking of women from Eastern Europe and Southeast Asia, and persecution of minority groups such as the Falon Gung, which are considered a religious cult, and the Uyghurs, a Muslim dissident group. Angela," he exclaimed, suddenly sitting up and leaning forward so close that he nearly bumped her forehead, "did you know that the Chinese stormed into the Xinjiang province and arrested Uyghur women who refused to follow the mandate not to wear the Muslim head covering?"

"But Mr. Tischner," Angela interrupted. "China's ability to keep Muslim uprisings in check within its own borders was exactly what prompted the U.N. to ask them to engage in peacekeeping in

Iraq. I fail to see the connection that has with the kidnapping of a CIA case officer."

"What about all the computer hacking the Chicoms have done to us?"

A choking sound came from the Director's direction.

"What about all those military bases they created out of hauled-in dirt deposits in the South Chinese Sea? Next let's talk about how China failed to reduce emissions in accordance with the Climate Peace Accord. They were supposed to peak in their emissions but they have completely failed to do their part in reducing the carbon footprint. We hold China responsible for environmental terrorism." Tyler Tischner was wound up and unable to stop. "Also, did you know that they continue to imprison internet bloggers who attempt to cross the Great Firewall? A columnist for an online newspaper was sent to a detention camp last month for exercising free expression—"

The CIA Director's eyes narrowed. "Does this guy have total diarrhea of the mouth? Who selected him for this operation? Was that you?" he asked the Deputy Director of National Clandestine Services.

The Deputy Director turned six shades of red. "Sir, he leads a popular humanitarian organization, and there was a team of us that selected him—"

"The buck stops with you. Your team put him on there to talk about releasing Evans from China. You didn't put him on there to go off on a tirade about all his damned racist opinions. Get Legal Support on the phone right away. Tell them to cancel Tischner for breach of contract!"

The bus from the Tube slowly rolled to a screeching stop in front of the austere brown brick four-story school building in Marylebone with its tall windows and little square window panes. The leaves on the trees in London were a deep green but with a faint suggestion of turning yellow-green. Nights were cooler, but afternoons were still warm.

Moving to London had been the perfect elixir. Being far away from McLean had helped Chelsea to get on with it. On Sundays she and Atalaya took the train and the bus from Marylebone to Oxford Hill and sometimes stayed to have lunch after church with Pastor Thorpe and his wife. She and Priya, her work friend and confidante, along with Atalaya, had taken two very fun weekend trips: one on the Eurostar to Paris and the other across the channel to Ireland.

Prepared if necessary to fly to Iraq to investigate a tip, Chelsea stayed in touch with the private investigator. But there had been no news lately and no tips or leads, and the U.S. Embassy in Baghdad was a stone wall. Other than necessary paperwork and brief correspondence with the Chair of the Senate Select Intelligence Committee, there had been little communication with the U.S. Government; it was as if she were living in a serene bubble, distantly insulated from the nearly unendurable stress in recent months.

She had reached the point of acceptance of ambiguous loss that Brittany had spoken about. She and Dane had communicated very little, but she thought about him at times, wondering at points if she had missed an opportunity. She even discussed it with Pastor Thorpe but ultimately she returned to her decision to commit her life to being a single mom. She lost seven pounds—"half a stone," as the Brits said, from moving and decorating, cutting out alcohol, halting her food intake when she wasn't hungry, and mostly from the constant walking in London to get to public transportation. Her clothes fit great and she felt good.

A new school term began. Often Chelsea left Oxford Street early, commuted to the school and worked on the way, accompanied Atalaya on the bus, and finished working at home. So far Atalaya seemed to be slowly adjusting. Atalaya had matured over the summer. She was no longer a little girl anymore, but a nine-year-old—helpful, thoughtful, and even beginning to understand jokes and sarcasm for the first time. The new school had been good for Atalaya. It was hard to pinpoint why. Sometimes it seemed to Chelsea that part of it was the formality of the British school, which emphasized rote memorization and more structure. School uniforms had at first seemed so quaint and boring, but they took the stress out of getting dressed each day and leveled the playing field with the diverse group of children. Atalaya had two girlfriends who liked to go with her to the park. The girls had been to each other's flats for birthday parties and recently even for a summer sleepover.

As Chelsea peered through the window of the bus and waved at her daughter, who was at the school bus stop just outside the bright blue gate in front of the high arched entry door preparing to board with her and go home, she felt her mobile buzzing. The caller ID on the mobile was for the *Good Morning America* offices. Quickly she slapped the mobile to her ear with an instant sense of foreboding. If Angela Stevens Giordano was calling, it could not be good.

It wasn't Angela, it was her assistant. "We have information that your husband is CIA. Would you like to come on air and comment?"

Her heart sank with a thud to the pit of her stomach, but she was prepared with a response. It was something all CIA wives were prepped for. "Why would you think something like that? Josh was an architect who disappeared while working on an archaeological dig site. He went missing five hundred ninety-two days ago." Atalaya stepped up into the bus with the other children, and instantly the noise level went up on the bus.

"It's on the internet. It's not something we can stop. It was in a *The New York Post* blog." Angela's assistant began to read the blog.

Fury and fear overtook her, and she felt the air begin to whirl and spin. Vaguely she heard Atalaya, who had sat down on the bus seat next to her and was trying to get her attention. "Mommy? Are we going to Costa today? I'm hungry for a snack."

"Do you care to comment? If you'd like to come on air, we'll give you the first opportunity," pressed the assistant.

"I'm picking up my child from school." Chelsea rudely cut off the conversation, hating the intense competition created between media outlets.

Did she really believe Josh was dead? If so, what did it matter that his cover was blown, and why get so upset about it?

But if he was still alive somewhere, his career with the CIA was officially ended. If he were rescued, at best he would be offered a boring desk job in a cubicle in Langley—something she knew he would hate. Or he might be such a liability and such a security risk that that CIA would have to officially terminate him.

And the odd thing: Angela had been very close to figuring out the story months ago. So why didn't she call Chelsea personally today to ask for the story? Was Angela too chicken, unwilling to face Chelsea?

Then she thought wildly of CEO Kelly Dunberry of Crestedon, Josh's international architectural firm that had provided his cover job. Mr. Dunberry was just trying to do his patriotic duty and assist the United States Government in a worthy cause. Now the international community would know that Mr. Dunberry's company was a party to espionage for the United States.

This story needed to be stopped!

The bus bumped to a metallic, screechy halt on York Street near their flat, and they exited down its steps, making their way up the sidewalk. In the United States it was nearly mid-day, and over the noise of the street, she called and left a message for Brick, the liaison at the CIA. Inside the brownstone (there would be no snacks or coffee drinks from Costa today), she instant messaged all the relatives and told them not to take calls from the press.

Then she did a search for the number for Governor Giordano's office. Tony Giordano had given her some of his own personal money to search for Josh. He had not forgotten their past relationship. He was the one person who could help her, probably the only person who could talk Angela out of doing this story. He was capable. He was authoritative. He was always in control.

She left a crisp, concise message with the person in the governor's office who took the call.

Brick was trying to reach her on the other line, the only time Chelsea remembered Brick ever doing anything in a hurry. "I am sorry to hear that the press has discovered your husband's true identity, and I know that makes you feel anxious. Others have felt the same way. In our experience, when this happens, we have found that if you—"

"Brick," Chelsea snapped impatiently, "you know, and I know, that you don't have any experience with this. You can stop with the retro 1980s Feel-Felt-Found stuff. I'm miles ahead of you." She disconnected in frustration.

That night she tossed and turned in bed, barely sleeping more than two hours, listening to the sound of cars passing by on York Street and occasional shouts of inebriated London partiers. She mourned the end of the chapter in their lives, the final break with the CIA. She and Josh had tried to serve their country. Unluckily, they had drawn the short straw. Everything had gone sour and backfired on them.

It was the next morning in London before the governor's office returned her call. It was the governor's chief of staff. He told her that she needed to brief him on the situation.

The most important, disastrous revelation of Josh's career, and she was stuck with the assistants for the Giordano family! "Please tell Tony that Angela is trying to do a story on my husband. It's—it's very damaging. Whether it's true or not, if Josh is still alive somewhere, it could endanger his life if people thought it was true. It will also compromise Crestedon, the private sector firm that provided the cover for the work he was doing. Please ask her to stop the story."

Surely now Tony would call her back himself!

But he did not. His chief of staff phoned her at the end of the business day, which was eleven o'clock p.m. London time. "The governor has spoken to his wife and outlined the gravity of the situation, but the news division is under obligation to its stockholders and executive management to report news, and there nothing he or his wife can specifically promise you."

She embargoed social media and London stations that reported American news. She refused to return any messages whose caller IDs she did not recognize. She simply couldn't bear it. The official ruination of Josh's career was second only to waiting for a verification of his death. She was grateful that she was thousands of miles away, buffered and insulated from direct contact with America.

Brittany was the one that called her at work and told her that the story had just aired on *Good Morning America with Milo and*

Giordano and was also published on Reuters. "It's out there. They pretty much told everything. Chelsea," Brittany gently warned, "Be prepared. You're going to be getting messages from astonished friends wondering how you and Josh could have kept a secret like this from them for all these years."

Chelsea thanked her friend, disconnected, and stared at the wall. After years of dodging questions, obfuscation about what she and Josh were doing, and outright lying, she felt a surreal mixture of sadness but also relief at the finality of it all. Unable to contain her curiosity, she went online and looked for the video clip. The video queued up, waiting to be played. Milo and Giordano sat frozen in front of the blue background—Angela with her perfectly coiffed blond hair and red dress, and Milo with his designer suit and bright blue tie. Chelsea took a deep breath, touched the little red arrow and started the video.

"In breaking news," Angela read the teleprompter, "A firefight occurred today between Iraqi soldiers and Chinese peacekeepers in Hillah, the old city part of Babylon Metro, after revelations that an undercover operation by the CIA to restore a portion of Saddam's palace had uncovered lost gold and antiquities called 'Nimrud's Treasure', some of which date back to the 9th century B.C. The Chinese will not release numbers, but thirty-five Iraqis are believed to be fatally wounded."

A fuzzy satellite image flashed on the screen with a scene of bloody carnage strewn along a sandy roadway, Chinese equestrian guards with AK-74Ms, and smoke drifting away in spiraling tendrils. The horses pawed and snorted as the Chinese barked instructions and angrily pointed their weapons. At the top of the hill, flanked by date palms and dusted with a film of smoke, was the familiar sight of Saddam's palace. Chinese military personnel in gas masks sprinted up and down the rocky, sandy hill.

The camera panned to Brett Milo. "The CIA operation used a non-profit by the name of 'Pyramids and Palaces Architectural Renovation' as a front, which, according to ABC's news files, was a cover for American citizen Josh Evans, who disappeared five hundred ninety-two days ago and has been missing ever since. Both the Iraqis and the Chinese are in a bitter fight over Ancient Babylon, and both issued statements today claiming to control Saddam's palace. The State Department released a statement today calling for peace and saying that all antiquities belong to the people of Iraq…."

On the crowded seventh floor at Langley, the closed circuit screen blipped and quickly popped into focus. Bleary-eyed analysts, techs and personnel who had worked with Case Officer Ryan Taylor, a/k/a Josh Evans, had been called out of bed at 0230 hours on a Saturday morning. Liu Chen and Josh's supervisor, Rich Novak, stood side by side, still in windbreakers, sipping bad coffee to try to stay alert.

Headquarters personnel at Langley couldn't be seen or heard, but they could watch the image on the video feed. "We've got full audio contact," announced one of the techs. The screen split, and the satellite image from China appeared.

"Holy shit," said Rich Novak painfully, shaking his head in disbelief.

Liu Chen's hand flew to her mouth at the nearly unrecognizably thin body in front of her with dark circles under the eyes and long, scraggly hair and beard with streaks of gray.

"Hello, Mr. Evans, I'm Lieutenant Brandon Jackson from Atlanta, Georgia. I'm talking to you by satellite from the State Department at Washington, D.C. How are you today?" The U.S. negotiator from Atlanta on the left side of the split screen had a distinctly southern drawl.

"Fine, sir." Ryan/Josh glanced at something off camera questioningly, and then turned his eyes back to the computer screen.

"The Chinese have granted permission to verify your condition, Mr. Evans. Are you in good health?"

"I am now." His hollow eyes darted off camera again, and they could only surmise that someone was likely standing there.

One of the operatives at Langley spoke into a mic, and Lieutenant Jackson wore an earbud that picked up the instructions. "Voice recognition analysis has begun," the operative noted.

The lieutenant began to ask basic questions. What city had Josh been born in? What elementary school did he attend? What was the name of his Kindergarten teacher?

"Confirmation that the subject is Ryan Taylor. Uh, Joshua David Evans," Liu said aloud, even before the voice recognition software had barely began to chart, its red lines creating a graph on the dark screen. She could not take her eyes off the screen, and she studied every detail. His soft-spoken voice was robotic, lacking the emotion and color and inflections from when they had trained together and worked together, but it was unmistakably him.

"Wow. Holy shit," was all Rich Novak could sputter.

Chelsea gets the word

L ittle droplets of water plopped softly to the sidewalk from the Saturday morning rain, and the watery light valiantly struggled to pierce through the fog, although in London you never knew how enduring that might be. Chelsea took off her raincoat and folded it over one arm. Atalaya's eyes were wide with excitement as the cab glided into place in front of her and the door opened with a soft whirr. The outgoing passengers exited the giant Ferris wheel that defined the London skyline on the Thames River across from 10 Downing Street and Westminster.

"Have a good weekend and thank you for riding the London Eye," said the attendant to them, and then he turned to Atalaya, who was first in the queue. "You may proceed up the boarding ramp."

Atalaya jumped up into the passenger capsule and clambered onto a seat inside. "Here, Mommy," she called, patting the place next to her, just like a little adult.

Chelsea sat down on the seat indicated by her daughter. "Your hair grows so fast." She reached for it and lovingly stroked it with her hands. The dark curls were, long, thick and flowing—Chelsea grinned to herself, remembering the scissors a couple years ago that were used to cut hair like Peppermint Pinkey. The passengers finished loading the observation wheel and the capsule began its slow ascension up into the sky.

"Look at all the boats in the river," Atalaya said excitedly as they rose up into the air. "I see Parliament and Big Ben!"

"Very good," said Chelsea. The other passengers, most of whom were tourists from all over the world, moved around the capsule, pointing out the glass observation windows and chatting in various languages while taking pictures. "Let's walk over there and I'll point the direction of our house." She studied the endless miles of buildings, trying to locate some sort of familiar landmark between them and Marylebone, when her mobile buzzed.

She took the call, and as the voice spoke, she dropped down on the nearest seat and hunched over her knees, listening intently. Purse dangling on her elbow, she raised her free hand to cover the other ear and block out the sounds of the passengers.

"Mommy, that's not polite." Atalaya tugged on the purse, but Chelsea did not hear. She tersely asked the caller several questions, then with her free hand rummaged through the purse for a pen and took notes.

When the call ended, she sat staring without seeing. She began to tremble and shake.

"Mommy, why don't you come and look out the windows?" implored Atalaya, puzzled.

It seemed the ride would never end....

After an interminable time, the London Eye glided to a stop. "Let's go!" Chelsea urged hoarsely. With her hand on Atalaya's back, she firmly guided her daughter out of the capsule, down the ramp, and onto the dock and towards the train. She punched a button on the phone. "Let's run, darling," she said.

"Why? Are we going to miss the train?" Atalaya asked worriedly.

"No."

She could hear the phone ringing several times.

Please answer.

Then Dr. Evans picked up, his voice thick with sleep. It was five-forty-five in the morning in Columbia.

She could hardly croak out the words. "Pop Evans, Josh is alive!" she exclaimed.

Saturday afternoon in London passed by as if they were in a daze. Headquarters only told Chelsea that Josh was to be released and would be flown to Landstuhl Airforce Base in Germany. She was to wait for confirmation. She tried to message Deep Throat, but there was no response.

And then definitive word came. Josh, Headquarters informed her, was en route from Beijing to Tel-Aviv, Israel, an eleven-hour flight.

There was no sleep that night. She made arrangements to leave the country, calling Atalaya's school and her boss, Ian Clarke, and packing suitcases. What if something went wrong? What if her hopes were dashed one more time?

The hour came for the plane to land in Tel-Aviv. In Columbia, her entire family drove to Josh's parents to be with each other while watching via webcam in the living room of Josh's parents' acreage. Josh's twin brother Jake in Kansas City woke up his wife and children, and they sat in the kitchen with their devices, watching and waiting as well. In the Marylebone flat, she and Atalaya waited for the confirmation call from Headquarters, listening to the excited voices of all of the family members.

She called Kimberly and Brittany, who were stunned and thrilled. Kimberly's voice boomed "Congratulations!" so loudly into the mic on web chat that Chelsea actually had to adjust the volume. Brittany burst into happy tears. "It was worth it, Chelsea, every minute in Babylon Metro, everything I went through with Jason. You see? It all worked out together for the good."

"Well, we actually have to get him back," Chelsea said practically, but she was still as joyous as Brittany.

She called Clinton, who retained his characteristic calm and responded amiably, "That's my chum Bags for you. I should have known he would land on his feet, just like a cat."

She called Brick, the liaison at the CIA. "I'm sorry I was so rude to you all those times. Thanks to you and the CIA family for your help."

Brick was very professional and very pleasant. "You're welcome. We have found that CIA family members who are under stress sometimes feel emotional. We feel the same way ourselves.

We have found that it helps to have a professional to talk to in order to process our feelings—" Eyes rolling, Chelsea quickly found a graceful way to end the conversation.

Time flew, and at the same time it dragged.

The Trade

The aircraft touched down on the runway and rattled to a noisy stop. A door opened, and Josh blinked at the lights that lit up the tarmac in the dark of night. From the cockpit, he could hear voices from the control tower.

Hebrew language…

His captors unshackled him, handed him a water bottle, and escorted him out of the plane. Gratefully he took huge gulps of water. His legs were so cramped he nearly fell down the stairs. The Chinese military soldiers held him by the arms and righted him. He stepped onto the tarmac. It was night, but in places there were bright lights on the airfield. An officer yanked him slightly to the left. His eyes adjusted, and he could see another military aircraft about a hundred yards away. In between was a small armored personnel carrier with a machine gun positioned on the roof.

"Zǒulù!" Walk. The officers accompanying him snapped open his shackles, gave him a hard shove, and pointed their guns up to the sky.

He walked.

A row of soldiers in camouflage flanked him, spaced about twenty yards apart on either side. About half-way down the tarmac, an ambulance idled along with a military convoy; its red light spun in unearthly circles. From the other aircraft a figure in an orange jumpsuit emerged and walked towards him. His heart began to thump.

With all of these soldiers, and with all of these weapons, all it would take is one misstep and they both would be in danger of being shot to death.

He continued to walk, his breath coming in short, ragged gasps as Hua Kalkai passed him in the semi-dark.

Briefly, their eyes met. They passed each other, only their footsteps making hollow noises on the concrete.

It was a prisoner swap! Had the negotiated prisoner release gone through diplomatic channels with America's allies, the Israelis?

As he approached the other aircraft, a small contingent of military with flashlights and weapons surrounded the steps leading up to the plane. He heard a voice with a southern accent call out in the night: "Case Officer Joshua David Evans, the United States of America welcomes you home."

As the servicemen offered him their arms to assist him up the stairs, he stopped. He swiveled to face the decal of the American flag on the side of the military aircraft. Drawing to his full height, he saluted.

In the Situation Room at the White House, applause broke out among the members of the national security team.

"Very good work today. Excellent negotiations on the part of the Israelis." President Maly stood up from the table, and the others at the table scrambled to stand up as well—Vice President Russo, the Chief of Staff, the Secretary of State, the Joint Special Operations Command, Homeland Security, the Director of National Intelligence. They gathered their things from the table.

President Maly slapped the back of his recently appointed Director of the CIA, who was celebrating his first year on the job and his most momentous gamble. "It was a tough choice, but a good call. You can't get lard unless you boil the hog. It worked, we got our boy back," drawled the president in his Texas accent.

"Thank you, Mr. President." The Director said.

Despite the president's casual use of idioms, he was indisputably one of the most brilliant politicians of the modern era, and this victory would only serve to solidify his legacy. The members of the team shook hands and congratulated each other.

The national security team began to pack up its things and file out of the room. Vice President Russo remained with his eyes fixed on the screen, watching the plane move into position for takeoff in the dark of night, its red tail lights glowing, carrying his former constituent to freedom, his mind drifting back to memories of his hometown of Columbia, and his best friend, Governor Tony Giordano.

At CIA headquarters in Langley, Liu Chen savored the moment of bittersweet success. She still could not take her eyes off the video feed. If normal classifications stayed in place, the vast amount of behind-the-scenes work on the part of herself and scores of other individuals would never be known to the media and to the public. Her friend Ryan, known to America as Josh Evans, probably would not even know the full scope of it.

The right things had been done.

She could sleep later. She took another swallow of coffee with a feeling of immense satisfaction for the quiet work she had done on her own, for the work her team had done in this late step in the negotiation, and most of all, for the privilege and opportunity to serve her country.

Chelsea's mobile buzzed. She snatched it up, her heart racing.

"Ma'am, Lieutenant Brandon Jackson here. The operation was successful...."

She let out a shriek. "THEY HAVE HIM!!!"

Atalaya jumped up and ran around the flat, bouncing and cheering. On the webcam the Evans and Steele families—both of their parents, all their brothers and sisters and nieces and nephews—screamed and cried and hugged.

The farm truck bumped and swerved so violently on the curving, mountainous road that Farah thought surely her teeth must fall out. The air was stuffy and she was wretchedly hot, so hot under the hay and the tarp, that she thought she must fall unconscious. The hay itched and scratched her skin. The stench of a dirty diaper permeated the hay. But the baby seemed not to mind as he sucked his milk eagerly.

The truck rolled to a stop, and she and her brother, who was crouched next to her under the hay, jerked to attention, listening intently. Was their transporter detained because of the authorities?

But they could hear no other vehicle and no other voices. The truck door opened. "Hurry!" they heard the farmer tersely order them.

They tossed the hay and the tarp out of the way and clambered out of the back of the pickup, gasping for fresh air. The baby made a sound of protest, for he was not quite sure that he was done with his supper. Farah fumbled through her bag for the cough medicine that would put him to sleep and keep him quiet.

Already her baby had the look of his father, Hakim. The hazel eyes, the perfectly symmetrical features.

"When the sun sets, you must run, down there." They stood on the precipice of a steep, woody incline, and the farmer pointed down to the valley in the north. The sun was setting in the west behind a steep mountain. Had the journey not been so terrifying, Farah would have acknowledged that with its stunning mountain peaks and setting sun, it must be one of the most beautiful places on earth. She peered down into the valley below. Row after row after endless row of white refugee tents stretched across the plateau. In the twilight she could see clotheslines strung with long, neat rows of colorful garments. Directly north of the refugee camp was the city of Çukurca, Turkey, with its inhabitants of ten thousand people, some of whom resided in precarious cliff-dwelling homes. Between them and the refugee camp was a steep embankment covered with trees and scrub, and an open plain where they could be visible from the road above.

They were so close! If Allah were gracious, they would soon be free from hunger, thirst, and dirt.

"Now, hide," the farmer instructed, pointing to the scrub. Quickly they clutched at their meager belongings, ducking down into the trees and bushes. *"Salaam alaikum."* Peace be upon you.

"Alaikum salaam." And upon you peace.

But the farmer didn't even hear them because he had already turned around and jumped back into his idling truck. All around them, it was quiet except for the sound of insects and birds in the trees. The instructions they had been given seemed accurate. There did not seem to be any border guards nearby at this hour.

Just a few more minutes and the sun would slide completely behind the mountain…

Farah stroked the curly head of her drowsy baby boy as he nestled against her breast, content with his meal. She crooned, "Someday, my dear one, if we are chosen in the lottery, we will make it to America, *inshallah*." Allah willing. "There we will be safe. Your father always said that we will have much food and water, and a nice house, and maybe even a swimming pool. Would you like a swimming pool, my little man? In America there will be no soldiers, and—" She clutched gently one baby hand and wrist in between her thumb and her index finger, trying to put out of her mind the gruesome image from the internet posted as a warning, that of her husband receiving his bloody punishment from Black Lightening. "And no one will ever cut off our hands in punishment!"

Her own stomach growled, and she took a meager sip of water, hoarding every drop. They were nearly out of provisions. Beside her, she could hear her brother's anxious and laborious breathing. The hay was terrible for his lungs. He squirted a precious bit of inhaler in his nostrils, sniffed the fresh air, and slowly his breathing began to calm.

"It is time!" he finally said as the golden orb set and darkness crept like cat feet across the plateau below. He jumped to his feet. "Let me hold my nephew. Come with me, my little man, we will run together."

She placed the precious treasure in his arms and hoisted her bag up over her shoulder. Her brother snuggled the little one to his chest and briefly buried his face on top of the small, fuzzy head.

And then they took off down the rocky embankment, sliding and stumbling towards the plateau.

Behind them, on the road, they heard the sound of an engine approaching. It was a heavy sound, that of a truck or a military vehicle. Frightened, they turned to look up and over their shoulders. Bright search lights appeared through the trees at the top of the embankment. Farah let out a wince of fear.

"Run, my sister, run!" Her brother clutched at her with his one free hand and burst into a sprint, dragging her in the direction of the white tents. The baby began to wail in fear. Little white dots of light on the edge of the encampment were turning on now for the night, and she thought surely her lungs would burst or she would fall and break her ankles.

Closer and closer the tents appeared as they widened the gap between border patrol and the refugee camp, huffing and puffing. A small knot of refugees clustered together to stare, and an American relief worker in a t-shirt with the logo of a cross stepped up to the group. "It's a baby!" she called out in shocked English.

As Farah and her brother ran towards the tents, the American relief worker held her arms out, and it seemed to them that it even though it was a final few steps, it took forever until finally they were there. The relief worker grabbed their arms and pulled them under the canopy. Farah's brother panted so hard he surely must be hyperventilating. Farah slid to her knees and began to weep, great hulking sobs of relief. The baby burst out in alarmed howls.

"I can't believe it. They ran through those mountains and got past the border patrol with a baby!" the American relief worker exclaimed in English, and then switched to Arabic. "Water. Take it and drink!" Another female, one of the refugees, took the baby, rocking him against her shoulder, trying to calm him, singing to him in Arabic.

Farah gulped the water thirstily and found herself shaking uncontrollably as the rescue worker wrapped her in a blanket and comfortingly rubbed her back. Next to her, her brother trembled and shook as well, so much so that he could hardly open the lid on the bottle of water.

"There, there. You are safe," the American relief worker reassured them, and repeated, "You are safe."

T he news broke worldwide on social media and television with Josh's photo. Chelsea had to change her voice message to tell the press to contact the hastily reactivated publicity firm. "We interrupt you for this special report," the weekend anchor for ABC announced. "American architect and CIA spy Joshua David Evans has been released from captivity in Beijing and is being airlifted to Landstuhl Airforce Base in Germany, where he will receive medical care and observation for a few weeks before being flown home."

The cut went live to their hometown of Columbia. Chelsea watched with mixed feelings the newscaster who had propelled Josh's blown identity story into the mainstream media. Angela Stevens Giordano stood in front of Riverfront Views Plaza, the rehabbed, brick, live-work building where their first condo and Josh's office had once been. A small crowd gathered, waving signs that read, "Welcome home, Josh!" Tall and distinguished, Governor Giordano stood next to her in the forefront of a crowd. Chelsea spotted several of the friends that had attended the fundraiser rally.

Angela held the mic up to Governor Giordano as he spoke. "We are gathered here to celebrate Josh's safe return, and acknowledge his service to the country," announced the governor in his deep, solemn voice.

Lucky Angela. No doubt on New Year's Eve, when news stations were trolling out their top ten stories of the year, Angela's breaking news about Josh Evans's release would be highlighted. She'd been able to combine a work trip with a weekend visit to Columbia and be with her husband, Governor Giordano. Chelsea couldn't help but wonder: how much longer until Tony Giordano decided to run for president?

"Israel negotiated the release," came Angela's voice as the camera panned the crowd in Columbia. "Israel has valiantly attempted in recent years to become an ally of China, selling it oil and bargaining for military protection against the increased violence and threats of annihilation that have come from the hostile Muslim countries surrounding them, although China has always taken a neutral stance—"

What a perfect circle, a providential irony, Chelsea thought. In his heart Josh had always been a friend of Israel. Israel, of course, didn't know that, or know him. Yet they had helped save him. She thought fondly of her former Jewish boss, Levi Mizrahi, who had been so generous. She could practically hear his whoops of exaltation across the ocean.

Just before the takeoff from Israel to Germany, the military and the CIA arranged a video call from Josh. Josh's appearance would be unfamiliar and possibly disturbing to Chelsea and their daughter, the CIA liaison Brick forewarned Chelsea, so Chelsea elected to take the call alone.

Her pulse raced as the moment came to speak to her husband for the first time in six-hundred-forty-one days. The picture was poor quality, and Chelsea was astounded at the nearly unrecognizable close-up in front of her. She caught herself just in time from flinching and grimaced her facial muscles into what she sincerely hoped was a smile. "Josh, honey, is that you?"

"Babe. It's you. Finally. There is a God. There really is." Josh's voice was dull and there was the background noise of an airport. His hair and beard were horrible, long fuzzy masses of dark brown tinged with ghastly streaks of gray. Inside the tangle of hair and beard were his brown eyes, but yet they were not his soft, warm brown eyes; they darted back and forth, wild and haunted and black. She would not have even been sure it was him if she did not hear his voice.

"Oh honey, you just have no idea how much I worried and how much I prayed," she said in a trembling voice. "There were times I lost hope, but somehow I just had a feeling, deep down, that some way, you would land on your feet." She tried not to let the tears spill, but they did. "Your dad, Clinton, Kimberly, a new friend named Brittany, and I came to look for you in Babylon Metro."

"You did?" the wild eyes looked surprised, flitting back and forth between her image on the screen and something in the airport. It was hard to hear; there was background noise.

"Are you injured or sick? How do you feel?" she asked.

"Better."

There was something odd about his voice. It was mechanical, flat, emotionless. She had expected him to be more expressive or something. She heard a rustle and then the camera wobbled. "Ok,

440

ma'am," came the voice of a military attaché. "It's time to load him on the plane."

Hours later the military plane carrying Chelsea, Atalaya and Pastor Thorpe landed in Ramstein, Germany and were met by a military detail and accompanied to Landstuhl Airforce Base, a short distance away. The unit took them to Air Force Inns where they ate a meal and checked into a pleasant room.

Landstuhl was a small town in a valley surrounded with trees, a lone castle, and a delightful cluster of prim, tidy white buildings with orange and brown roofs. It was not, Chelsea thought, the context in which she would have imagined visiting Germany for the first time on a long weekend with Atalaya.

Three hours later, Dr. Evans and Judge Mary Duncan-Evans arrived at the hotel. Dr. Evans clasped Chelsea in his arms in a massive bear hug. The judge also hugged her, her skinny arms awkwardly encircling Chelsea's shoulders. As much as Chelsea disliked her mother-in-law, she could not help but admire the woman's straight posture and poise during what was most certainly one of the most defining moments in her life.

The CIA and the military prepped them, warning them about surprise they might have at Josh's appearance and responses. Josh would have to be debriefed to see if he shared sensitive secrets with enemy nations. It was unfortunate but it was necessary. Once again Chelsea felt the slow burn of resentment at her country for putting her husband in an impossible situation and then doubting his character.

A convoy drove them to the Landstuhl Regional Medical Center, an endless sprawl of metal and white concrete, and assisted them through the security clearance, and they were led through the massive building, past throngs of doctors in blue scrubs and military people in fatigues, into the wing and up to the floor where Josh's hospital room was. They walked in a line, following the staff officer assigned to their case, their feet padding down the endless white tile hallways with blue baseboard. Chelsea went in front. Behind her was Dr. Evans, who was holding his granddaughter's hand, then the Judge, and then Pastor Thorpe. A nurse brought up the rear; the nurse was pulling the little cart with the cooler of dry ice and a gift from A Pizza Me restaurant in his hometown of Columbia. When asked what food he would most like to have, Josh had mentioned Thick Crust Pepperoni from his favorite restaurant, A Pizza Me, and chocolate chip cookies. The restaurant immediately had pizzas packed in dry ice to be sent to Germany along with fresh baked chocolate chip cookies.

The staffer led them to a small waiting area with soft, padded benches just outside the nurses' station on the floor.

In a few minutes, she would begin to get answers. Answers about where Josh had been, what had happened to him, who he thought it was that betrayed him.

"Mrs. Evans and her daughter will meet with the patient first, and then they will call the rest of the family in," said the staff officer.

"Go ahead, my dears," Dr. Evans. He nudged Atalaya in Chelsea's direction. Chelsea took her daughter's hand and followed the officer down the corridor to the room, her heart racing with anticipation.

"Mr. Evans, your family is here," said the staff officer, tapping on the door.

It swung open.

Eagerly she stepped inside, but then halted. A hospital tech partially obscured her view of Josh, leaning over him with an electric shaver, shaving off the ugly long locks of fuzzy hair and giving him a military buzz cut.

The razor shut off, and the tech straightened up and turned around, leaving one-third of Josh's head yet unshaven with long, unkempt curls streaming down one side. "Oh, hello. Come on in. We're just getting trimmed up," the tech said cheerily. "We thought we'd be done before you got here."

Josh's eyes met hers.

He had shaved his beard, or someone had shaved him. His skin was pulled tight over hallow, skeletal cheekbones, and his lips were chapped and dry. Every bone in his slight, slim body protruded from yellowish skin. His toe nails were horribly long and yellow and dirty. He may have seemed somewhat normal in the online chat yesterday—bearded and heavier on a camera—but in person he was utterly weak and frail.

She swallowed hard, trying to process the scene in front of her. "Josh, honey!" she said in what she hoped was a natural tone of voice.

"That's not Daddy," she heard Atalaya say from down beside her. "Mommy, who is that man—"

"Shhhh," Chelsea cautioned sharply, pinching Atalaya on the trapezius muscle. "Would you like to wait while Mommy gives Daddy a hug?"

She forced herself to cross the room and went to him. Without saying a word his scrawny arms and hands clutched at her, as if they were bird-like claws, and he grabbed her and drew her close to his bony body, without speaking. She could hear his labored breath.

It was as if a thousand thoughts raced through her mind in a second.

We're finally reunited, after all this time.

I hate Omar Al Ghamdi for what he did to my husband.

The man in that hospital bed is thin and ugly and broken and horrible. I can't stand to touch him. This isn't my husband, it's only a hollowed-out shell of him that's left.

He's changed. This isn't the man I loved and married.

Chelsea tossed and turned in the hotel bed that night, the searing image of her weakened husband haunting her brain.

What if every woman whose husband went to war and came back injured had these thoughts? We would have no country, no society.

This is the worse part they talk about in for better or for worse, to love and to cherish, as long as you both shall live.

The hospital staff talked to her about classic symptoms of POWs: hypervigilance, bursts of anger, bad dreams, personality swings, unwillingness to talk about the experiences while imprisoned. Since being freed, Josh was in the process of receiving medical exams, an exam by a psychologist from the CIA who had flown to Germany in less than 24 hours, and endless debriefs by Agency and State personnel that had streamed through the small hospital room. The Director of the CIA had phoned him, then the Director of National Intelligence. President Maly was expected to call at 3:00 p.m. Central European Summer Time.

Angela Stevens Giordano messaged her five times requesting an interview, and after talking it over with Kimberly, Chelsea finally responded affirmatively. Angela hadn't really blown Josh's identity, she'd reported what was already circulating on the internet. The story would be taped this evening and air tomorrow. The hospital had its hands full with every major news media in the world interested in covering the story.

Clinton flew to Germany in a private plane from San Francisco to Zweibrücken airport, the closest airport to the base. In Chelsea's eyes, Clinton had made the necessary steps to redeem himself.

"Hey, Bags," Clinton said, giving the softest of pretend punches to Josh's shoulder. "You numpty, running off and getting lost, you scared the—" He glanced at Pastor Thorpe, standing under the TV in the hospital room, and changed the word. "—the poo out of us."

"Balls," had been Josh's flat, dull response, but with a twinge of a grin. "You big eejit."

This morning they all sat in a lovely garden on the hospital patio, delighted at the sight of the trees just beginning to turn colors. Southwest Germany was cooler than London, but with sleeves or a light jacket, the mid-day sun made it comfortable to be outside. A nurse brought Josh's medication and urged him to take it. He swallowed the pill reluctantly. "I hate taking those things. They alter the composition of your brain. The sooner I can get off them, the better," he complained. It was no surprise. Josh held a contempt for addictions.

"You must look at it as help for this point in time," Pastor Thorpe said encouragingly. "You are surrounded by help. The CIA will pay for all your medical care and therapy. You have friends and family with you. Most importantly, there is spiritual aid available."

Within a few minutes of taking the pills, Josh's eyes dilated and he became less monosyllabic and more talkative. It became easier to get answers out of him. She broached the question that had nagged at her night and day for months. "Honey, I always believed that Omar Al Ghamdi was the one that betrayed you. Did the Agency inform you yet that he was killed by Black Lightening? They said he was gunned down and his body found in the Euphrates."

"Omar was killed? Last I knew, he was missing. Before I got captured, they doubted that he really turned. They believed he was hiding and they were trying to get to him and protect him."

It made her angry at the Agency again, that they were so nonchalant about the prime suspect to have betrayed Josh. But Josh didn't believe Omar betrayed him, either! If not Omar, then who….

"So, Bags," Clinton asked. "What exactly were you doing out there in Ancient Babylon with antiquities? Where did they come from?"

"It's likely that Uday Hussein, Saddam's oldest son, stole the antiquities from the Central Bank in Baghdad just before the first American invasion and hid them down under the Ancient Babylon ruins. He knew they were less likely to be uncovered there. He and his father had a stormy relationship. Uday was every bit of a bat-crazy brute as Saddam." There was something uneasily robotic about her husband; he rattled off facts like an encyclopedia which he had heard from somewhere. "Uday tortured and raped and murdered and stole everything from heroin to Rolls Royces and paintings. He had an illegal trade op going on with Iran before the U.S. assassinated him in 2003. Absolutely none of this is classified that I'm telling you, by the way. It's all open sources."

"I remember when Saddam's sons were killed," Dr. Evans mused. "They were sadists. Uday had his own personal zoo at his palace, and they found starving lions and cheetahs."

Josh was starting to look drowsy, and Chelsea asked the other question she had been so curious about. "Josh, honey, there is something your dad and I were always curious about. Were you also working with sarin gas? Is that what the C-H-F-O-P stands for?"

Josh hesitated, then seemed uncomfortable. "The Agency never gave me specific intel about biochem targets."

A bird fluttered to the patio, clearly expecting the hospital guests to drop crumbs on the ground. Josh continued, "I observed some weird-shaped containers in the palace ruins surrounding the antiquities. They had American flag decals on them. My guess was they were some sort of American weapons of mass destruction that Uday got ahold of. At any rate, my instructions were to notify the military division if I ran across any antiquities cached with weapons and get out of there. Since I really didn't know for sure what it was, my interrogators couldn't get any reliable intel out of me."

"You see, it was for the best that your superiors didn't tell you," said Josh's mother, bobbing her graying auburn head up and down eagerly.

Chelsea felt a flash of anger towards her mother-in-law for her knee-jerk defense of the CIA. There was nothing 'for the best' about it; Josh had been set up and used by the Agency and experienced imprisonment and torture. Now his character was in question. He was going to be subjected to a lie detector test to see if he was a spy.

"My cover still got blown, but I guess I'm alive, right?" he shrugged in agreement with his mother.

Atalaya jumped up onto the little brick curved sidewalk bordered by flower beds, trying to catch a butterfly in her hands. As she passed by, Josh suddenly began to sing a ditty from the Peppermint Pinkey television show. Then he did an impression of Peppermint Pinkey—a stream of conversational Chinese in a high-pitched little girl voice, long Mandarin sentences Chelsea had never heard him speak before, with the same cadence and rhythm to his voice as the television character. Atalaya stopped and turned around. She approached her father curiously and listened with wide brown eyes. Then she began to giggle. "You're silly, Daddy. I'm too old for Peppermint Pinkey." She turned and went along the path again, looking for another butterfly to capture.

"Thank God," he muttered. "On my honor, I never want to see Pepto-Bismol pink again as long as I live."

The dry humor was, Chelsea thought hopefully, the first glimmer of the old Josh. "Honey," she asked, "Did your captors find out that you had a daughter with a Peppermint Pinkey toy? That's how we knew that reports of you were real. They sent us a picture of a Talky Watch. Then I remembered it had GPS."

"Serious? There was a holiday party in Baghdad at the embassy. I found Atalaya's Talky Watch from Clinton in my tux pocket the same night I was arrested," he said.

Dr. Evans picked up the subject of the sarin gas again. "Son, sarin doesn't usually have a long shelf life. So it wouldn't have protected the antiquities for very long and it wouldn't be dangerous anymore."

"That's not always the case. It's pretty general knowledge in the military that Iraqis experimented with stabilizers to keep sarin from breaking down. They also experimented with binary weapons. You know, that's where you take the components of WMDs and store them separately side by side, and then combine them when you are actually ready to shoot them off. Anybody who actually served in the military knew that fragments of all kinds of weapons were scattered all over Iraq and never removed. There were servicemen who came back with suspicious symptoms and talked about it to the media and got treated by the VA. I was terrified of what might be in those containers, and I was nervous that we had Crestedon employees working around that stuff."

All of a sudden everything made total sense to Chelsea. "So THAT is the real reason why the CIA wanted this operation!" she exploded angrily. "They weren't trying to rebuild Ancient Babylon out of the goodness of their hearts! They didn't really care about returning the antiquities to the Iraqi people! They were just afraid the Chinese would discover WMDs, and the United States would be humiliated!"

447

Judge Mary-Duncan Evans spoke. "Interestingly, it would be far more of a humiliation to those partisan Americans who staked a dogged political position, which lasted for decades, that there were never any weapons of mass destruction in Iraq. That would matter far more than what the Chinese thought of us."

"Well, of course, you are absolutely right, dear," said Dr. Evans, nodding thoughtfully. "Everyone was obsessed with whether or not the maniacal father had WMDs, but remember, there was never an interrogation of his sons about their role with WMDs or what they might have done with them. All we know was that there was a gun battle and TOW missiles, an Army task force blew the sons to bits, and that was the end of them."

Sometimes, Chelsea thought with grudging admiration, her critical, blunt mother-in-law, with her acute perception and sharply-honed judgment, was the most insightful of anyone.

"I don't want to talk about it anymore," Josh suddenly snapped irritably, and they all realized he had been asked too much too soon by too many people.

"I am prompted," Pastor Thorpe said kindly and tactfully, "to be thankful to our Lord for all of those people in both of our governments, those who roles are significant and also those who are seemingly insignificant, who work to protect all of us. Especially you today, Josh."

"Hear, hear," said Dr. Evans.

Chelsea soaked in the rays of autumn sunshine, her mind whirling with endless questions, wishing she had point blank asked Josh who he thought it was that betrayed him before he became frustrated and wanted to stop talking. A squirrel ran by, but it looked different than the squirrels back in the United States. It was redder, and the hair on its ears was so long it looked like bird feathers.

"Hey, Bags, want to start a NoitaLever tourney?" Clinton offered lightly.

Josh smiled crookedly and then slowly shook his head. "No, Balls, I think I finally broke that addiction."

"Me, too, actually," said Clinton. "When you went missing, I quit the game. I left it up to my developers to sort everything all out. Actually, NoitaLever has fallen behind quite a bit to Jihadi Janna video game lately. The gravy train with the State Department has broken wheels."

Josh said wistfully, "Germany is nice and everything, but when we get back to the United States, I will get down on my knees and kiss the ground."

In spite of everything that the CIA and his country had put him through? Even though his integrity was being questioned and the CIA was investigating to see if he had turned into a spy for the Chinese? "Josh," Chelsea ventured carefully, "Of course we'll take you back to see everyone in the United States just as soon as possible, but…Atalaya and I have an apartment in London. I'm working for Goldberger Hewitt. I wanted to be closer in case they found you."

"Really? Then it all works out. When I get better, I'll find some sort of work in London. I don't think I have much of a future with the CIA anymore."

"Oh dear!" Josh's mother made a little choking sound.

"Move back to London to live and work? Are you sure that is what you would like to do next?" Chelsea was still careful, not wanting to overly excite him, but hardly able to believe her ears.

"For a while," Josh replied. "Maybe for a few years, while we're still young. U.K. is where it all began: the history, the freedom we have, our system of government—it was birthed there and passed onto us, and I love the U.K. I love the energy in London. I'm glad Attie has a chance to live there. But," he conceded, "I wouldn't want to live there forever. No offense, Pastor Thorpe, but there's no place like the United States. It's the greatest country in the world. No matter what they think of me or what they think I did, I'll want to go back home to live eventually."

No one seemed quite sure what to say about this. Josh's mother opened her mouth but closed it again. Clinton took it in with equanimity. Dr. Evans smiled ruefully as if he expected this.

Atalaya, noting that the adults had fallen quiet, came up to Chelsea. She grasped a lock of her mother's hair with one hand and twirled it in the finger of her other hand, regarding Josh shyly. They were strangers to each other. They would have to get acquainted in a different way.

A new beginning, a fresh start. A breeze from the north blew, cooling the heat of the concrete patio, and they were all there. Together, finally.

Vice President Russo
The Rose Garden

The morning sunshine streamed into garden as President Maly and Vice President Russo shared their weekly breakfast. The suffocating mugginess of Washington was abating and gorgeous fall weather was setting in. The end of weekly breakfasts between the top two leaders in the United States was on the horizon; President Maly was term limited.

"I'm hearing that our friend, Governor Tony Giordano, has been making calls to donors," President Maly warned his vice president. "He wants to enter the race."

"He and I are best friends from the same hometown and we go back a lot of years. If anyone can persuade him to step aside, it's me. He'll listen to our positions and he'll support our campaign," Vice President Russo replied with egotistical bravado.

"Take it from someone who rode hard running for president and got put up wet," President Maly counselled, "your best friend in politics is eventually your next opponent. Don't overestimate his loyalty or underestimate his ambition. I've kept tabs on Governor Giordano. He works harder than a one-legged man in a butt-kicking contest."

"His wife doesn't want him to run. She would have to give up the *Good Morning America* gig. Her contract this year is for $9 million."

"If he wants it, he'll appeal to her ambition and patriotism and get her to walk away."

"We'll be calling Mr. Evans in one hour," said Vice President Russo, checking the time and changing the uncomfortable subject.

"Excellent. I look forward to speaking to him. Joshua David Evans was lucky as a blind man crossing the street. It's a good thing the Chinese like Israeli oil and the Israelis have been trying to make nice with the Chinese for military protection." President Maly, to the continual frustration of his political opponents, consistently managed to discover political advantage in every seeming mis-opportunity; this incident would be no different.

"They are interviewing him to see if he gave up secrets to the Chinese, or turned. They haven't done the lie detector test yet," said the vice president. "Remember when we flew in and met them in Columbia during our first campaign after they evacuated from London during that Muslim uprising? His wife did some local volunteer work on my campaigns. Hard to imagine him as a traitor to the good old USA. Solid, resolute, clean-cut guy."

"I remember the couple. Until he's cleared, the safe thing to do is thank him for his service to the Agency and ask about his health." The president took a drink of coffee and shook his head. "Unfortunately for him, even if he did stay loyal and didn't become a spy for the Chinese, it doesn't matter if he wants to go back into espionage. That dog won't hunt."

"Which is something I wanted to bring up with you." The vice president presented a letter out of a file to President Maly. "This is a letter from his wife. She's a firecracker, full of energy. She said that they always wanted to return to London. I made some calls to move her visa along, so she moved back there a few months ago to be closer to Iraq in case he was found alive. Before he disappeared, he made several requests to his supervisors for a Western Europe position."

He handed it to the president, who scanned it quickly.

"So if his results turn out okay and he's cleared, what do you think about diplomat, or some sort of position with the State Department in the London embassy?" pressed Vice President Russo.

"If Evans is innocent, don't you think he'll probably write his memoirs? Make a movie deal? Run for Congress or Senate?" The president handed his empty coffee cup to the staff waiter, who set it on a silver tray and moved silently away.

"I don't know. I don't think he's like that. I don't think either one of them are really like that," said Vice President Russo.

"Hmm." As the second half of the second term had ticked on, legacy had become important. President Maly had been gracious lately, pardoning prisoners and attending to small acts of justice that personally touched him. "We'll wait to see the results back from the CIA. If he's clean, let me talk to the Secretary of State. There's probably something we can do."

"If he's clean, then he's a true patriot," agreed Vice President Russo. Then he added, "We should do everything for him that we can."

POSTSCRIPT
Six hundred fifty days earlier

In the American Embassy in Baghdad, fifty-seven miles north of Babylon Metro, in the marble foyer with the huge holiday wreath situated between the entrance containing security booth Number Two and the main lobby with security checkpoint Number Three, Ana took the mop and plopped it into a bucket of water. She slid the yellow "CAUTION" stanchion across the wet marble entrance floor. Hearing a guest enter, she stood up and turned around. A long piece of hair fell in front of her eyes, and with a sweaty hand she pushed it away, tucking it inside the burka she was wearing around her head.

Their eyes met in an immediate flash of recognition.

"Oh, hi," the American said to her, startled.

"*Buna seara,*" she mumbled back in Romanian.

"I know you. What are you doing here?" he started to ask.

Her pulse raced and she felt her mouth grow dry, but she immediately recognized not only him but also an opportunity. "*Scuza ma.*" Her pulse raced and her thoughts exploded, trying to decide what to do. She melted away behind a large, thick column, watching as he walked inside. Then she exited the building.

She took off around the wall outside the compound, hastily shoving her employee I.D. in the lanyard around her neck at the Chinese officers and American Marine Guard patrolling the embassy with their AK-74Ms and M16 rifles, and into the Green Zone. Taking off into a run, she dashed across the employee parking lot in the direction of the bus stop, the lanyard slapping against her chest. Panting, she pulled out the burn phone that had been provided to her by the Iraqi Black Lightening resistance on the Baghdad police force. She dialed the number of the private investigator's office.

"It is Ana," the prostitute replied to the voice on the other line. "I have information for you about one of my customer. He is not who he say he is. He is CIA. He is at American Embassy tonight."

The Iraqi voice on the other end rapid-fired skeptical questions.

She snapped into the phone, "So what, you say many kinds of Americans come to Embassy for Christmas party? You do not believe me that he is CIA? That is your stupid decision then. I give

452

you good informations in exchange for freedom. I will hang up for this shit and you will not know who he is."

She listened for a moment and then replied hotly, "How much you pay me?"

When the voice answered and she said, "Good, I will wait to see you deposit the monies. Then I will call you back."

She disconnected, logged in to check her account, and then she called his phone number back. "You have his business card. You steal it from me when you arrest me at my pimp's house. His business card say 'Palaces' on it, in the English. He is American who builds buildings in Babylon Metro."

There was a question and she replied, "He is short, not big like most Americans, brown eyes. Dark curly hair, very thick. Release my money now, yes?"

From the police station in Baghdad, a call was made to a fellow Black Lightening insurgent on the detective force in Babylon Metro.

A van was dispatched with three detectives. The van pulled out of the underground garage in the Babylon Metro police station and into the dark night. Its tail lights gleamed red as it threaded through the streets towards the Tomorrow Globe Financial Center and past the gleaming white digital billboard up on the freeway with the cartoon image of a fat, cheerful, benevolent queen with a scepter in her hand, blessing the Governorate of Babil with her a colorful kaleidoscope of seven exploding stars signifying prosperity, and declaring, *"Welcome to Babylon Metro, Forever a Happy Place!"*

AUTHOR'S NOTES:

News sources indicate that Saddam Hussein attempted to rebuild Ancient Babylon over a twenty-year period and spent half a billion dollars before being driven out by American tanks. Hussein's attempts to restore the city are depicted accurately in the book, although my description of the kitchen and underground prison area was fictionalized. To view pictures of Hussein's restoration depicted on the book, see
http://www.cnn.com/2013/04/04/world/meast/iraq-babylon-tourism/

The Pentagon, in the late 2000s, invented a computer game called "Native Echo," which used down-loaded computer games to both propagandize Middle East youths with affirmative messages about the United States, and also collect computer data on them for espionage purposes. The British government spy agency, Government Communications Headquarters, placed spy recruitment ads on, and mined gamer's data from, Xbox. For more information on the Pentagon's computer games, see
http://www.washingtonian.com/blogs/dead_drop/cia/in-2005-a-pentagon-employee.php

The imagery and characters depicted in Clinton's propaganda NoitaLever game are from Revelation 9, written in the late first century A.D. The text has generally been interpreted to predict that 200,000 troops (a number potentially necessitating at least some participation by China) will conceivably gather in Iraq and eradicate one third of the world's population.

Isaiah 13, Revelation 17 and 18, and the Apocryphal book of 2 Esdras 15 predict the spectacular destruction in the end of days of a world-wide economic trading center and ring of prostitution called Babylon. Scholars vigorously disagree on whether this is literally Ancient Babylon, or figurative language for another modern-day city such as Jerusalem, Dubai, Mecca, or Rome.

The reference to the Muslim prophecy about an apocalyptical battle over a mountain of gold in the Euphrates is found in the Sahih Muslim Hadith, an accompaniment to the Quran.

During the Saddam Hussein era, Iraqis experimented with stabilizing agents and binary munitions for sarin nerve gas. American soldiers discovered artillery shells during the second Gulf War, and ISIS took possession of an old chemical weapons munitions plant.

http://www.nytimes.com/interactive/2014/10/14/world/middleeast/100000003173431.mobile.html?_r=1
http://www.huffingtonpost.com/2014/10/13/isis-chemical-weapons_n_5979848.html
http://www.theguardian.com/world/2014/jul/09/isis-seizes-chemical-weapons-plant-muthanna-iraq

At publishing time of this book, China, while the number one customer for Iraq oil, and in spite of its shared concern about Muslim extremism within its own borders, has thus far refrained from delving overtly into Iraq peacekeeping and politics.

http://www.washingtontimes.com/news/2016/jan/13/inside-ring-china-may-join-russia-war-against-isla/

ACKNOWLEDGEMENTS:

Julian Tyler, who helped with the British English in the previous books, suggested that this novel be written from Josh Evan's perspective. I decided Josh should officially join the CIA and so I went to the library and checked out a stack of books. The inspiration for the plot came from a chapter about the Pentagon's experiment with computer games in the book *The Way of the Knife: The CIA, a Secret Army, and a War at the Ends of the Earth,* by *New York Times* national security correspondent Mark Mazzetti.

Colonel Matthew Bogdanos of the U.S. Marines authored an autobiography in my stack of library books about the theft of antiquities from the Iraqi National Museum in his book "Thieves of Baghdad" and his attempts to recover some of them. He took time with me to provide feedback on this book. His book can be purchased at http://www.amazon.com/Thieves-Baghdad-Matthew-Bogdanos-ebook/dp/B002TTICDM/ref=sr_1_1?ie=UTF8&qid=1421988464&sr=8-1&keywords=thieves+of+bagdad

Thanks to my Reader Review committee:
Sue Bittfield
Joanie Bittner
Gary Blackshear
Don Harris
Pam Harris
Barb Tyler
"Z"

Jeff Beckenbach, graphic arts

And to Keith Heckman

www.ingramcontent.com/pod-product-compliance
Lightning Source LLC
Chambersburg PA
CBHW060136260626
47160CB00001B/1